Fights, Flights, and the Chosen Ones

ZONDERVAN®

Fights, Flights, and the Chosen Ones
Copyright © 2008 by Lamp Post, Inc.

Library of Congress Cataloging-in-Publication Data
Lee, Young Shin.
Fights, flights, and the chosen ones / edited by Brett Burner and J.S. Earls ; original story and art by Young Shin Lee and Jung Sun Hwang.
    p. cm. -- (The manga Bible ; bk. 3)
  ISBN-13: 978-0-310-71289-3 (softcover : alk. paper)
  ISBN-10: 0-310-71289-0 (softcover : alk. paper)
  1. Bible stories, English--O.T. Samuel. I. Burner, Brett A., 1969- II. Earls, J. S. III. Hwang, Jung Sun. IV. Title.
  BS551.3.L42 2007
  222'.409505--dc22

                  2007031182

Requests for information should be addressed to: Grand Rapids, Michigan 49530

This book published in conjunction with Lamp Post, Inc.; 8367 Lemon Avenue, La Mesa, CA 91941

Series Editor: Bud Rogers
Managing Editor: Bruce Nuffer
Managing Art Director: Sarah Molegraaf

Printed in United States
08 09 10 11 • 7 6 5 4 3 2 1

GRAPHIC NOVELS

MANGA BIBLE

Fights, Flights, and the Chosen Ones

1 Samuel–2 Samuel

Series Editor: Bud Rogers
Edited by: Brett Burner and JS Earls
Story by Young Shin Lee
Art by Jung Sun Hwang

ZONDERVAN®

ZONDERVAN.com/
AUTHORTRACKER
follow your favorite authors

FIRST SAMUEL

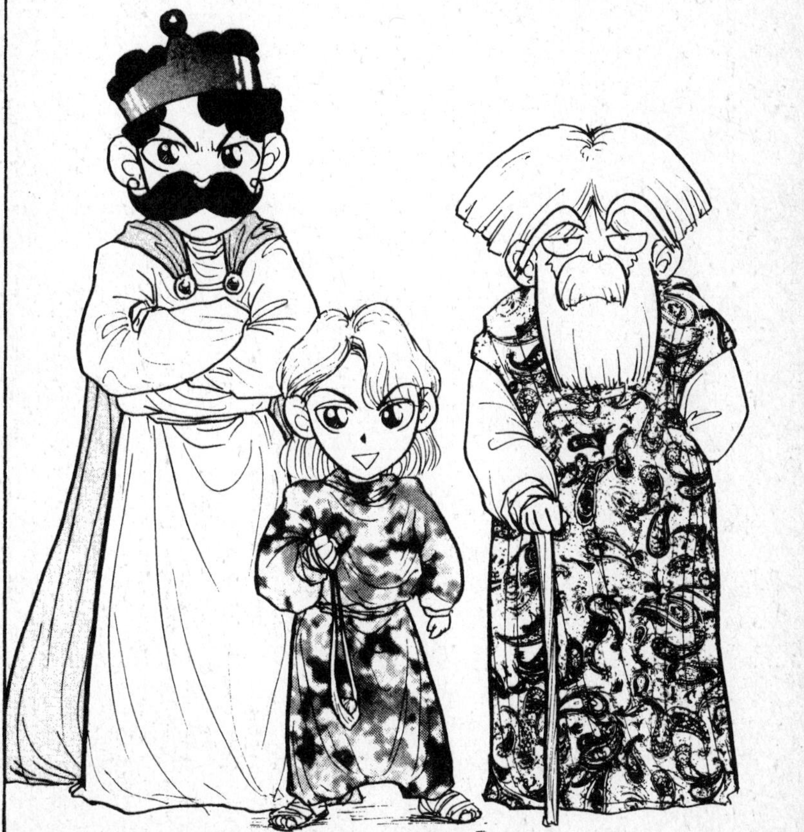

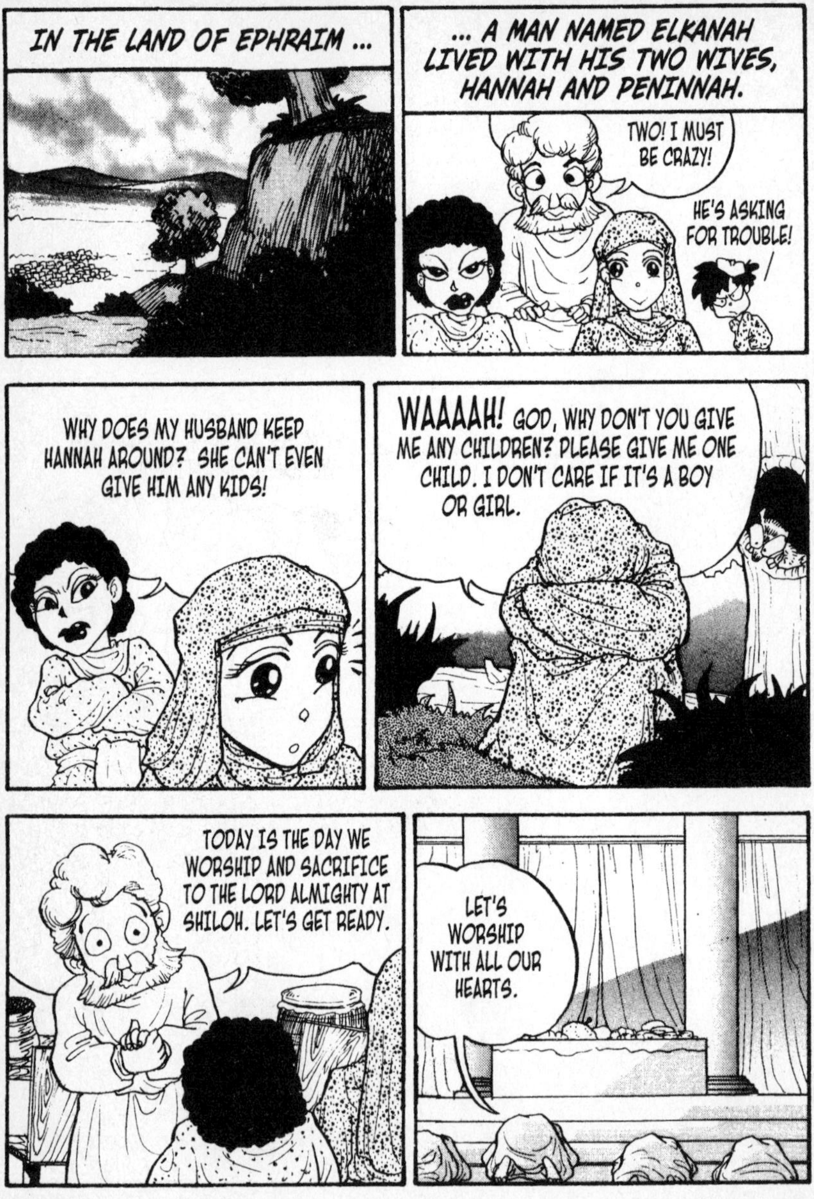
IN THE LAND OF EPHRAIM ...
... A MAN NAMED ELKANAH LIVED WITH HIS TWO WIVES, HANNAH AND PENINNAH.
TWO! I MUST BE CRAZY!
HE'S ASKING FOR TROUBLE!
WHY DOES MY HUSBAND KEEP HANNAH AROUND? SHE CAN'T EVEN GIVE HIM ANY KIDS!
WAAAAH! GOD, WHY DON'T YOU GIVE ME ANY CHILDREN? PLEASE GIVE ME ONE CHILD. I DON'T CARE IF IT'S A BOY OR GIRL.
TODAY IS THE DAY WE WORSHIP AND SACRIFICE TO THE LORD ALMIGHTY AT SHILOH. LET'S GET READY.
LET'S WORSHIP WITH ALL OUR HEARTS.

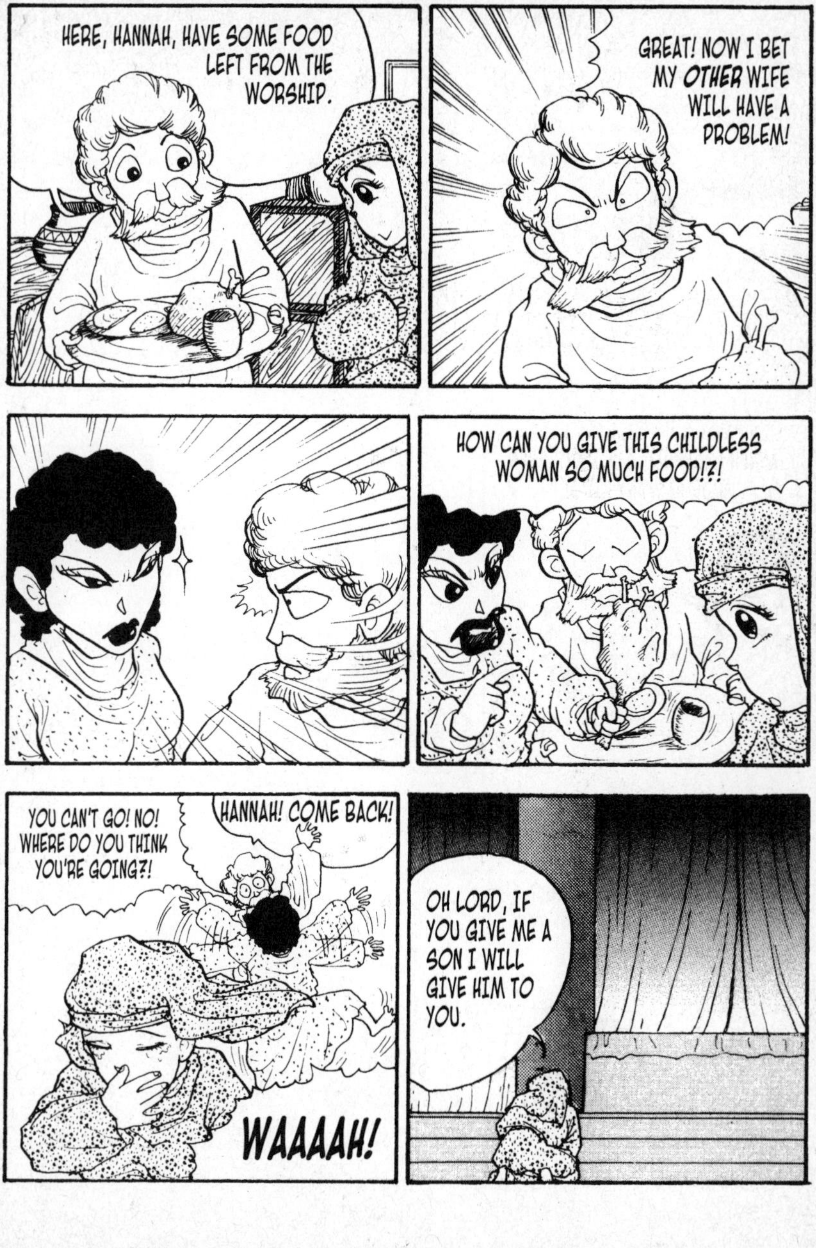
HERE, HANNAH, HAVE SOME FOOD LEFT FROM THE WORSHIP.
GREAT! NOW I BET MY OTHER WIFE WILL HAVE A PROBLEM!
HOW CAN YOU GIVE THIS CHILDLESS WOMAN SO MUCH FOOD!?!
YOU CAN'T GO! NO! WHERE DO YOU THINK YOU'RE GOING?!
HANNAH! COME BACK!
WAAAAH!
OH LORD, IF YOU GIVE ME A SON I WILL GIVE HIM TO YOU.

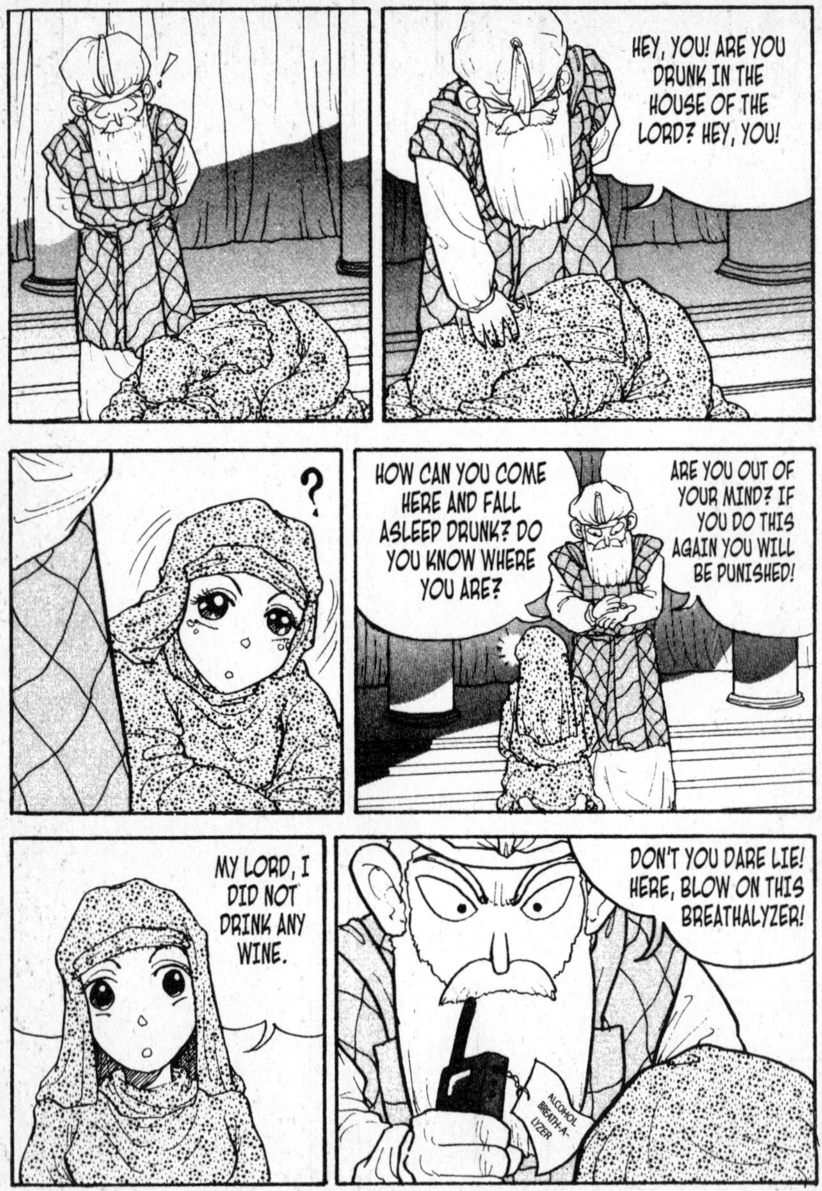
HEY, YOU! ARE YOU DRUNK IN THE HOUSE OF THE LORD? HEY, YOU!
?
HOW CAN YOU COME HERE AND FALL ASLEEP DRUNK? DO YOU KNOW WHERE YOU ARE?
ARE YOU OUT OF YOUR MIND? IF YOU DO THIS AGAIN YOU WILL BE PUNISHED!
MY LORD, I DID NOT DRINK ANY WINE.
DON'T YOU DARE LIE! HERE, BLOW ON THIS BREATHALYZER!
ALCOHOL BREATH-A-LYZER

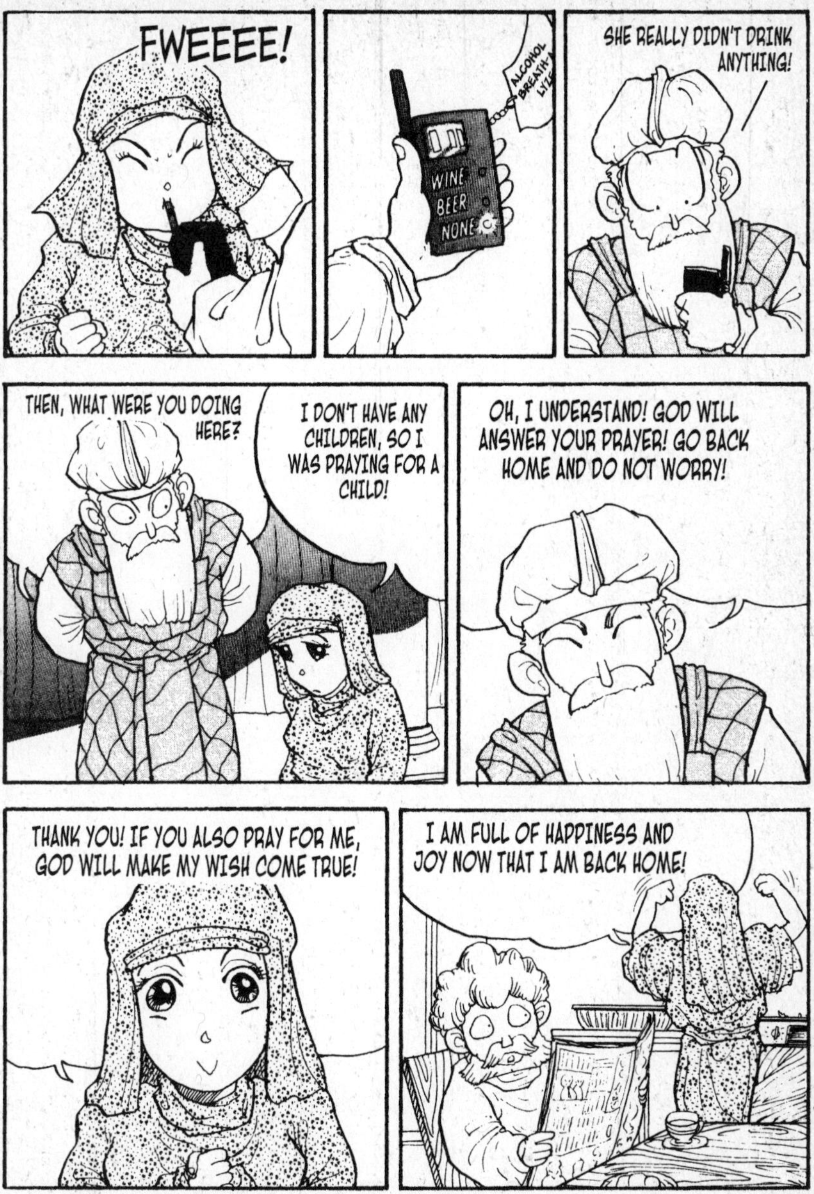
FWEEEE!
ALCOHOL
0.00
WINE
BEER
NONE
SHE REALLY DIDN'T DRINK ANYTHING!
THEN, WHAT WERE YOU DOING HERE?
I DON'T HAVE ANY CHILDREN, SO I WAS PRAYING FOR A CHILD!
OH, I UNDERSTAND! GOD WILL ANSWER YOUR PRAYER! GO BACK HOME AND DO NOT WORRY!
THANK YOU! IF YOU ALSO PRAY FOR ME, GOD WILL MAKE MY WISH COME TRUE!
I AM FULL OF HAPPINESS AND JOY NOW THAT I AM BACK HOME!

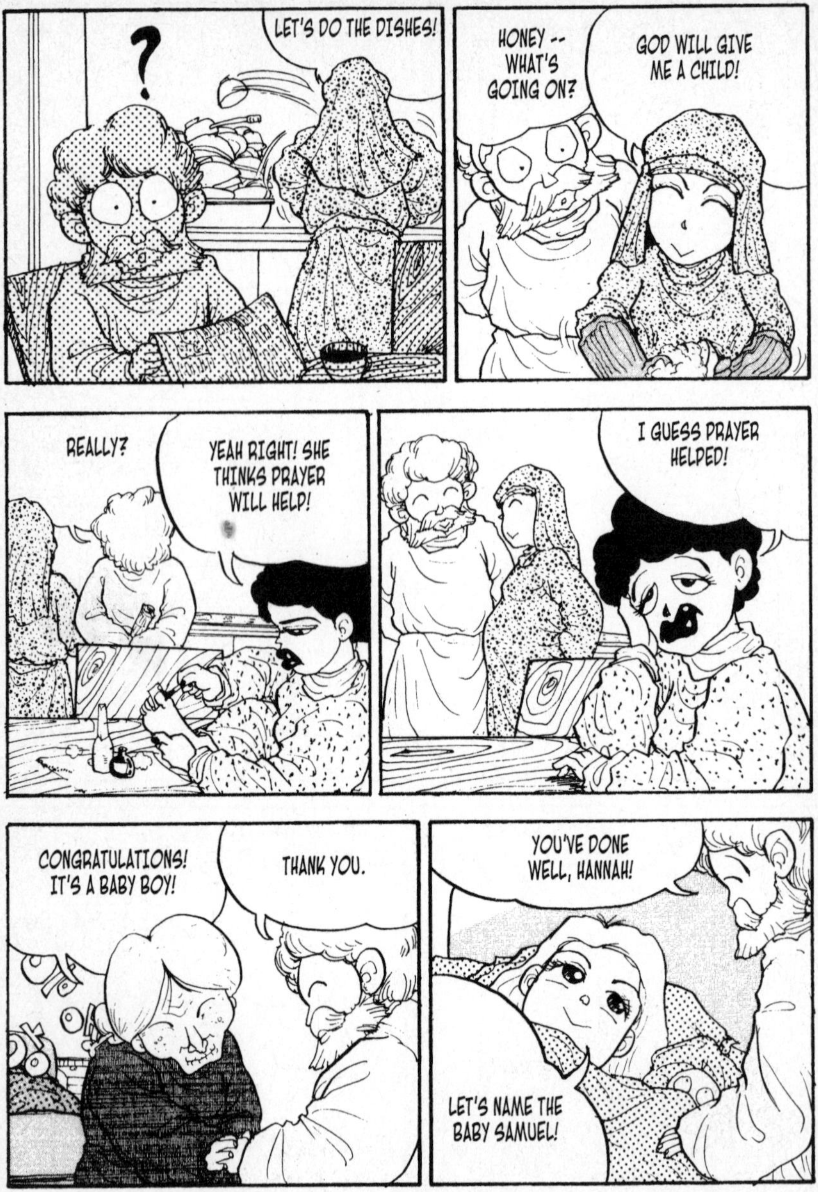
?
LET'S DO THE DISHES!
HONEY -- WHAT'S GOING ON?
GOD WILL GIVE ME A CHILD!
REALLY?
YEAH RIGHT! SHE THINKS PRAYER WILL HELP!
I GUESS PRAYER HELPED!
CONGRATULATIONS! IT'S A BABY BOY!
THANK YOU.
YOU'VE DONE WELL, HANNAH!
LET'S NAME THE BABY SAMUEL!

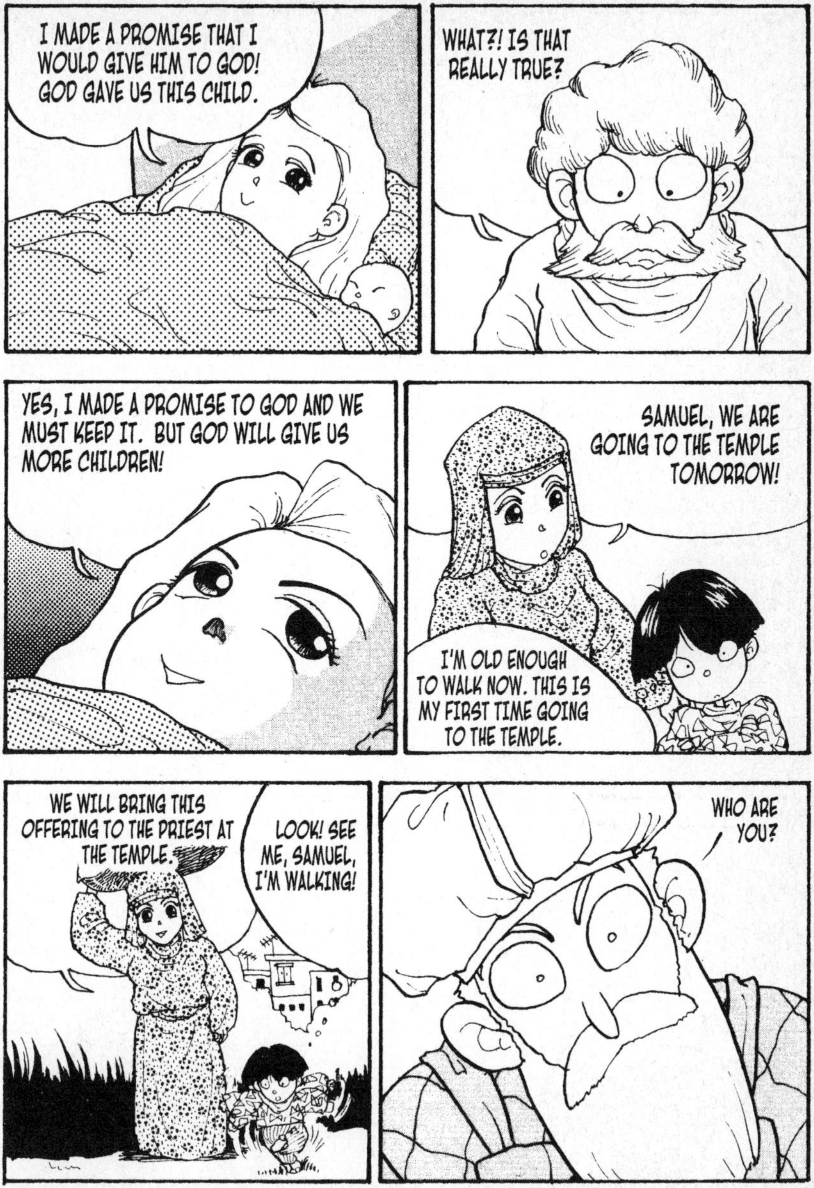

I MADE A PROMISE THAT I WOULD GIVE HIM TO GOD! GOD GAVE US THIS CHILD.
WHAT?! IS THAT REALLY TRUE?
YES, I MADE A PROMISE TO GOD AND WE MUST KEEP IT. BUT GOD WILL GIVE US MORE CHILDREN!
SAMUEL, WE ARE GOING TO THE TEMPLE TOMORROW!
I'M OLD ENOUGH TO WALK NOW. THIS IS MY FIRST TIME GOING TO THE TEMPLE.
WE WILL BRING THIS OFFERING TO THE PRIEST AT THE TEMPLE.
LOOK! SEE ME, SAMUEL, I'M WALKING!
WHO ARE YOU?

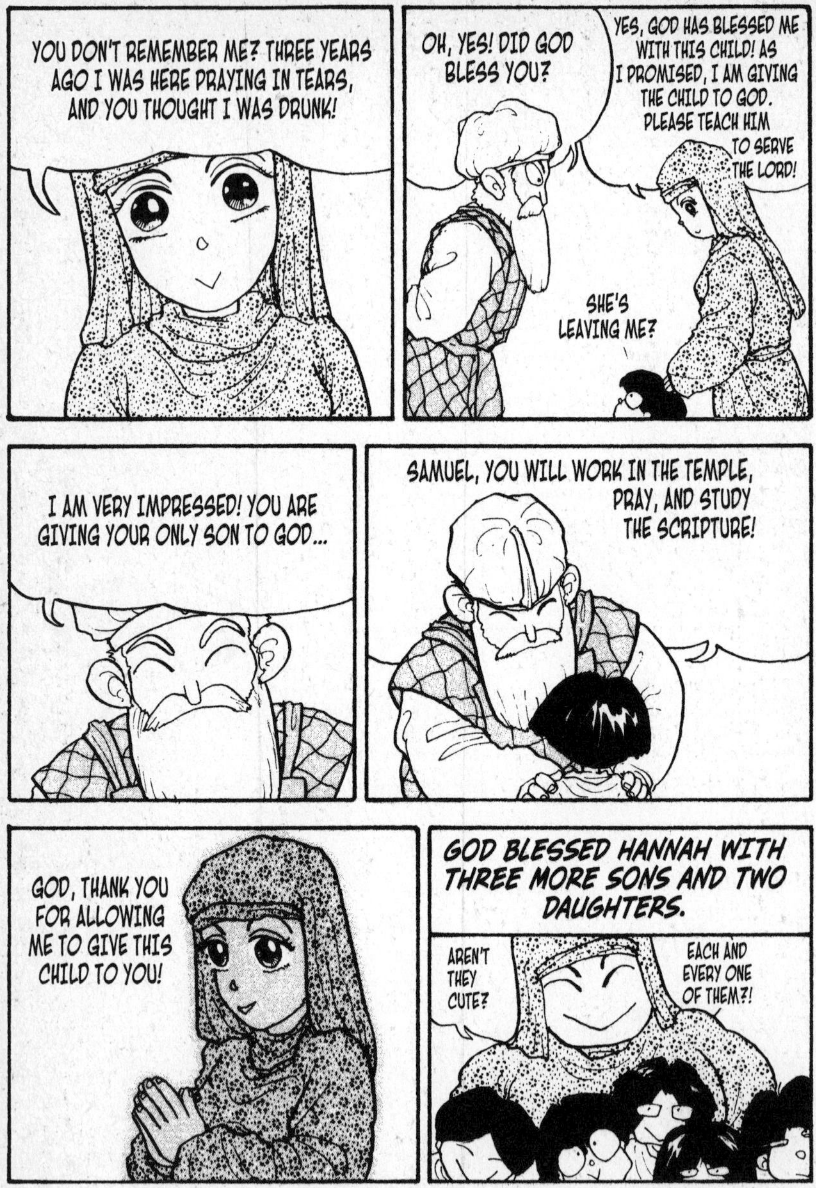
YOU DON'T REMEMBER ME? THREE YEARS AGO I WAS HERE PRAYING IN TEARS, AND YOU THOUGHT I WAS DRUNK!
OH, YES! DID GOD BLESS YOU?
YES, GOD HAS BLESSED ME WITH THIS CHILD! AS I PROMISED, I AM GIVING THE CHILD TO GOD. PLEASE TEACH HIM TO SERVE THE LORD!
SHE'S LEAVING ME?
I AM VERY IMPRESSED! YOU ARE GIVING YOUR ONLY SON TO GOD...
SAMUEL, YOU WILL WORK IN THE TEMPLE, PRAY, AND STUDY THE SCRIPTURE!
GOD, THANK YOU FOR ALLOWING ME TO GIVE THIS CHILD TO YOU!
GOD BLESSED HANNAH WITH THREE MORE SONS AND TWO DAUGHTERS.
AREN'T THEY CUTE?
EACH AND EVERY ONE OF THEM?!

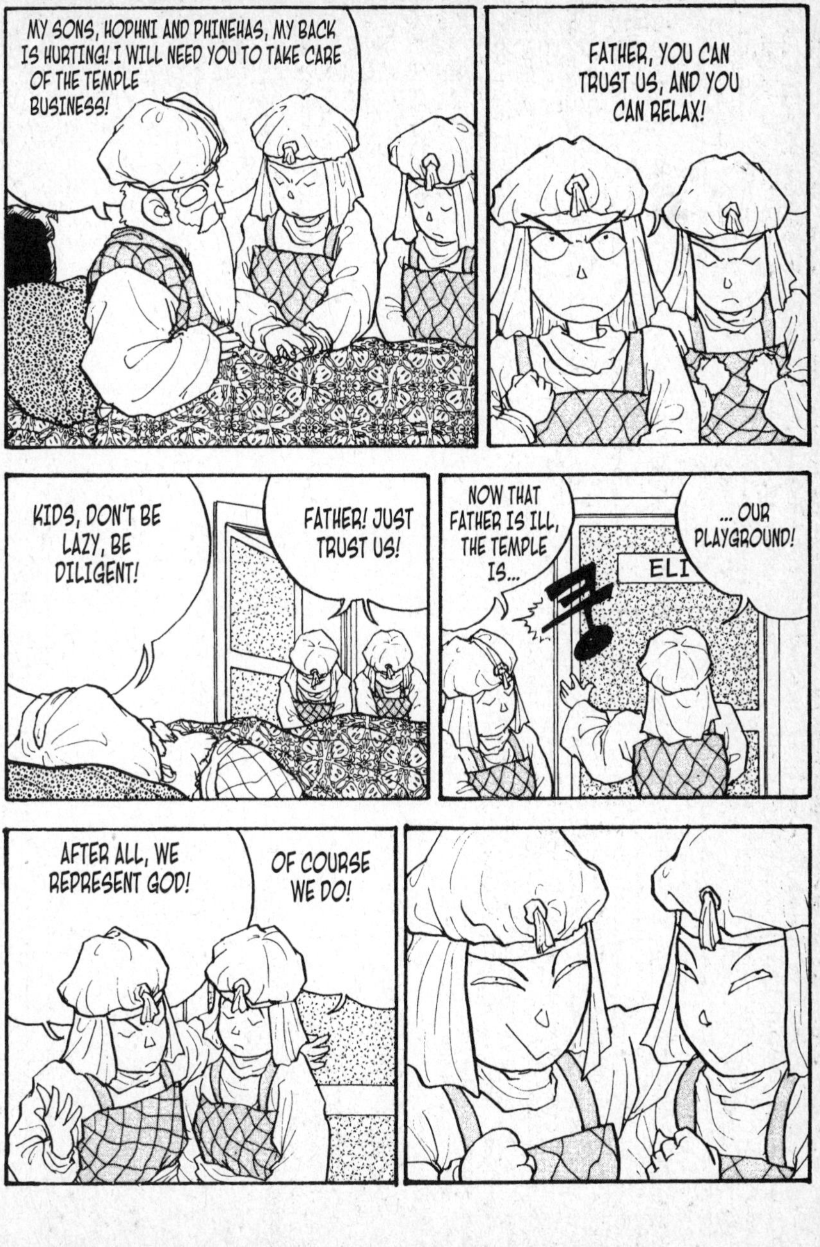
MY SONS, HOPHNI AND PHINEHAS, MY BACK IS HURTING! I WILL NEED YOU TO TAKE CARE OF THE TEMPLE BUSINESS!
FATHER, YOU CAN TRUST US, AND YOU CAN RELAX!
KIDS, DON'T BE LAZY, BE DILIGENT!
FATHER! JUST TRUST US!
NOW THAT FATHER IS ILL, THE TEMPLE IS...
ELI
... OUR PLAYGROUND!
AFTER ALL, WE REPRESENT GOD!
OF COURSE WE DO!

HEY, LET'S SPEND SOME TIME TOGETHER!
STOP!
YUM -- THIS MEAT FROM THE OFFERING TABLE IS FIRST CLASS!
HOW DARE YOU!
YOU CAN'T DO THIS --
FATHER IS ALL TALK. HE WON'T PUNISH US!
THEN WHICH WOMAN SHOULD WE BOTHER TODAY?
SOB -- MY LORD, I CANNOT WORK IN THE TEMPLE BECAUSE OF YOUR SONS. PLEASE MAKE THEM STOP!
I TOLD THEM TO STOP...
GOOD PARENTING

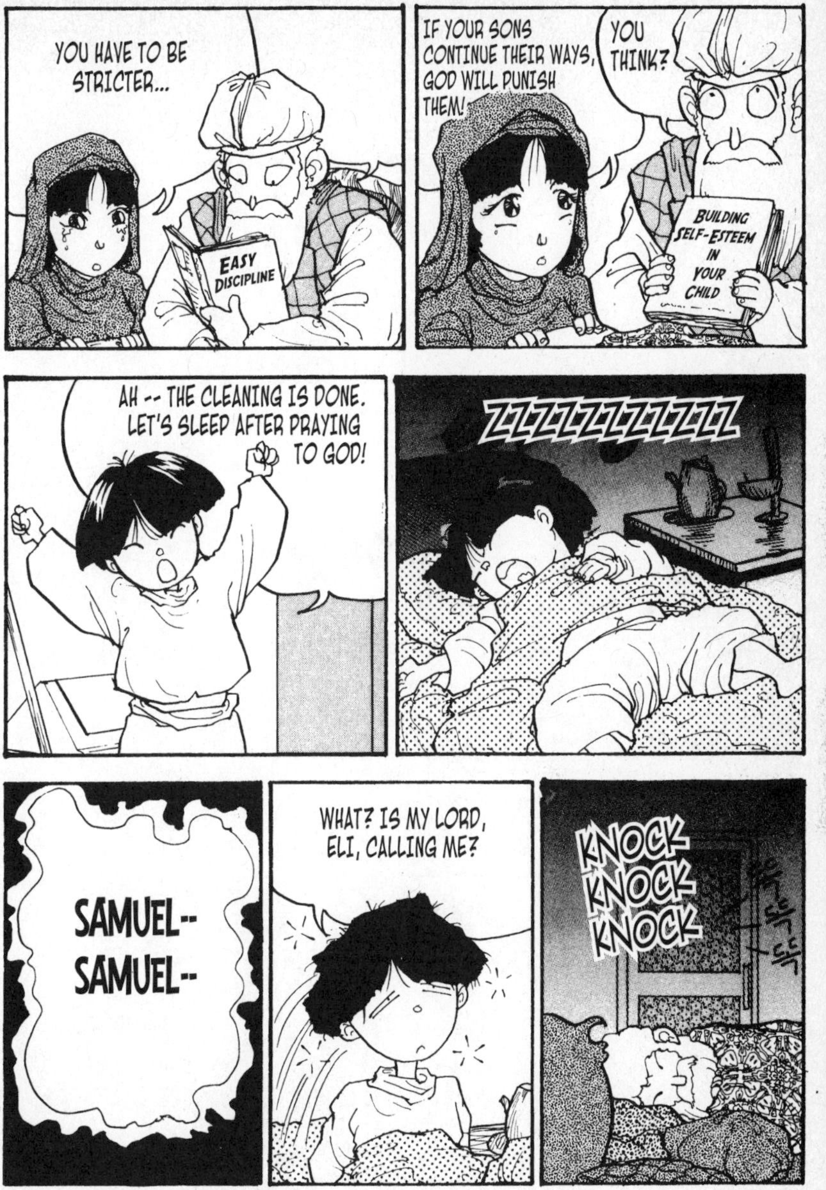
YOU HAVE TO BE STRICTER...
EASY DISCIPLINE
IF YOUR SONS CONTINUE THEIR WAYS, GOD WILL PUNISH THEM!
YOU THINK?
BUILDING SELF-ESTEEM IN YOUR CHILD
AH -- THE CLEANING IS DONE. LET'S SLEEP AFTER PRAYING TO GOD!
ZZZZZZZZZZZZZ
SAMUEL-- SAMUEL--
WHAT? IS MY LORD, ELI, CALLING ME?
KNOCK KNOCK KNOCK

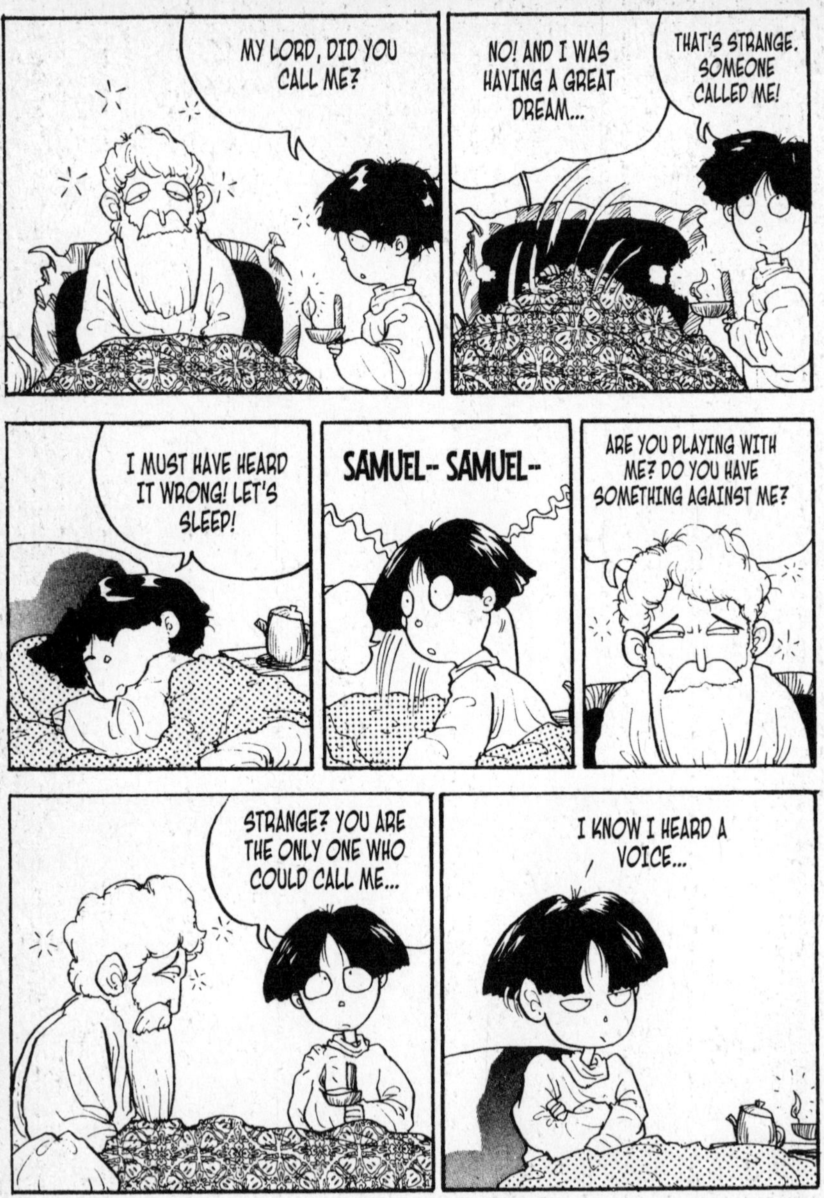
MY LORD, DID YOU CALL ME?
NO! AND I WAS HAVING A GREAT DREAM...
THAT'S STRANGE. SOMEONE CALLED ME!
I MUST HAVE HEARD IT WRONG! LET'S SLEEP!
SAMUEL-- SAMUEL--
ARE YOU PLAYING WITH ME? DO YOU HAVE SOMETHING AGAINST ME?
STRANGE? YOU ARE THE ONLY ONE WHO COULD CALL ME...
I KNOW I HEARD A VOICE...

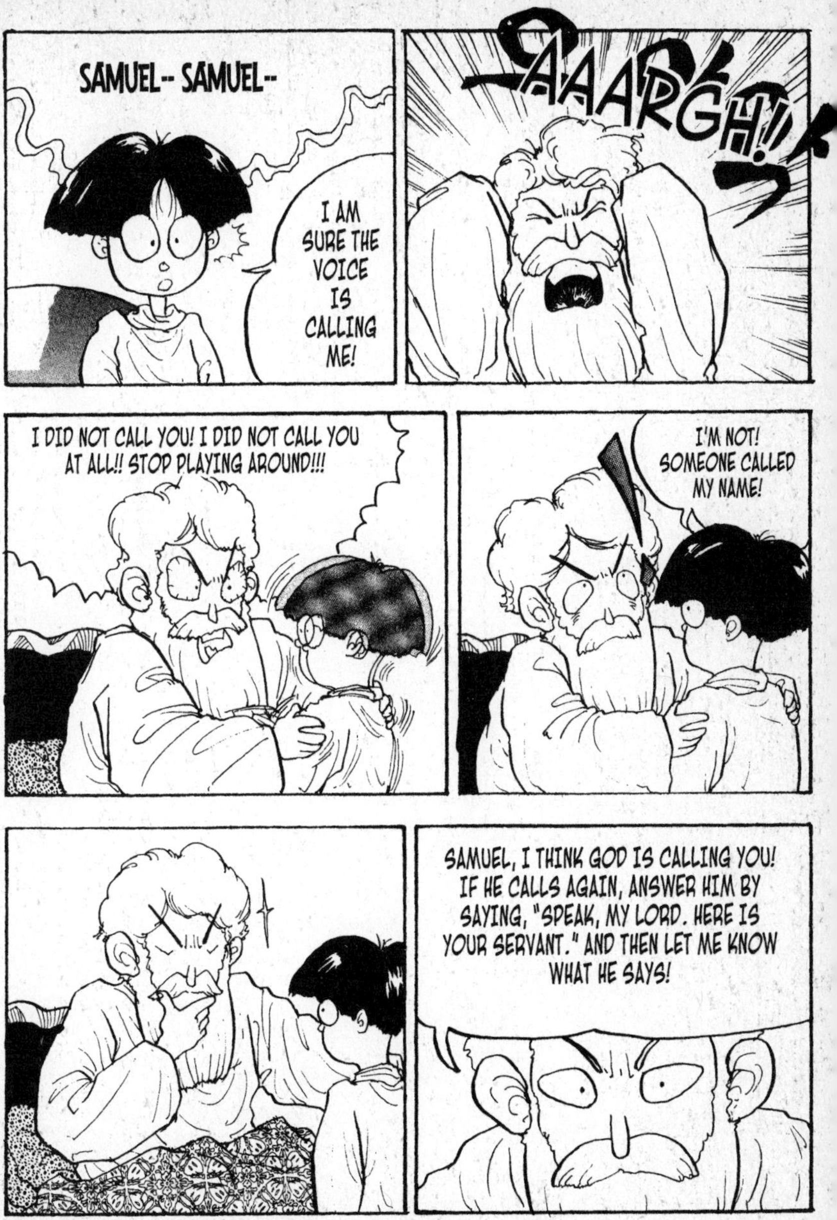
SAMUEL-- SAMUEL--
I AM SURE THE VOICE IS CALLING ME!
AAAARGH!!
I DID NOT CALL YOU! I DID NOT CALL YOU AT ALL!! STOP PLAYING AROUND!!!
I'M NOT! SOMEONE CALLED MY NAME!
SAMUEL, I THINK GOD IS CALLING YOU! IF HE CALLS AGAIN, ANSWER HIM BY SAYING, "SPEAK, MY LORD. HERE IS YOUR SERVANT." AND THEN LET ME KNOW WHAT HE SAYS!

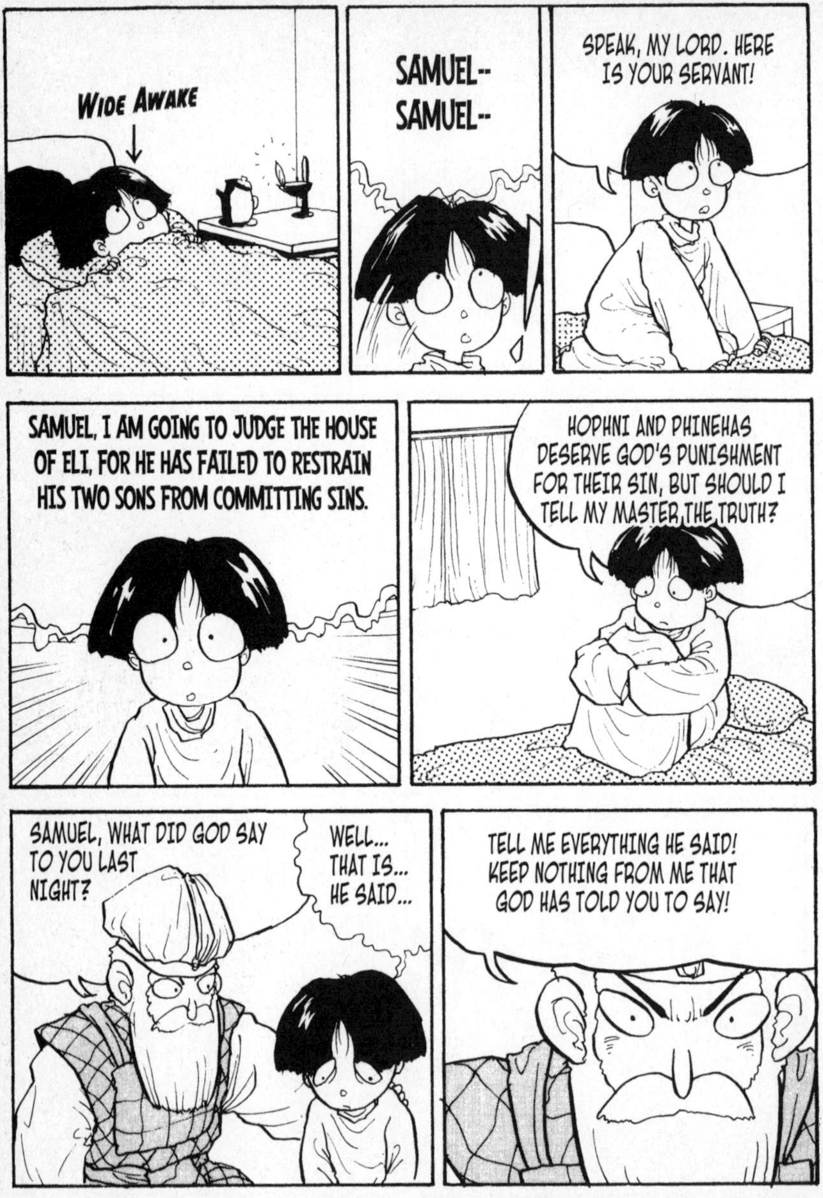
WIDE AWAKE
SAMUEL-- SAMUEL--
SPEAK, MY LORD. HERE IS YOUR SERVANT!
SAMUEL, I AM GOING TO JUDGE THE HOUSE OF ELI, FOR HE HAS FAILED TO RESTRAIN HIS TWO SONS FROM COMMITTING SINS.
HOPHNI AND PHINEHAS DESERVE GOD'S PUNISHMENT FOR THEIR SIN, BUT SHOULD I TELL MY MASTER THE TRUTH?
SAMUEL, WHAT DID GOD SAY TO YOU LAST NIGHT?
WELL... THAT IS... HE SAID...
TELL ME EVERYTHING HE SAID! KEEP NOTHING FROM ME THAT GOD HAS TOLD YOU TO SAY!

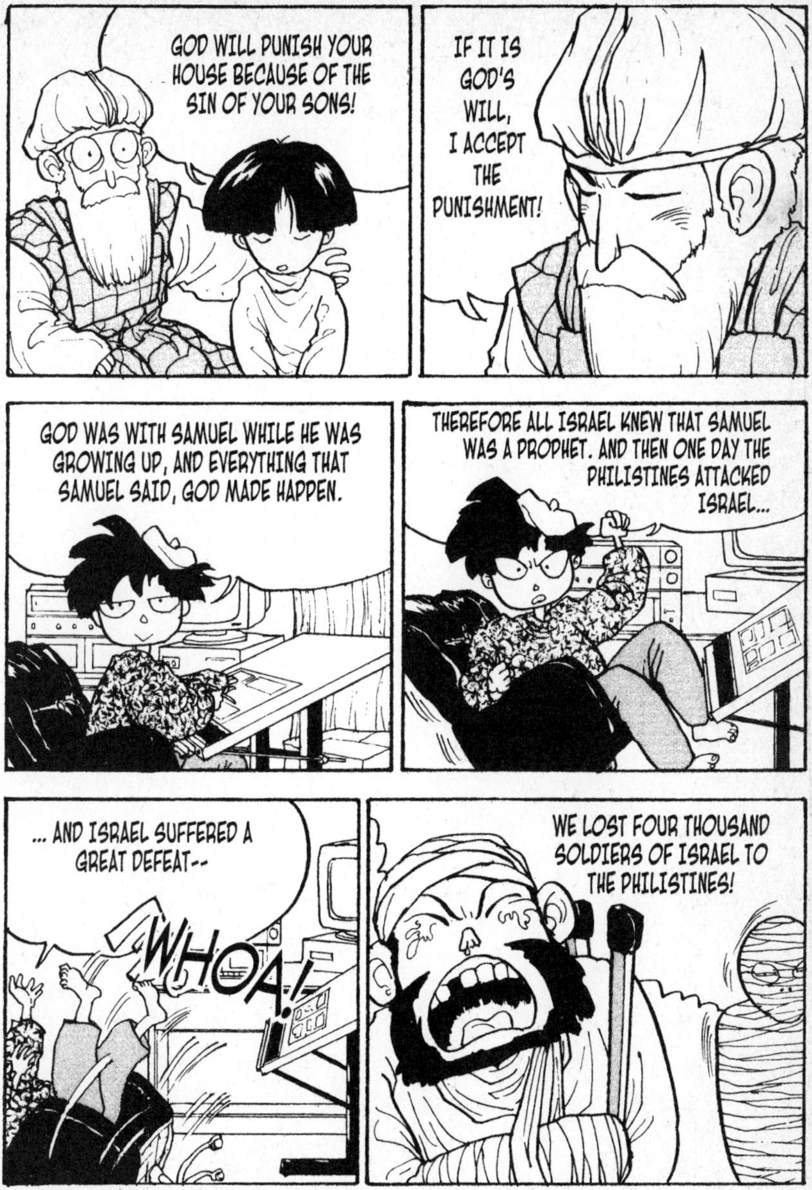
GOD WILL PUNISH YOUR HOUSE BECAUSE OF THE SIN OF YOUR SONS!
IF IT IS GOD'S WILL, I ACCEPT THE PUNISHMENT!
GOD WAS WITH SAMUEL WHILE HE WAS GROWING UP, AND EVERYTHING THAT SAMUEL SAID, GOD MADE HAPPEN.
THEREFORE ALL ISRAEL KNEW THAT SAMUEL WAS A PROPHET. AND THEN ONE DAY THE PHILISTINES ATTACKED ISRAEL...
... AND ISRAEL SUFFERED A GREAT DEFEAT--
WHOA!
WE LOST FOUR THOUSAND SOLDIERS OF ISRAEL TO THE PHILISTINES!

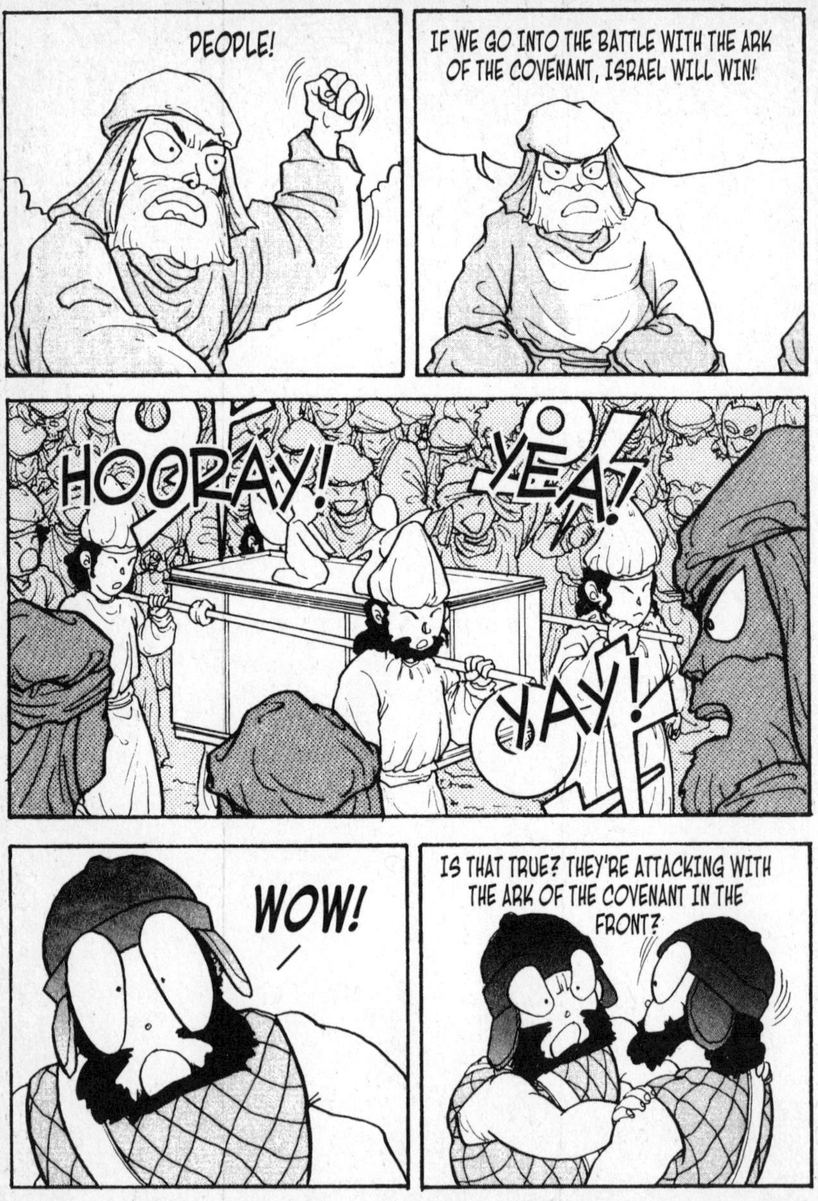
PEOPLE!
IF WE GO INTO THE BATTLE WITH THE ARK OF THE COVENANT, ISRAEL WILL WIN!
HOORAY!
YEA!
YAY!
WOW!
IS THAT TRUE? THEY'RE ATTACKING WITH THE ARK OF THE COVENANT IN THE FRONT?

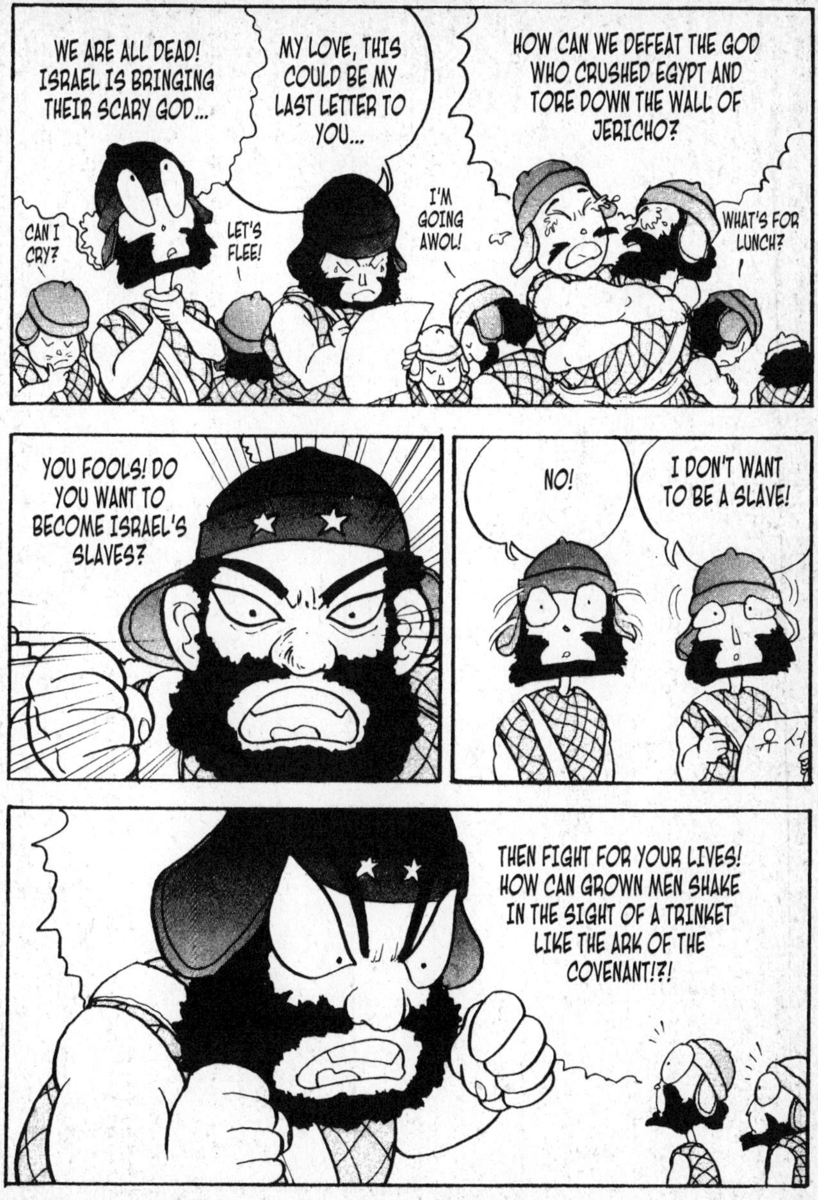
WE ARE ALL DEAD! ISRAEL IS BRINGING THEIR SCARY GOD...
MY LOVE, THIS COULD BE MY LAST LETTER TO YOU...
HOW CAN WE DEFEAT THE GOD WHO CRUSHED EGYPT AND TORE DOWN THE WALL OF JERICHO?
CAN I CRY?
LET'S FLEE!
I'M GOING AWOL!
WHAT'S FOR LUNCH?
YOU FOOLS! DO YOU WANT TO BECOME ISRAEL'S SLAVES?
NO!
I DON'T WANT TO BE A SLAVE!
유서
THEN FIGHT FOR YOUR LIVES! HOW CAN GROWN MEN SHAKE IN THE SIGHT OF A TRINKET LIKE THE ARK OF THE COVENANT!?!

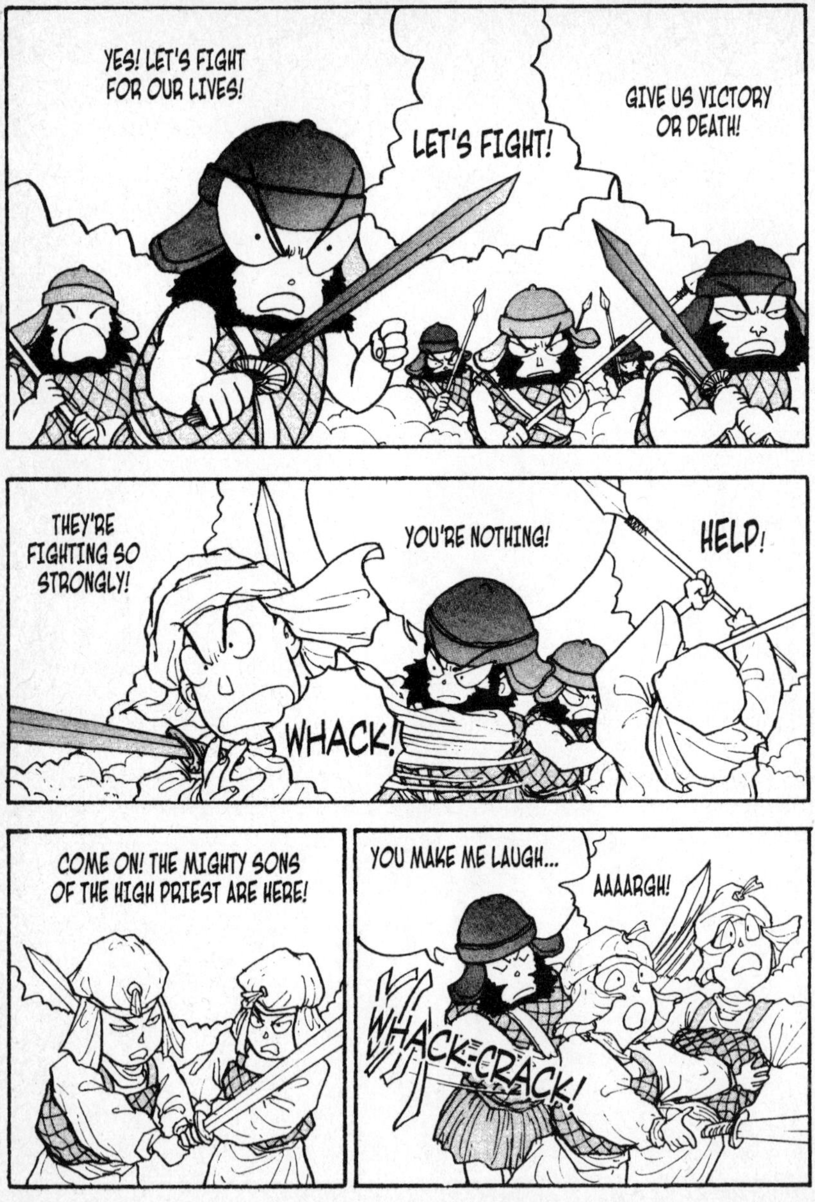
YES! LET'S FIGHT FOR OUR LIVES!
LET'S FIGHT!
GIVE US VICTORY OR DEATH!
THEY'RE FIGHTING SO STRONGLY!
YOU'RE NOTHING!
HELP!
WHACK!
COME ON! THE MIGHTY SONS OF THE HIGH PRIEST ARE HERE!
YOU MAKE ME LAUGH...
AAAARGH!
WHACK-CRACK!

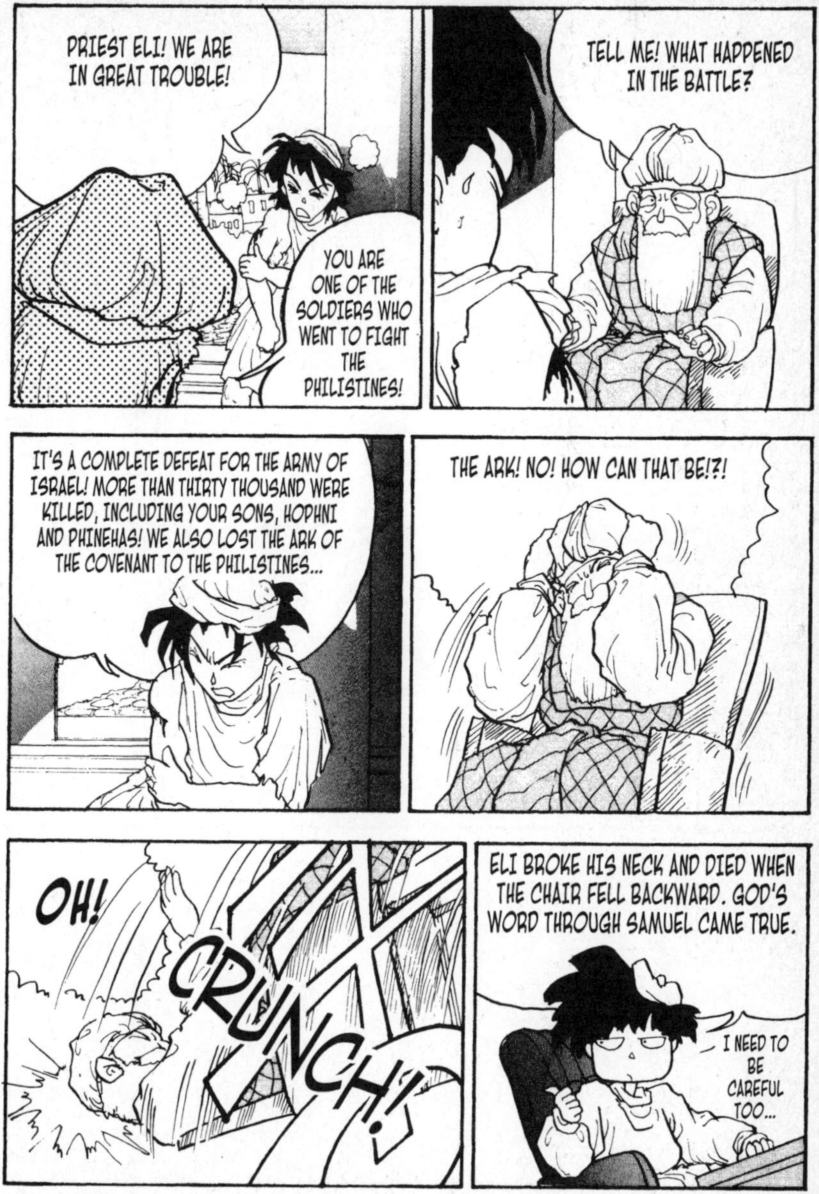
PRIEST ELI! WE ARE IN GREAT TROUBLE!
YOU ARE ONE OF THE SOLDIERS WHO WENT TO FIGHT THE PHILISTINES!
TELL ME! WHAT HAPPENED IN THE BATTLE?
IT'S A COMPLETE DEFEAT FOR THE ARMY OF ISRAEL! MORE THAN THIRTY THOUSAND WERE KILLED, INCLUDING YOUR SONS, HOPHNI AND PHINEHAS! WE ALSO LOST THE ARK OF THE COVENANT TO THE PHILISTINES...
THE ARK! NO! HOW CAN THAT BE!?!
OH!
CRUNCH!
ELI BROKE HIS NECK AND DIED WHEN THE CHAIR FELL BACKWARD. GOD'S WORD THROUGH SAMUEL CAME TRUE.
I NEED TO BE CAREFUL TOO...

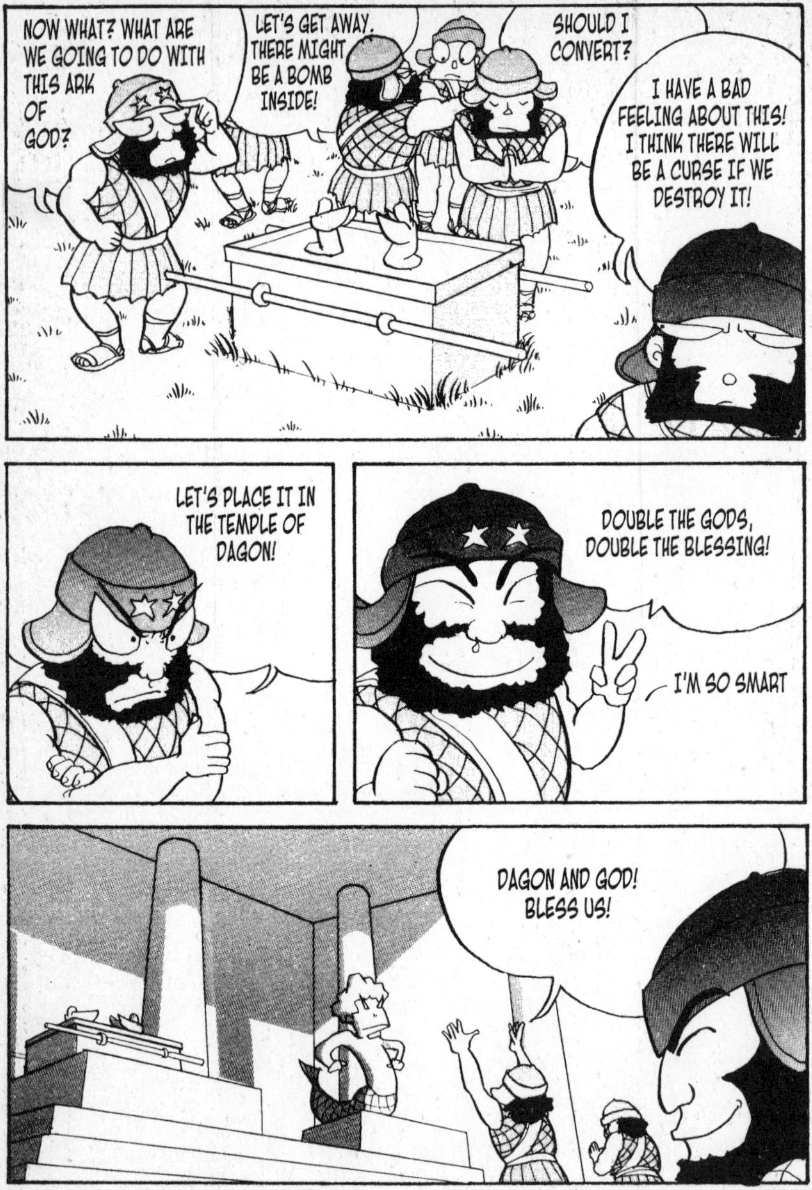
NOW WHAT? WHAT ARE WE GOING TO DO WITH THIS ARK OF GOD?
LET'S GET AWAY. THERE MIGHT BE A BOMB INSIDE!
SHOULD I CONVERT?
I HAVE A BAD FEELING ABOUT THIS! I THINK THERE WILL BE A CURSE IF WE DESTROY IT!
LET'S PLACE IT IN THE TEMPLE OF DAGON!
DOUBLE THE GODS, DOUBLE THE BLESSING!
I'M SO SMART
DAGON AND GOD! BLESS US!

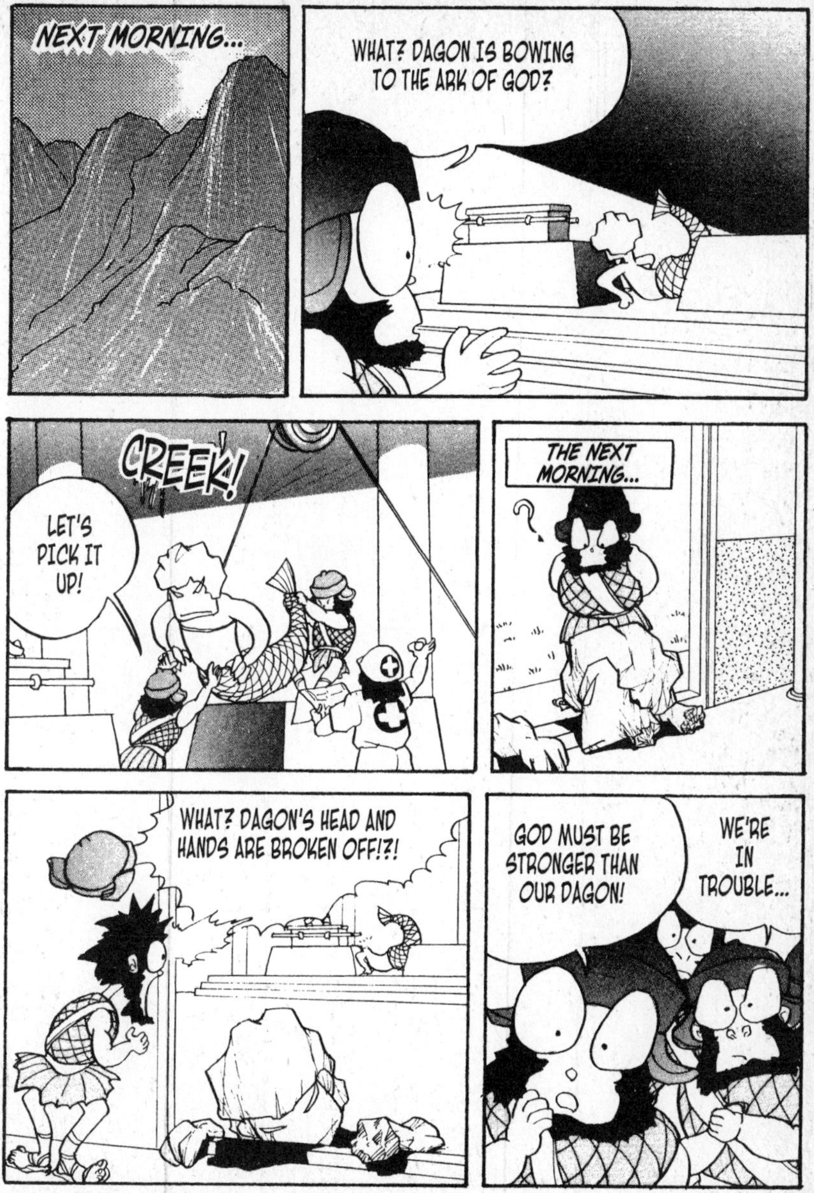
NEXT MORNING...
WHAT? DAGON IS BOWING TO THE ARK OF GOD?
CREEK!
LET'S PICK IT UP!
THE NEXT MORNING...
WHAT? DAGON'S HEAD AND HANDS ARE BROKEN OFF!?!
GOD MUST BE STRONGER THAN OUR DAGON!
WE'RE IN TROUBLE...

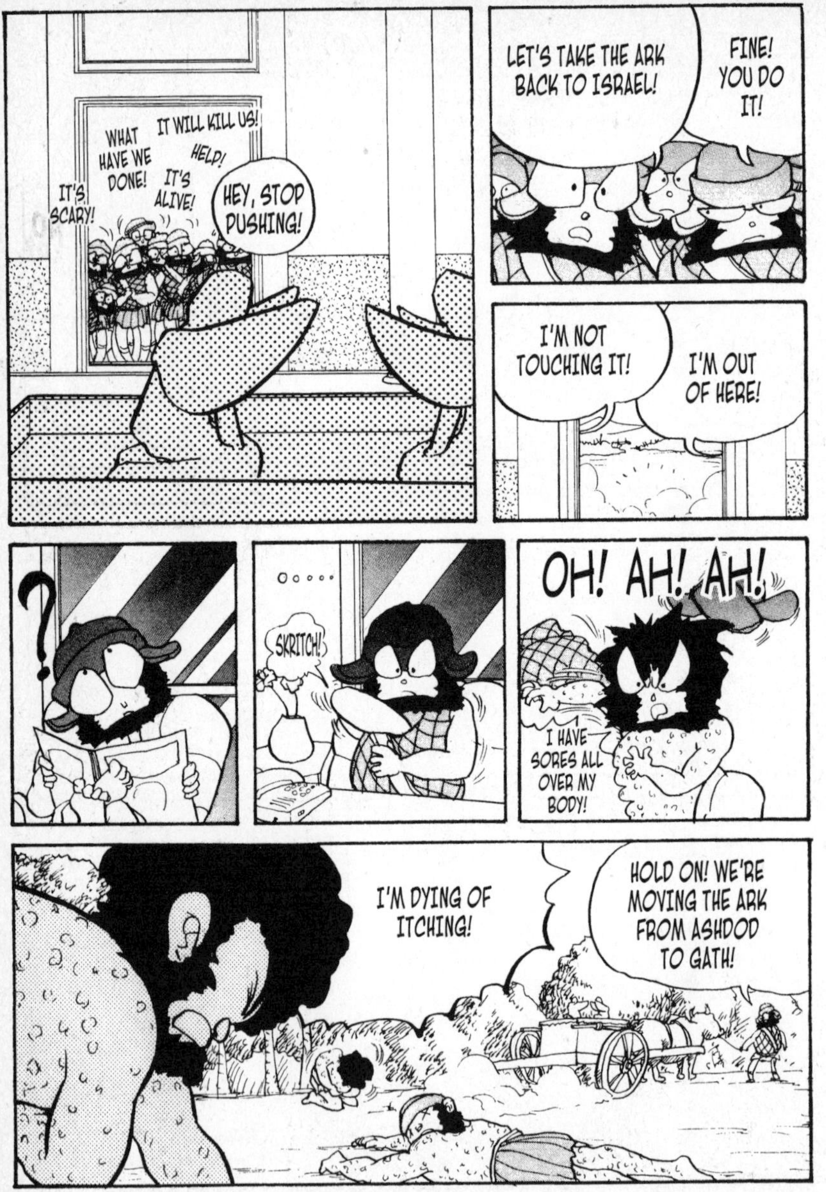
IT'S SCARY!
WHAT HAVE WE DONE!
IT WILL KILL US!
IT'S ALIVE!
HELP!
HEY, STOP PUSHING!
LET'S TAKE THE ARK BACK TO ISRAEL!
FINE! YOU DO IT!
I'M NOT TOUCHING IT!
I'M OUT OF HERE!
?
SKRITCH!
Ooooo
OH! AH! AH!
I HAVE SORES ALL OVER MY BODY!
I'M DYING OF ITCHING!
HOLD ON! WE'RE MOVING THE ARK FROM ASHDOD TO GATH!

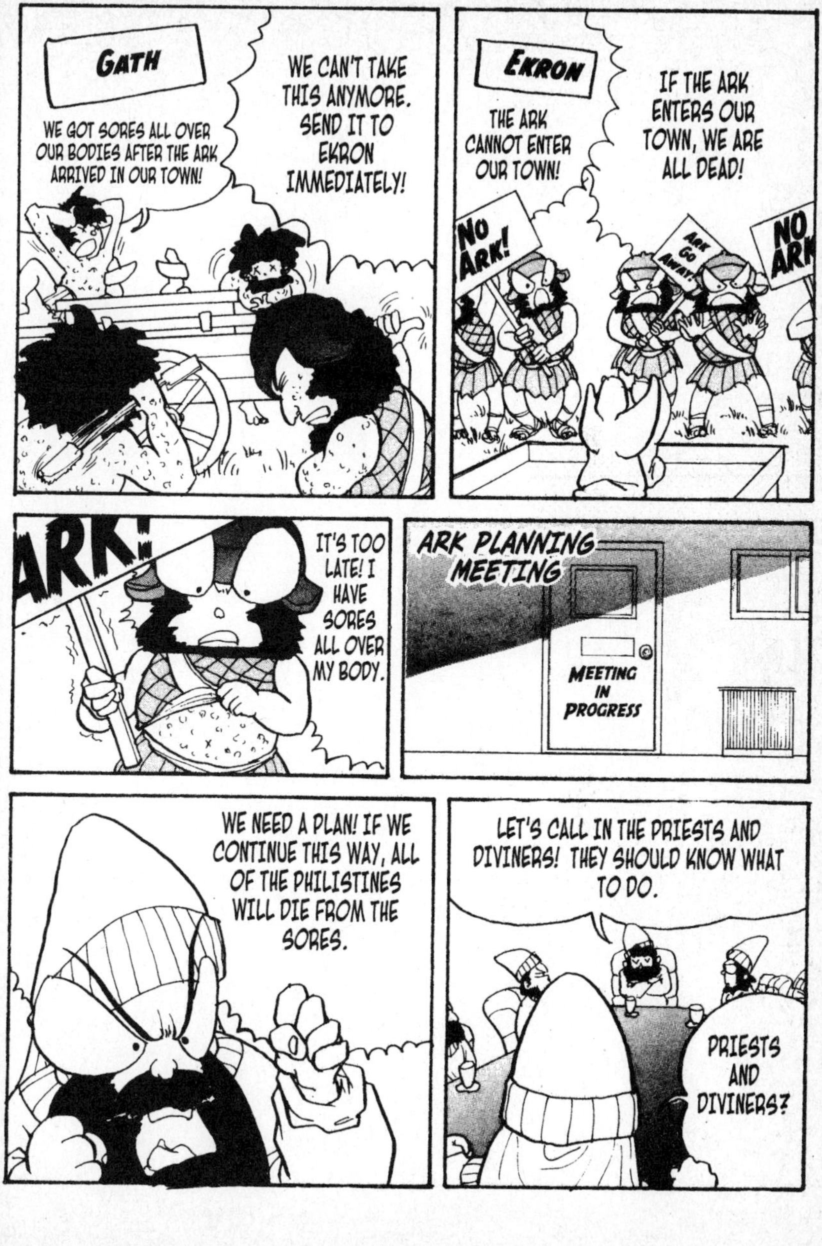
GATH
WE GOT SORES ALL OVER OUR BODIES AFTER THE ARK ARRIVED IN OUR TOWN!
WE CAN'T TAKE THIS ANYMORE. SEND IT TO EKRON IMMEDIATELY!
EKRON
THE ARK CANNOT ENTER OUR TOWN!
IF THE ARK ENTERS OUR TOWN, WE ARE ALL DEAD!
NO ARK!
ARK GO AWAY!
NO ARK
ARK!
IT'S TOO LATE! I HAVE SORES ALL OVER MY BODY.
ARK PLANNING MEETING
MEETING IN PROGRESS
WE NEED A PLAN! IF WE CONTINUE THIS WAY, ALL OF THE PHILISTINES WILL DIE FROM THE SORES.
LET'S CALL IN THE PRIESTS AND DIVINERS! THEY SHOULD KNOW WHAT TO DO.
PRIESTS AND DIVINERS?

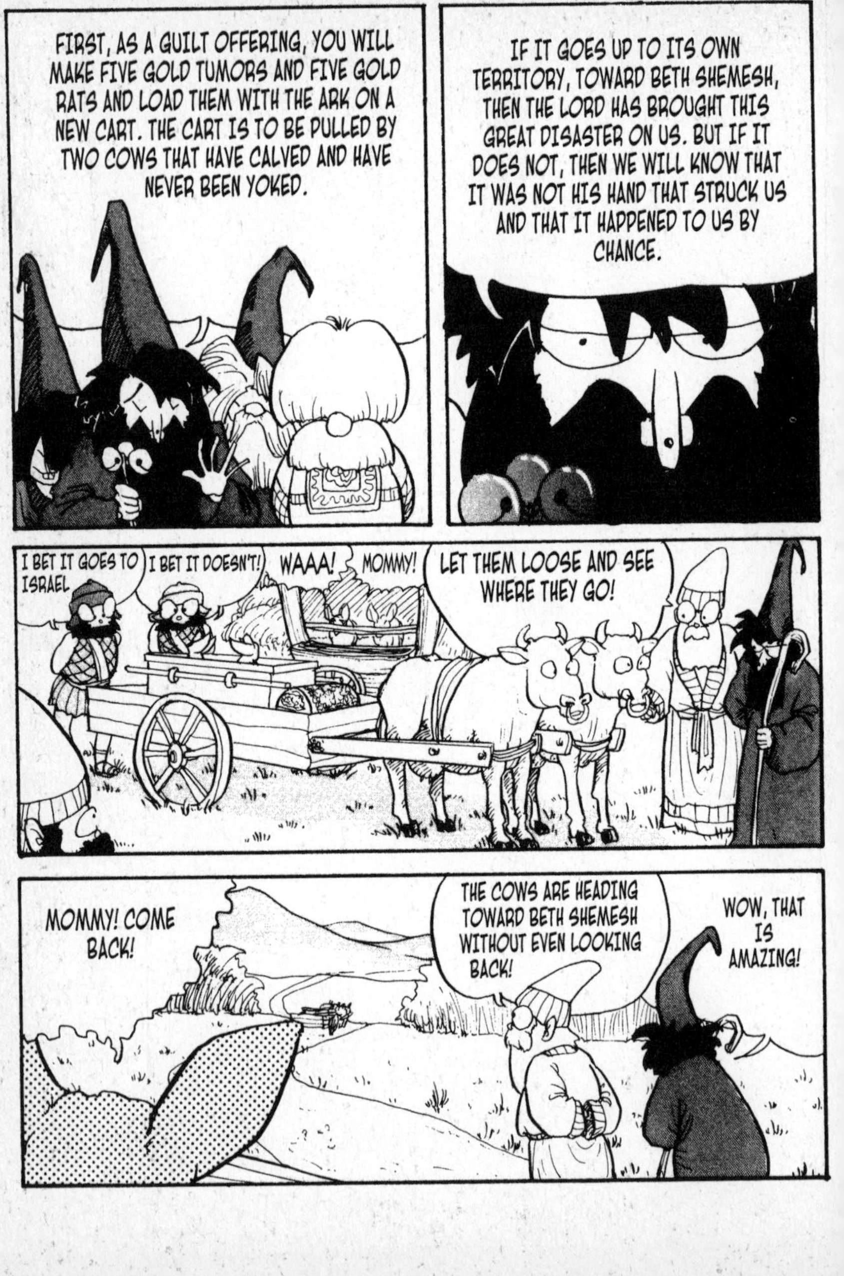

FIRST, AS A GUILT OFFERING, YOU WILL MAKE FIVE GOLD TUMORS AND FIVE GOLD RATS AND LOAD THEM WITH THE ARK ON A NEW CART. THE CART IS TO BE PULLED BY TWO COWS THAT HAVE CALVED AND HAVE NEVER BEEN YOKED.
IF IT GOES UP TO ITS OWN TERRITORY, TOWARD BETH SHEMESH, THEN THE LORD HAS BROUGHT THIS GREAT DISASTER ON US. BUT IF IT DOES NOT, THEN WE WILL KNOW THAT IT WAS NOT HIS HAND THAT STRUCK US AND THAT IT HAPPENED TO US BY CHANCE.
I BET IT GOES TO ISRAEL
I BET IT DOESN'T!
WAAA!
MOMMY!
LET THEM LOOSE AND SEE WHERE THEY GO!
MOMMY! COME BACK!
THE COWS ARE HEADING TOWARD BETH SHEMESH WITHOUT EVEN LOOKING BACK!
WOW, THAT IS AMAZING!

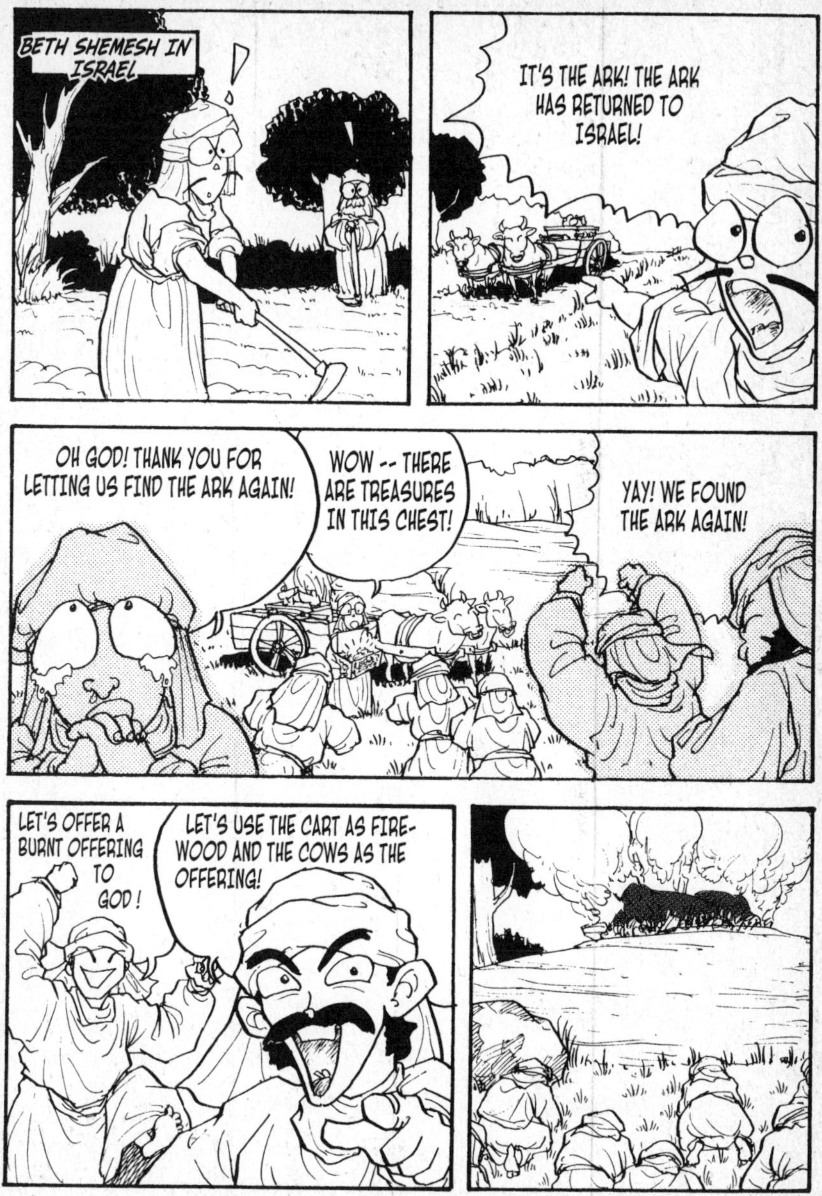
BETH SHEMESH IN ISRAEL
IT'S THE ARK! THE ARK HAS RETURNED TO ISRAEL!
OH GOD! THANK YOU FOR LETTING US FIND THE ARK AGAIN!
WOW -- THERE ARE TREASURES IN THIS CHEST!
YAY! WE FOUND THE ARK AGAIN!
LET'S OFFER A BURNT OFFERING TO GOD !
LET'S USE THE CART AS FIRE-WOOD AND THE COWS AS THE OFFERING!

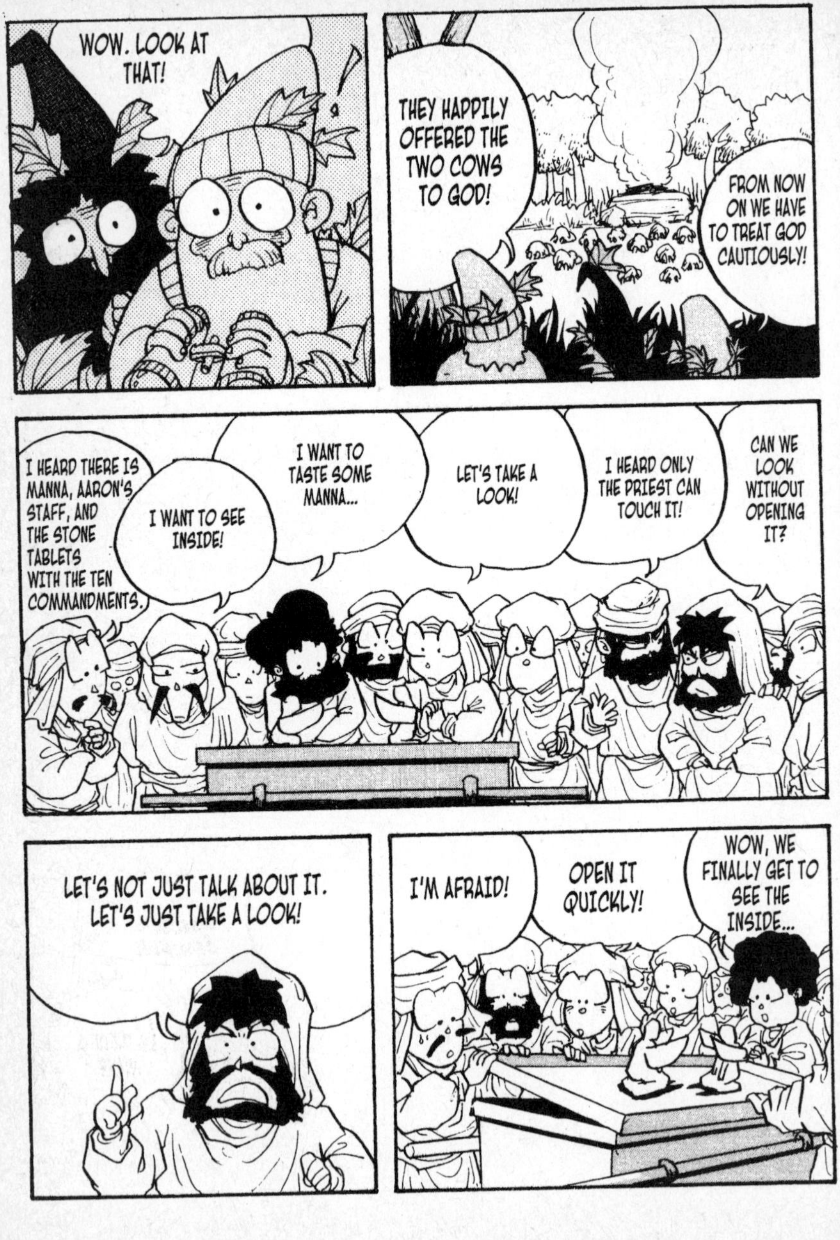
WOW. LOOK AT THAT!
!
THEY HAPPILY OFFERED THE TWO COWS TO GOD!
FROM NOW ON WE HAVE TO TREAT GOD CAUTIOUSLY!
I HEARD THERE IS MANNA, AARON'S STAFF, AND THE STONE TABLETS WITH THE TEN COMMANDMENTS.
I WANT TO SEE INSIDE!
I WANT TO TASTE SOME MANNA...
LET'S TAKE A LOOK!
I HEARD ONLY THE PRIEST CAN TOUCH IT!
CAN WE LOOK WITHOUT OPENING IT?
LET'S NOT JUST TALK ABOUT IT. LET'S JUST TAKE A LOOK!
I'M AFRAID!
OPEN IT QUICKLY!
WOW, WE FINALLY GET TO SEE THE INSIDE...

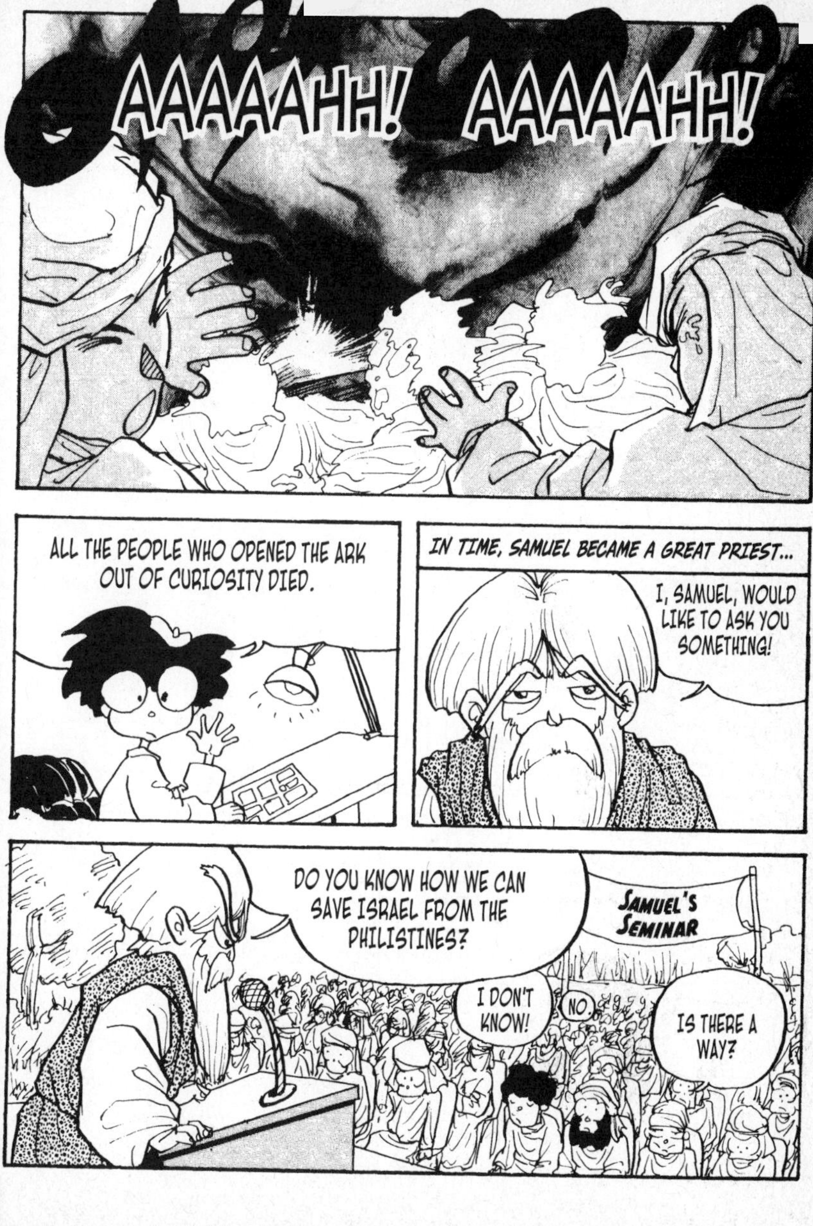
AAAAAHH! AAAAAHH!
ALL THE PEOPLE WHO OPENED THE ARK OUT OF CURIOSITY DIED.
IN TIME, SAMUEL BECAME A GREAT PRIEST...
I, SAMUEL, WOULD LIKE TO ASK YOU SOMETHING!
DO YOU KNOW HOW WE CAN SAVE ISRAEL FROM THE PHILISTINES?
SAMUEL'S SEMINAR
I DON'T KNOW!
NO.
IS THERE A WAY?

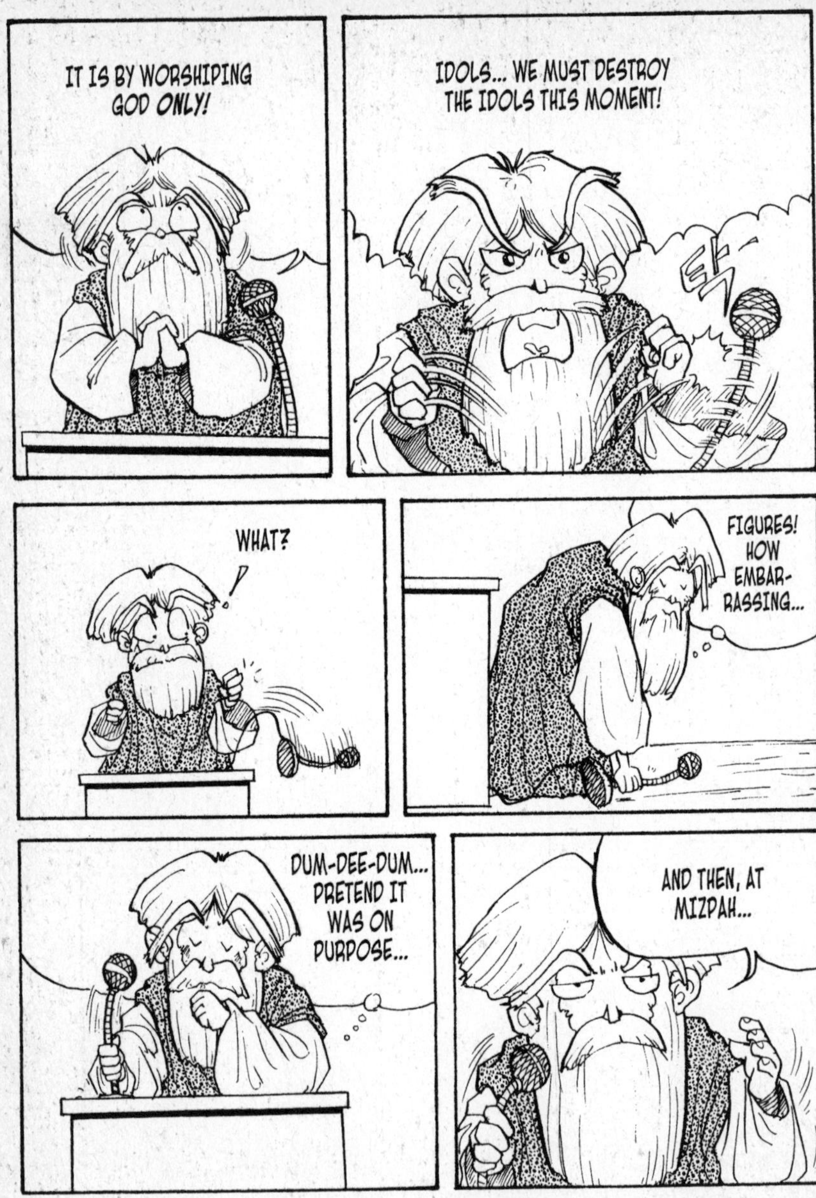
IT IS BY WORSHIPING GOD ONLY!
IDOLS... WE MUST DESTROY THE IDOLS THIS MOMENT!
WHAT?
!
FIGURES! HOW EMBAR-RASSING...
DUM-DEE-DUM... PRETEND IT WAS ON PURPOSE...
AND THEN, AT MIZPAH...

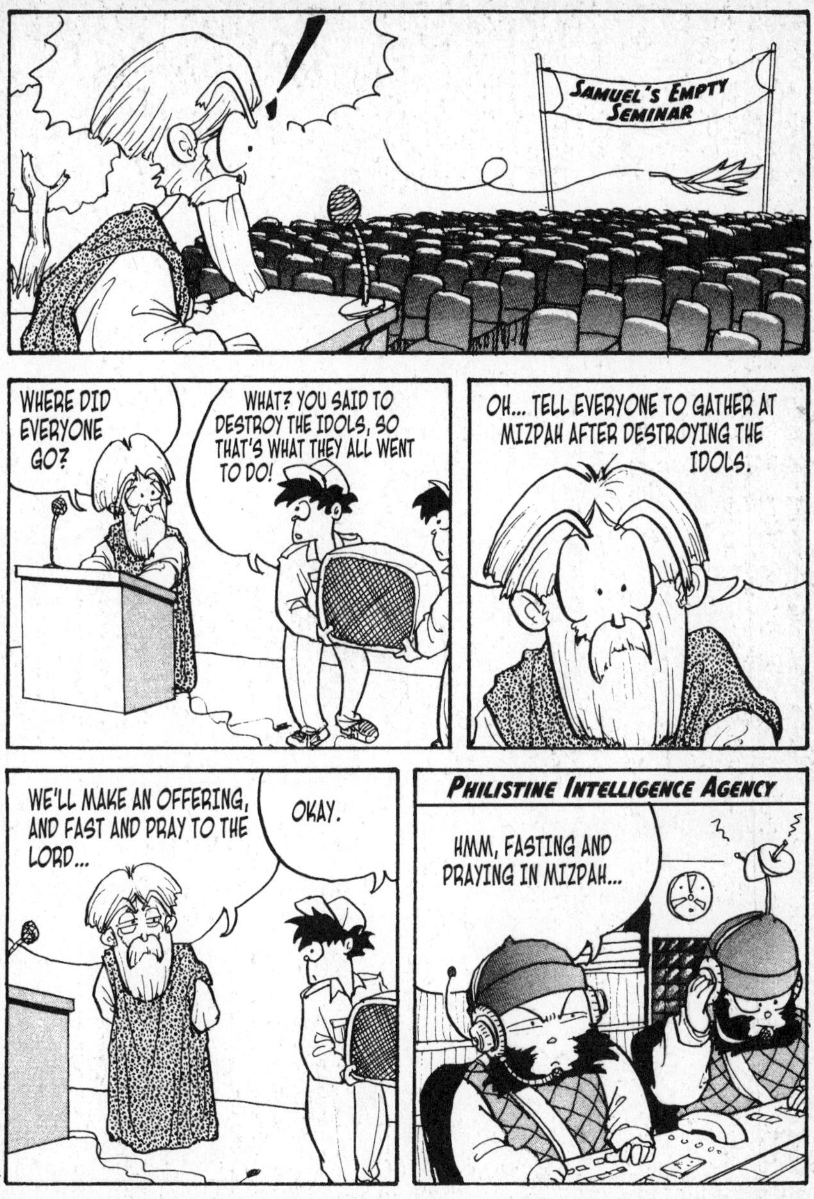
!
SAMUEL'S EMPTY SEMINAR
WHERE DID EVERYONE GO?
WHAT? YOU SAID TO DESTROY THE IDOLS, SO THAT'S WHAT THEY ALL WENT TO DO!
OH... TELL EVERYONE TO GATHER AT MIZPAH AFTER DESTROYING THE IDOLS.
WE'LL MAKE AN OFFERING, AND FAST AND PRAY TO THE LORD...
OKAY.
PHILISTINE INTELLIGENCE AGENCY
HMM, FASTING AND PRAYING IN MIZPAH...

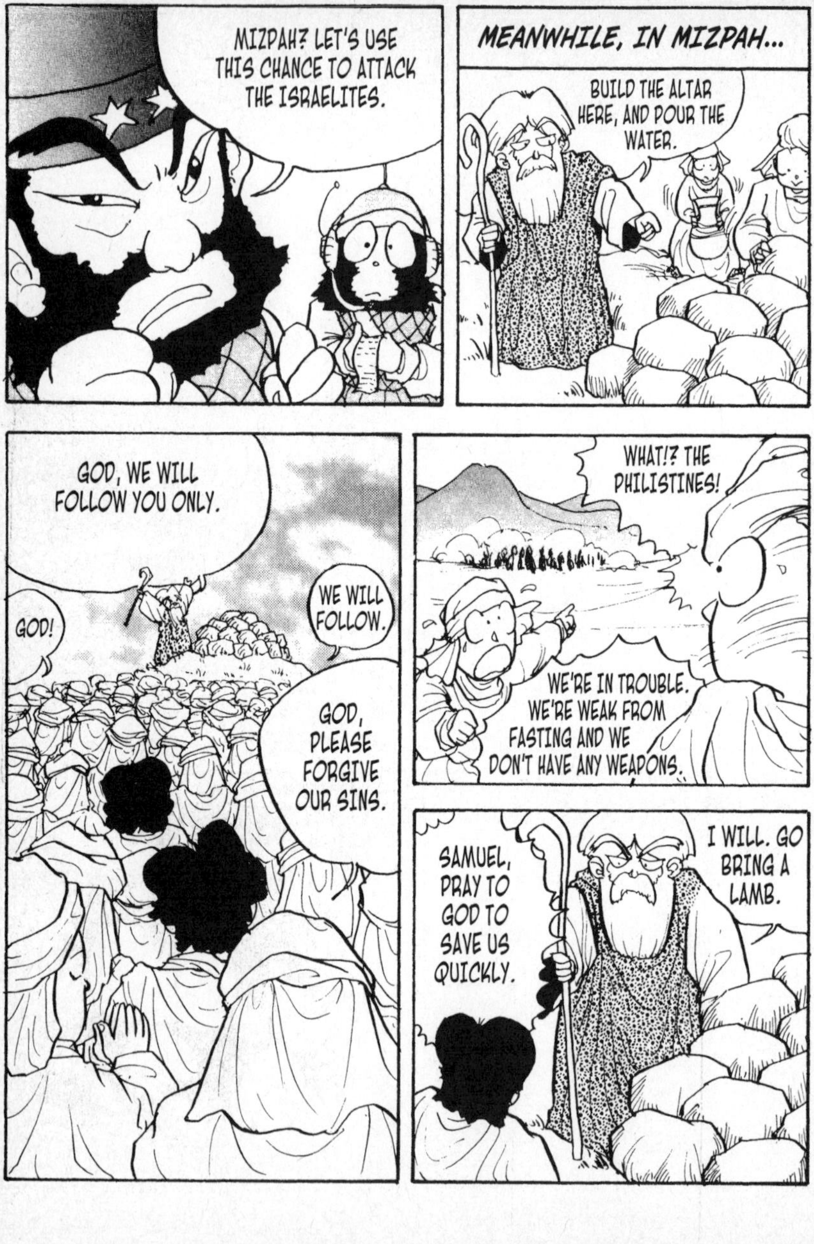
MIZPAH? LET'S USE THIS CHANCE TO ATTACK THE ISRAELITES.
MEANWHILE, IN MIZPAH...
BUILD THE ALTAR HERE, AND POUR THE WATER.
GOD, WE WILL FOLLOW YOU ONLY.
GOD!
WE WILL FOLLOW.
GOD, PLEASE FORGIVE OUR SINS.
WHAT!? THE PHILISTINES!
WE'RE IN TROUBLE. WE'RE WEAK FROM FASTING AND WE DON'T HAVE ANY WEAPONS.
SAMUEL, PRAY TO GOD TO SAVE US QUICKLY.
I WILL. GO BRING A LAMB.

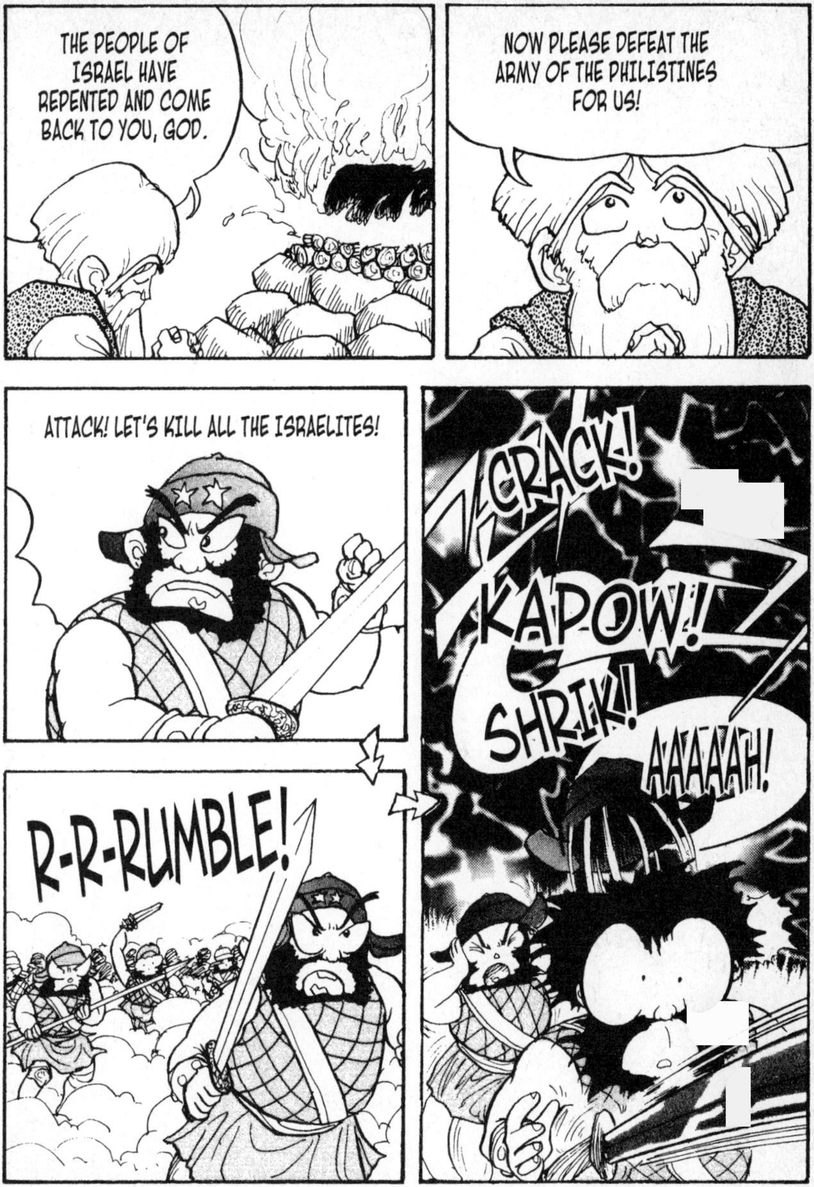
THE PEOPLE OF ISRAEL HAVE REPENTED AND COME BACK TO YOU, GOD.
NOW PLEASE DEFEAT THE ARMY OF THE PHILISTINES FOR US!
ATTACK! LET'S KILL ALL THE ISRAELITES!
R-R-RUMBLE!
CRACK!
KAPOW!
SHRIK!
AAAAAH!

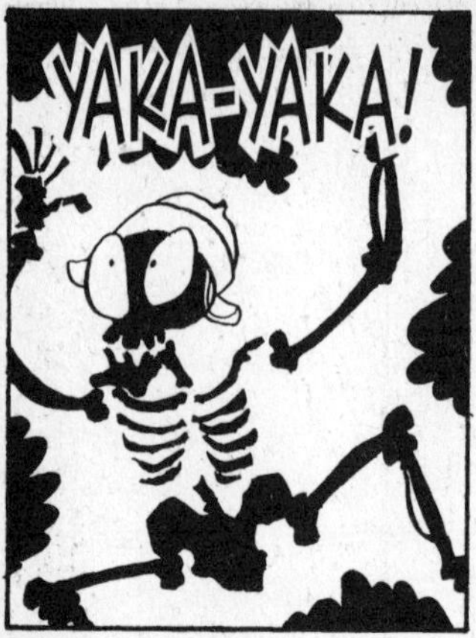
YAKA-YAKA!

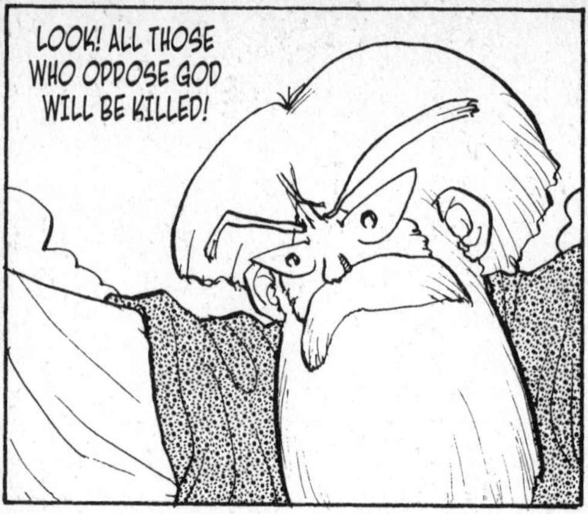
LOOK! ALL THOSE WHO OPPOSE GOD WILL BE KILLED!

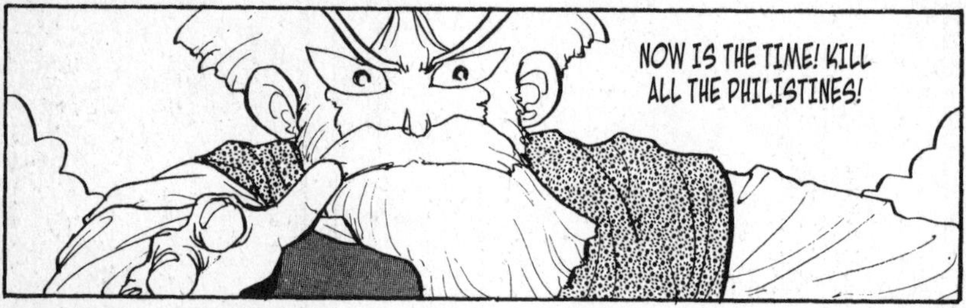
NOW IS THE TIME! KILL ALL THE PHILISTINES!

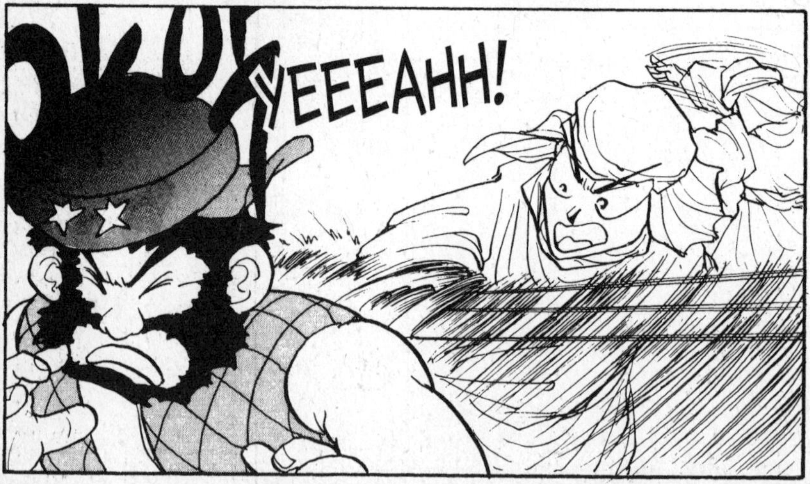
YEEEAHH!

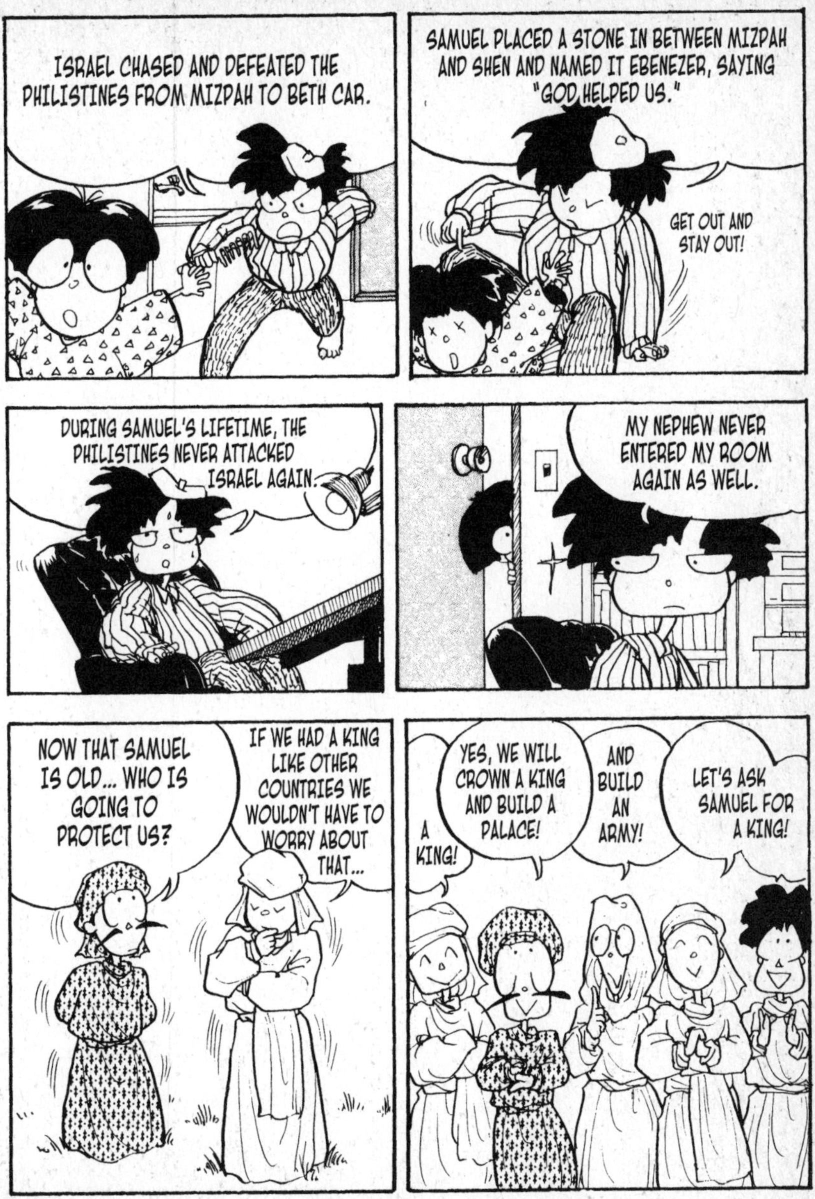
ISRAEL CHASED AND DEFEATED THE PHILISTINES FROM MIZPAH TO BETH CAR.
SAMUEL PLACED A STONE IN BETWEEN MIZPAH AND SHEN AND NAMED IT EBENEZER, SAYING "GOD HELPED US."
GET OUT AND STAY OUT!
DURING SAMUEL'S LIFETIME, THE PHILISTINES NEVER ATTACKED ISRAEL AGAIN.
MY NEPHEW NEVER ENTERED MY ROOM AGAIN AS WELL.
NOW THAT SAMUEL IS OLD... WHO IS GOING TO PROTECT US?
IF WE HAD A KING LIKE OTHER COUNTRIES WE WOULDN'T HAVE TO WORRY ABOUT THAT...
A KING!
YES, WE WILL CROWN A KING AND BUILD A PALACE!
AND BUILD AN ARMY!
LET'S ASK SAMUEL FOR A KING!

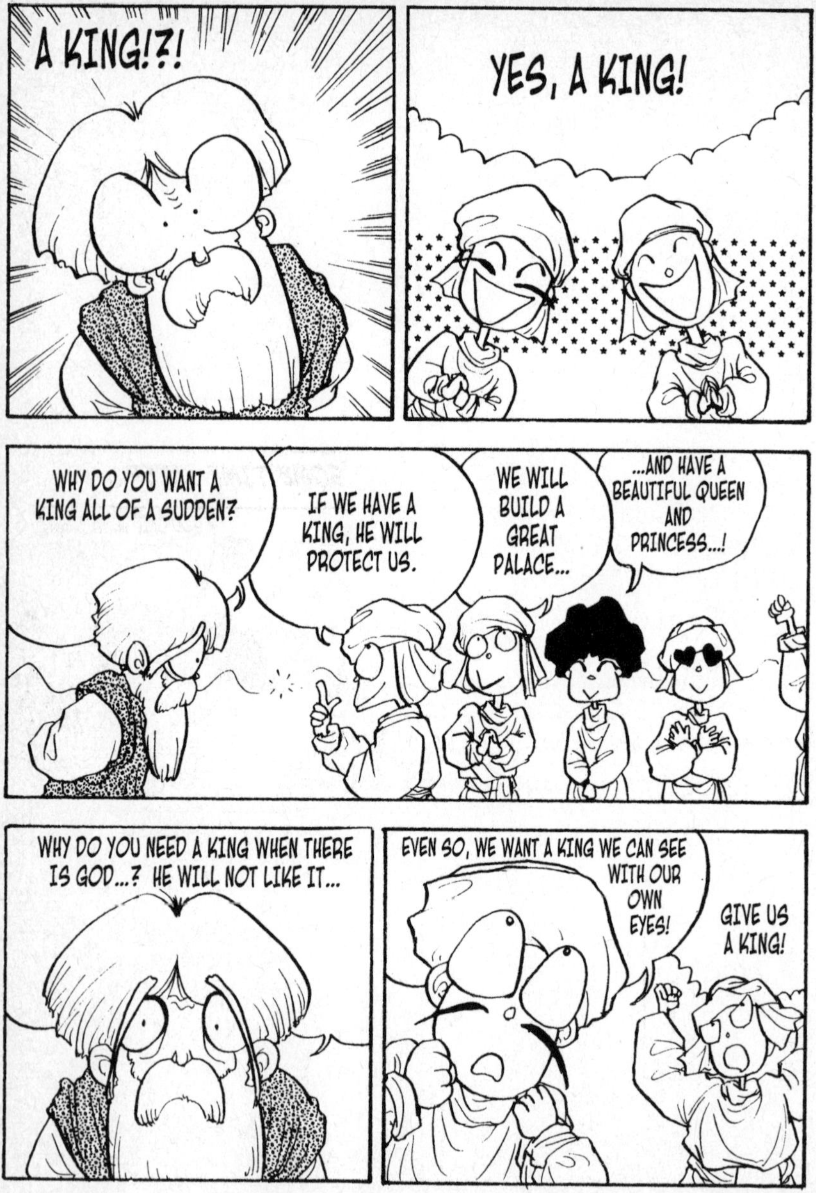
A KING!?!
YES, A KING!
WHY DO YOU WANT A KING ALL OF A SUDDEN?
IF WE HAVE A KING, HE WILL PROTECT US.
WE WILL BUILD A GREAT PALACE...
...AND HAVE A BEAUTIFUL QUEEN AND PRINCESS...!
WHY DO YOU NEED A KING WHEN THERE IS GOD...? HE WILL NOT LIKE IT...
EVEN SO, WE WANT A KING WE CAN SEE WITH OUR OWN EYES!
GIVE US A KING!

ALL RIGHT. GO BACK AND WAIT. I WILL PRAY AND SEEK GOD'S WILL.

A KING! A KING!

A KING!

GOD, THE PEOPLE WANT A KING...

LISTEN TO ALL THAT THE PEOPLE ARE SAYING TO YOU; IT IS NOT YOU THEY HAVE REJECTED, BUT THEY HAVE REJECTED ME AS THEIR KING. NOW LISTEN TO THEM; BUT WARN THEM WHAT THE KING WHO WILL REIGN OVER THEM WILL DO. I WILL SEND YOU A MAN FROM THE LAND OF BENJAMIN. ANOINT HIM LEADER OVER MY PEOPLE, ISRAEL, AND HE WILL DELIVER THEM FROM THE PHILISTINES.

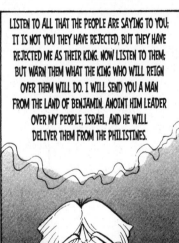

SOME TIME LATER...

GOD SAID HE WILL SEND SOMEONE TO BE KING...

EXCUSE ME, CAN I ASK YOU SOMETHING?

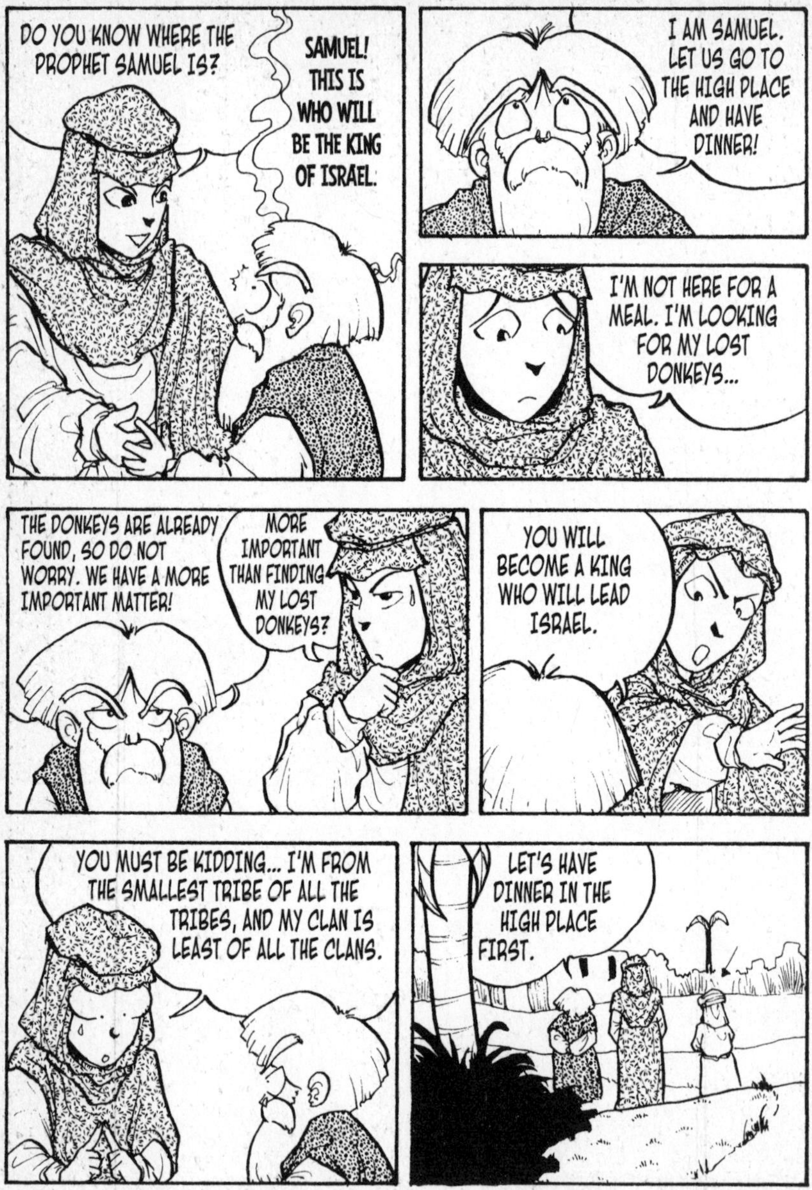
DO YOU KNOW WHERE THE PROPHET SAMUEL IS?
SAMUEL! THIS IS WHO WILL BE THE KING OF ISRAEL.
I AM SAMUEL. LET US GO TO THE HIGH PLACE AND HAVE DINNER!
I'M NOT HERE FOR A MEAL. I'M LOOKING FOR MY LOST DONKEYS...
THE DONKEYS ARE ALREADY FOUND, SO DO NOT WORRY. WE HAVE A MORE IMPORTANT MATTER!
MORE IMPORTANT THAN FINDING MY LOST DONKEYS?
YOU WILL BECOME A KING WHO WILL LEAD ISRAEL.
YOU MUST BE KIDDING... I'M FROM THE SMALLEST TRIBE OF ALL THE TRIBES, AND MY CLAN IS LEAST OF ALL THE CLANS.
LET'S HAVE DINNER IN THE HIGH PLACE FIRST.

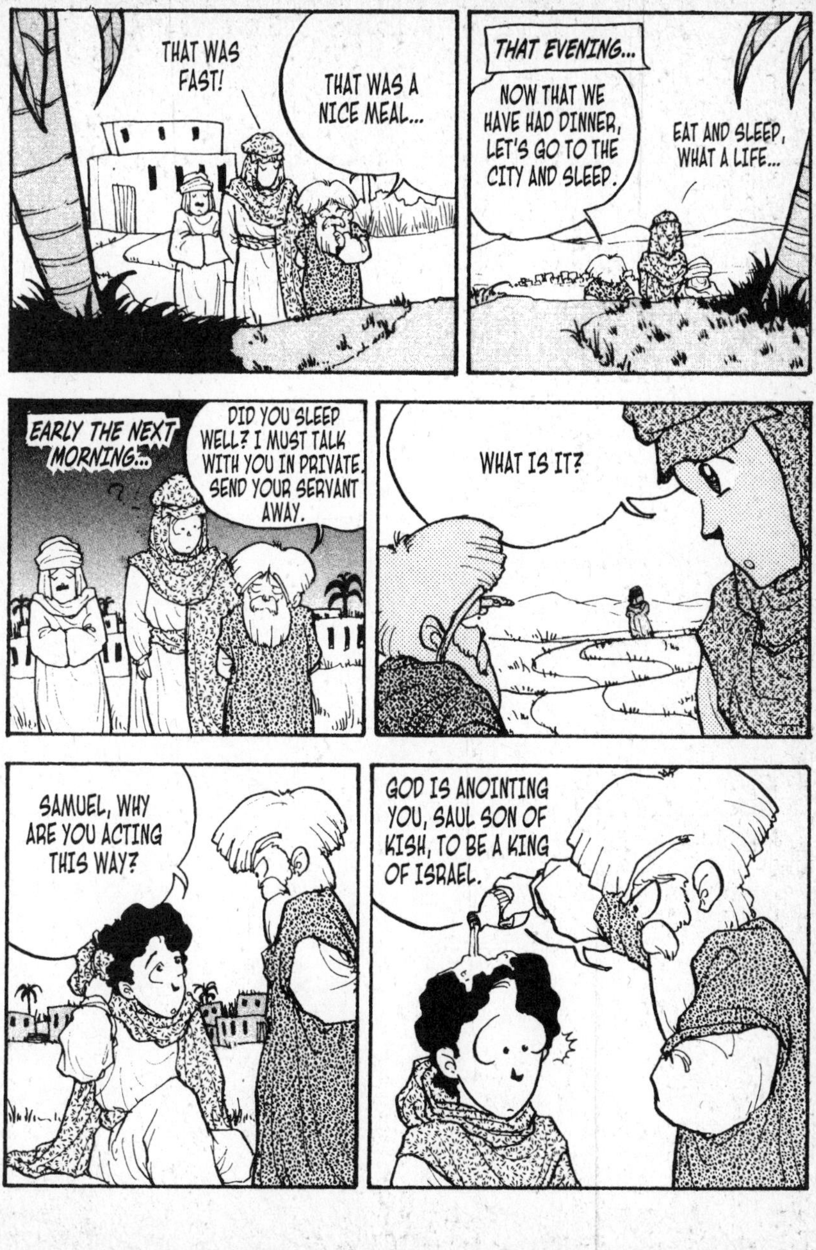
THAT WAS FAST!
THAT WAS A NICE MEAL...
THAT EVENING...
NOW THAT WE HAVE HAD DINNER, LET'S GO TO THE CITY AND SLEEP.
EAT AND SLEEP, WHAT A LIFE...
EARLY THE NEXT MORNING...
DID YOU SLEEP WELL? I MUST TALK WITH YOU IN PRIVATE. SEND YOUR SERVANT AWAY.
WHAT IS IT?
SAMUEL, WHY ARE YOU ACTING THIS WAY?
GOD IS ANOINTING YOU, SAUL SON OF KISH, TO BE A KING OF ISRAEL.

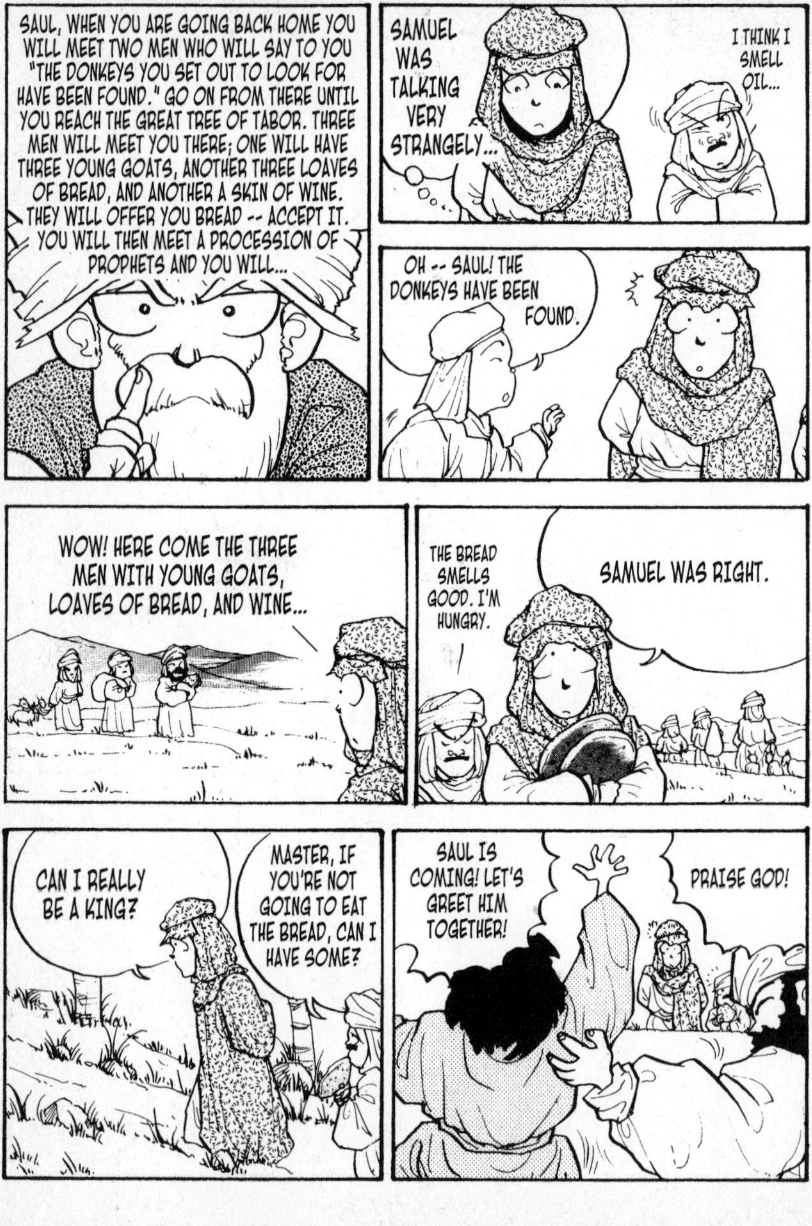
SAUL, WHEN YOU ARE GOING BACK HOME YOU WILL MEET TWO MEN WHO WILL SAY TO YOU "THE DONKEYS YOU SET OUT TO LOOK FOR HAVE BEEN FOUND." GO ON FROM THERE UNTIL YOU REACH THE GREAT TREE OF TABOR. THREE MEN WILL MEET YOU THERE; ONE WILL HAVE THREE YOUNG GOATS, ANOTHER THREE LOAVES OF BREAD, AND ANOTHER A SKIN OF WINE. THEY WILL OFFER YOU BREAD -- ACCEPT IT. YOU WILL THEN MEET A PROCESSION OF PROPHETS AND YOU WILL...
SAMUEL WAS TALKING VERY STRANGELY...
I THINK I SMELL OIL...
OH -- SAUL! THE DONKEYS HAVE BEEN FOUND.
WOW! HERE COME THE THREE MEN WITH YOUNG GOATS, LOAVES OF BREAD, AND WINE...
THE BREAD SMELLS GOOD. I'M HUNGRY.
SAMUEL WAS RIGHT.
CAN I REALLY BE A KING?
MASTER, IF YOU'RE NOT GOING TO EAT THE BREAD, CAN I HAVE SOME?
SAUL IS COMING! LET'S GREET HIM TOGETHER!
PRAISE GOD!

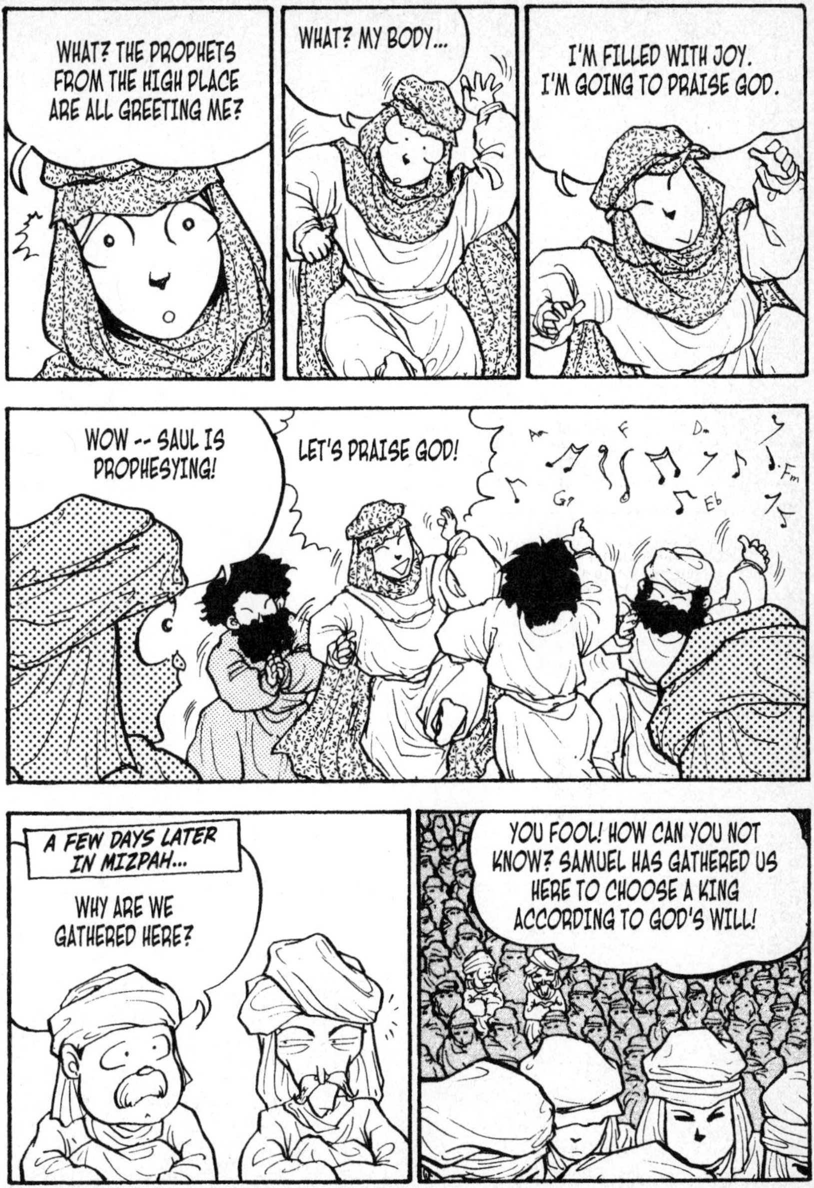

WHAT? THE PROPHETS FROM THE HIGH PLACE ARE ALL GREETING ME?
WHAT? MY BODY...
I'M FILLED WITH JOY. I'M GOING TO PRAISE GOD.
WOW -- SAUL IS PROPHESYING!
LET'S PRAISE GOD!
A FEW DAYS LATER IN MIZPAH...
WHY ARE WE GATHERED HERE?
YOU FOOL! HOW CAN YOU NOT KNOW? SAMUEL HAS GATHERED US HERE TO CHOOSE A KING ACCORDING TO GOD'S WILL!

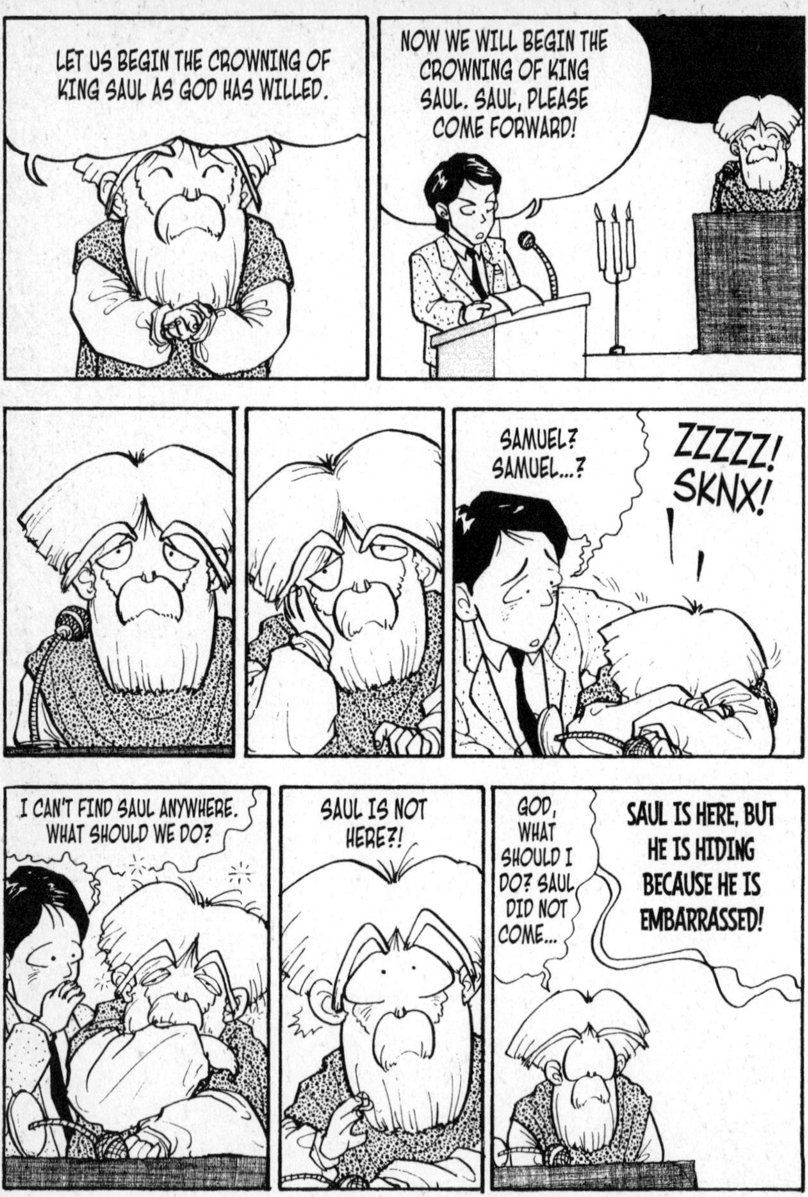
LET US BEGIN THE CROWNING OF KING SAUL AS GOD HAS WILLED.
NOW WE WILL BEGIN THE CROWNING OF KING SAUL. SAUL, PLEASE COME FORWARD!
SAMUEL? SAMUEL...?
ZZZZZ! SKNX!
I CAN'T FIND SAUL ANYWHERE. WHAT SHOULD WE DO?
SAUL IS NOT HERE?!
GOD, WHAT SHOULD I DO? SAUL DID NOT COME...
SAUL IS HERE, BUT HE IS HIDING BECAUSE HE IS EMBARRASSED!

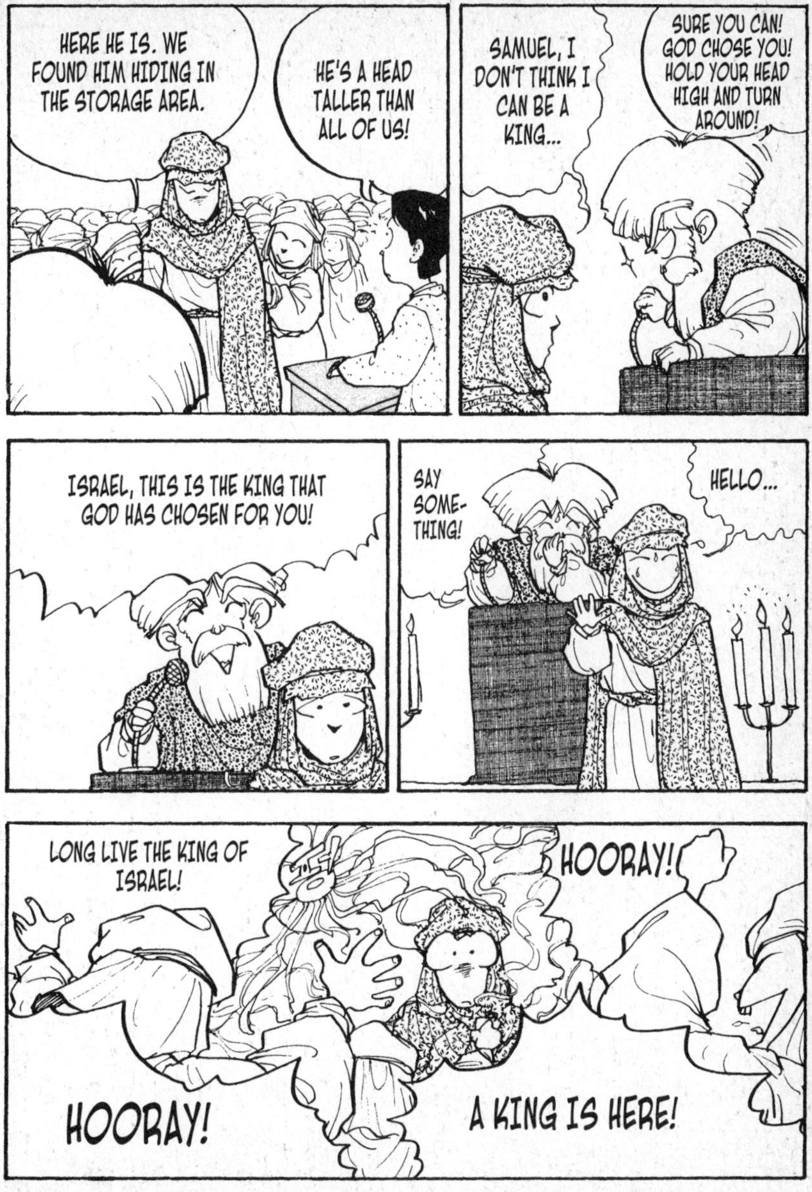
HERE HE IS. WE FOUND HIM HIDING IN THE STORAGE AREA.
HE'S A HEAD TALLER THAN ALL OF US!
SAMUEL, I DON'T THINK I CAN BE A KING...
SURE YOU CAN! GOD CHOSE YOU! HOLD YOUR HEAD HIGH AND TURN AROUND!
ISRAEL, THIS IS THE KING THAT GOD HAS CHOSEN FOR YOU!
SAY SOME-THING!
HELLO...
LONG LIVE THE KING OF ISRAEL!
HOORAY!
HOORAY!
A KING IS HERE!

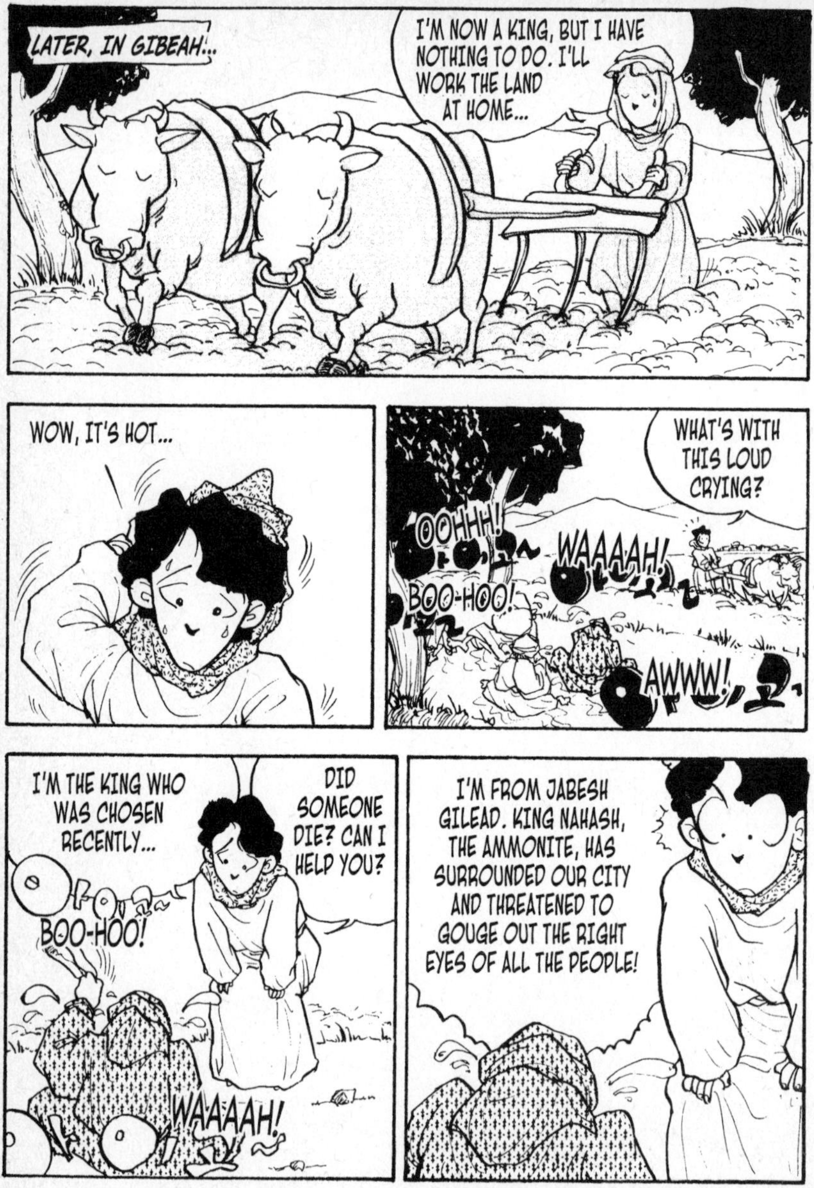
LATER, IN GIBEAH...
I'M NOW A KING, BUT I HAVE NOTHING TO DO. I'LL WORK THE LAND AT HOME...
WOW, IT'S HOT...
WHAT'S WITH THIS LOUD CRYING?
OOHHH!
WAAAAH!
BOO-HOO!
AWWW!
I'M THE KING WHO WAS CHOSEN RECENTLY...
DID SOMEONE DIE? CAN I HELP YOU?
BOO-HOO!
WAAAAH!
I'M FROM JABESH GILEAD. KING NAHASH, THE AMMONITE, HAS SURROUNDED OUR CITY AND THREATENED TO GOUGE OUT THE RIGHT EYES OF ALL THE PEOPLE!

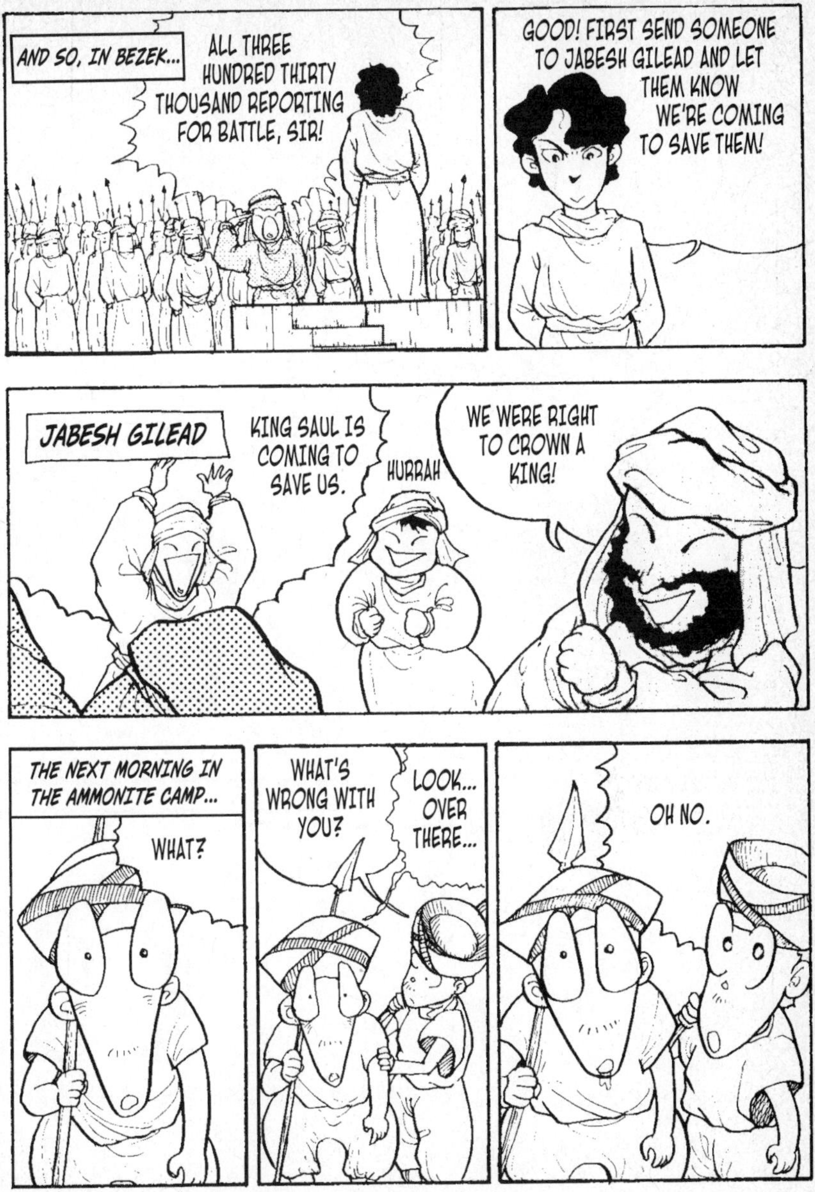
AND SO, IN BEZEK...
ALL THREE HUNDRED THIRTY THOUSAND REPORTING FOR BATTLE, SIR!
GOOD! FIRST SEND SOMEONE TO JABESH GILEAD AND LET THEM KNOW WE'RE COMING TO SAVE THEM!
JABESH GILEAD
KING SAUL IS COMING TO SAVE US.
HURRAH
WE WERE RIGHT TO CROWN A KING!
THE NEXT MORNING IN THE AMMONITE CAMP...
WHAT?
WHAT'S WRONG WITH YOU?
LOOK... OVER THERE...
OH NO.

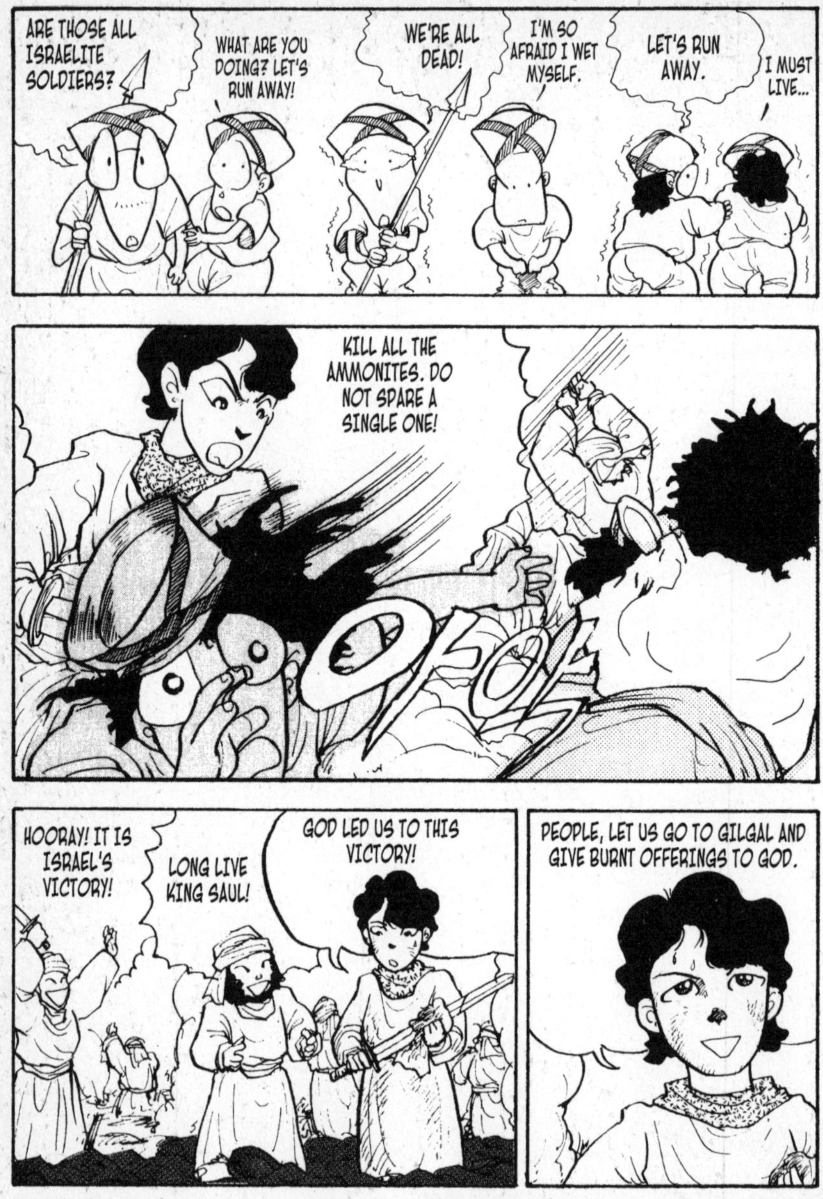
ARE THOSE ALL ISRAELITE SOLDIERS?
WHAT ARE YOU DOING? LET'S RUN AWAY!
WE'RE ALL DEAD!
I'M SO AFRAID I WET MYSELF.
LET'S RUN AWAY.
I MUST LIVE...
KILL ALL THE AMMONITES. DO NOT SPARE A SINGLE ONE!
HOORAY! IT IS ISRAEL'S VICTORY!
LONG LIVE KING SAUL!
GOD LED US TO THIS VICTORY!
PEOPLE, LET US GO TO GILGAL AND GIVE BURNT OFFERINGS TO GOD.

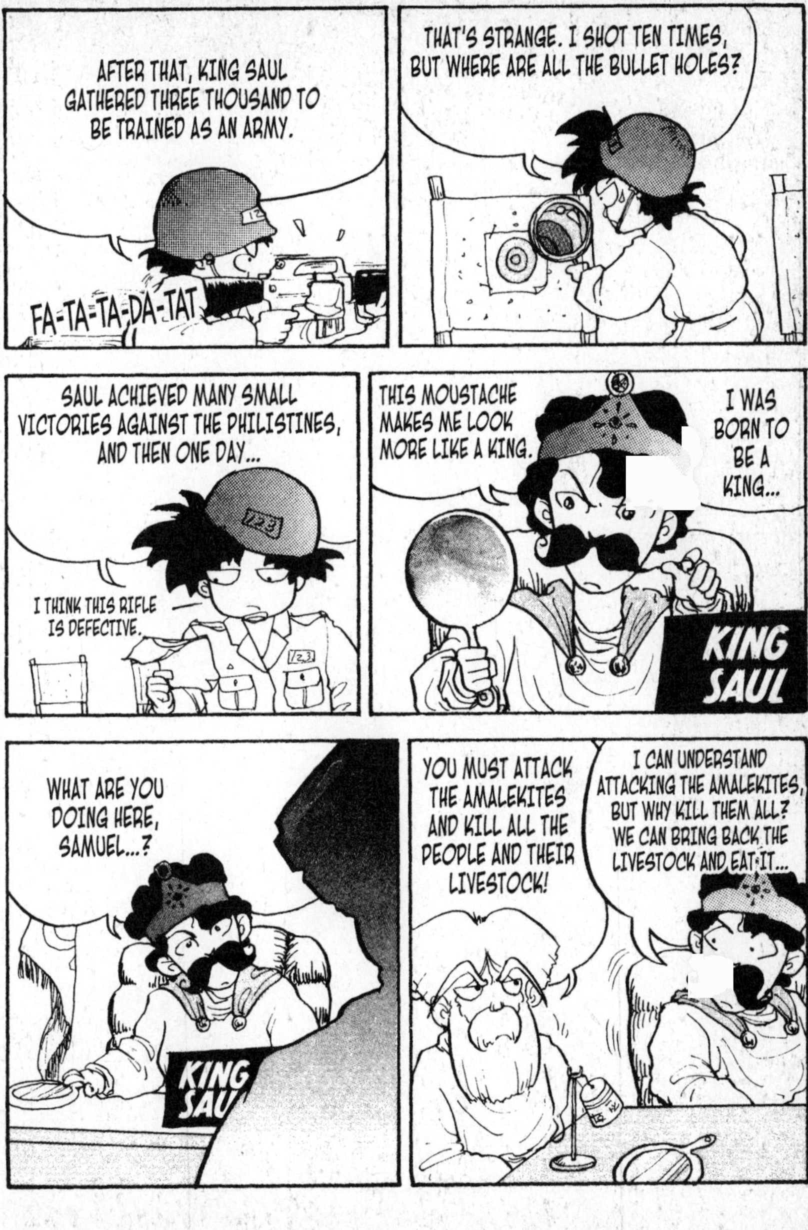
AFTER THAT, KING SAUL GATHERED THREE THOUSAND TO BE TRAINED AS AN ARMY.
FA-TA-TA-DA-TAT
THAT'S STRANGE. I SHOT TEN TIMES, BUT WHERE ARE ALL THE BULLET HOLES?
SAUL ACHIEVED MANY SMALL VICTORIES AGAINST THE PHILISTINES, AND THEN ONE DAY...
I THINK THIS RIFLE IS DEFECTIVE.
THIS MOUSTACHE MAKES ME LOOK MORE LIKE A KING.
I WAS BORN TO BE A KING...
KING SAUL
WHAT ARE YOU DOING HERE, SAMUEL...?
KING SAU
YOU MUST ATTACK THE AMALEKITES AND KILL ALL THE PEOPLE AND THEIR LIVESTOCK!
I CAN UNDERSTAND ATTACKING THE AMALEKITES, BUT WHY KILL THEM ALL? WE CAN BRING BACK THE LIVESTOCK AND EAT IT...

IT IS GOD'S COMMAND. YOU MUST OBEY!

OKAY! I WILL.

HEY, WE'RE GOING TO ATTACK THE AMALEKITES. READY THE MEN.

KING SAUL! IT'S A COMPLETE VICTORY. WHAT SHOULD WE DO WITH THE PRISONERS AND LIVESTOCK?

YEAH!

HOORAY! IT'S ISRAEL'S VICTORY!

WARNING!

TAKE THE GOOD LIVESTOCK AND KILL THE REST!

KEEP THE COWS.

A FEW DAYS LATER...

SAMUEL! SAMUEL!

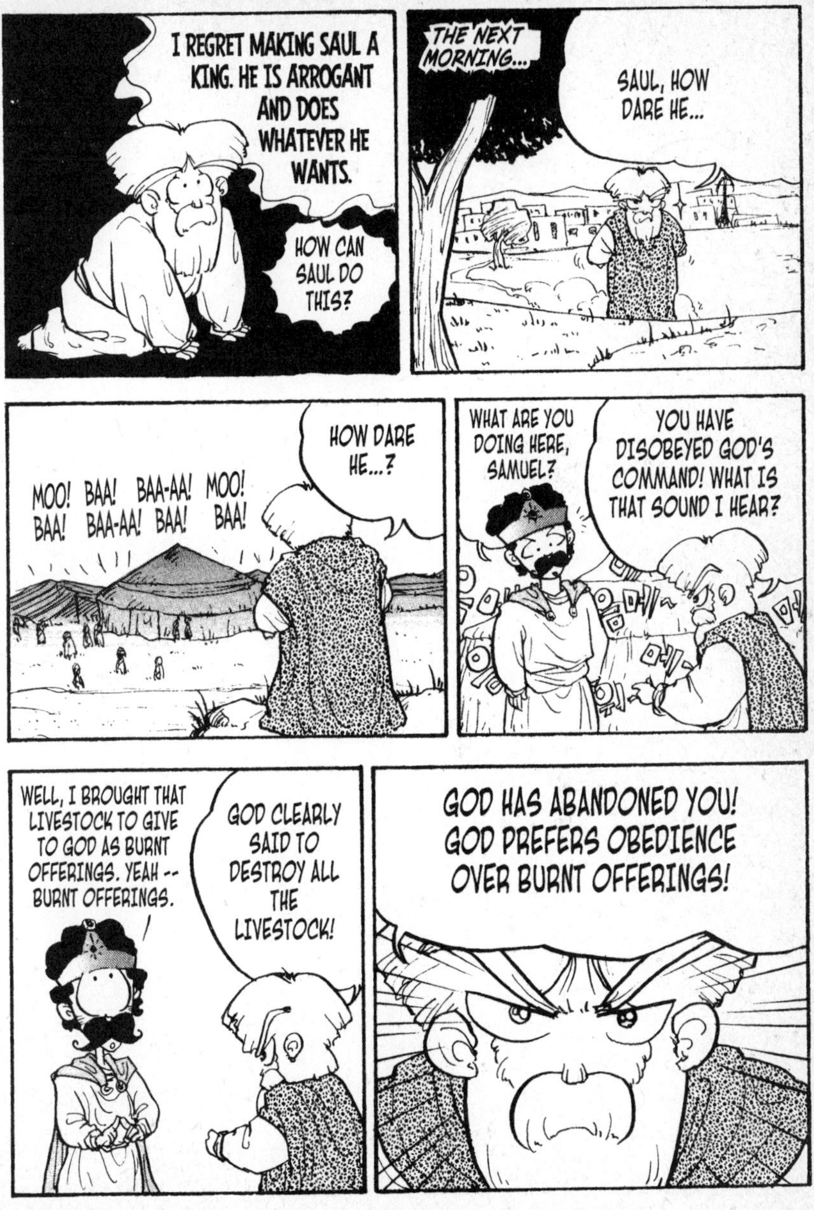
I REGRET MAKING SAUL A KING. HE IS ARROGANT AND DOES WHATEVER HE WANTS.
HOW CAN SAUL DO THIS?
THE NEXT MORNING...
SAUL, HOW DARE HE...
MOO! BAA! BAA-AA! MOO! BAA! BAA-AA! BAA! BAA!
HOW DARE HE...?
WHAT ARE YOU DOING HERE, SAMUEL?
YOU HAVE DISOBEYED GOD'S COMMAND! WHAT IS THAT SOUND I HEAR?
WELL, I BROUGHT THAT LIVESTOCK TO GIVE TO GOD AS BURNT OFFERINGS. YEAH -- BURNT OFFERINGS.
GOD CLEARLY SAID TO DESTROY ALL THE LIVESTOCK!
GOD HAS ABANDONED YOU! GOD PREFERS OBEDIENCE OVER BURNT OFFERINGS!

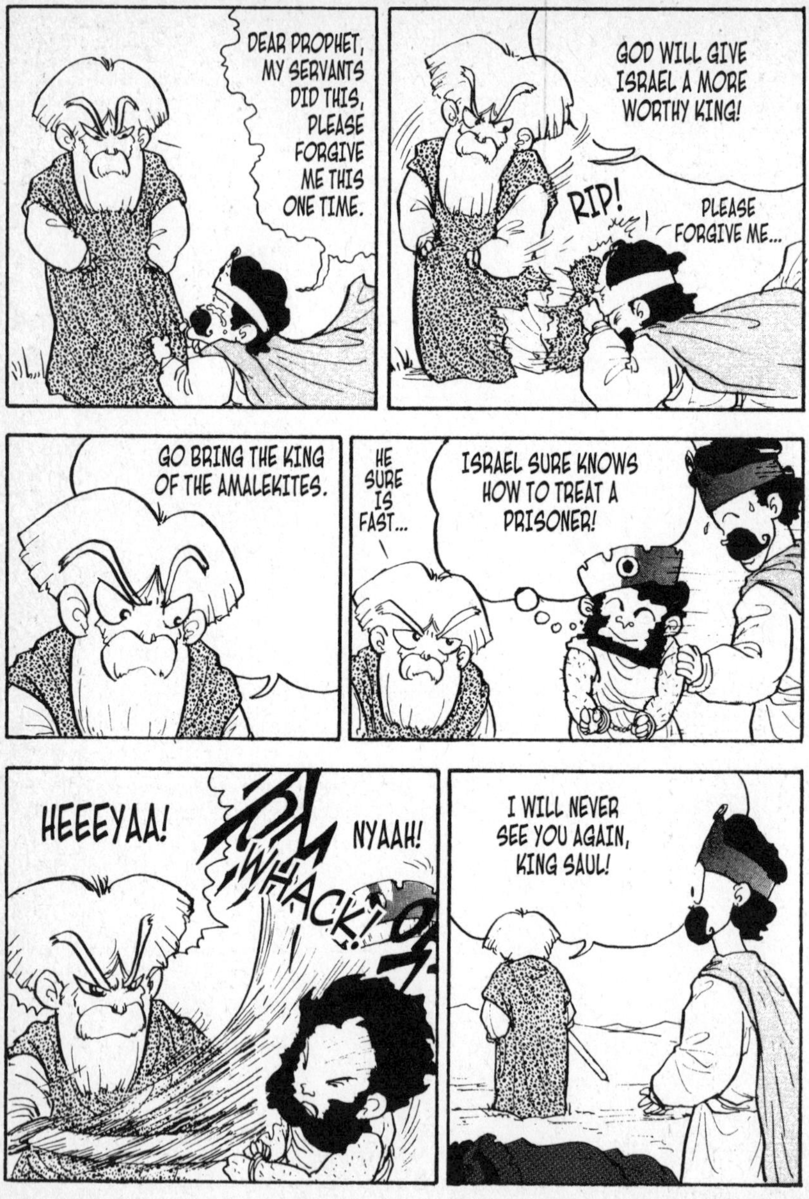
DEAR PROPHET, MY SERVANTS DID THIS, PLEASE FORGIVE ME THIS ONE TIME.
GOD WILL GIVE ISRAEL A MORE WORTHY KING!
RIP!
PLEASE FORGIVE ME...
GO BRING THE KING OF THE AMALEKITES.
HE SURE IS FAST...
ISRAEL SURE KNOWS HOW TO TREAT A PRISONER!
HEEEYAA!
WHACK!
NYAAH!
I WILL NEVER SEE YOU AGAIN, KING SAUL!

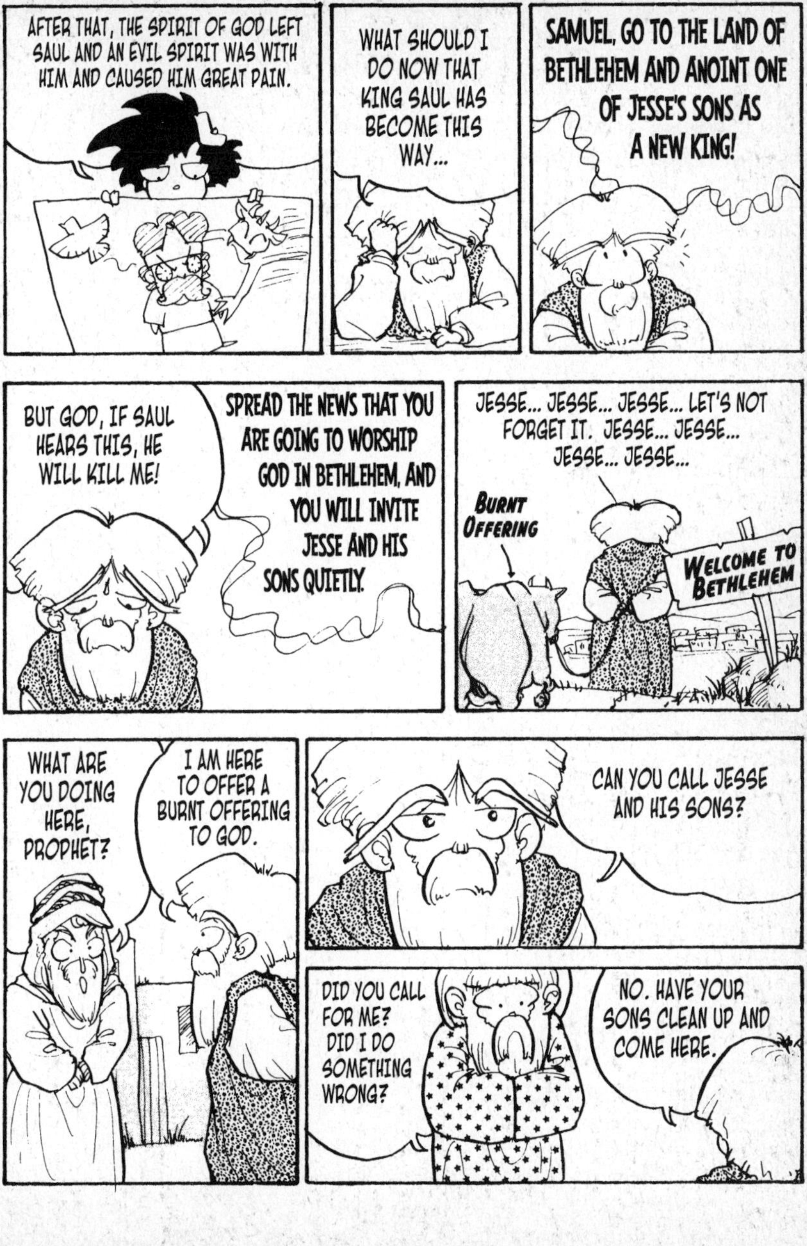
AFTER THAT, THE SPIRIT OF GOD LEFT SAUL AND AN EVIL SPIRIT WAS WITH HIM AND CAUSED HIM GREAT PAIN.
WHAT SHOULD I DO NOW THAT KING SAUL HAS BECOME THIS WAY...
SAMUEL, GO TO THE LAND OF BETHLEHEM AND ANOINT ONE OF JESSE'S SONS AS A NEW KING!
BUT GOD, IF SAUL HEARS THIS, HE WILL KILL ME!
SPREAD THE NEWS THAT YOU ARE GOING TO WORSHIP GOD IN BETHLEHEM, AND YOU WILL INVITE JESSE AND HIS SONS QUIETLY.
JESSE... JESSE... JESSE... LET'S NOT FORGET IT. JESSE... JESSE... JESSE... JESSE...
BURNT OFFERING
WELCOME TO BETHLEHEM
WHAT ARE YOU DOING HERE, PROPHET?
I AM HERE TO OFFER A BURNT OFFERING TO GOD.
CAN YOU CALL JESSE AND HIS SONS?
DID YOU CALL FOR ME? DID I DO SOMETHING WRONG?
NO. HAVE YOUR SONS CLEAN UP AND COME HERE.

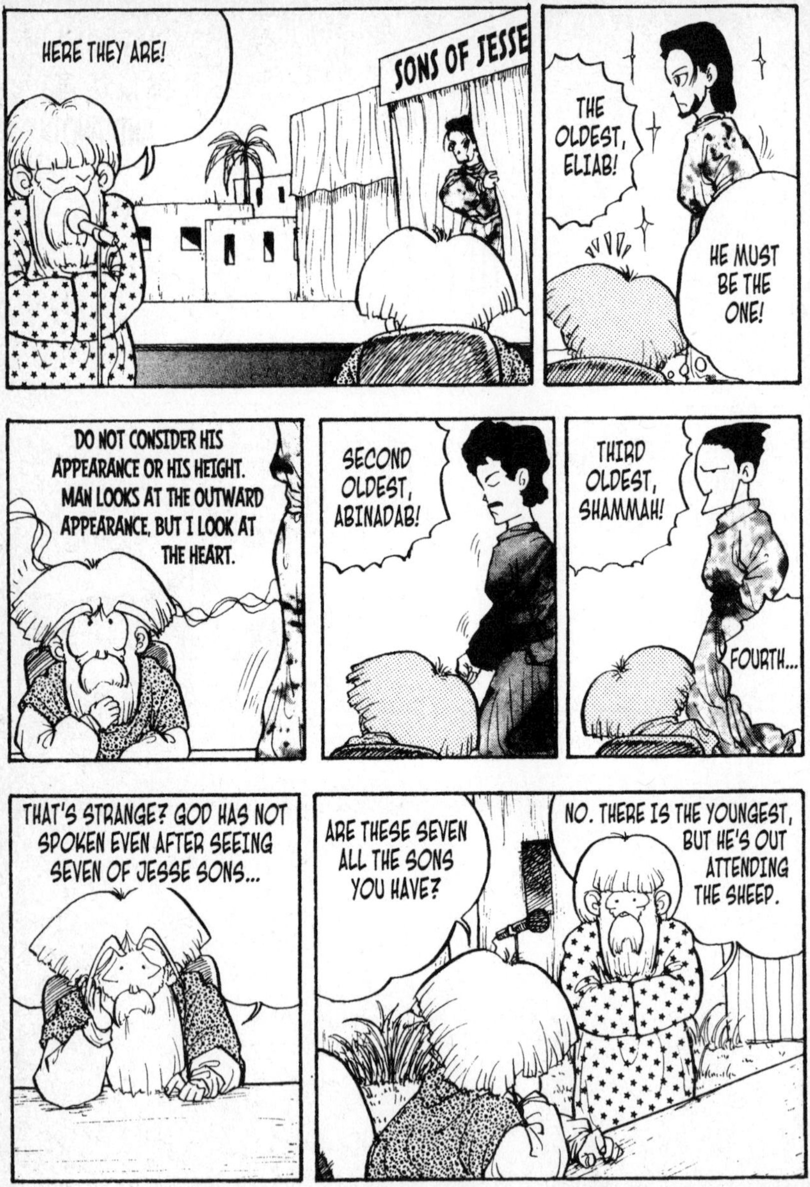
HERE THEY ARE!
SONS OF JESSE
THE OLDEST, ELIAB!
HE MUST BE THE ONE!
DO NOT CONSIDER HIS APPEARANCE OR HIS HEIGHT. MAN LOOKS AT THE OUTWARD APPEARANCE, BUT I LOOK AT THE HEART.
SECOND OLDEST, ABINADAB!
THIRD OLDEST, SHAMMAH!
FOURTH...
THAT'S STRANGE? GOD HAS NOT SPOKEN EVEN AFTER SEEING SEVEN OF JESSE SONS...
ARE THESE SEVEN ALL THE SONS YOU HAVE?
NO. THERE IS THE YOUNGEST, BUT HE'S OUT ATTENDING THE SHEEP.

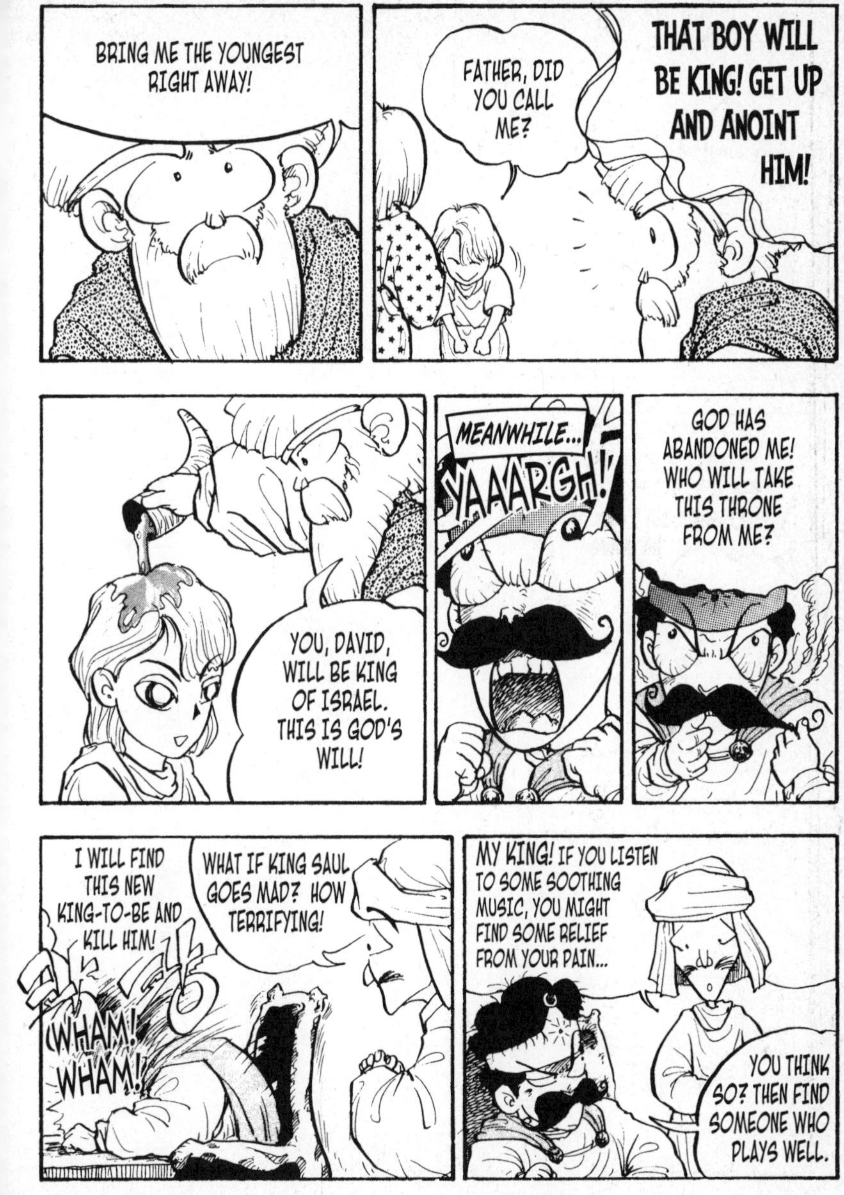
BRING ME THE YOUNGEST RIGHT AWAY!
FATHER, DID YOU CALL ME?
THAT BOY WILL BE KING! GET UP AND ANOINT HIM!
YOU, DAVID, WILL BE KING OF ISRAEL. THIS IS GOD'S WILL!
MEANWHILE...
YAAARGH!
GOD HAS ABANDONED ME! WHO WILL TAKE THIS THRONE FROM ME?
I WILL FIND THIS NEW KING-TO-BE AND KILL HIM!
WHAT IF KING SAUL GOES MAD? HOW TERRIFYING!
WHAM! WHAM!
MY KING! IF YOU LISTEN TO SOME SOOTHING MUSIC, YOU MIGHT FIND SOME RELIEF FROM YOUR PAIN...
YOU THINK SO? THEN FIND SOMEONE WHO PLAYS WELL.

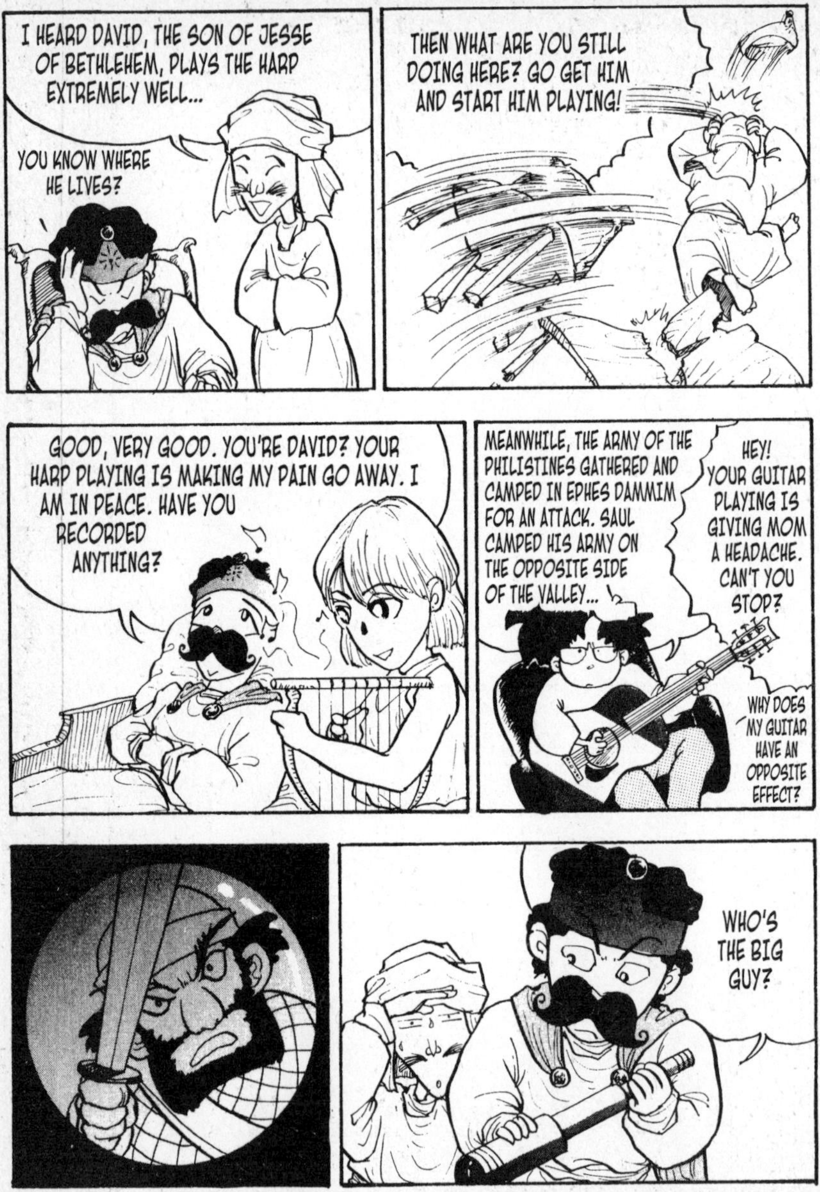
I HEARD DAVID, THE SON OF JESSE OF BETHLEHEM, PLAYS THE HARP EXTREMELY WELL...
YOU KNOW WHERE HE LIVES?
THEN WHAT ARE YOU STILL DOING HERE? GO GET HIM AND START HIM PLAYING!
GOOD, VERY GOOD. YOU'RE DAVID? YOUR HARP PLAYING IS MAKING MY PAIN GO AWAY. I AM IN PEACE. HAVE YOU RECORDED ANYTHING?
MEANWHILE, THE ARMY OF THE PHILISTINES GATHERED AND CAMPED IN EPHES DAMMIM FOR AN ATTACK. SAUL CAMPED HIS ARMY ON THE OPPOSITE SIDE OF THE VALLEY...
HEY! YOUR GUITAR PLAYING IS GIVING MOM A HEADACHE. CAN'T YOU STOP?
WHY DOES MY GUITAR HAVE AN OPPOSITE EFFECT?
WHO'S THE BIG GUY?

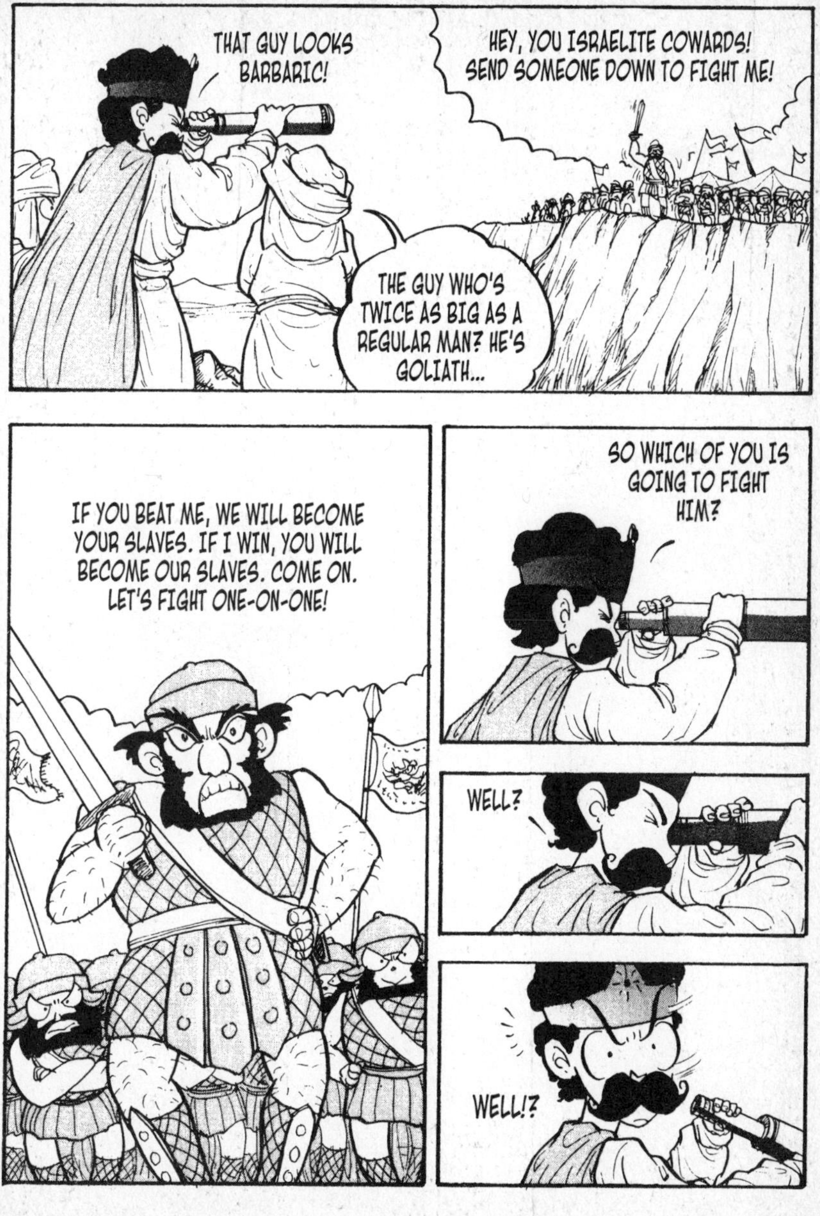
THAT GUY LOOKS BARBARIC!
HEY, YOU ISRAELITE COWARDS! SEND SOMEONE DOWN TO FIGHT ME!
THE GUY WHO'S TWICE AS BIG AS A REGULAR MAN? HE'S GOLIATH...
IF YOU BEAT ME, WE WILL BECOME YOUR SLAVES. IF I WIN, YOU WILL BECOME OUR SLAVES. COME ON. LET'S FIGHT ONE-ON-ONE!
SO WHICH OF YOU IS GOING TO FIGHT HIM?
WELL?
WELL!?

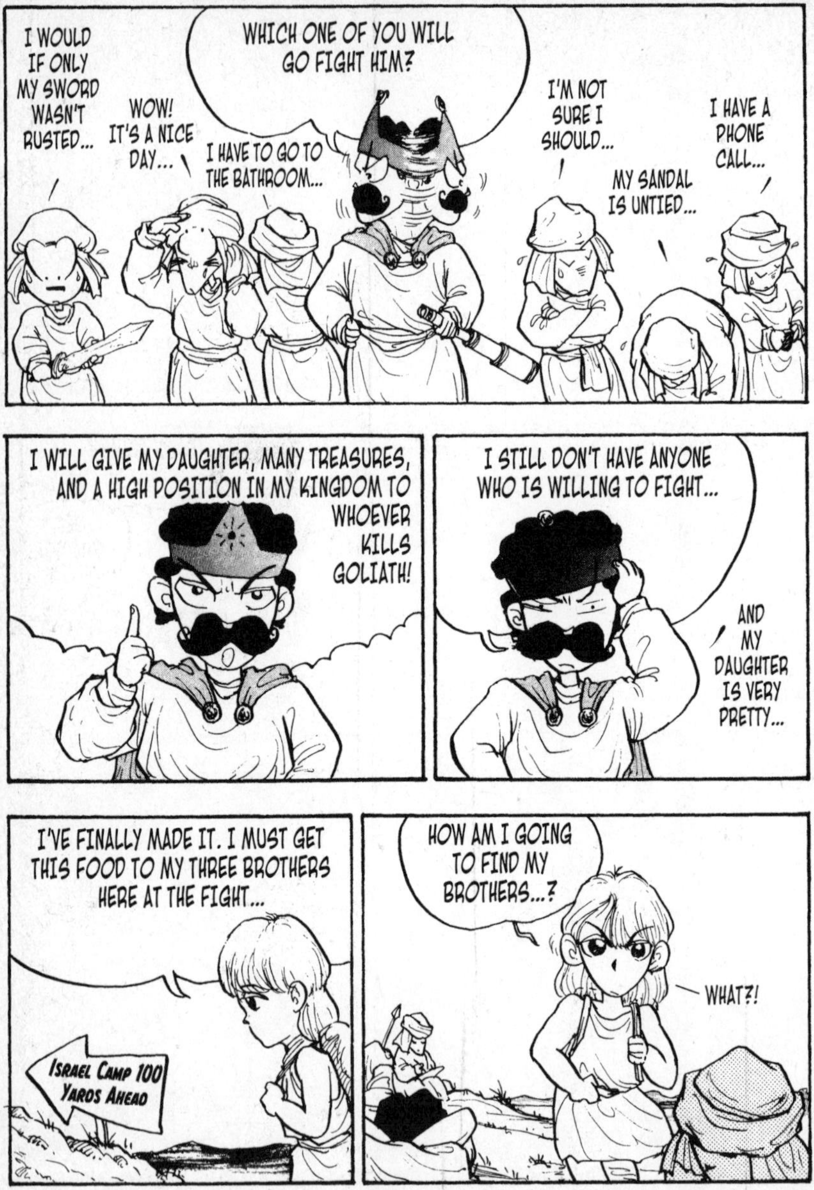
I WOULD IF ONLY MY SWORD WASN'T RUSTED...
WOW! IT'S A NICE DAY...
WHICH ONE OF YOU WILL GO FIGHT HIM?
I HAVE TO GO TO THE BATHROOM...
I'M NOT SURE I SHOULD...
MY SANDAL IS UNTIED...
I HAVE A PHONE CALL...
I WILL GIVE MY DAUGHTER, MANY TREASURES, AND A HIGH POSITION IN MY KINGDOM TO WHOEVER KILLS GOLIATH!
I STILL DON'T HAVE ANYONE WHO IS WILLING TO FIGHT...
AND MY DAUGHTER IS VERY PRETTY...
I'VE FINALLY MADE IT. I MUST GET THIS FOOD TO MY THREE BROTHERS HERE AT THE FIGHT...
ISRAEL CAMP 100 YARDS AHEAD
HOW AM I GOING TO FIND MY BROTHERS...?
WHAT?!

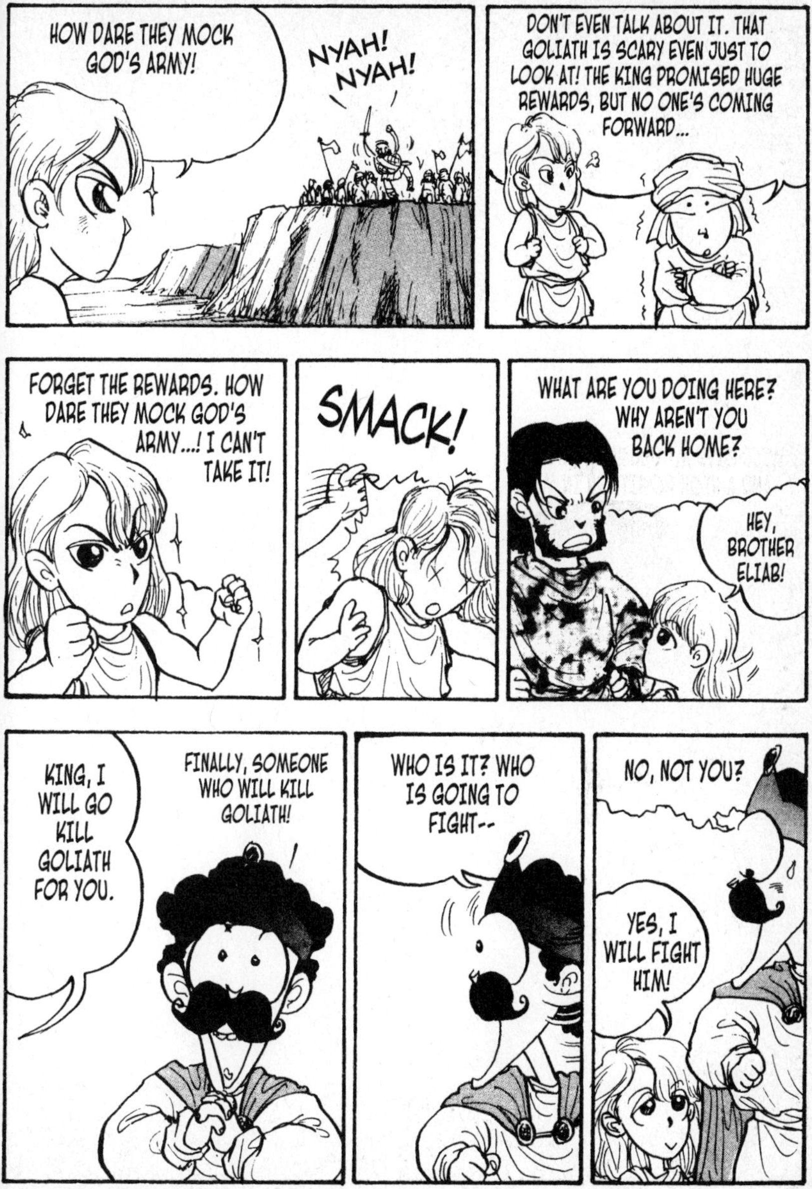
HOW DARE THEY MOCK GOD'S ARMY!
NYAH! NYAH!
DON'T EVEN TALK ABOUT IT. THAT GOLIATH IS SCARY EVEN JUST TO LOOK AT! THE KING PROMISED HUGE REWARDS, BUT NO ONE'S COMING FORWARD...
FORGET THE REWARDS. HOW DARE THEY MOCK GOD'S ARMY...! I CAN'T TAKE IT!
SMACK!
WHAT ARE YOU DOING HERE? WHY AREN'T YOU BACK HOME?
HEY, BROTHER ELIAB!
KING, I WILL GO KILL GOLIATH FOR YOU.
FINALLY, SOMEONE WHO WILL KILL GOLIATH!
WHO IS IT? WHO IS GOING TO FIGHT--
NO, NOT YOU?
YES, I WILL FIGHT HIM!

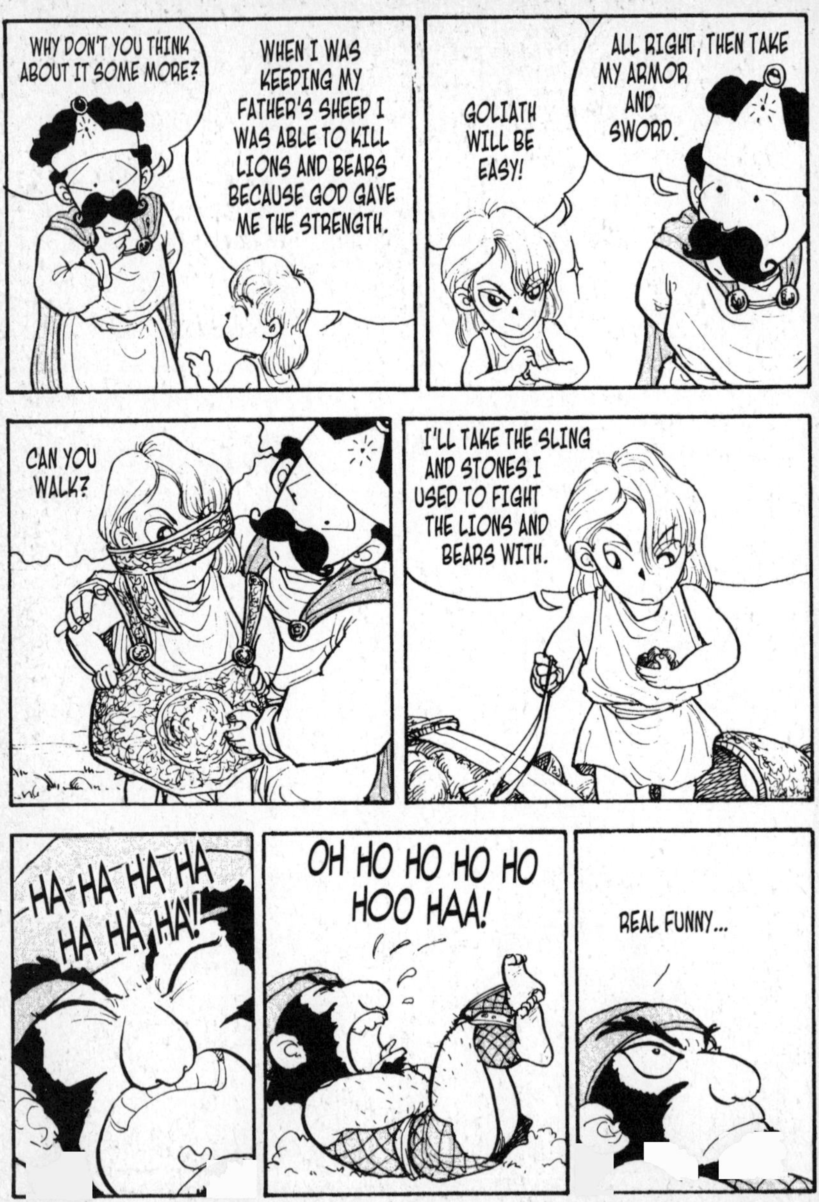
WHY DON'T YOU THINK ABOUT IT SOME MORE?
WHEN I WAS KEEPING MY FATHER'S SHEEP I WAS ABLE TO KILL LIONS AND BEARS BECAUSE GOD GAVE ME THE STRENGTH.
GOLIATH WILL BE EASY!
ALL RIGHT, THEN TAKE MY ARMOR AND SWORD.
CAN YOU WALK?
I'LL TAKE THE SLING AND STONES I USED TO FIGHT THE LIONS AND BEARS WITH.
HA-HA-HA-HA HA HA HA!
OH HO HO HO HO HOO HAA!
REAL FUNNY...

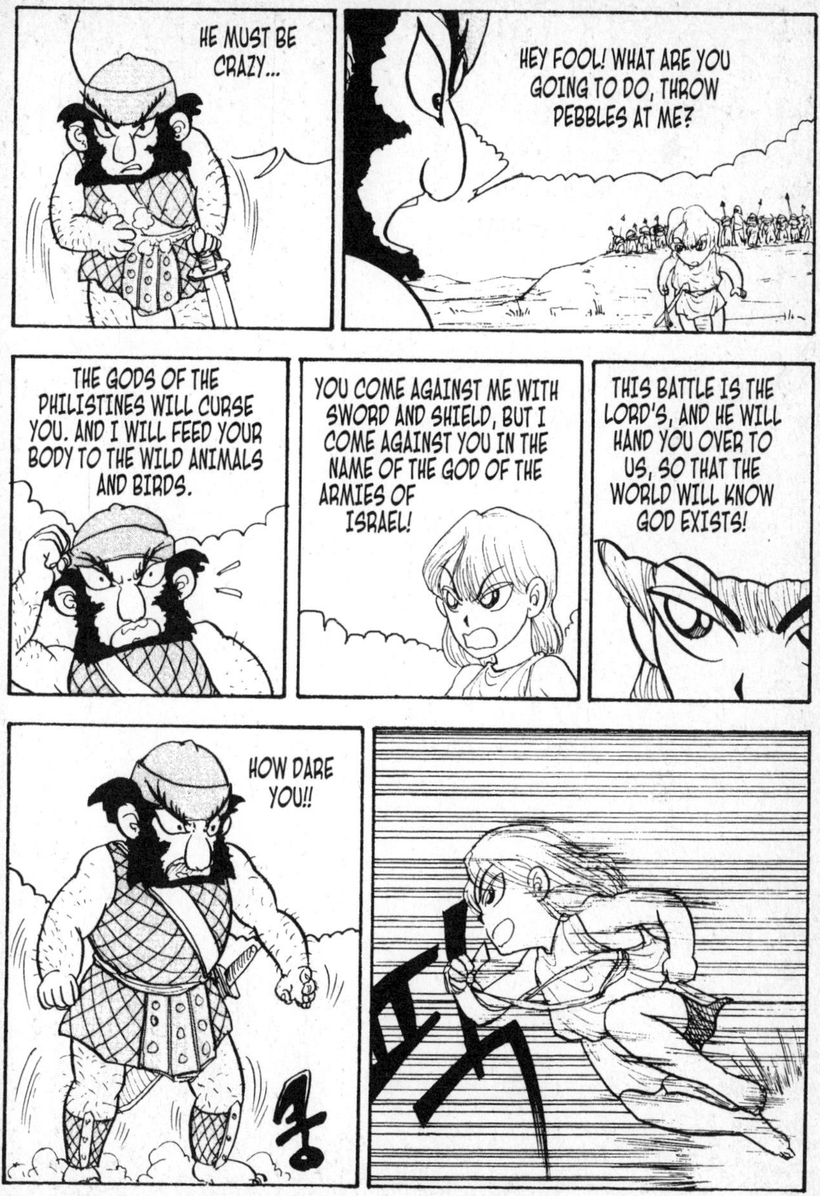
HE MUST BE CRAZY...
HEY FOOL! WHAT ARE YOU GOING TO DO, THROW PEBBLES AT ME?
THE GODS OF THE PHILISTINES WILL CURSE YOU. AND I WILL FEED YOUR BODY TO THE WILD ANIMALS AND BIRDS.
YOU COME AGAINST ME WITH SWORD AND SHIELD, BUT I COME AGAINST YOU IN THE NAME OF THE GOD OF THE ARMIES OF ISRAEL!
THIS BATTLE IS THE LORD'S, AND HE WILL HAND YOU OVER TO US, SO THAT THE WORLD WILL KNOW GOD EXISTS!
HOW DARE YOU!!

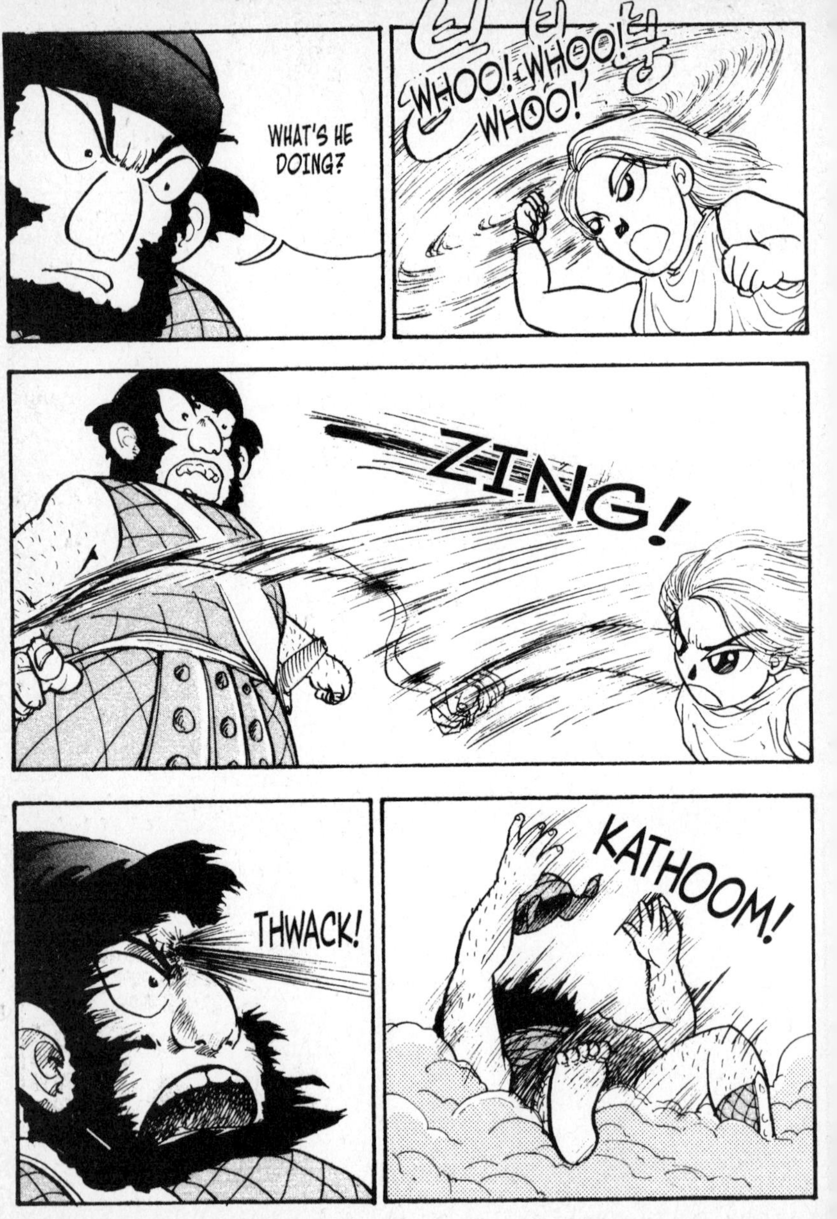
WHAT'S HE DOING?
WHOO! WHOO! WHOO!
ZING!
THWACK!
KATHOOM!

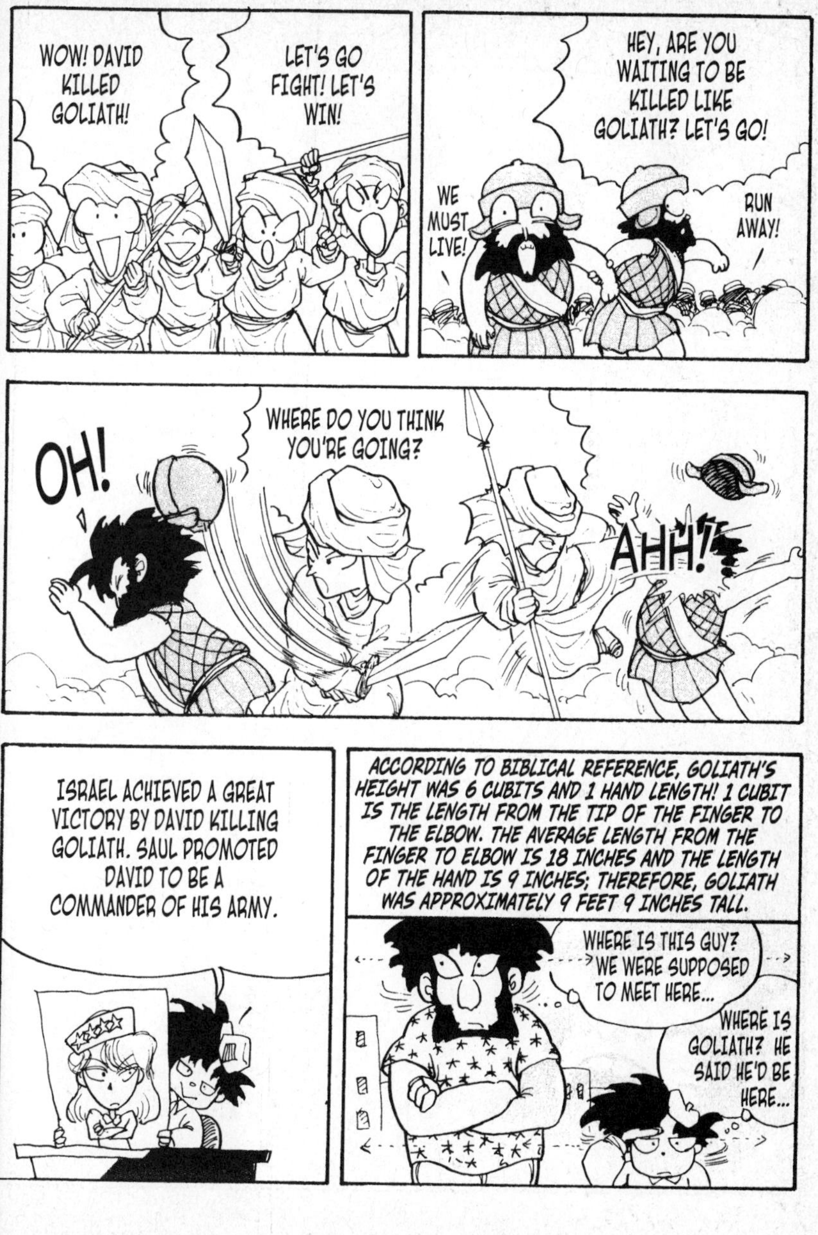
WOW! DAVID KILLED GOLIATH!
LET'S GO FIGHT! LET'S WIN!
HEY, ARE YOU WAITING TO BE KILLED LIKE GOLIATH? LET'S GO!
WE MUST LIVE!
RUN AWAY!
OH!
WHERE DO YOU THINK YOU'RE GOING?
AHH!?
ISRAEL ACHIEVED A GREAT VICTORY BY DAVID KILLING GOLIATH. SAUL PROMOTED DAVID TO BE A COMMANDER OF HIS ARMY.
ACCORDING TO BIBLICAL REFERENCE, GOLIATH'S HEIGHT WAS 6 CUBITS AND 1 HAND LENGTH! 1 CUBIT IS THE LENGTH FROM THE TIP OF THE FINGER TO THE ELBOW. THE AVERAGE LENGTH FROM THE FINGER TO ELBOW IS 18 INCHES AND THE LENGTH OF THE HAND IS 9 INCHES; THEREFORE, GOLIATH WAS APPROXIMATELY 9 FEET 9 INCHES TALL.
WHERE IS THIS GUY? WE WERE SUPPOSED TO MEET HERE...
WHERE IS GOLIATH? HE SAID HE'D BE HERE...

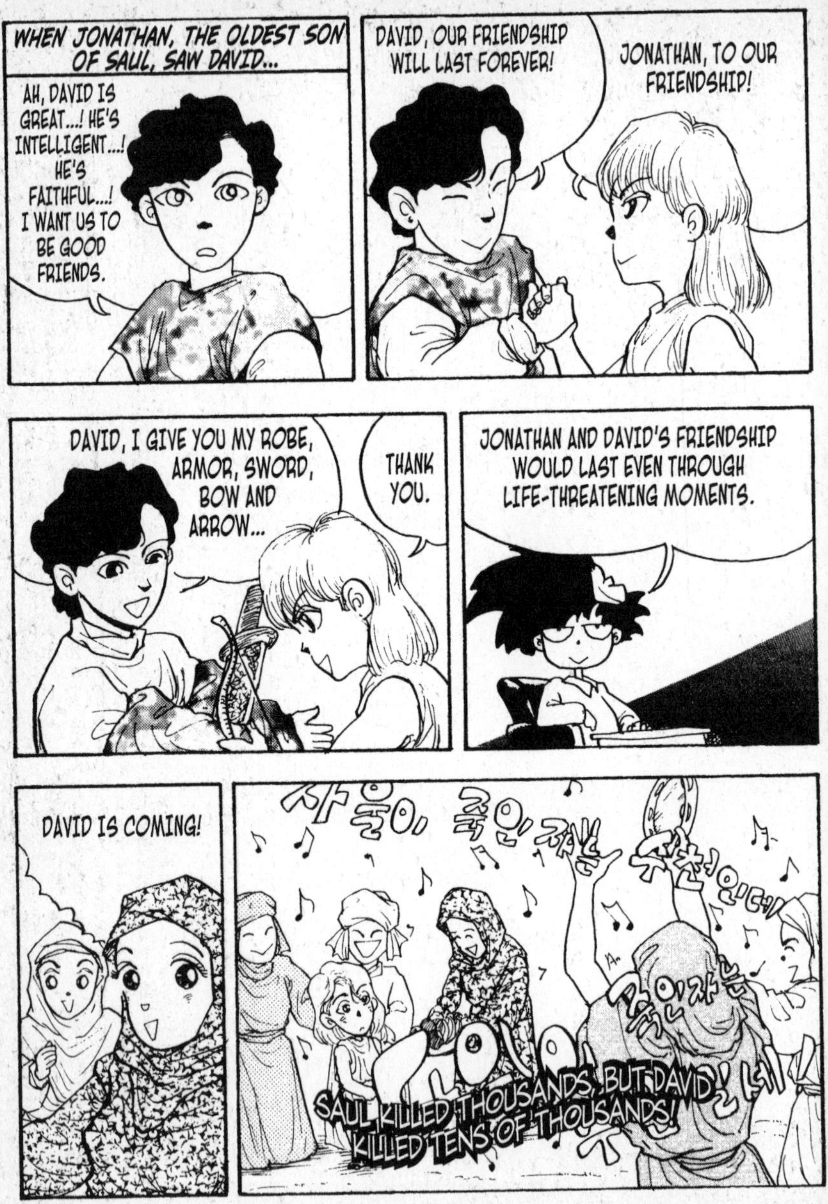

WHEN JONATHAN, THE OLDEST SON OF SAUL, SAW DAVID...
AH, DAVID IS GREAT...! HE'S INTELLIGENT...! HE'S FAITHFUL...! I WANT US TO BE GOOD FRIENDS.
DAVID, OUR FRIENDSHIP WILL LAST FOREVER!
JONATHAN, TO OUR FRIENDSHIP!
DAVID, I GIVE YOU MY ROBE, ARMOR, SWORD, BOW AND ARROW...
THANK YOU.
JONATHAN AND DAVID'S FRIENDSHIP WOULD LAST EVEN THROUGH LIFE-THREATENING MOMENTS.
DAVID IS COMING!
SAUL KILLED THOUSANDS, BUT DAVID KILLED TENS OF THOUSANDS!

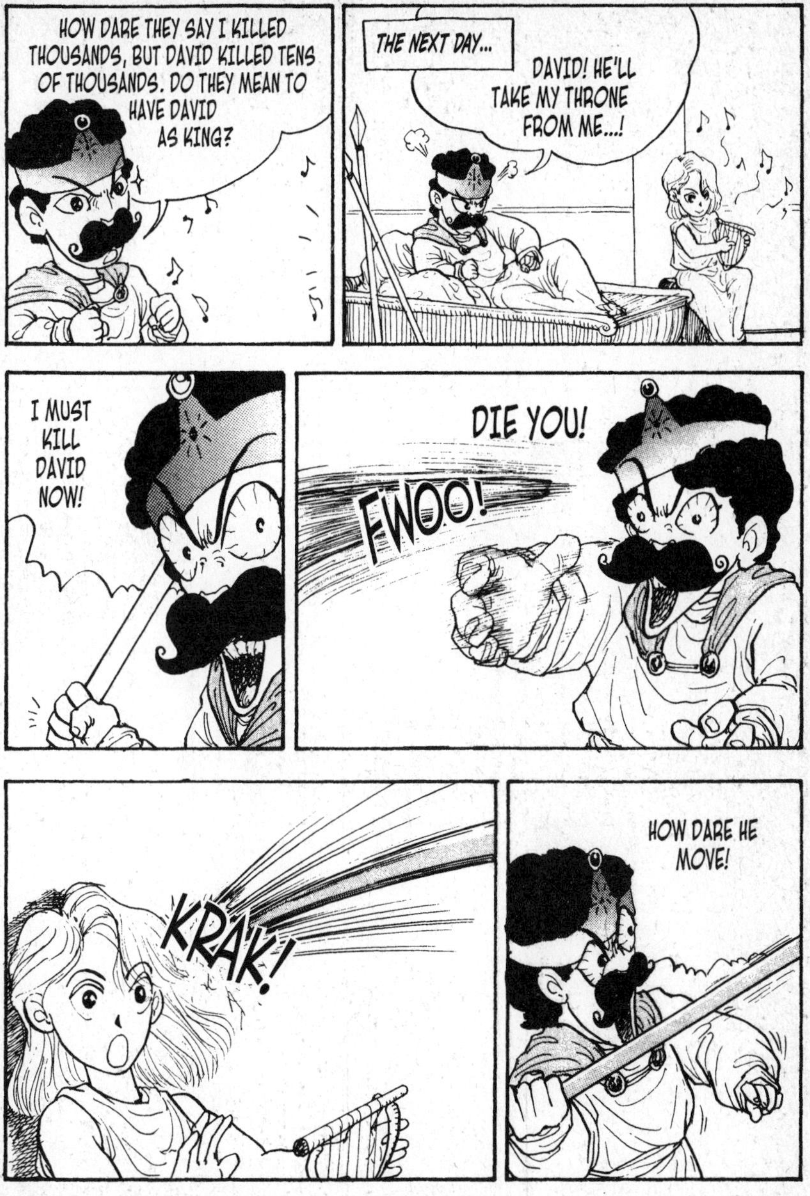
HOW DARE THEY SAY I KILLED THOUSANDS, BUT DAVID KILLED TENS OF THOUSANDS. DO THEY MEAN TO HAVE DAVID AS KING?
THE NEXT DAY...
DAVID! HE'LL TAKE MY THRONE FROM ME...!
I MUST KILL DAVID NOW!
DIE YOU!
FWOO!
KRAK!
HOW DARE HE MOVE!

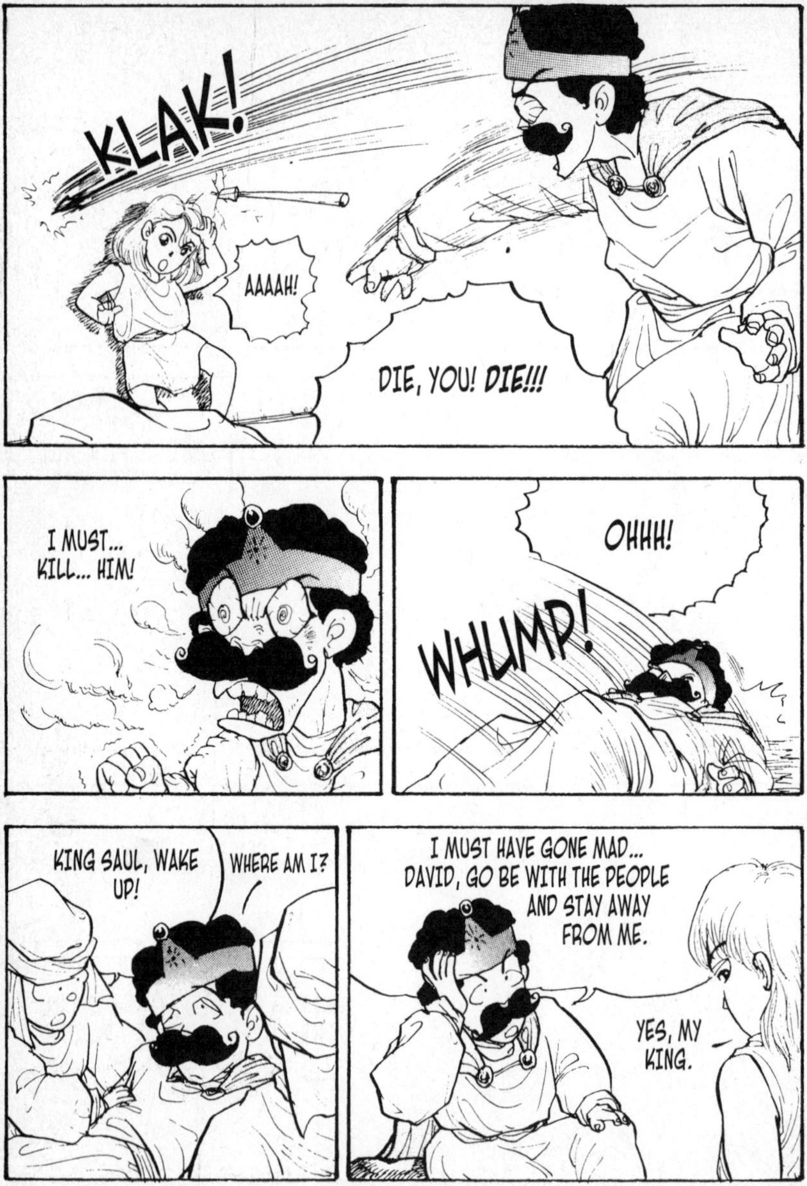
KLAK!
AAAAH!
DIE, YOU! DIE!!!
I MUST... KILL... HIM!
OHHH!
WHUMP!
KING SAUL, WAKE UP!
WHERE AM I?
I MUST HAVE GONE MAD... DAVID, GO BE WITH THE PEOPLE AND STAY AWAY FROM ME.
YES, MY KING.

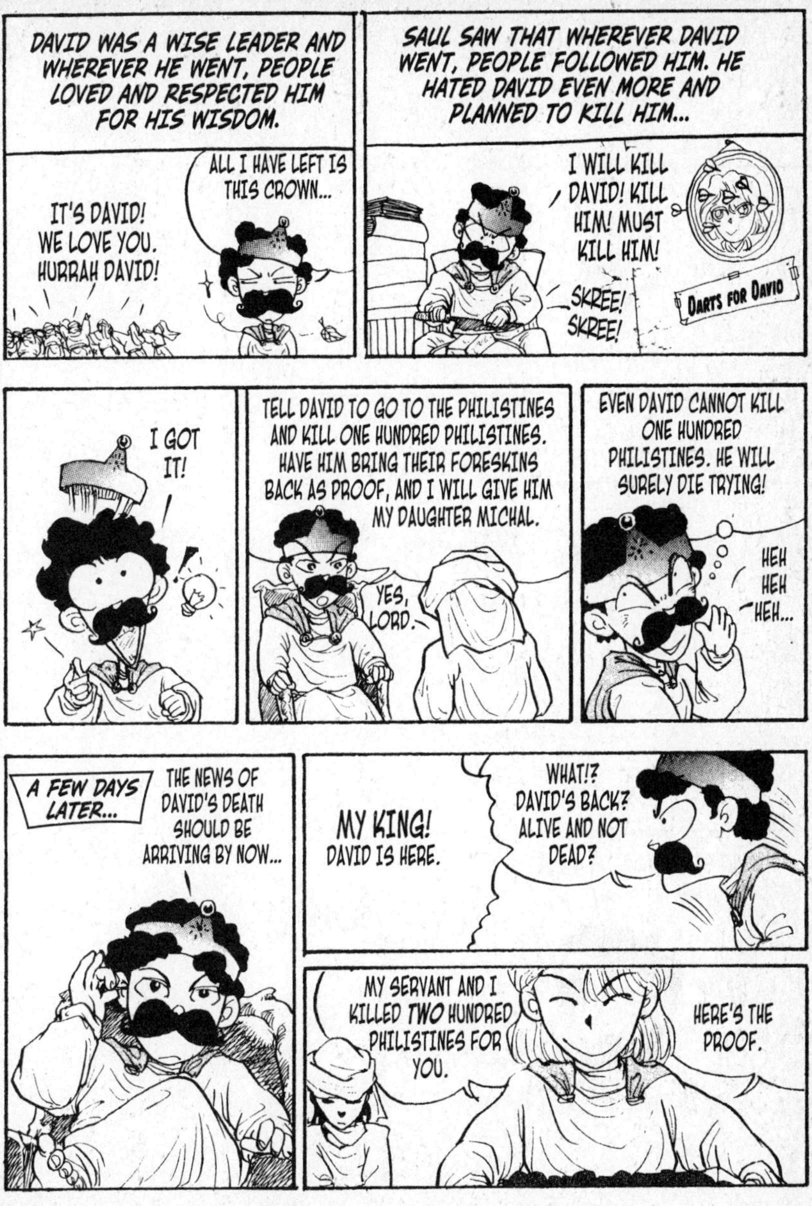
DAVID WAS A WISE LEADER AND WHEREVER HE WENT, PEOPLE LOVED AND RESPECTED HIM FOR HIS WISDOM.
IT'S DAVID! WE LOVE YOU. HURRAH DAVID!
ALL I HAVE LEFT IS THIS CROWN...
SAUL SAW THAT WHEREVER DAVID WENT, PEOPLE FOLLOWED HIM. HE HATED DAVID EVEN MORE AND PLANNED TO KILL HIM...
I WILL KILL DAVID! KILL HIM! MUST KILL HIM!
SKREE! SKREE!
DARTS FOR DAVID
I GOT IT!
TELL DAVID TO GO TO THE PHILISTINES AND KILL ONE HUNDRED PHILISTINES. HAVE HIM BRING THEIR FORESKINS BACK AS PROOF, AND I WILL GIVE HIM MY DAUGHTER MICHAL.
YES, LORD.
EVEN DAVID CANNOT KILL ONE HUNDRED PHILISTINES. HE WILL SURELY DIE TRYING!
HEH HEH HEH...
A FEW DAYS LATER...
THE NEWS OF DAVID'S DEATH SHOULD BE ARRIVING BY NOW...
MY KING! DAVID IS HERE.
WHAT!? DAVID'S BACK? ALIVE AND NOT DEAD?
MY SERVANT AND I KILLED *TWO* HUNDRED PHILISTINES FOR YOU.
HERE'S THE PROOF.

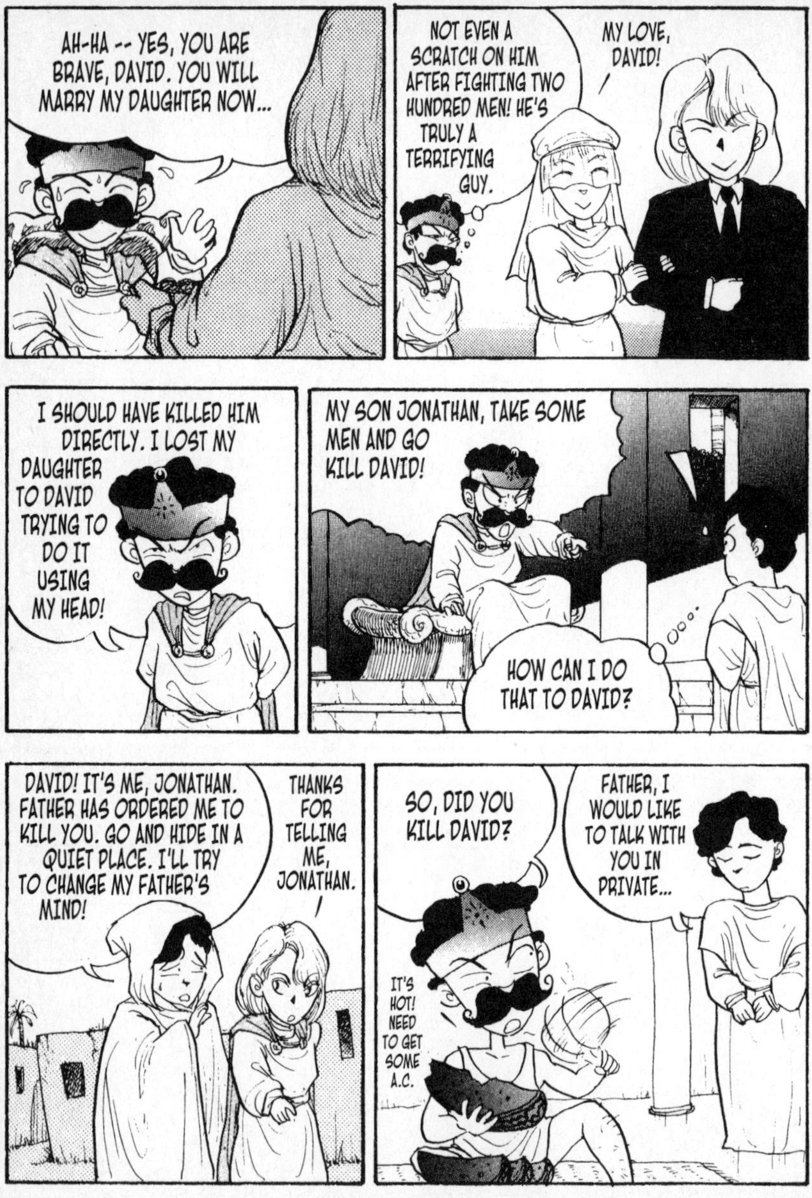
AH-HA -- YES, YOU ARE BRAVE, DAVID. YOU WILL MARRY MY DAUGHTER NOW...
NOT EVEN A SCRATCH ON HIM AFTER FIGHTING TWO HUNDRED MEN! HE'S TRULY A TERRIFYING GUY.
MY LOVE, DAVID!
I SHOULD HAVE KILLED HIM DIRECTLY. I LOST MY DAUGHTER TO DAVID TRYING TO DO IT USING MY HEAD!
MY SON JONATHAN, TAKE SOME MEN AND GO KILL DAVID!
HOW CAN I DO THAT TO DAVID?
DAVID! IT'S ME, JONATHAN. FATHER HAS ORDERED ME TO KILL YOU. GO AND HIDE IN A QUIET PLACE. I'LL TRY TO CHANGE MY FATHER'S MIND!
THANKS FOR TELLING ME, JONATHAN.
SO, DID YOU KILL DAVID?
IT'S HOT! NEED TO GET SOME A.C.
FATHER, I WOULD LIKE TO TALK WITH YOU IN PRIVATE...

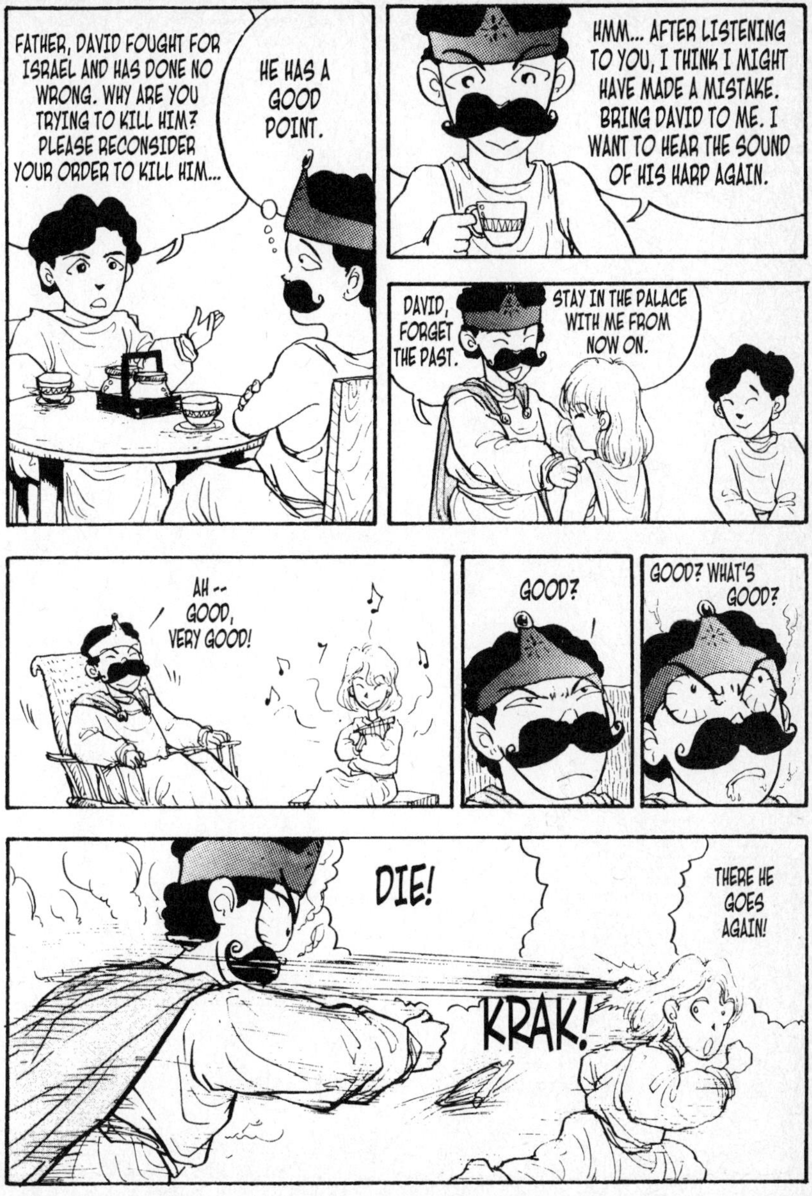
FATHER, DAVID FOUGHT FOR ISRAEL AND HAS DONE NO WRONG. WHY ARE YOU TRYING TO KILL HIM? PLEASE RECONSIDER YOUR ORDER TO KILL HIM...
HE HAS A GOOD POINT.
HMM... AFTER LISTENING TO YOU, I THINK I MIGHT HAVE MADE A MISTAKE. BRING DAVID TO ME. I WANT TO HEAR THE SOUND OF HIS HARP AGAIN.
DAVID, FORGET THE PAST.
STAY IN THE PALACE WITH ME FROM NOW ON.
AH -- GOOD, VERY GOOD!
GOOD?
GOOD? WHAT'S GOOD?
DIE!
THERE HE GOES AGAIN!
KRAK!

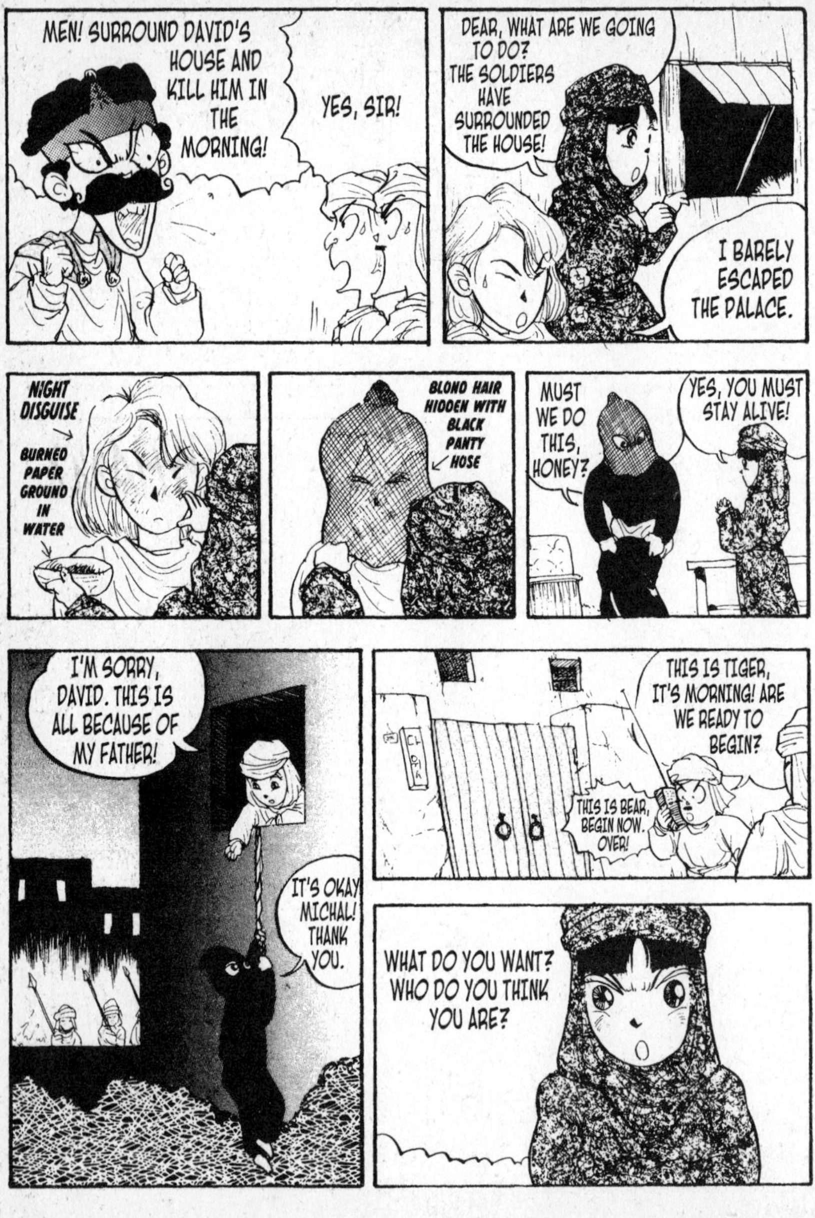
MEN! SURROUND DAVID'S HOUSE AND KILL HIM IN THE MORNING!
YES, SIR!
DEAR, WHAT ARE WE GOING TO DO? THE SOLDIERS HAVE SURROUNDED THE HOUSE!
I BARELY ESCAPED THE PALACE.
NIGHT DISGUISE
BURNED PAPER GROUND IN WATER
BLOND HAIR HIDDEN WITH BLACK PANTY HOSE
MUST WE DO THIS, HONEY?
YES, YOU MUST STAY ALIVE!
I'M SORRY, DAVID. THIS IS ALL BECAUSE OF MY FATHER!
IT'S OKAY MICHAL! THANK YOU.
THIS IS TIGER, IT'S MORNING! ARE WE READY TO BEGIN?
THIS IS BEAR, BEGIN NOW. OVER!
WHAT DO YOU WANT? WHO DO YOU THINK YOU ARE?

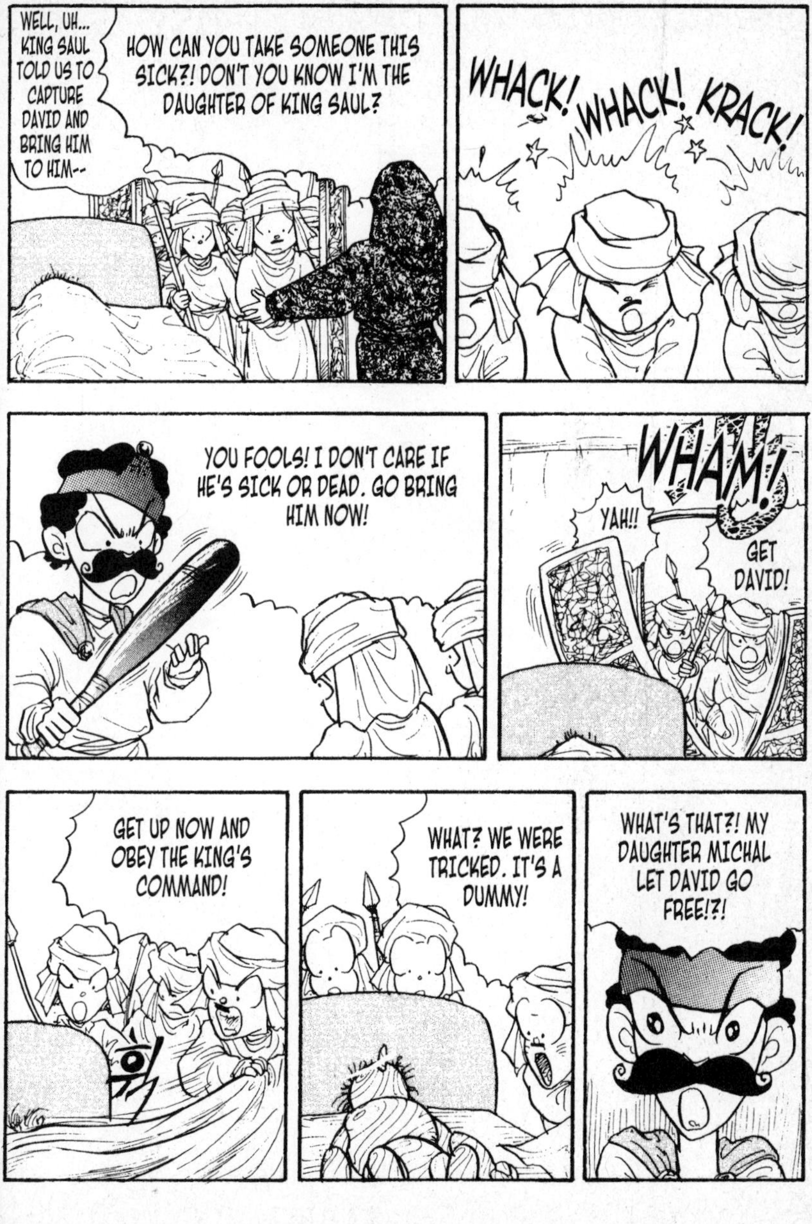

WELL, UH... KING SAUL TOLD US TO CAPTURE DAVID AND BRING HIM TO HIM--
HOW CAN YOU TAKE SOMEONE THIS SICK?! DON'T YOU KNOW I'M THE DAUGHTER OF KING SAUL?
WHACK! WHACK! KRACK!
YOU FOOLS! I DON'T CARE IF HE'S SICK OR DEAD. GO BRING HIM NOW!
WHAM!
YAH!!
GET DAVID!
GET UP NOW AND OBEY THE KING'S COMMAND!
WHAT? WE WERE TRICKED. IT'S A DUMMY!
WHAT'S THAT?! MY DAUGHTER MICHAL LET DAVID GO FREE!?!

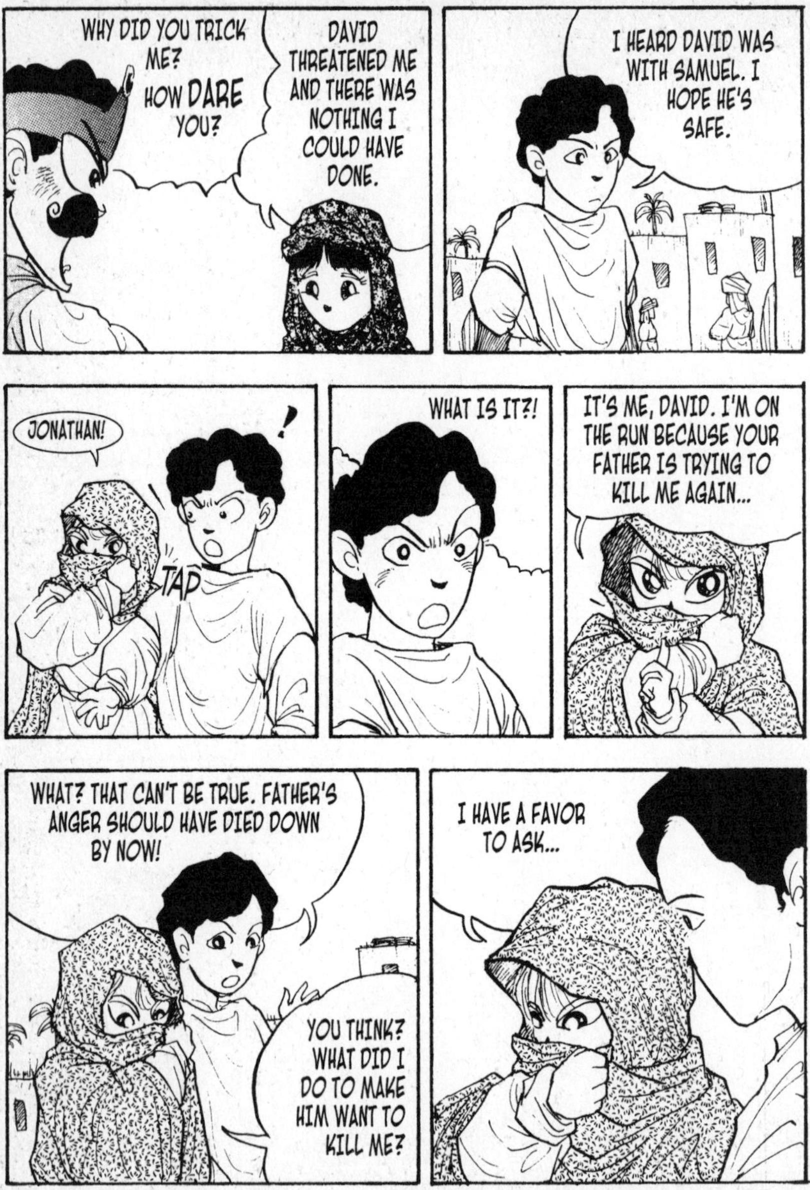
WHY DID YOU TRICK ME? HOW DARE YOU?
DAVID THREATENED ME AND THERE WAS NOTHING I COULD HAVE DONE.
I HEARD DAVID WAS WITH SAMUEL. I HOPE HE'S SAFE.
JONATHAN!
!
TAP
WHAT IS IT?!
IT'S ME, DAVID. I'M ON THE RUN BECAUSE YOUR FATHER IS TRYING TO KILL ME AGAIN...
WHAT? THAT CAN'T BE TRUE. FATHER'S ANGER SHOULD HAVE DIED DOWN BY NOW!
YOU THINK? WHAT DID I DO TO MAKE HIM WANT TO KILL ME?
I HAVE A FAVOR TO ASK...

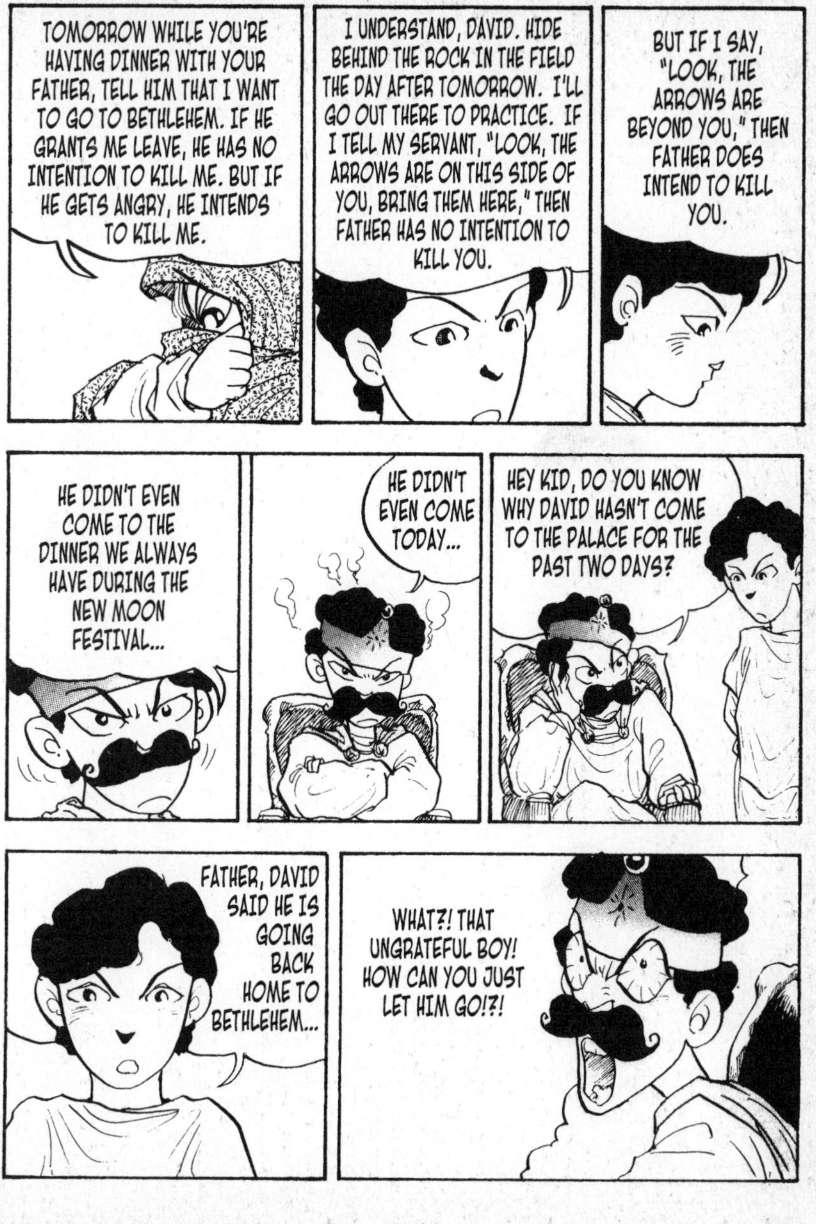
TOMORROW WHILE YOU'RE HAVING DINNER WITH YOUR FATHER, TELL HIM THAT I WANT TO GO TO BETHLEHEM. IF HE GRANTS ME LEAVE, HE HAS NO INTENTION TO KILL ME. BUT IF HE GETS ANGRY, HE INTENDS TO KILL ME.
I UNDERSTAND, DAVID. HIDE BEHIND THE ROCK IN THE FIELD THE DAY AFTER TOMORROW. I'LL GO OUT THERE TO PRACTICE. IF I TELL MY SERVANT, "LOOK, THE ARROWS ARE ON THIS SIDE OF YOU, BRING THEM HERE," THEN FATHER HAS NO INTENTION TO KILL YOU.
BUT IF I SAY, "LOOK, THE ARROWS ARE BEYOND YOU," THEN FATHER DOES INTEND TO KILL YOU.
HE DIDN'T EVEN COME TO THE DINNER WE ALWAYS HAVE DURING THE NEW MOON FESTIVAL...
HE DIDN'T EVEN COME TODAY...
HEY KID, DO YOU KNOW WHY DAVID HASN'T COME TO THE PALACE FOR THE PAST TWO DAYS?
FATHER, DAVID SAID HE IS GOING BACK HOME TO BETHLEHEM...
WHAT?! THAT UNGRATEFUL BOY! HOW CAN YOU JUST LET HIM GO!?!

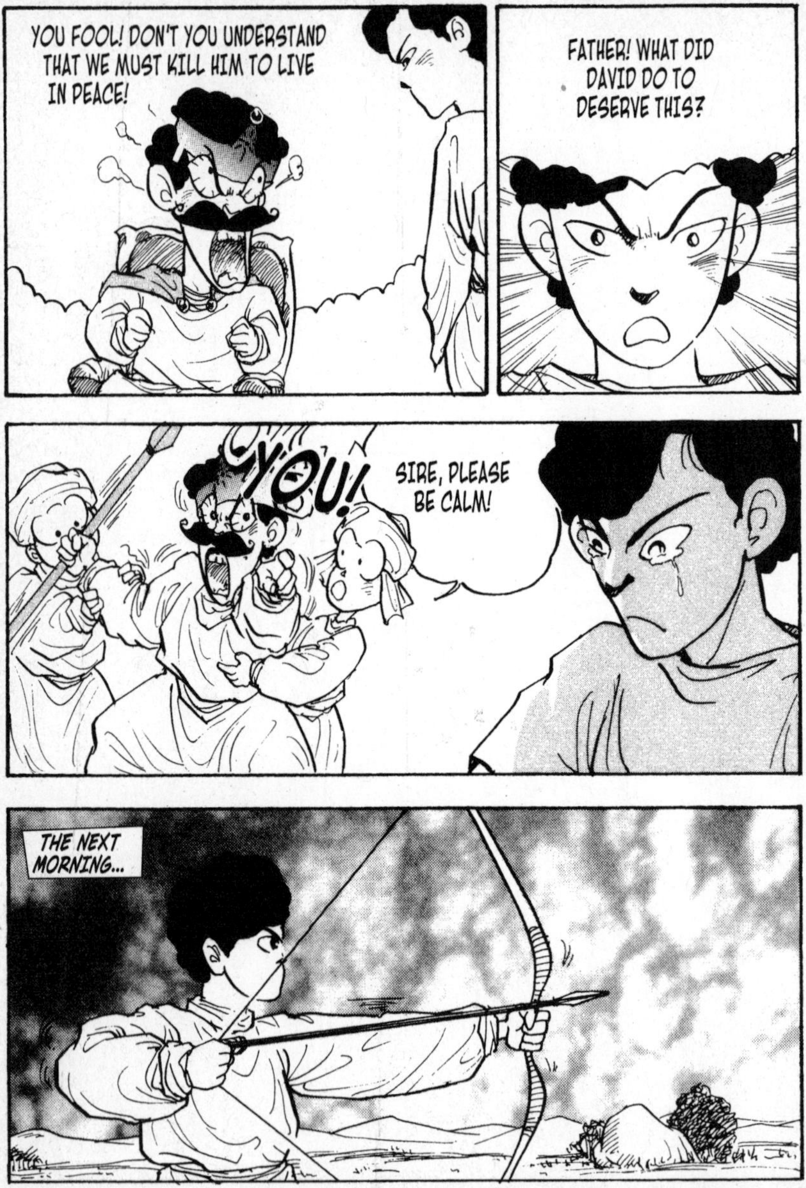
YOU FOOL! DON'T YOU UNDERSTAND THAT WE MUST KILL HIM TO LIVE IN PEACE!
FATHER! WHAT DID DAVID DO TO DESERVE THIS?
YOU!
SIRE, PLEASE BE CALM!
THE NEXT MORNING...

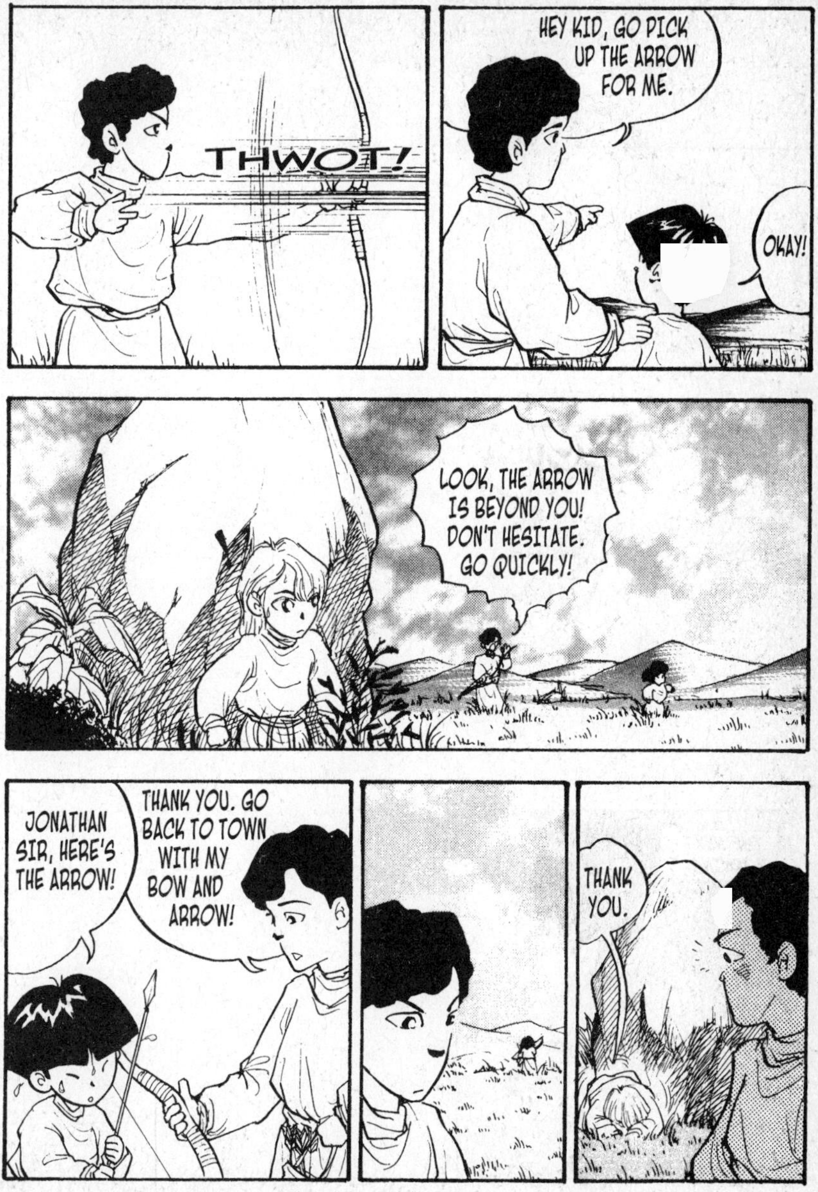
THWOT!
HEY KID, GO PICK UP THE ARROW FOR ME.
OKAY!
LOOK, THE ARROW IS BEYOND YOU! DON'T HESITATE. GO QUICKLY!
JONATHAN SIR, HERE'S THE ARROW!
THANK YOU. GO BACK TO TOWN WITH MY BOW AND ARROW!
THANK YOU.

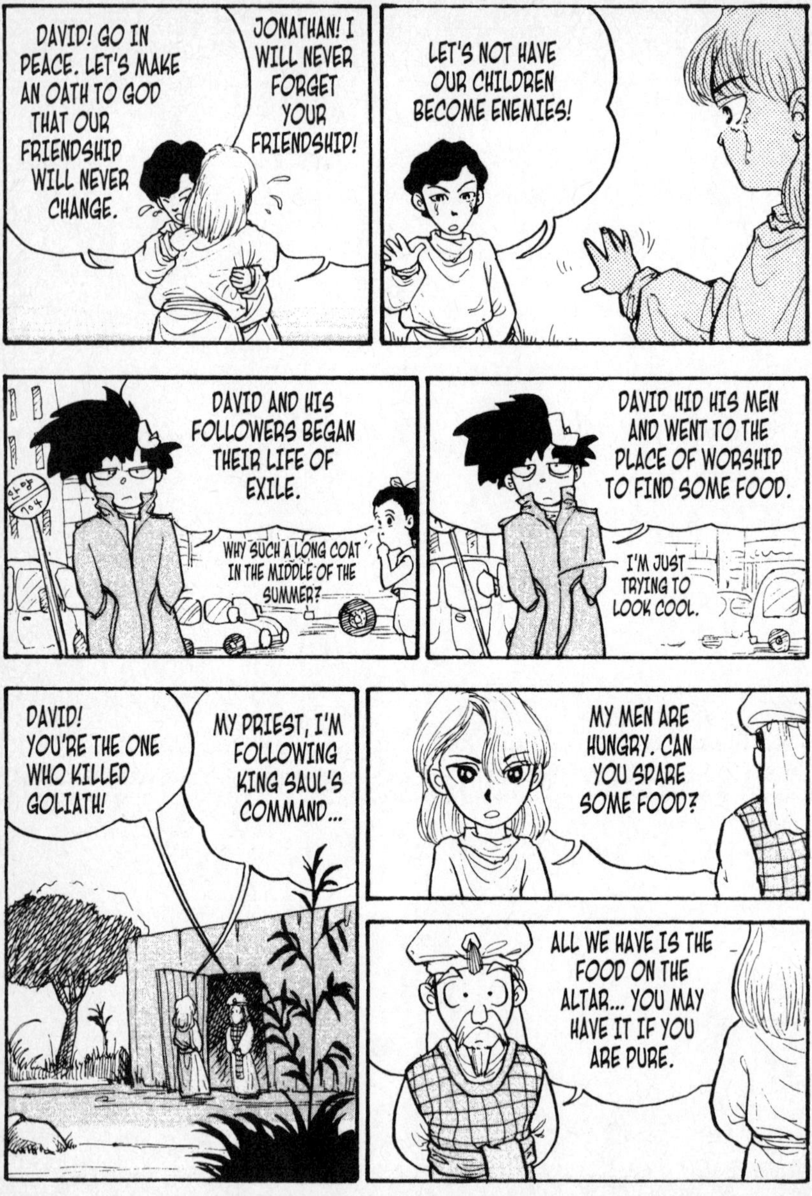
DAVID! GO IN PEACE. LET'S MAKE AN OATH TO GOD THAT OUR FRIENDSHIP WILL NEVER CHANGE.
JONATHAN! I WILL NEVER FORGET YOUR FRIENDSHIP!
LET'S NOT HAVE OUR CHILDREN BECOME ENEMIES!
DAVID AND HIS FOLLOWERS BEGAN THEIR LIFE OF EXILE.
WHY SUCH A LONG COAT IN THE MIDDLE OF THE SUMMER?
DAVID HID HIS MEN AND WENT TO THE PLACE OF WORSHIP TO FIND SOME FOOD.
I'M JUST TRYING TO LOOK COOL.
DAVID! YOU'RE THE ONE WHO KILLED GOLIATH!
MY PRIEST, I'M FOLLOWING KING SAUL'S COMMAND...
MY MEN ARE HUNGRY. CAN YOU SPARE SOME FOOD?
ALL WE HAVE IS THE FOOD ON THE ALTAR... YOU MAY HAVE IT IF YOU ARE PURE.

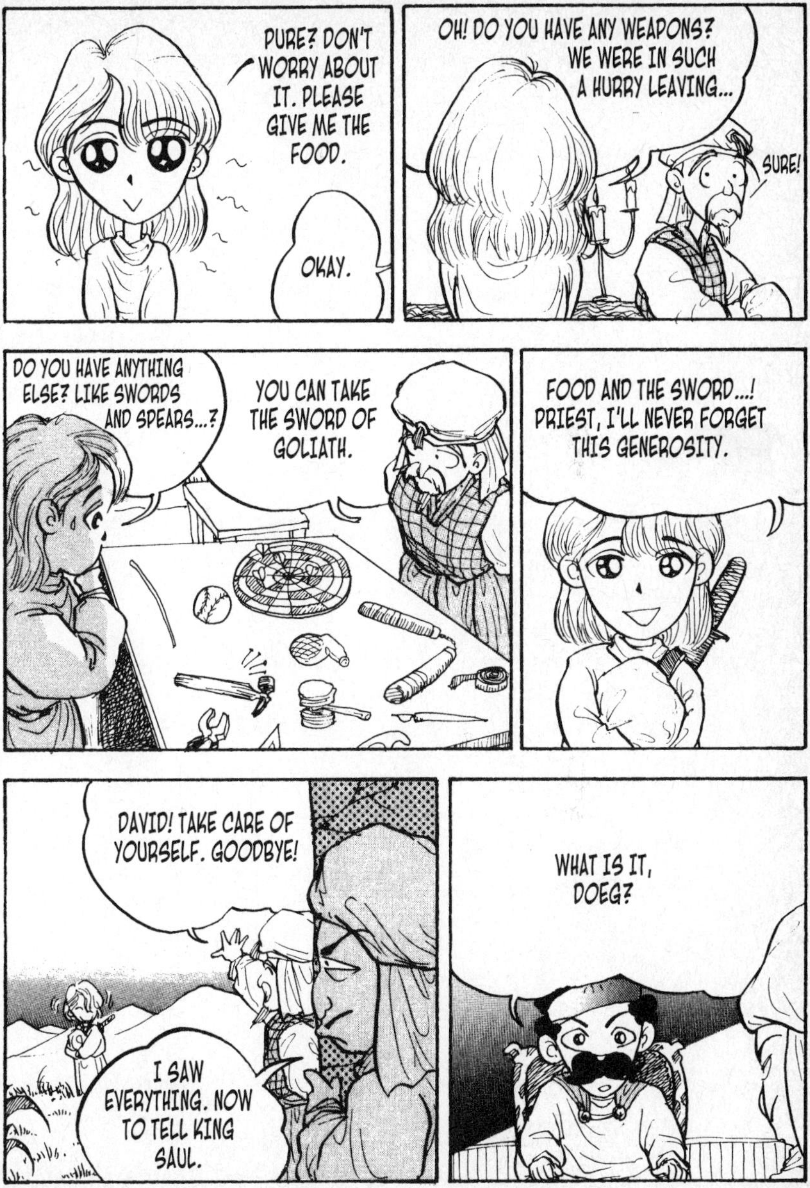
PURE? DON'T WORRY ABOUT IT. PLEASE GIVE ME THE FOOD.
OKAY.
OH! DO YOU HAVE ANY WEAPONS? WE WERE IN SUCH A HURRY LEAVING...
SURE!
DO YOU HAVE ANYTHING ELSE? LIKE SWORDS AND SPEARS...?
YOU CAN TAKE THE SWORD OF GOLIATH.
FOOD AND THE SWORD...! PRIEST, I'LL NEVER FORGET THIS GENEROSITY.
DAVID! TAKE CARE OF YOURSELF. GOODBYE!
I SAW EVERYTHING. NOW TO TELL KING SAUL.
WHAT IS IT, DOEG?

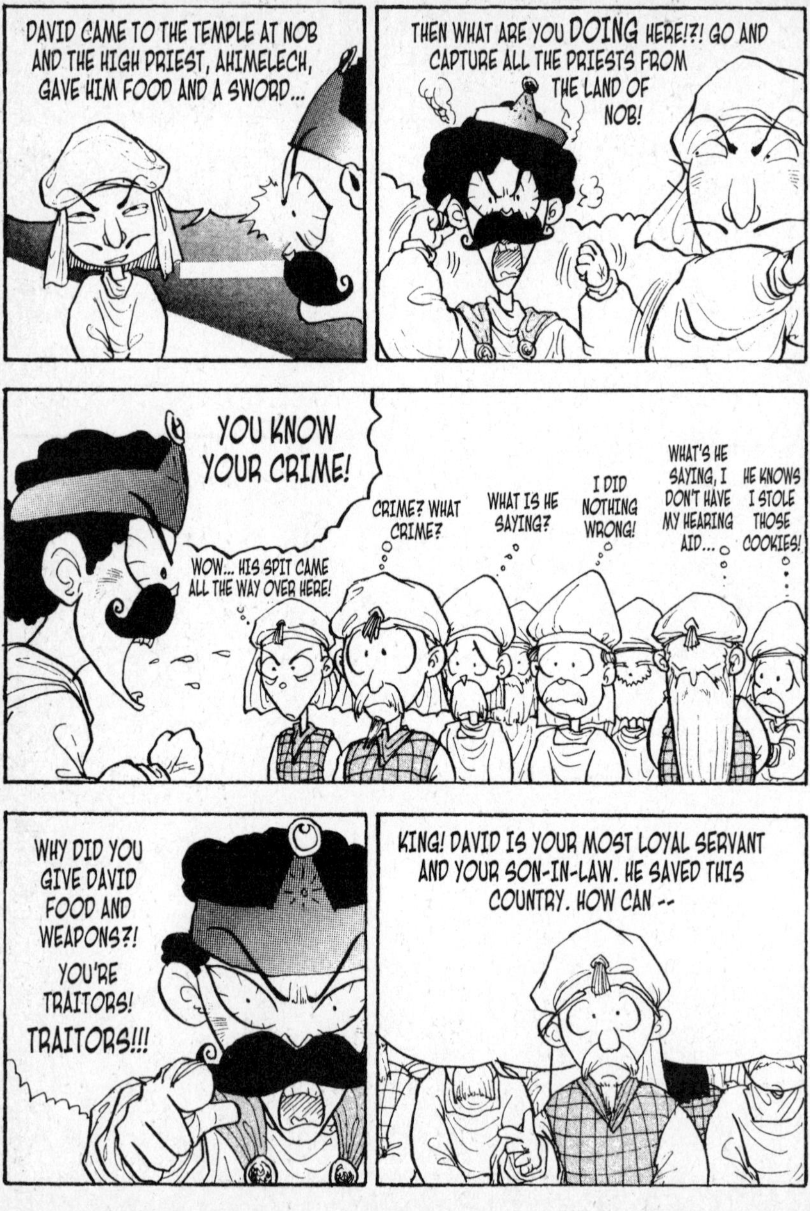
DAVID CAME TO THE TEMPLE AT NOB AND THE HIGH PRIEST, AHIMELECH, GAVE HIM FOOD AND A SWORD...
THEN WHAT ARE YOU DOING HERE!?! GO AND CAPTURE ALL THE PRIESTS FROM THE LAND OF NOB!
YOU KNOW YOUR CRIME!
WOW... HIS SPIT CAME ALL THE WAY OVER HERE!
CRIME? WHAT CRIME?
WHAT IS HE SAYING?
I DID NOTHING WRONG!
WHAT'S HE SAYING, I DON'T HAVE MY HEARING AID...
HE KNOWS I STOLE THOSE COOKIES!
WHY DID YOU GIVE DAVID FOOD AND WEAPONS?!
YOU'RE TRAITORS!
TRAITORS!!!
KING! DAVID IS YOUR MOST LOYAL SERVANT AND YOUR SON-IN-LAW. HE SAVED THIS COUNTRY. HOW CAN --

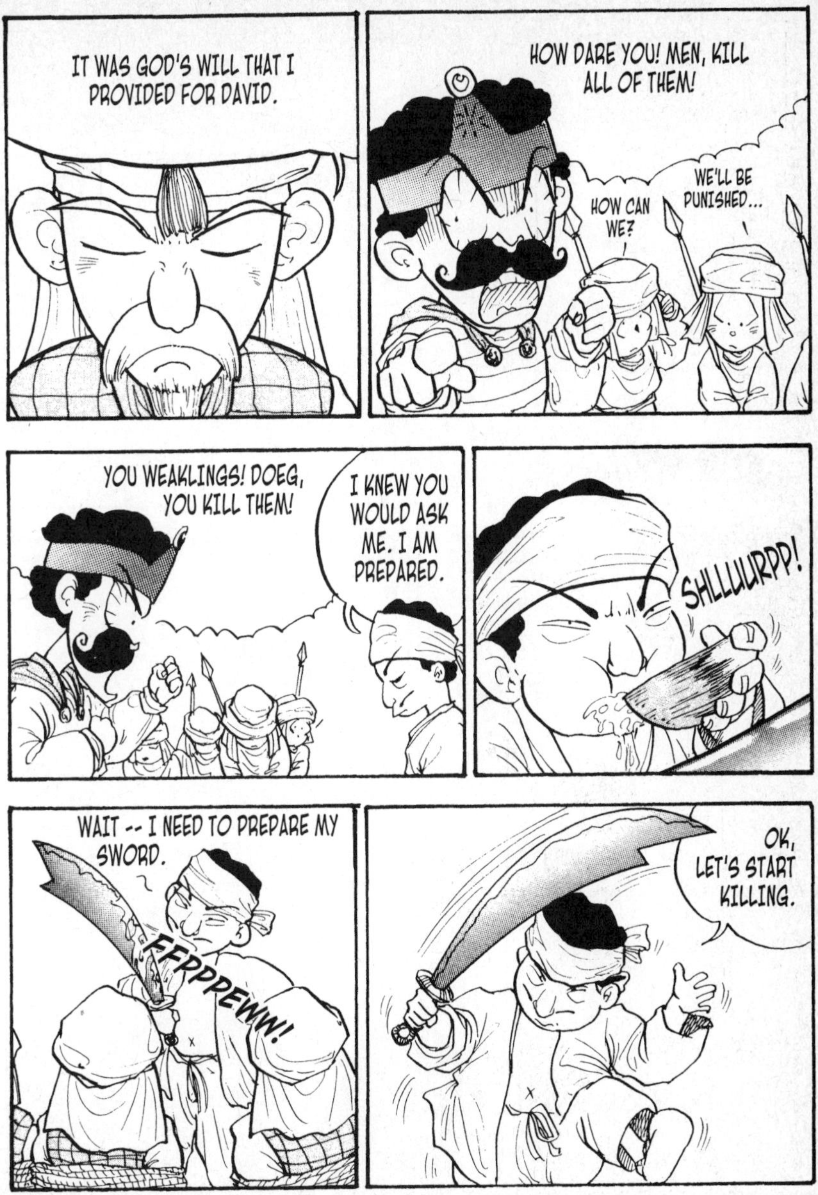
IT WAS GOD'S WILL THAT I PROVIDED FOR DAVID.
HOW DARE YOU! MEN, KILL ALL OF THEM!
HOW CAN WE?
WE'LL BE PUNISHED...
YOU WEAKLINGS! DOEG, YOU KILL THEM!
I KNEW YOU WOULD ASK ME. I AM PREPARED.
SHLLUURPP!
WAIT -- I NEED TO PREPARE MY SWORD.
FFRPPPEWW!
OK, LET'S START KILLING.

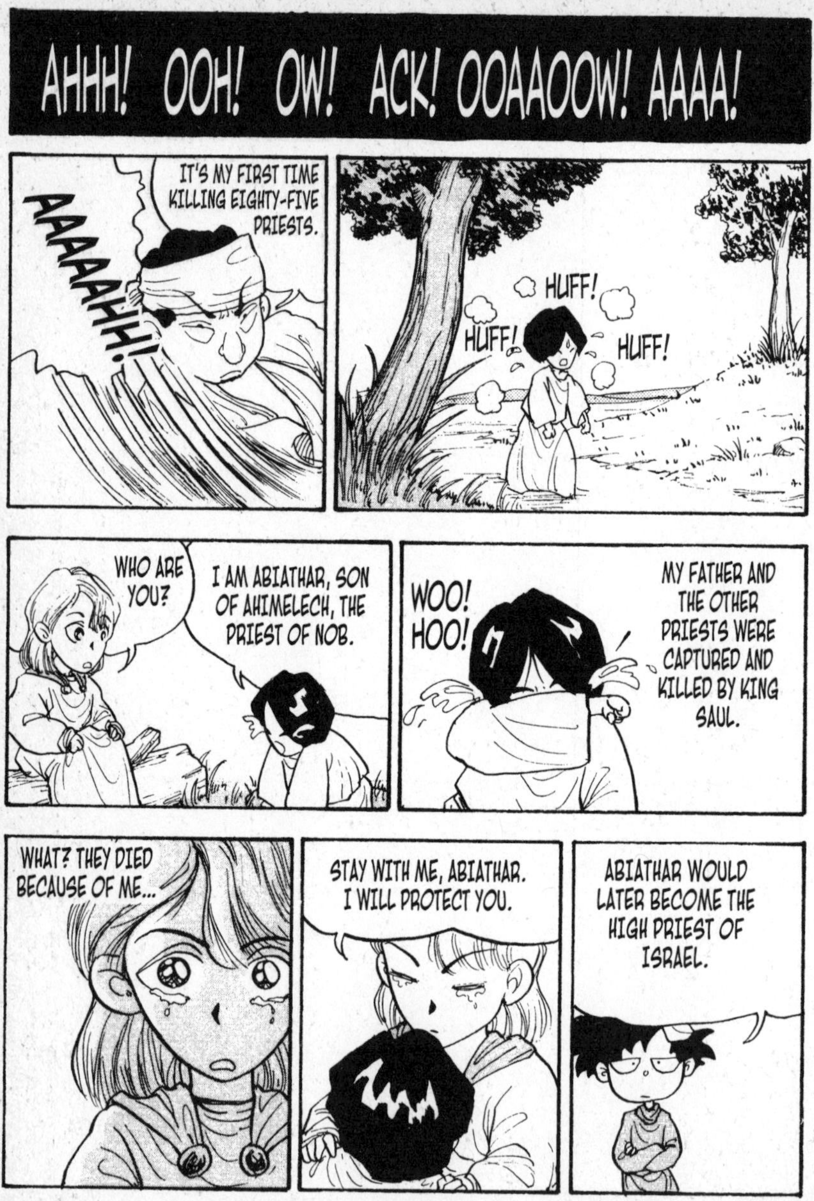
AHHH! OOH! OW! ACK! OOAAOOW! AAAA!
IT'S MY FIRST TIME KILLING EIGHTY-FIVE PRIESTS.
AAAAAHH!
HUFF!
HUFF!
HUFF!
WHO ARE YOU?
I AM ABIATHAR, SON OF AHIMELECH, THE PRIEST OF NOB.
WOO! HOO!
MY FATHER AND THE OTHER PRIESTS WERE CAPTURED AND KILLED BY KING SAUL.
WHAT? THEY DIED BECAUSE OF ME...
STAY WITH ME, ABIATHAR. I WILL PROTECT YOU.
ABIATHAR WOULD LATER BECOME THE HIGH PRIEST OF ISRAEL.

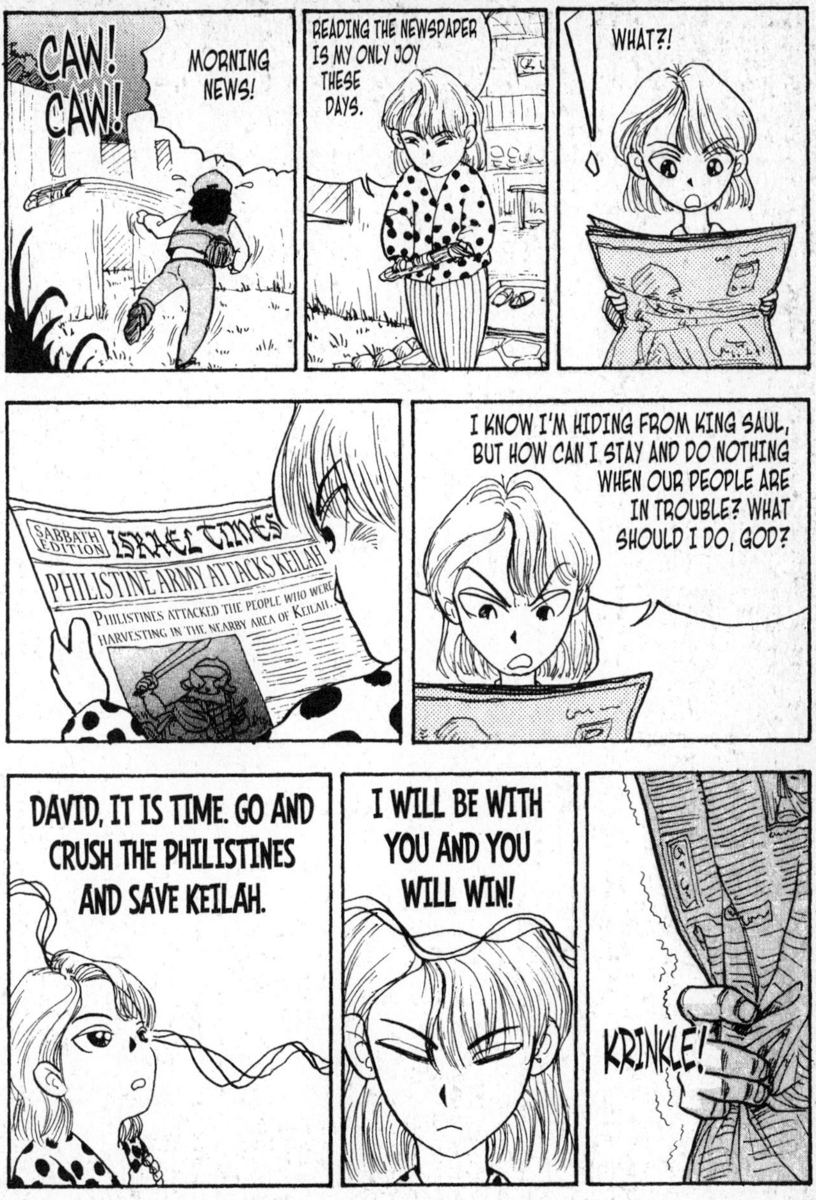
CAW! CAW!
MORNING NEWS!
READING THE NEWSPAPER IS MY ONLY JOY THESE DAYS.
WHAT?!
SABBATH EDITION
ISRAEL TIMES
PHILISTINE ARMY ATTACKS KEILAH
PHILISTINES ATTACKED THE PEOPLE WHO WERE HARVESTING IN THE NEARBY AREA OF KEILAH...
I KNOW I'M HIDING FROM KING SAUL, BUT HOW CAN I STAY AND DO NOTHING WHEN OUR PEOPLE ARE IN TROUBLE? WHAT SHOULD I DO, GOD?
DAVID, IT IS TIME. GO AND CRUSH THE PHILISTINES AND SAVE KEILAH.
I WILL BE WITH YOU AND YOU WILL WIN!
KRINKLE!

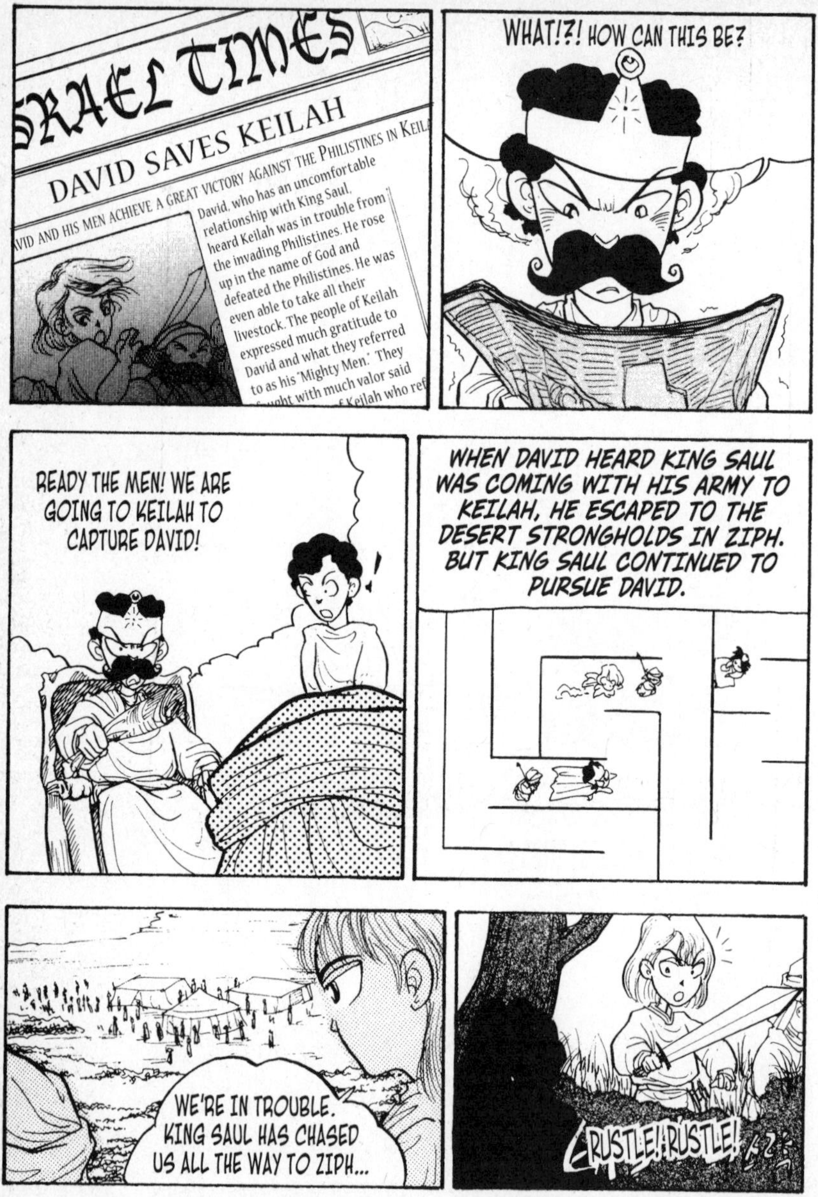
SRAEL TIMES
DAVID SAVES KEILAH
DAVID AND HIS MEN ACHIEVE A GREAT VICTORY AGAINST THE PHILISTINES IN KEILA
David, who has an uncomfortable
relationship with King Saul,
heard Keilah was in trouble from
the invading Philistines. He rose
up in the name of God and
defeated the Philistines. He was
even able to take all their
livestock. The people of Keilah
expressed much gratitude to
David and what they referred
to as his "Mighty Men." They
WHAT!?! HOW CAN THIS BE?
READY THE MEN! WE ARE GOING TO KEILAH TO CAPTURE DAVID!
WHEN DAVID HEARD KING SAUL WAS COMING WITH HIS ARMY TO KEILAH, HE ESCAPED TO THE DESERT STRONGHOLDS IN ZIPH. BUT KING SAUL CONTINUED TO PURSUE DAVID.
WE'RE IN TROUBLE. KING SAUL HAS CHASED US ALL THE WAY TO ZIPH...
RUSTLE! RUSTLE!

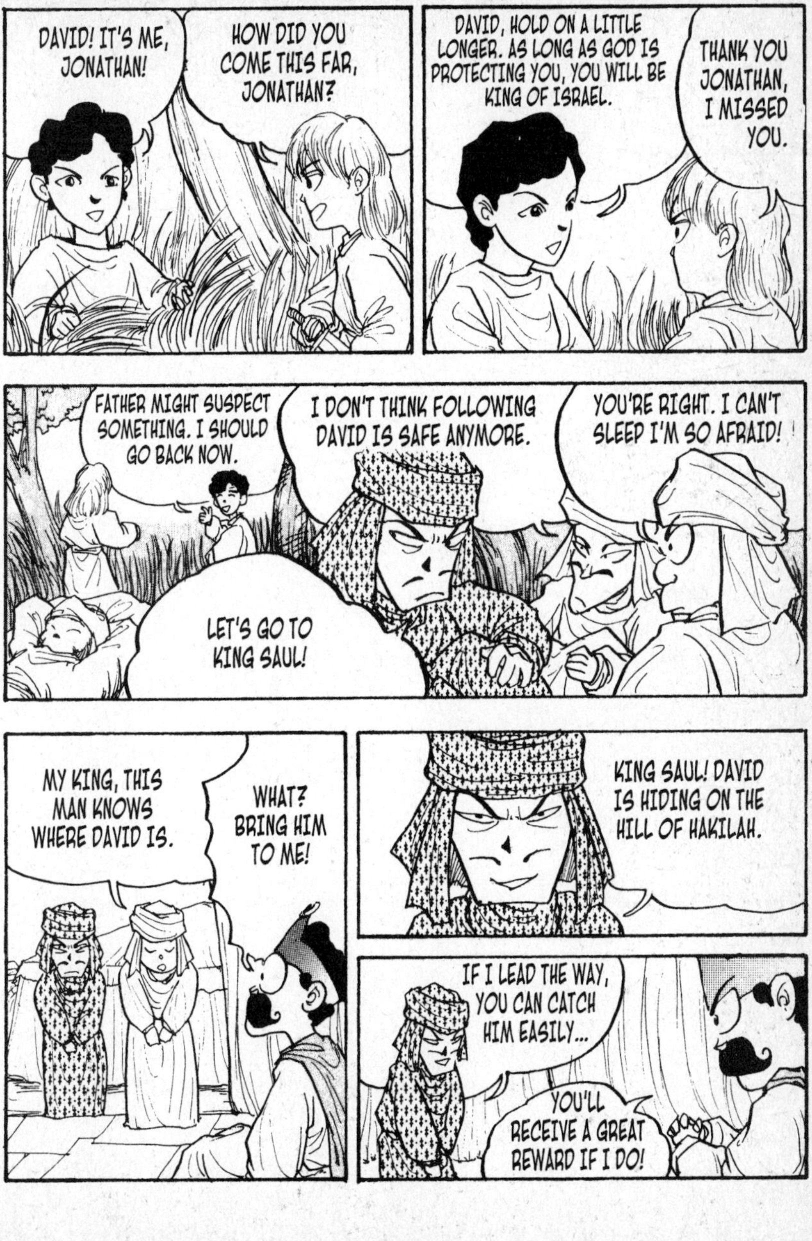
DAVID! IT'S ME, JONATHAN!
HOW DID YOU COME THIS FAR, JONATHAN?
DAVID, HOLD ON A LITTLE LONGER. AS LONG AS GOD IS PROTECTING YOU, YOU WILL BE KING OF ISRAEL.
THANK YOU JONATHAN, I MISSED YOU.
FATHER MIGHT SUSPECT SOMETHING. I SHOULD GO BACK NOW.
I DON'T THINK FOLLOWING DAVID IS SAFE ANYMORE.
YOU'RE RIGHT. I CAN'T SLEEP I'M SO AFRAID!
LET'S GO TO KING SAUL!
MY KING, THIS MAN KNOWS WHERE DAVID IS.
WHAT? BRING HIM TO ME!
KING SAUL! DAVID IS HIDING ON THE HILL OF HAKILAH.
IF I LEAD THE WAY, YOU CAN CATCH HIM EASILY...
YOU'LL RECEIVE A GREAT REWARD IF I DO!

DAVID! I KNOW YOU'RE HIDING THERE!
HOW DID HE KNOW?
GENERAL DAVID, WE'RE IN TROUBLE. SAUL'S MEN ARE BEHIND US AS WELL.
우린 죽었다
NOW YOU'RE DEAD, DAVID.
KING SAUL, I HAVE TERRIBLE NEWS!
THE PHILISTINE ARMY HAS ATTACKED. YOU MUST RETURN AND DEFEND THE LAND....
WHAT...?! WHY NOW?
WE MUST GO AND FIGHT THE PHILISTINES!
(SIGH) -- WE'RE SAVED.
GOD! THANK YOU FOR PROTECTING ME FROM SAUL.

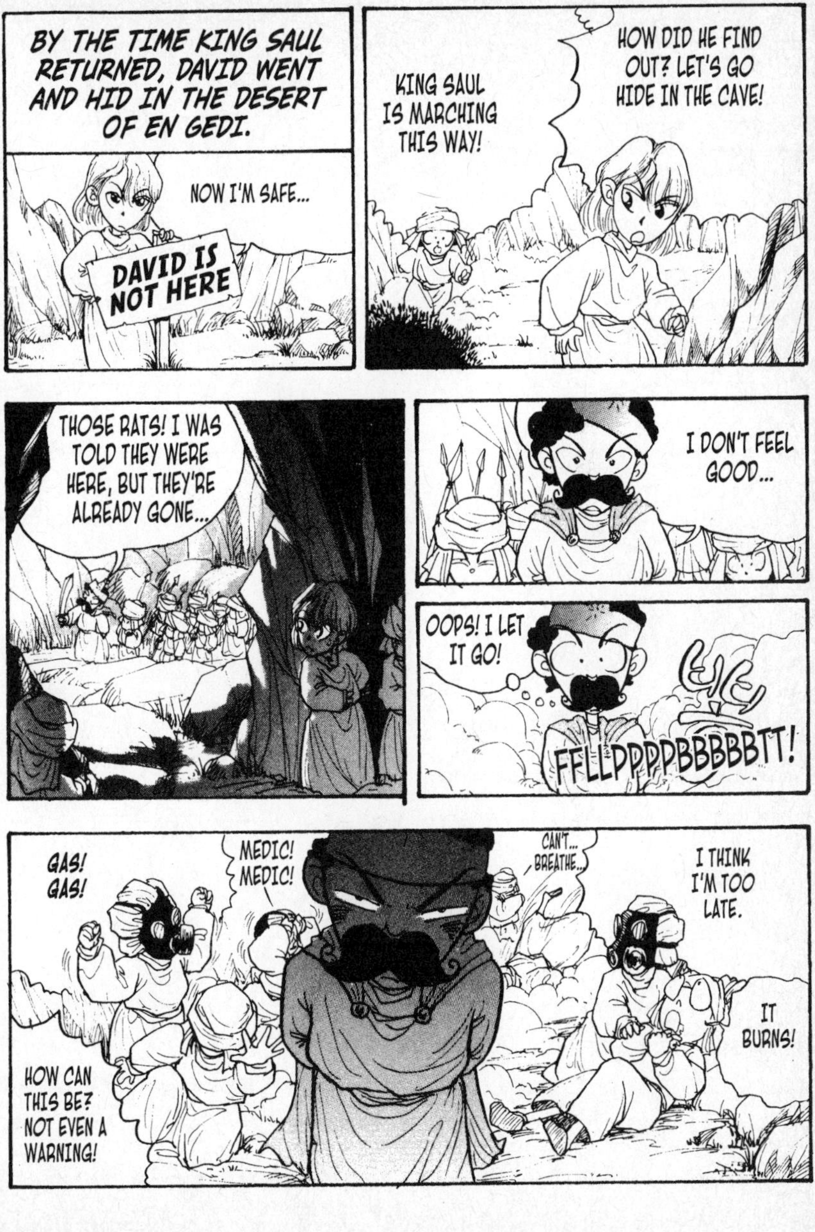
BY THE TIME KING SAUL RETURNED, DAVID WENT AND HID IN THE DESERT OF EN GEDI.
NOW I'M SAFE...
DAVID IS NOT HERE
KING SAUL IS MARCHING THIS WAY!
HOW DID HE FIND OUT? LET'S GO HIDE IN THE CAVE!
THOSE RATS! I WAS TOLD THEY WERE HERE, BUT THEY'RE ALREADY GONE...
I DON'T FEEL GOOD...
OOPS! I LET IT GO!
FFLLPPPPBBBBBTT!
GAS! GAS!
MEDIC! MEDIC!
CAN'T... BREATHE...
I THINK I'M TOO LATE.
IT BURNS!
HOW CAN THIS BE? NOT EVEN A WARNING!

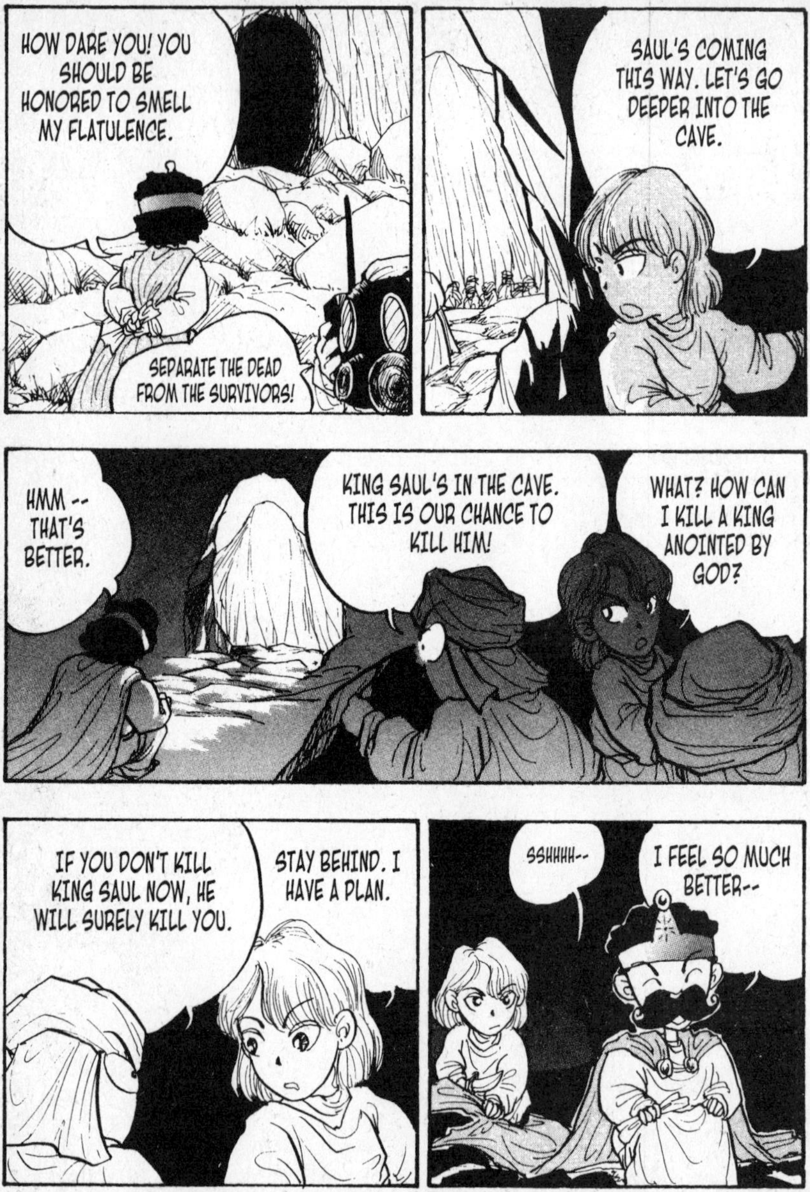
HOW DARE YOU! YOU SHOULD BE HONORED TO SMELL MY FLATULENCE.
SEPARATE THE DEAD FROM THE SURVIVORS!
SAUL'S COMING THIS WAY. LET'S GO DEEPER INTO THE CAVE.
HMM -- THAT'S BETTER.
KING SAUL'S IN THE CAVE. THIS IS OUR CHANCE TO KILL HIM!
WHAT? HOW CAN I KILL A KING ANOINTED BY GOD?
IF YOU DON'T KILL KING SAUL NOW, HE WILL SURELY KILL YOU.
STAY BEHIND. I HAVE A PLAN.
SSHHHH--
I FEEL SO MUCH BETTER--

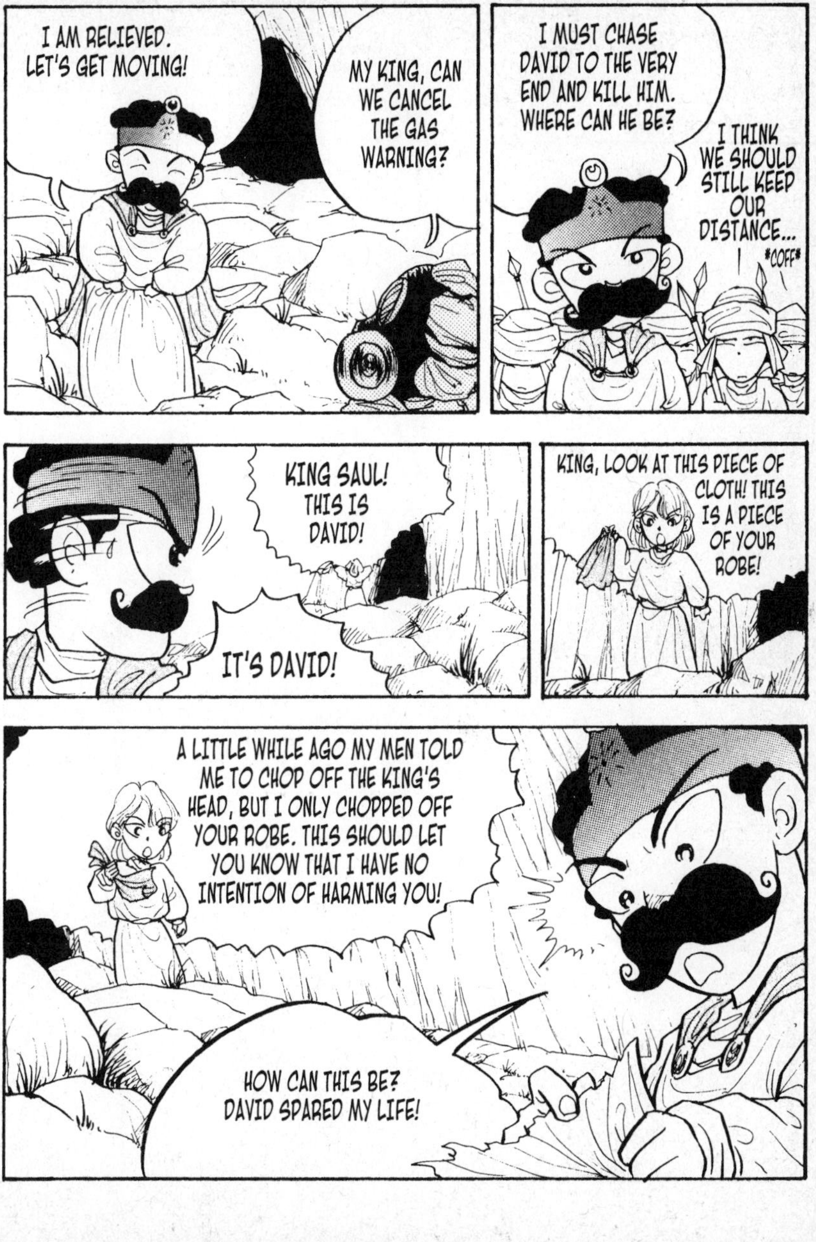
I AM RELIEVED. LET'S GET MOVING!
MY KING, CAN WE CANCEL THE GAS WARNING?
I MUST CHASE DAVID TO THE VERY END AND KILL HIM. WHERE CAN HE BE?
I THINK WE SHOULD STILL KEEP OUR DISTANCE...
!
COFF
KING SAUL! THIS IS DAVID!
IT'S DAVID!
KING, LOOK AT THIS PIECE OF CLOTH! THIS IS A PIECE OF YOUR ROBE!
A LITTLE WHILE AGO MY MEN TOLD ME TO CHOP OFF THE KING'S HEAD, BUT I ONLY CHOPPED OFF YOUR ROBE. THIS SHOULD LET YOU KNOW THAT I HAVE NO INTENTION OF HARMING YOU!
HOW CAN THIS BE? DAVID SPARED MY LIFE!

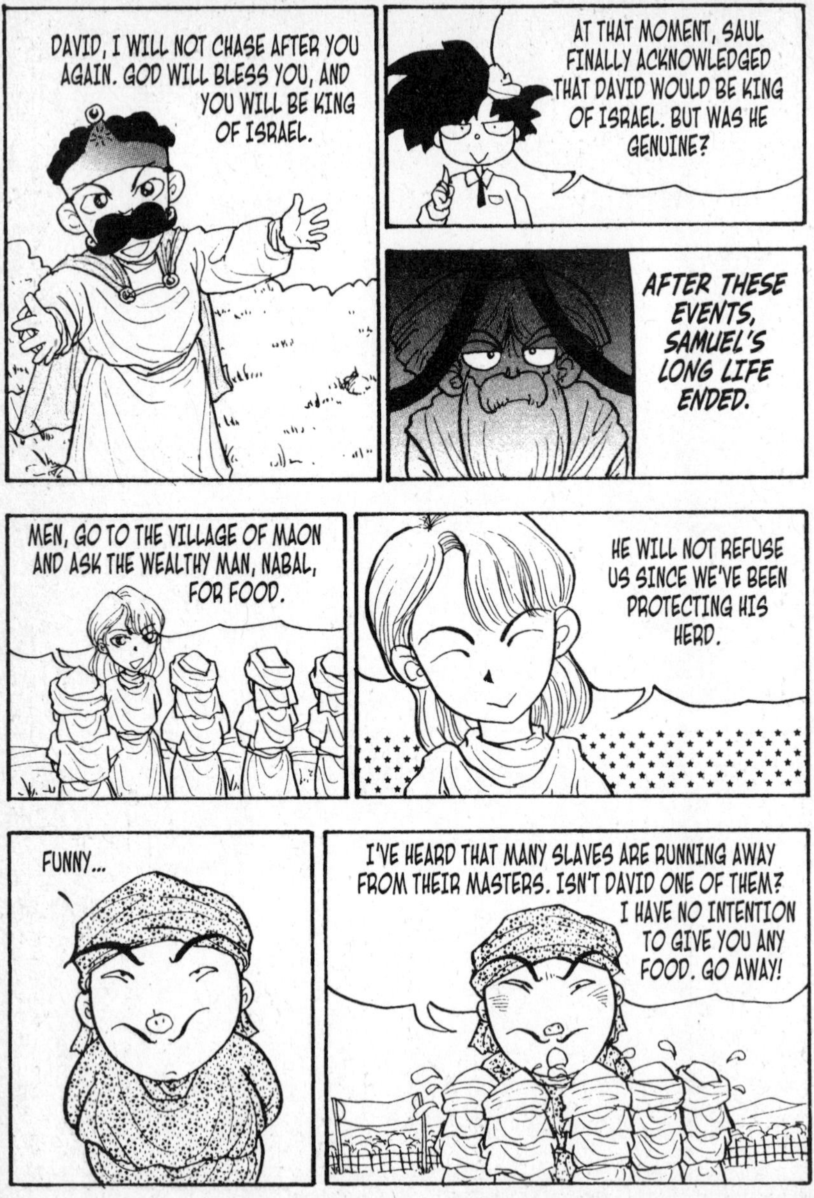
DAVID, I WILL NOT CHASE AFTER YOU AGAIN. GOD WILL BLESS YOU, AND YOU WILL BE KING OF ISRAEL.
AT THAT MOMENT, SAUL FINALLY ACKNOWLEDGED THAT DAVID WOULD BE KING OF ISRAEL. BUT WAS HE GENUINE?
AFTER THESE EVENTS, SAMUEL'S LONG LIFE ENDED.
MEN, GO TO THE VILLAGE OF MAON AND ASK THE WEALTHY MAN, NABAL, FOR FOOD.
HE WILL NOT REFUSE US SINCE WE'VE BEEN PROTECTING HIS HERD.
FUNNY...
I'VE HEARD THAT MANY SLAVES ARE RUNNING AWAY FROM THEIR MASTERS. ISN'T DAVID ONE OF THEM?
I HAVE NO INTENTION TO GIVE YOU ANY FOOD. GO AWAY!

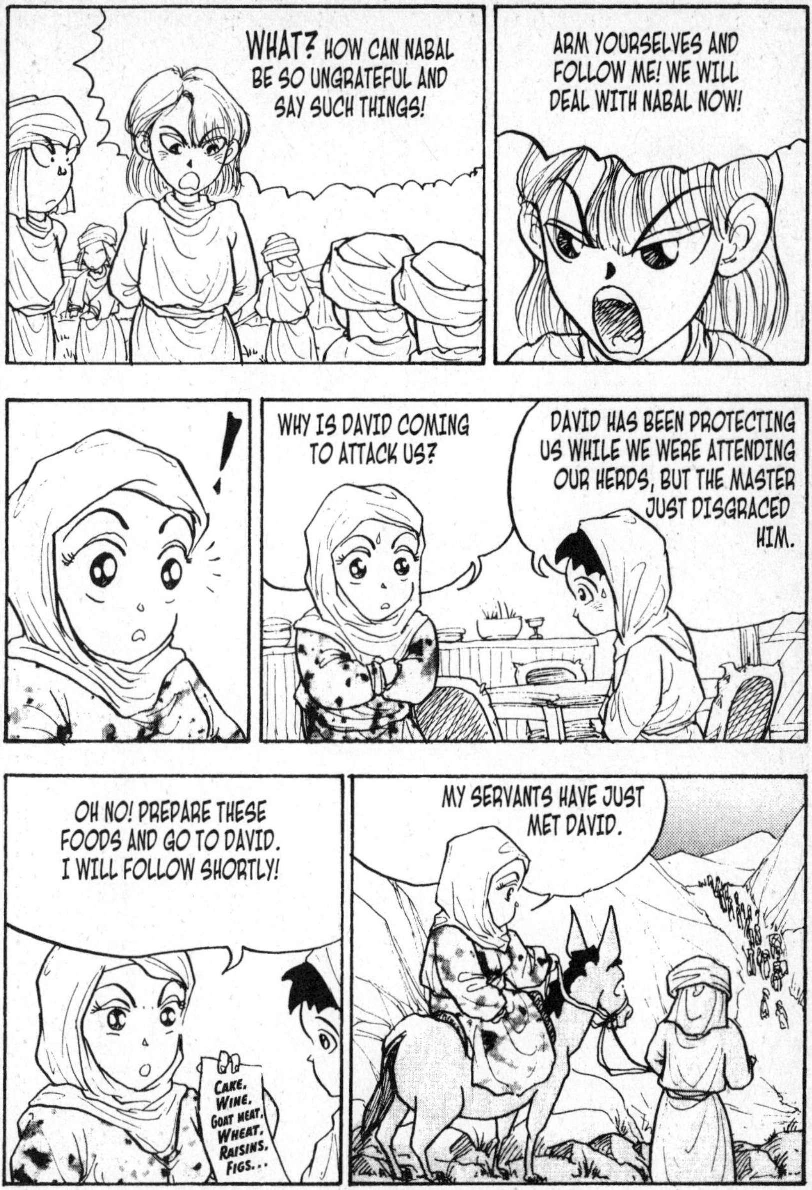
WHAT? HOW CAN NABAL BE SO UNGRATEFUL AND SAY SUCH THINGS!
ARM YOURSELVES AND FOLLOW ME! WE WILL DEAL WITH NABAL NOW!
!
WHY IS DAVID COMING TO ATTACK US?
DAVID HAS BEEN PROTECTING US WHILE WE WERE ATTENDING OUR HERDS, BUT THE MASTER JUST DISGRACED HIM.
OH NO! PREPARE THESE FOODS AND GO TO DAVID. I WILL FOLLOW SHORTLY!
CAKE, WINE, GOAT MEAT, WHEAT, RAISINS, FIGS...
MY SERVANTS HAVE JUST MET DAVID.

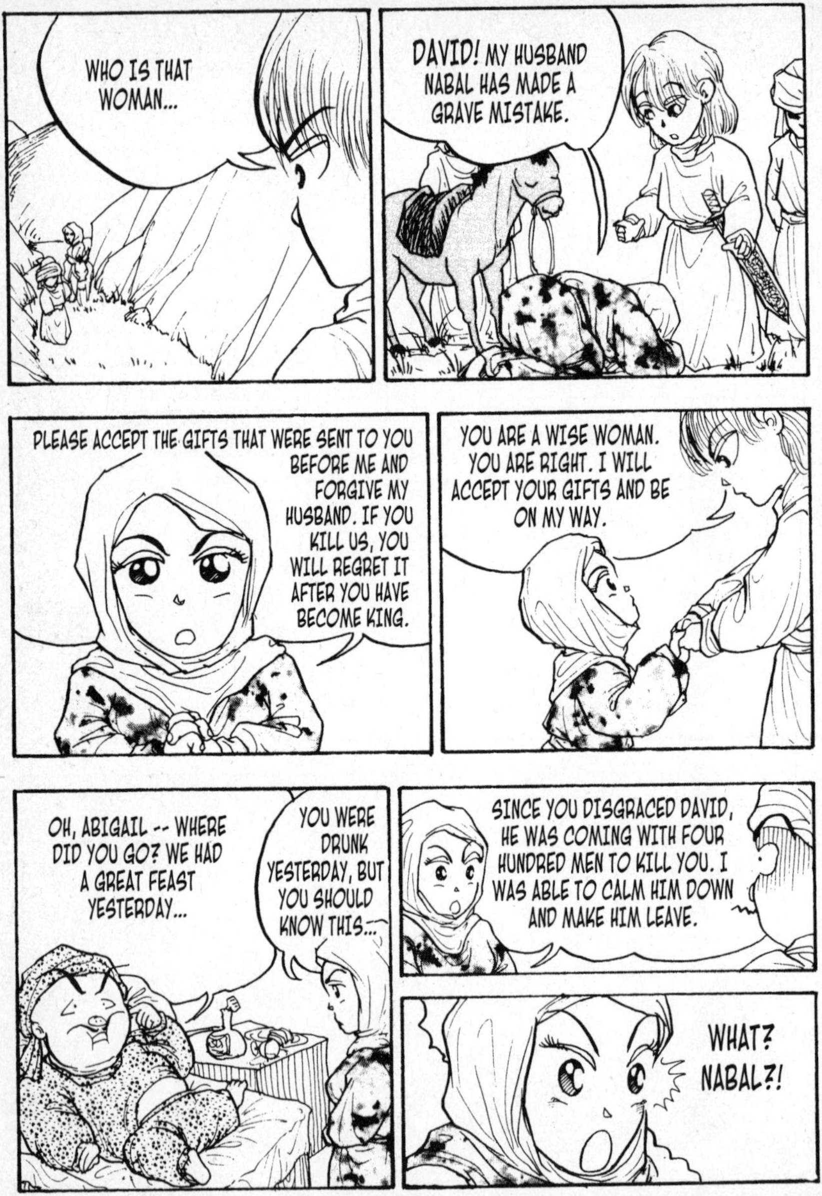
WHO IS THAT WOMAN...
DAVID! MY HUSBAND NABAL HAS MADE A GRAVE MISTAKE.
PLEASE ACCEPT THE GIFTS THAT WERE SENT TO YOU BEFORE ME AND FORGIVE MY HUSBAND. IF YOU KILL US, YOU WILL REGRET IT AFTER YOU HAVE BECOME KING.
YOU ARE A WISE WOMAN. YOU ARE RIGHT. I WILL ACCEPT YOUR GIFTS AND BE ON MY WAY.
OH, ABIGAIL -- WHERE DID YOU GO? WE HAD A GREAT FEAST YESTERDAY...
YOU WERE DRUNK YESTERDAY, BUT YOU SHOULD KNOW THIS...
SINCE YOU DISGRACED DAVID, HE WAS COMING WITH FOUR HUNDRED MEN TO KILL YOU. I WAS ABLE TO CALM HIM DOWN AND MAKE HIM LEAVE.
WHAT? NABAL?!

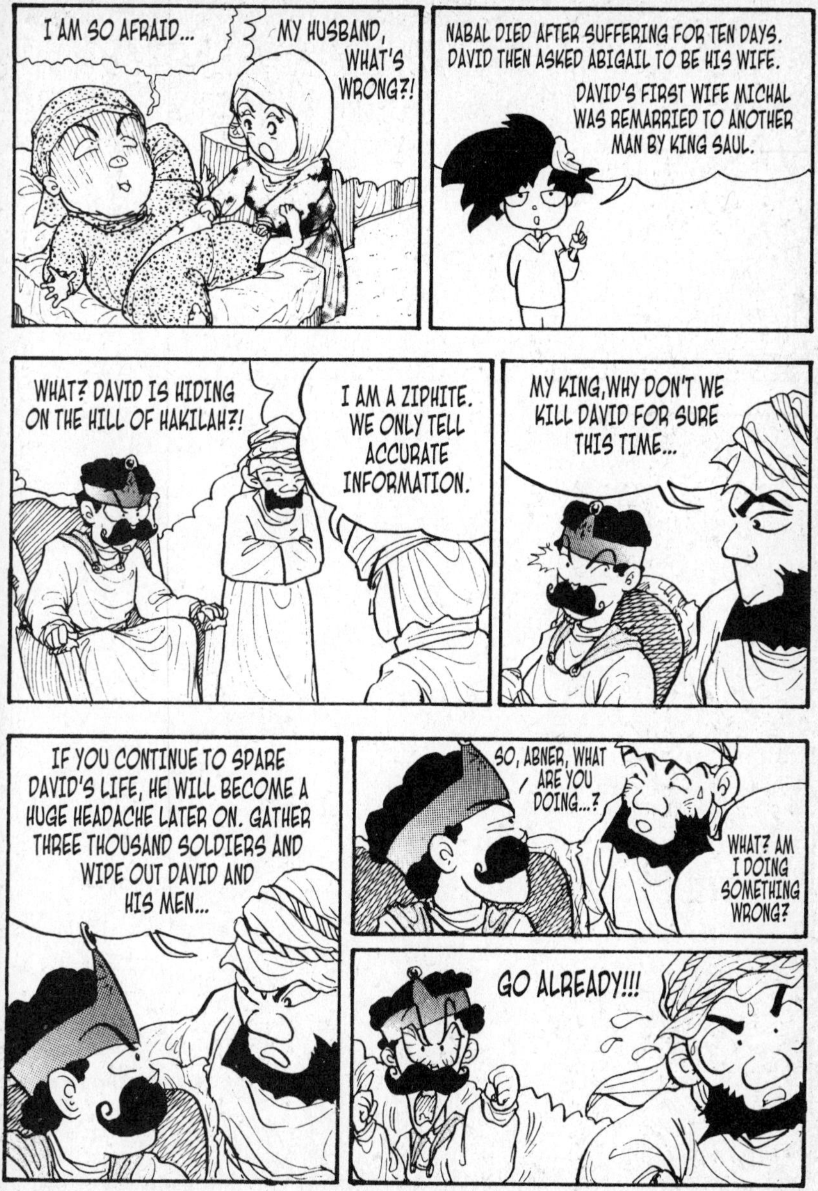
I AM SO AFRAID...
MY HUSBAND, WHAT'S WRONG?!
NABAL DIED AFTER SUFFERING FOR TEN DAYS. DAVID THEN ASKED ABIGAIL TO BE HIS WIFE.
DAVID'S FIRST WIFE MICHAL WAS REMARRIED TO ANOTHER MAN BY KING SAUL.
WHAT? DAVID IS HIDING ON THE HILL OF HAKILAH?!
I AM A ZIPHITE. WE ONLY TELL ACCURATE INFORMATION.
MY KING, WHY DON'T WE KILL DAVID FOR SURE THIS TIME...
IF YOU CONTINUE TO SPARE DAVID'S LIFE, HE WILL BECOME A HUGE HEADACHE LATER ON. GATHER THREE THOUSAND SOLDIERS AND WIPE OUT DAVID AND HIS MEN...
SO, ABNER, WHAT ARE YOU DOING...?
WHAT? AM I DOING SOMETHING WRONG?
GO ALREADY!!!

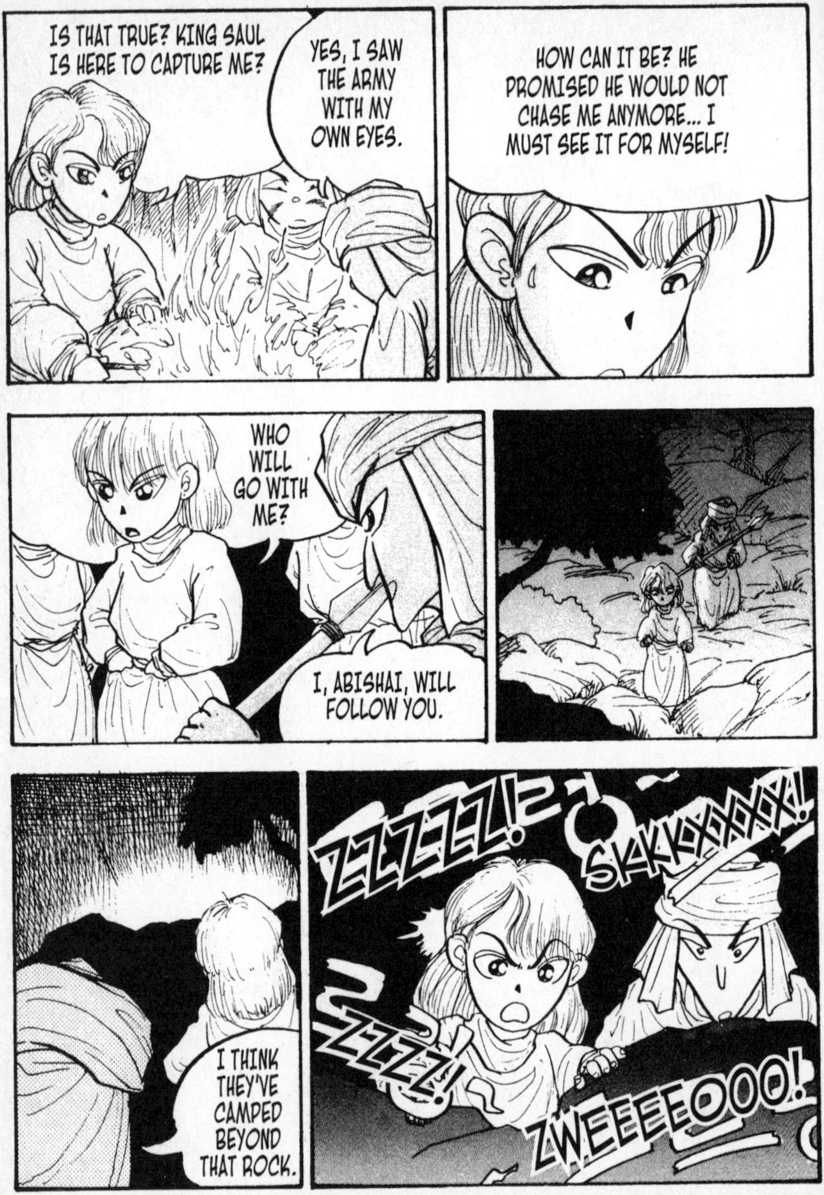
IS THAT TRUE? KING SAUL IS HERE TO CAPTURE ME?
YES, I SAW THE ARMY WITH MY OWN EYES.
HOW CAN IT BE? HE PROMISED HE WOULD NOT CHASE ME ANYMORE... I MUST SEE IT FOR MYSELF!
WHO WILL GO WITH ME?
I, ABISHAI, WILL FOLLOW YOU.
I THINK THEY'VE CAMPED BEYOND THAT ROCK.
ZZZZZZZ!
SKKKOOOOOX!
ZZZZ!
ZWEEEEEOOO!

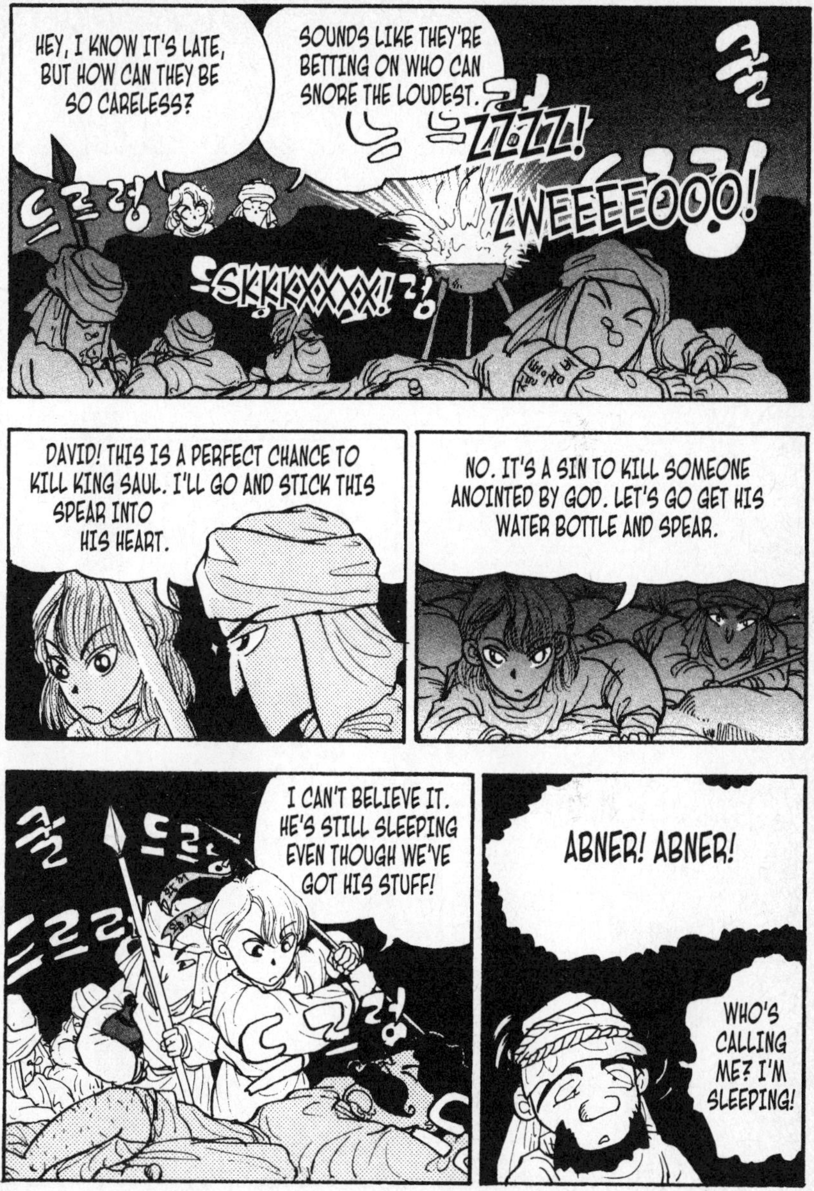
HEY, I KNOW IT'S LATE, BUT HOW CAN THEY BE SO CARELESS?
SOUNDS LIKE THEY'RE BETTING ON WHO CAN SNORE THE LOUDEST.
ZZZZ!
ZWEEEEEOOO!
SKKKXXXX!
DAVID! THIS IS A PERFECT CHANCE TO KILL KING SAUL. I'LL GO AND STICK THIS SPEAR INTO HIS HEART.
NO. IT'S A SIN TO KILL SOMEONE ANOINTED BY GOD. LET'S GO GET HIS WATER BOTTLE AND SPEAR.
I CAN'T BELIEVE IT. HE'S STILL SLEEPING EVEN THOUGH WE'VE GOT HIS STUFF!
ABNER! ABNER!
WHO'S CALLING ME? I'M SLEEPING!

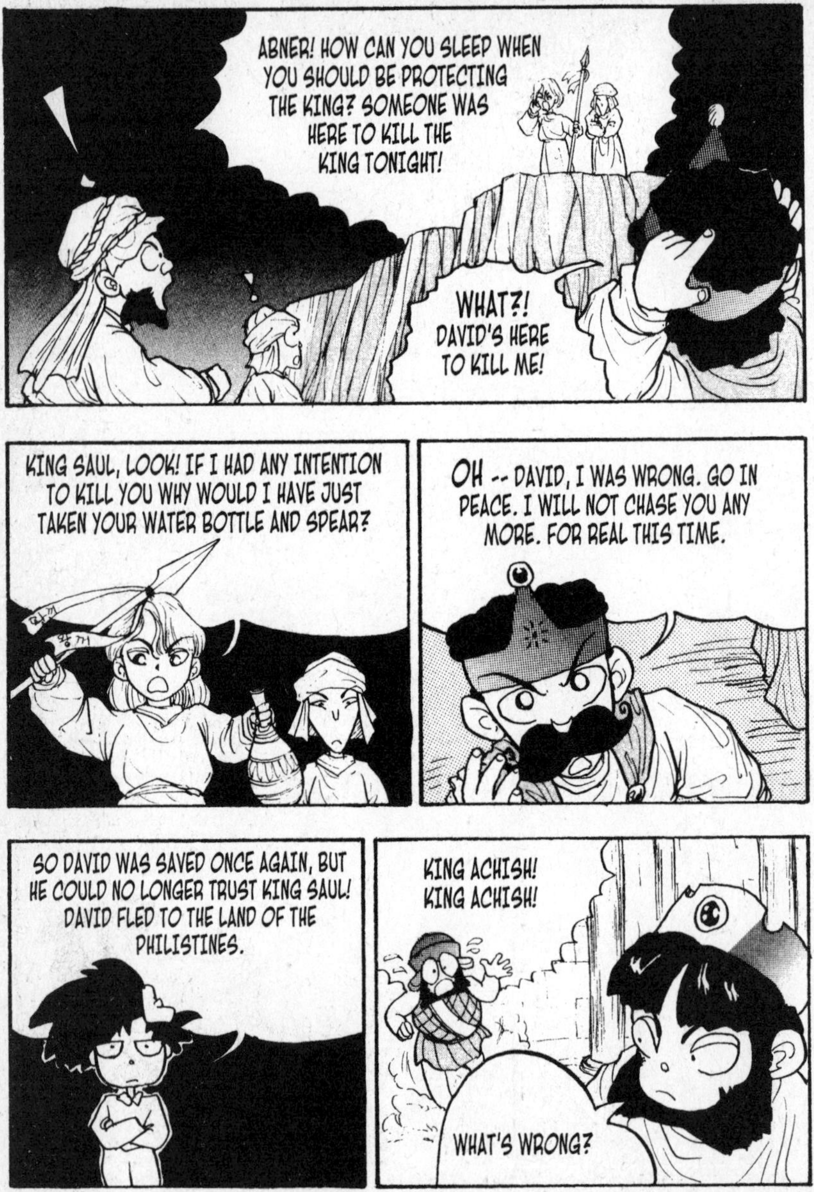
ABNER! HOW CAN YOU SLEEP WHEN YOU SHOULD BE PROTECTING THE KING? SOMEONE WAS HERE TO KILL THE KING TONIGHT!
WHAT?! DAVID'S HERE TO KILL ME!
KING SAUL, LOOK! IF I HAD ANY INTENTION TO KILL YOU WHY WOULD I HAVE JUST TAKEN YOUR WATER BOTTLE AND SPEAR?
OH -- DAVID, I WAS WRONG. GO IN PEACE. I WILL NOT CHASE YOU ANY MORE. FOR REAL THIS TIME.
SO DAVID WAS SAVED ONCE AGAIN, BUT HE COULD NO LONGER TRUST KING SAUL! DAVID FLED TO THE LAND OF THE PHILISTINES.
KING ACHISH! KING ACHISH!
WHAT'S WRONG?

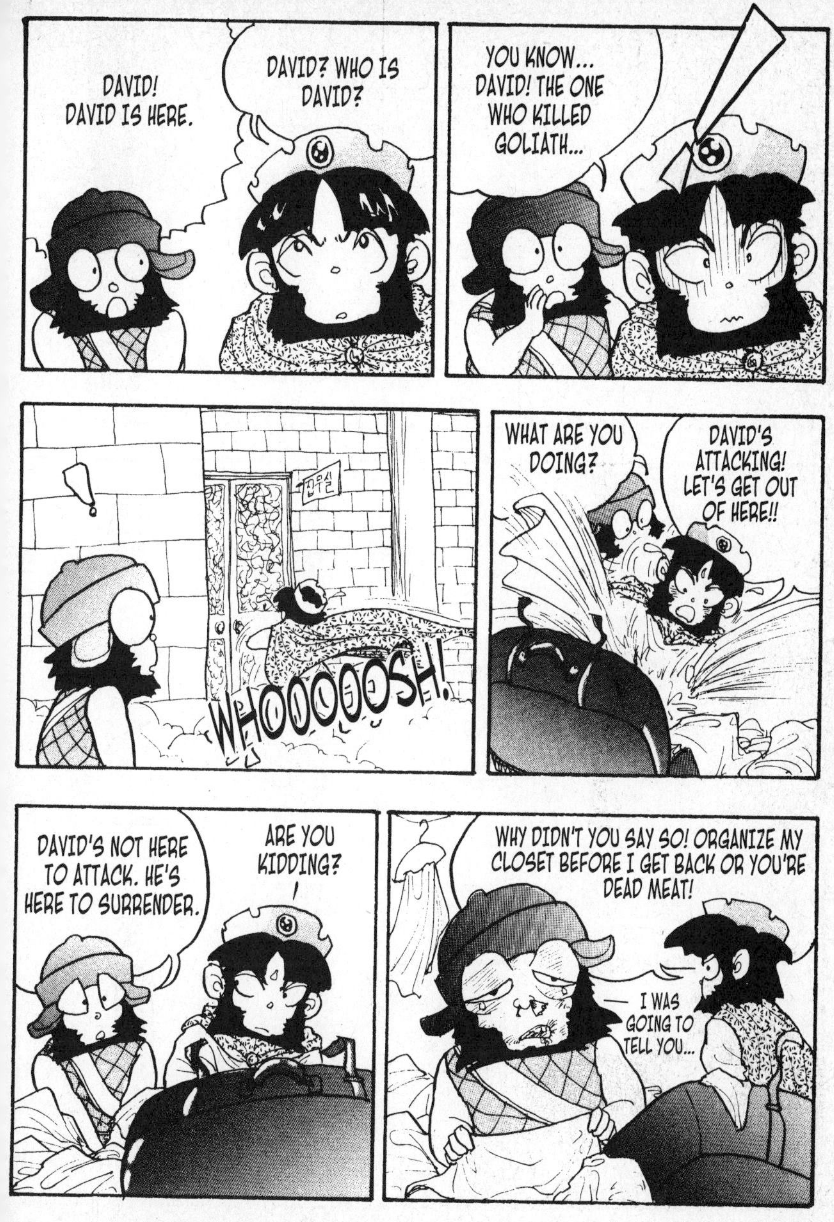

DAVID! DAVID IS HERE.
DAVID? WHO IS DAVID?
YOU KNOW... DAVID! THE ONE WHO KILLED GOLIATH...
WHOOOOOSH!
WHAT ARE YOU DOING?
DAVID'S ATTACKING! LET'S GET OUT OF HERE!!
DAVID'S NOT HERE TO ATTACK. HE'S HERE TO SURRENDER.
ARE YOU KIDDING?
WHY DIDN'T YOU SAY SO! ORGANIZE MY CLOSET BEFORE I GET BACK OR YOU'RE DEAD MEAT!
I WAS GOING TO TELL YOU...

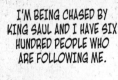

I'M BEING CHASED BY KING SAUL AND I HAVE SIX HUNDRED PEOPLE WHO ARE FOLLOWING ME.

IF YOU LEND ME A CASTLE, I WILL BECOME YOUR SERVANT AND FIGHT FOR YOU.

WHAT A LUCKY BREAK!

DAVID, WHO KILLED THE MIGHTY COMMANDER GOLIATH, IS WILLING TO BECOME MY SERVANT? MWWOOOO-HA! HA! HA! HAAAA!

ALL RIGHT! I WILL GIVE YOU THE CASTLE AT ZIKLAG. YOU MAY LIVE THERE!

THEREFORE DAVID SETTLED IN THE CASTLE AT ZIKLAG.

NOW THAT WE ARE SETTLED, LET'S ATTACK THE AMALEKITES!

OH! DAVID IS NOW RETURNING FROM A BATTLE!

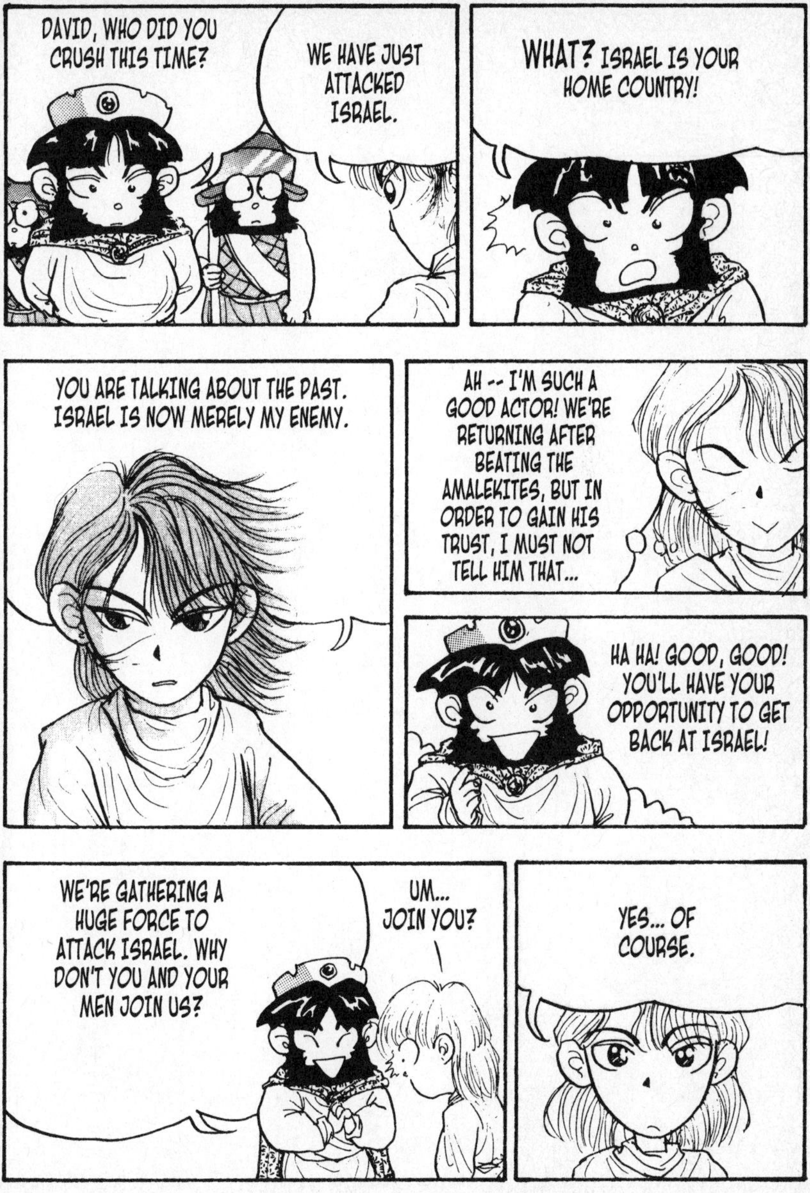
DAVID, WHO DID YOU CRUSH THIS TIME?
WE HAVE JUST ATTACKED ISRAEL.
WHAT? ISRAEL IS YOUR HOME COUNTRY!
YOU ARE TALKING ABOUT THE PAST. ISRAEL IS NOW MERELY MY ENEMY.
AH -- I'M SUCH A GOOD ACTOR! WE'RE RETURNING AFTER BEATING THE AMALEKITES, BUT IN ORDER TO GAIN HIS TRUST, I MUST NOT TELL HIM THAT...
HA HA! GOOD, GOOD! YOU'LL HAVE YOUR OPPORTUNITY TO GET BACK AT ISRAEL!
WE'RE GATHERING A HUGE FORCE TO ATTACK ISRAEL. WHY DON'T YOU AND YOUR MEN JOIN US?
UM... JOIN YOU?
YES... OF COURSE.

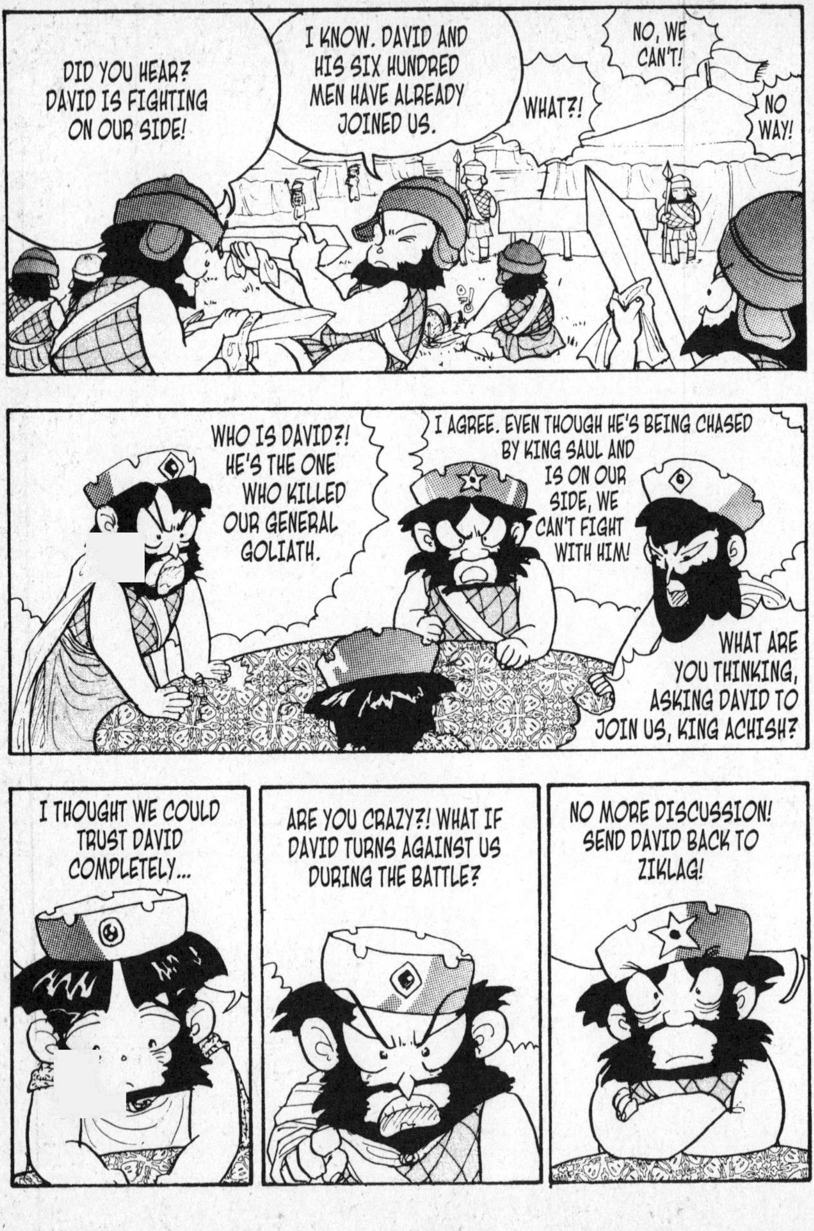
DID YOU HEAR? DAVID IS FIGHTING ON OUR SIDE!
I KNOW. DAVID AND HIS SIX HUNDRED MEN HAVE ALREADY JOINED US.
WHAT?!
NO, WE CAN'T!
NO WAY!
WHO IS DAVID?! HE'S THE ONE WHO KILLED OUR GENERAL GOLIATH.
I AGREE. EVEN THOUGH HE'S BEING CHASED BY KING SAUL AND IS ON OUR SIDE, WE CAN'T FIGHT WITH HIM!
WHAT ARE YOU THINKING, ASKING DAVID TO JOIN US, KING ACHISH?
I THOUGHT WE COULD TRUST DAVID COMPLETELY...
ARE YOU CRAZY?! WHAT IF DAVID TURNS AGAINST US DURING THE BATTLE?
NO MORE DISCUSSION! SEND DAVID BACK TO ZIKLAG!

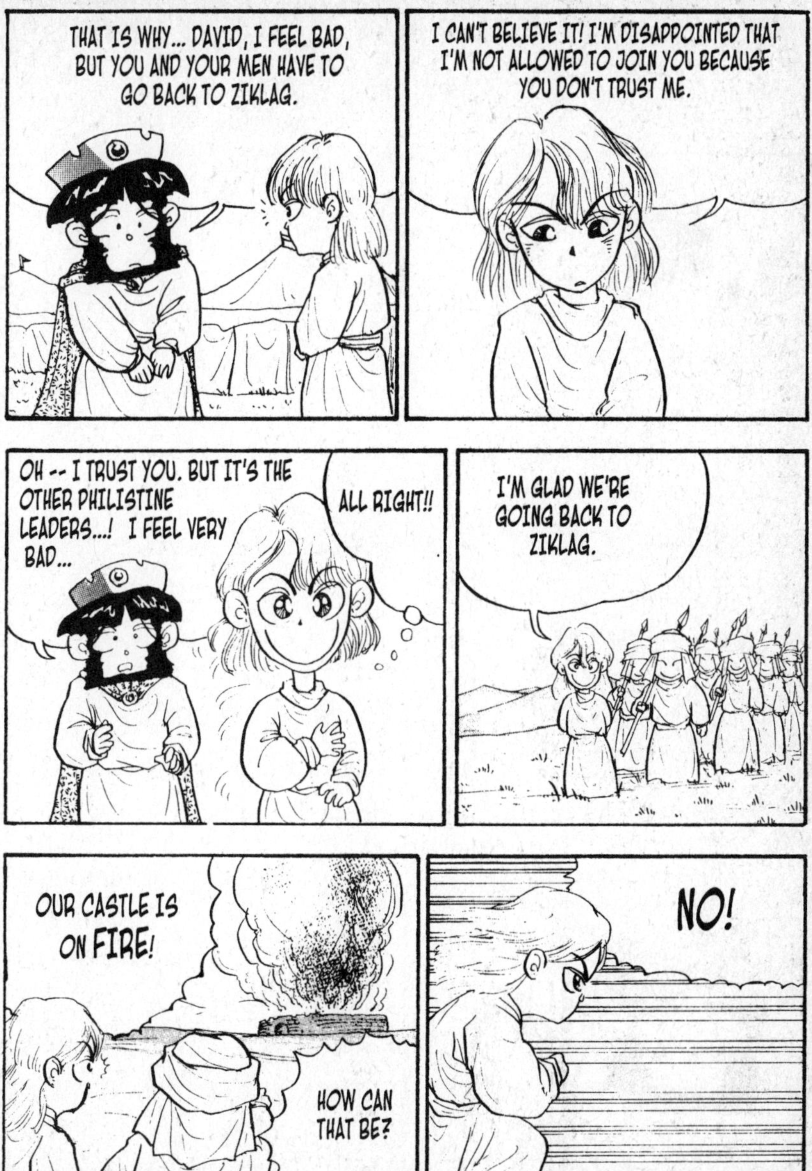
THAT IS WHY... DAVID, I FEEL BAD, BUT YOU AND YOUR MEN HAVE TO GO BACK TO ZIKLAG.
I CAN'T BELIEVE IT! I'M DISAPPOINTED THAT I'M NOT ALLOWED TO JOIN YOU BECAUSE YOU DON'T TRUST ME.
OH -- I TRUST YOU. BUT IT'S THE OTHER PHILISTINE LEADERS...! I FEEL VERY BAD...
ALL RIGHT!!
I'M GLAD WE'RE GOING BACK TO ZIKLAG.
OUR CASTLE IS ON FIRE!
HOW CAN THAT BE?
NO!

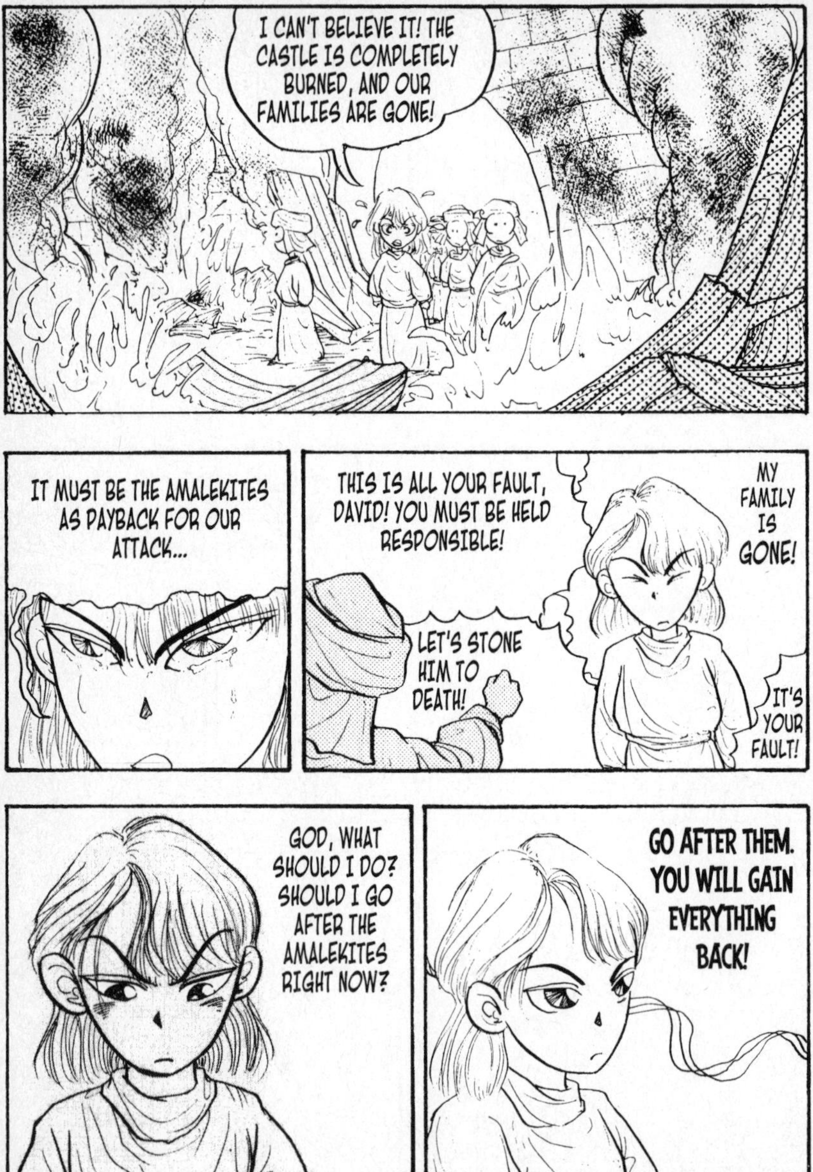
I CAN'T BELIEVE IT! THE CASTLE IS COMPLETELY BURNED, AND OUR FAMILIES ARE GONE!
IT MUST BE THE AMALEKITES AS PAYBACK FOR OUR ATTACK...
THIS IS ALL YOUR FAULT, DAVID! YOU MUST BE HELD RESPONSIBLE!
LET'S STONE HIM TO DEATH!
MY FAMILY IS GONE!
IT'S YOUR FAULT!
GOD, WHAT SHOULD I DO? SHOULD I GO AFTER THE AMALEKITES RIGHT NOW?
GO AFTER THEM. YOU WILL GAIN EVERYTHING BACK!

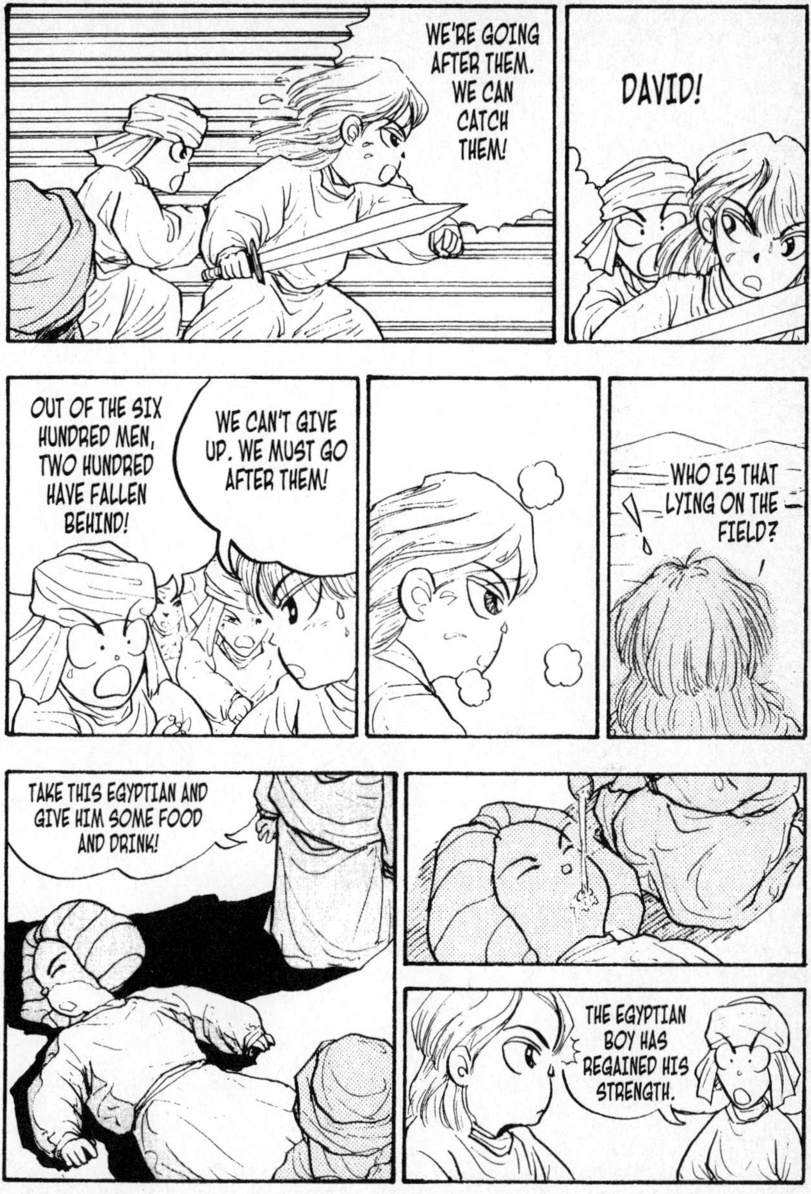
WE'RE GOING AFTER THEM. WE CAN CATCH THEM!
DAVID!
OUT OF THE SIX HUNDRED MEN, TWO HUNDRED HAVE FALLEN BEHIND!
WE CAN'T GIVE UP. WE MUST GO AFTER THEM!
WHO IS THAT LYING ON THE FIELD?
TAKE THIS EGYPTIAN AND GIVE HIM SOME FOOD AND DRINK!
THE EGYPTIAN BOY HAS REGAINED HIS STRENGTH.

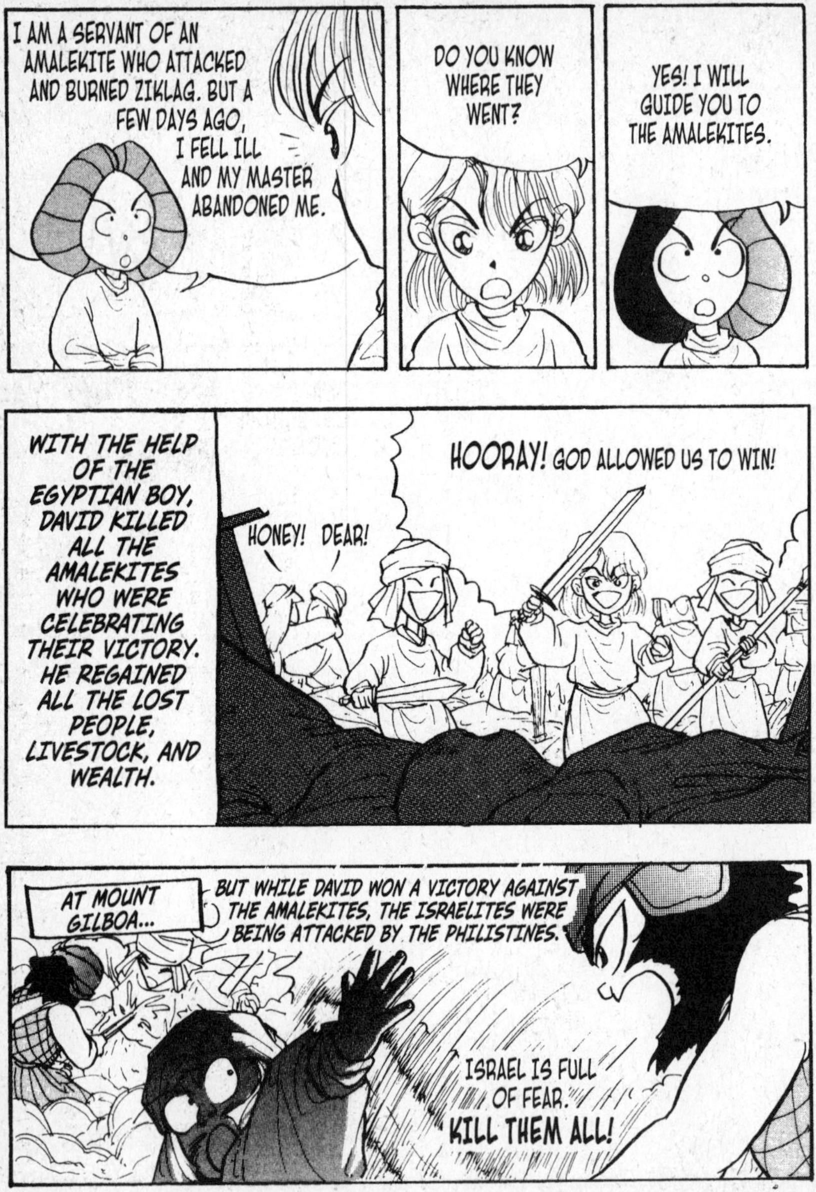
I AM A SERVANT OF AN AMALEKITE WHO ATTACKED AND BURNED ZIKLAG. BUT A FEW DAYS AGO, I FELL ILL AND MY MASTER ABANDONED ME.
DO YOU KNOW WHERE THEY WENT?
YES! I WILL GUIDE YOU TO THE AMALEKITES.
WITH THE HELP OF THE EGYPTIAN BOY, DAVID KILLED ALL THE AMALEKITES WHO WERE CELEBRATING THEIR VICTORY. HE REGAINED ALL THE LOST PEOPLE, LIVESTOCK, AND WEALTH.
HONEY!
DEAR!
HOORAY! GOD ALLOWED US TO WIN!
AT MOUNT GILBOA...
BUT WHILE DAVID WON A VICTORY AGAINST THE AMALEKITES, THE ISRAELITES WERE BEING ATTACKED BY THE PHILISTINES.
ISRAEL IS FULL OF FEAR. KILL THEM ALL!

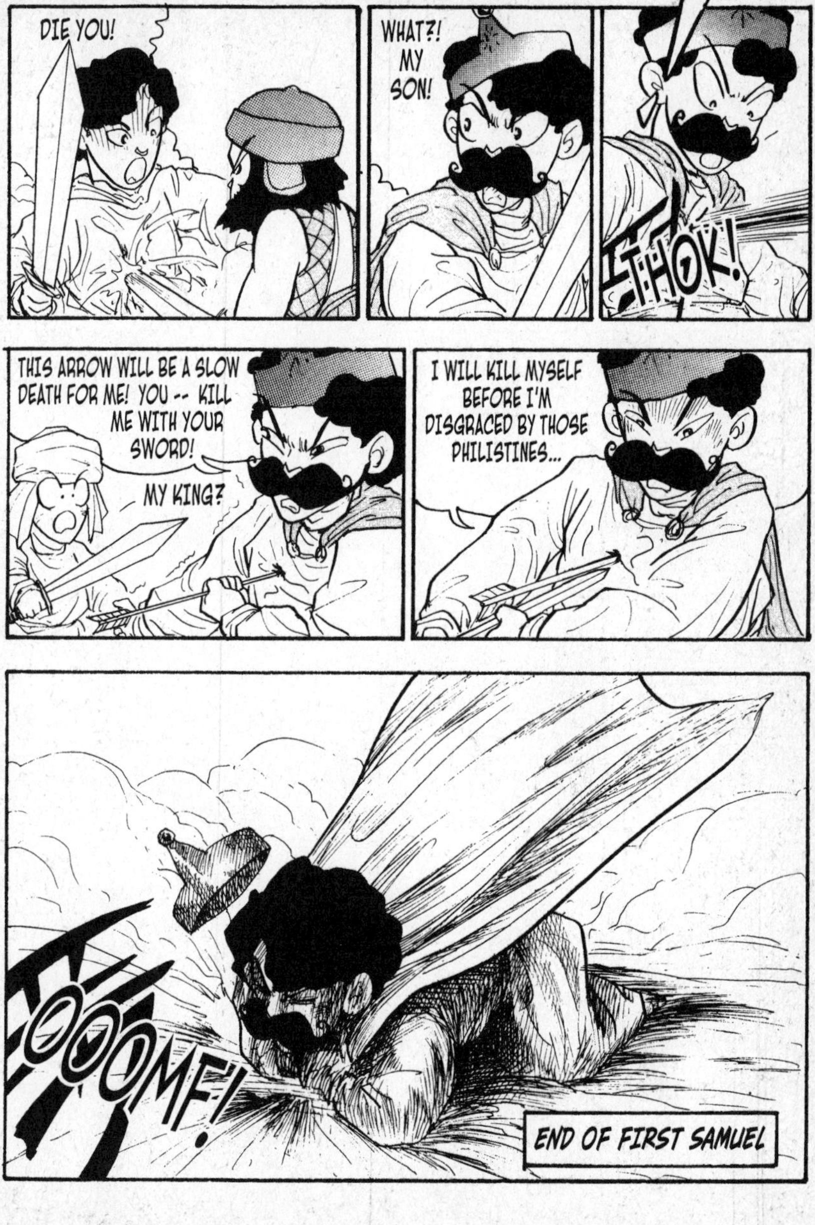
DIE YOU!
WHAT?! MY SON!
THOK!
THIS ARROW WILL BE A SLOW DEATH FOR ME! YOU -- KILL ME WITH YOUR SWORD!
MY KING?
I WILL KILL MYSELF BEFORE I'M DISGRACED BY THOSE PHILISTINES...
FOOOMF!
END OF FIRST SAMUEL

SECOND SAMUEL

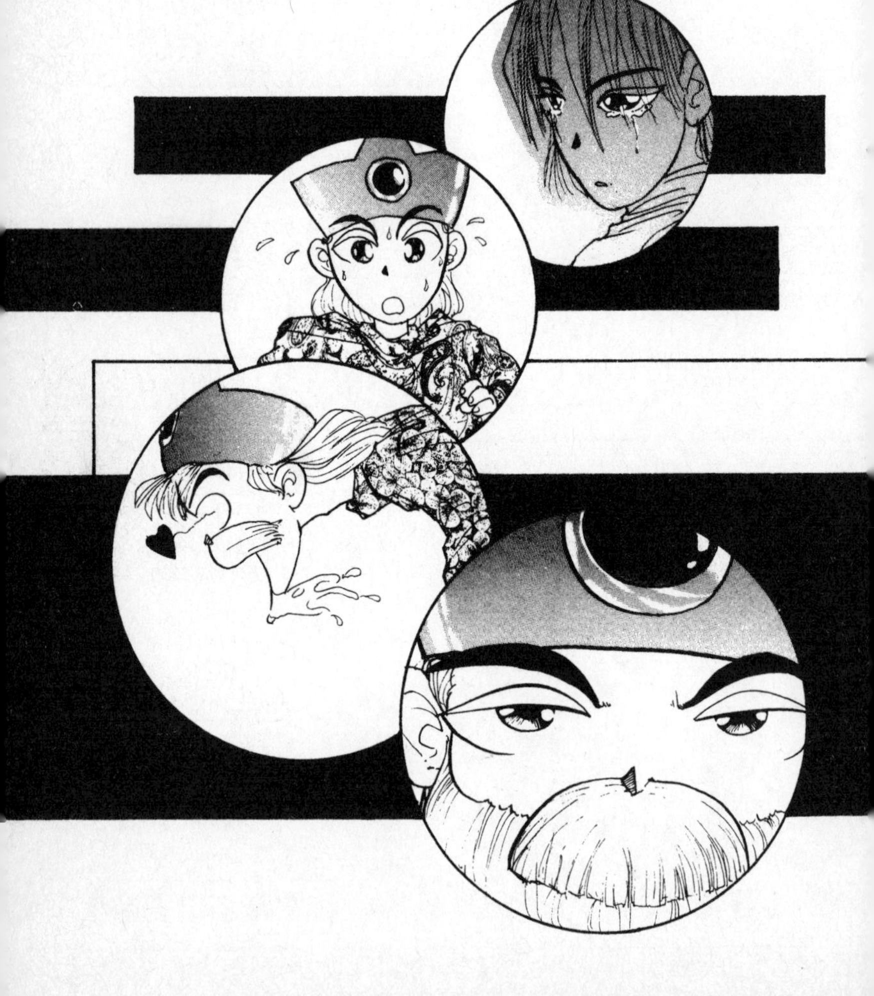

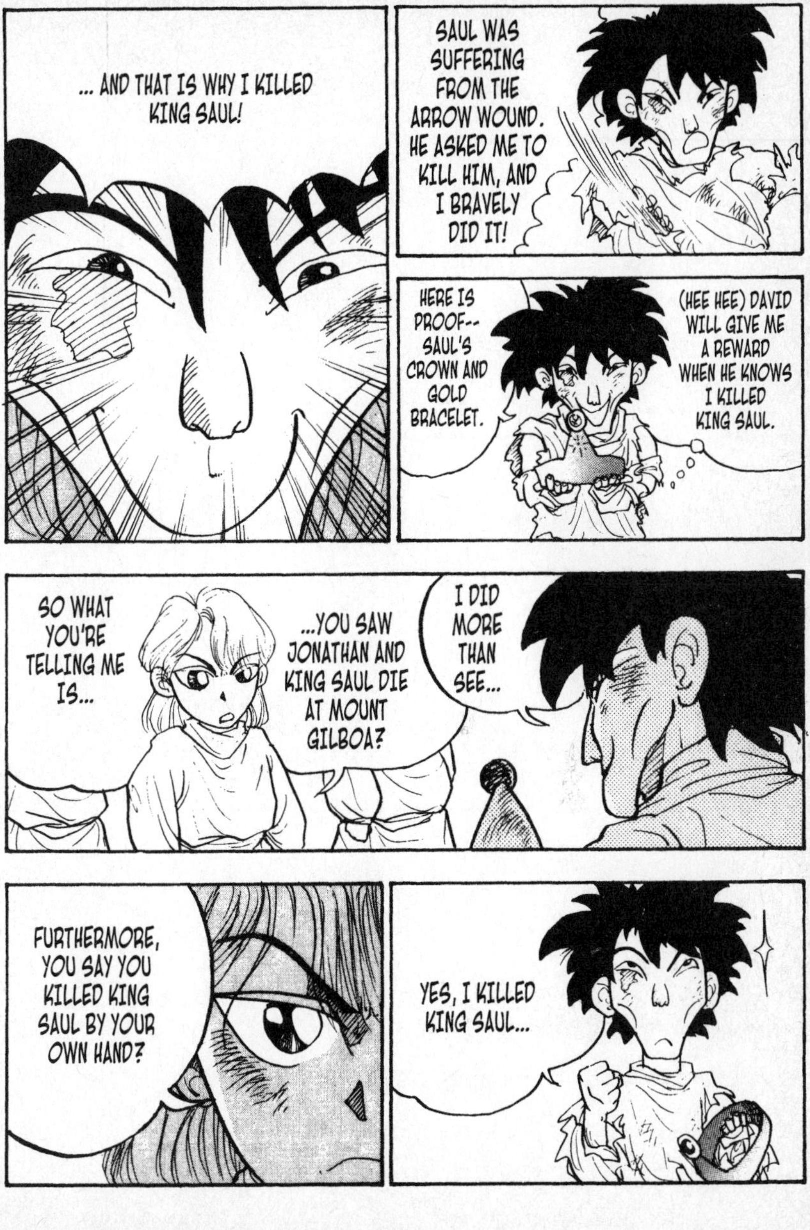
... AND THAT IS WHY I KILLED KING SAUL!
SAUL WAS SUFFERING FROM THE ARROW WOUND. HE ASKED ME TO KILL HIM, AND I BRAVELY DID IT!
HERE IS PROOF-- SAUL'S CROWN AND GOLD BRACELET.
(HEE HEE) DAVID WILL GIVE ME A REWARD WHEN HE KNOWS I KILLED KING SAUL.
SO WHAT YOU'RE TELLING ME IS...
...YOU SAW JONATHAN AND KING SAUL DIE AT MOUNT GILBOA?
I DID MORE THAN SEE...
FURTHERMORE, YOU SAY YOU KILLED KING SAUL BY YOUR OWN HAND?
YES, I KILLED KING SAUL...

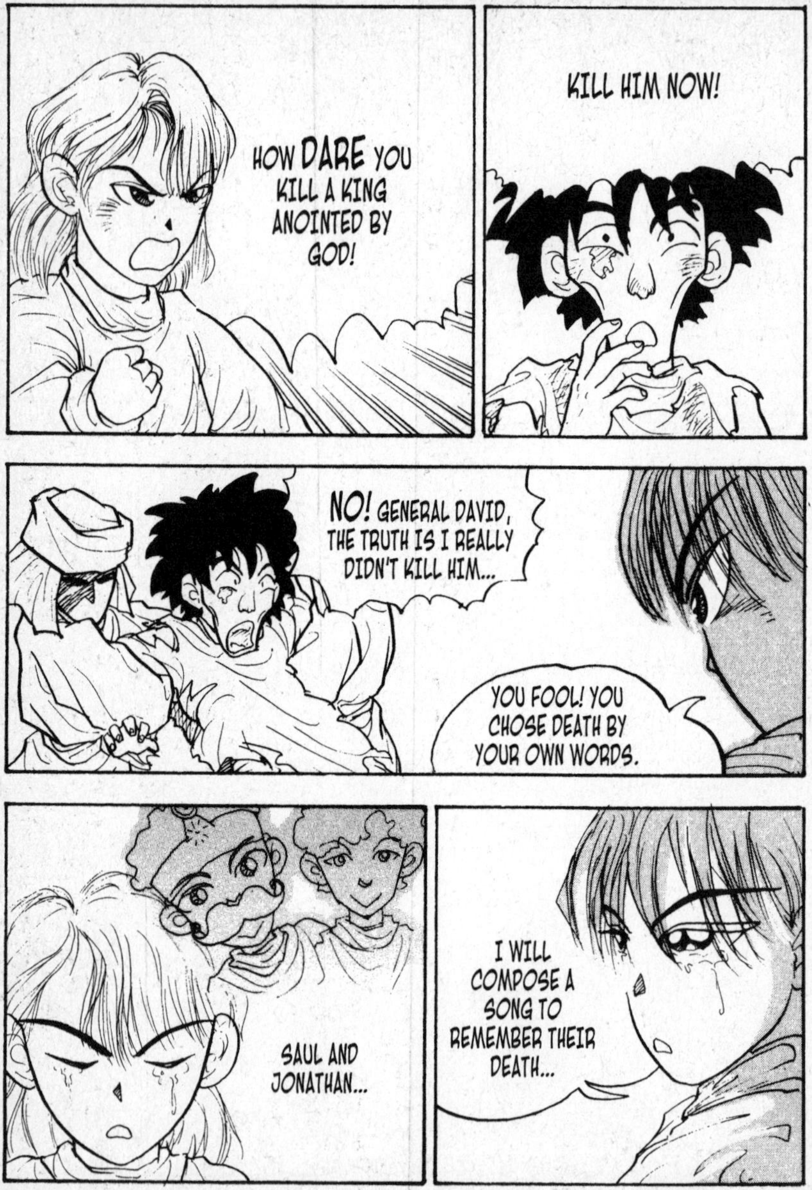
HOW DARE YOU KILL A KING ANOINTED BY GOD!
KILL HIM NOW!
NO! GENERAL DAVID, THE TRUTH IS I REALLY DIDN'T KILL HIM...
YOU FOOL! YOU CHOSE DEATH BY YOUR OWN WORDS.
SAUL AND JONATHAN...
I WILL COMPOSE A SONG TO REMEMBER THEIR DEATH...

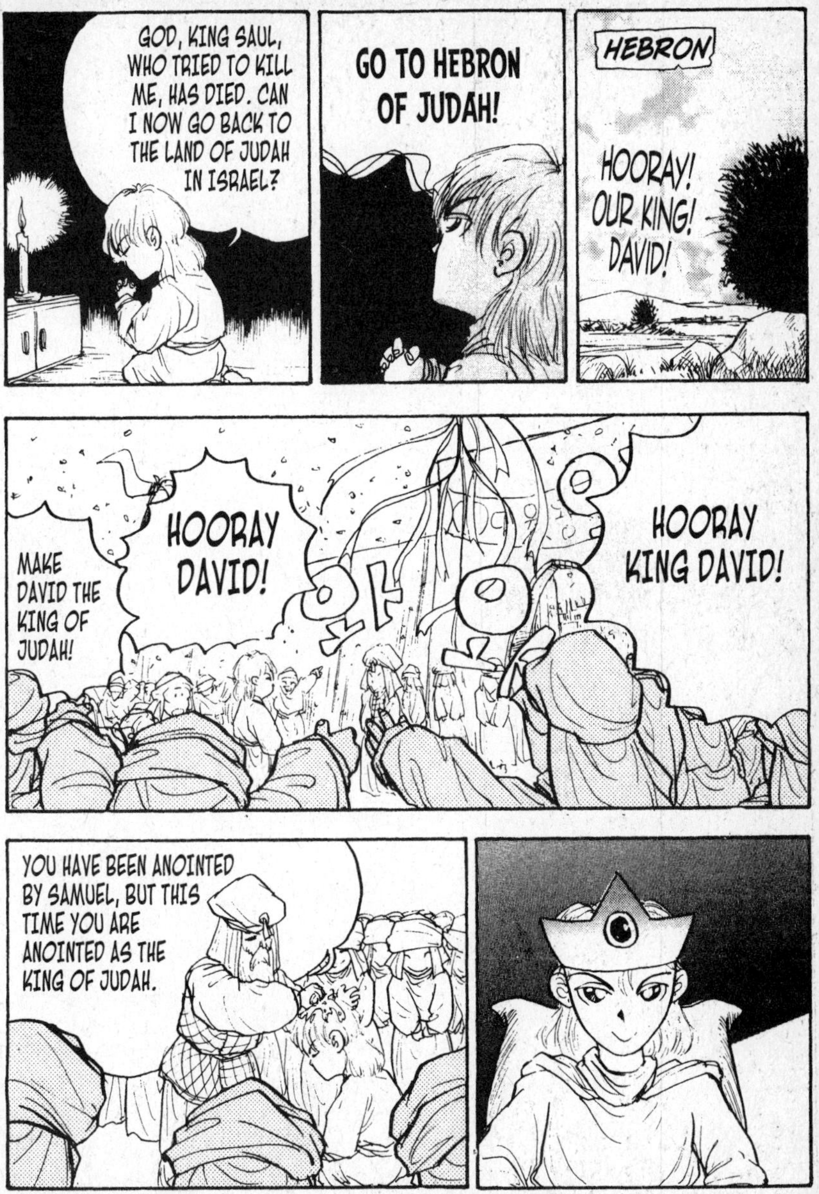
GOD, KING SAUL, WHO TRIED TO KILL ME, HAS DIED. CAN I NOW GO BACK TO THE LAND OF JUDAH IN ISRAEL?
GO TO HEBRON OF JUDAH!
HEBRON
HOORAY! OUR KING! DAVID!
MAKE DAVID THE KING OF JUDAH!
HOORAY DAVID!
HOORAY KING DAVID!
YOU HAVE BEEN ANOINTED BY SAMUEL, BUT THIS TIME YOU ARE ANOINTED AS THE KING OF JUDAH.

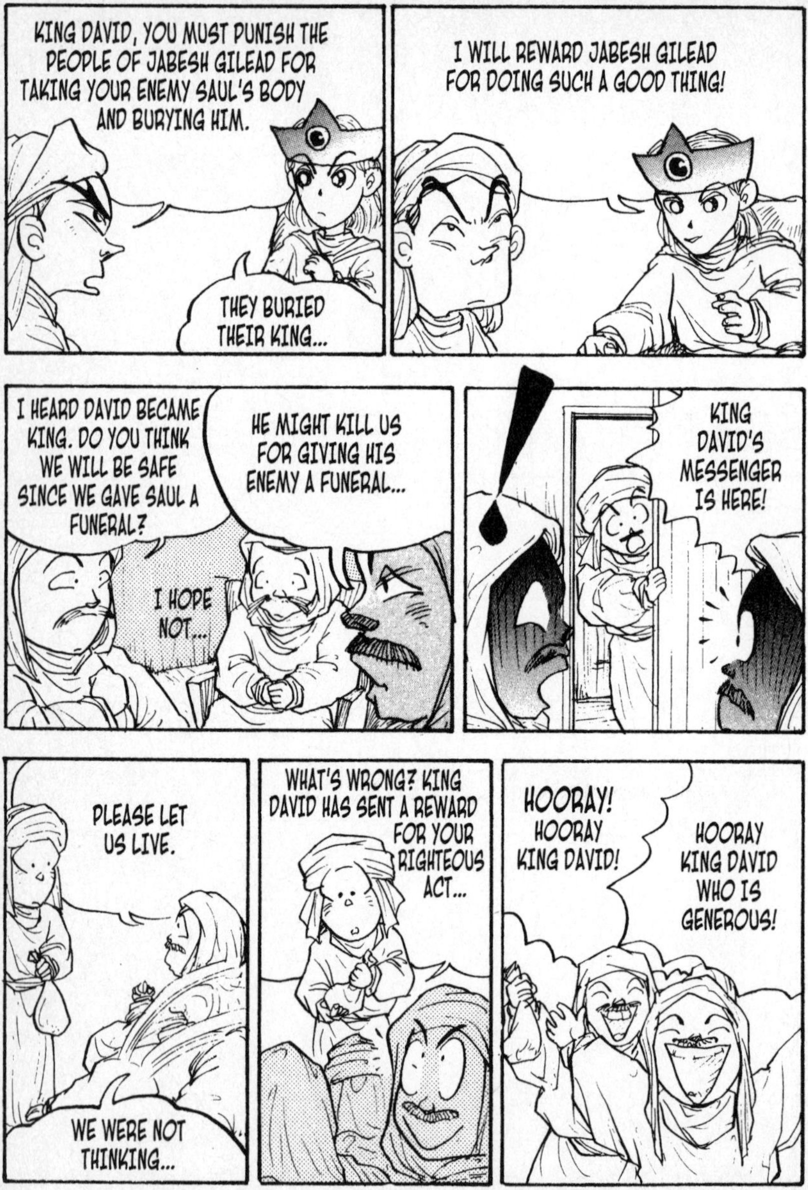
KING DAVID, YOU MUST PUNISH THE PEOPLE OF JABESH GILEAD FOR TAKING YOUR ENEMY SAUL'S BODY AND BURYING HIM.
THEY BURIED THEIR KING...
I WILL REWARD JABESH GILEAD FOR DOING SUCH A GOOD THING!
I HEARD DAVID BECAME KING. DO YOU THINK WE WILL BE SAFE SINCE WE GAVE SAUL A FUNERAL?
I HOPE NOT...
HE MIGHT KILL US FOR GIVING HIS ENEMY A FUNERAL...
!
KING DAVID'S MESSENGER IS HERE!
PLEASE LET US LIVE.
WE WERE NOT THINKING...
WHAT'S WRONG? KING DAVID HAS SENT A REWARD FOR YOUR RIGHTEOUS ACT...
HOORAY! HOORAY KING DAVID!
HOORAY KING DAVID WHO IS GENEROUS!

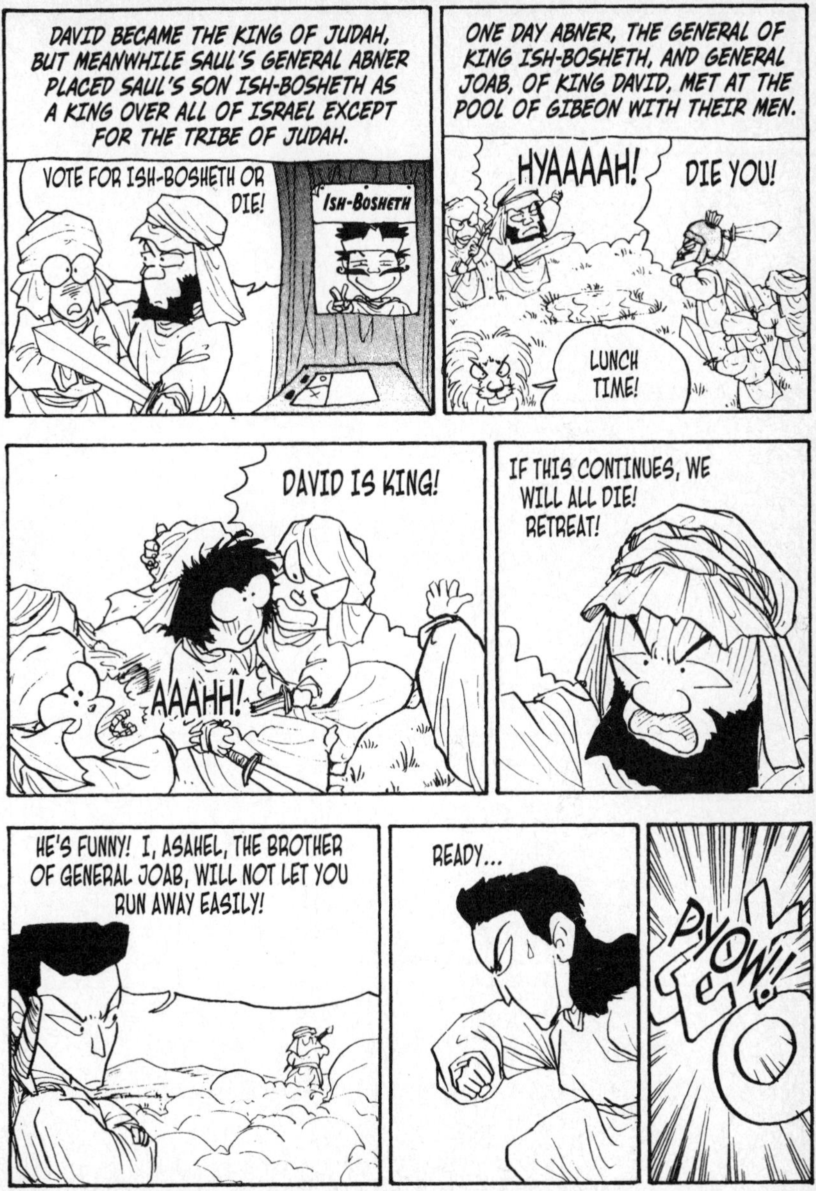
DAVID BECAME THE KING OF JUDAH, BUT MEANWHILE SAUL'S GENERAL ABNER PLACED SAUL'S SON ISH-BOSHETH AS A KING OVER ALL OF ISRAEL EXCEPT FOR THE TRIBE OF JUDAH.
VOTE FOR ISH-BOSHETH OR DIE!
ISH-BOSHETH
ONE DAY ABNER, THE GENERAL OF KING ISH-BOSHETH, AND GENERAL JOAB, OF KING DAVID, MET AT THE POOL OF GIBEON WITH THEIR MEN.
HYAAAAH!
DIE YOU!
LUNCH TIME!
DAVID IS KING!
AAAHH!
IF THIS CONTINUES, WE WILL ALL DIE! RETREAT!
HE'S FUNNY! I, ASAHEL, THE BROTHER OF GENERAL JOAB, WILL NOT LET YOU RUN AWAY EASILY!
READY...
PYOW!

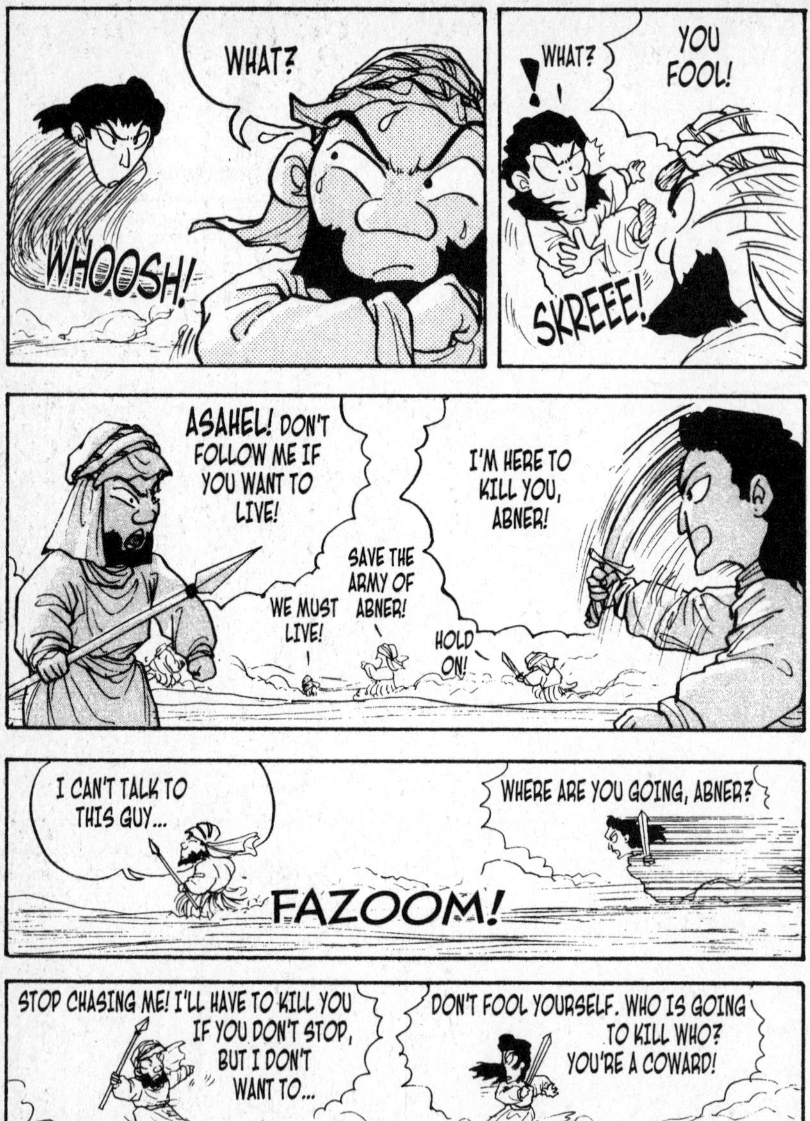
WHAT?
WHOOSH!
WHAT?
YOU FOOL!
SKREEE!
ASAHEL! DON'T FOLLOW ME IF YOU WANT TO LIVE!
WE MUST LIVE!
SAVE THE ARMY OF ABNER!
HOLD ON!
I'M HERE TO KILL YOU, ABNER!
I CAN'T TALK TO THIS GUY...
FAZOOM!
WHERE ARE YOU GOING, ABNER?
STOP CHASING ME! I'LL HAVE TO KILL YOU IF YOU DON'T STOP, BUT I DON'T WANT TO...
DON'T FOOL YOURSELF. WHO IS GOING TO KILL WHO? YOU'RE A COWARD!

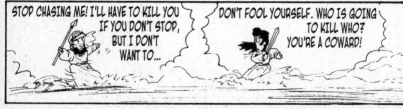

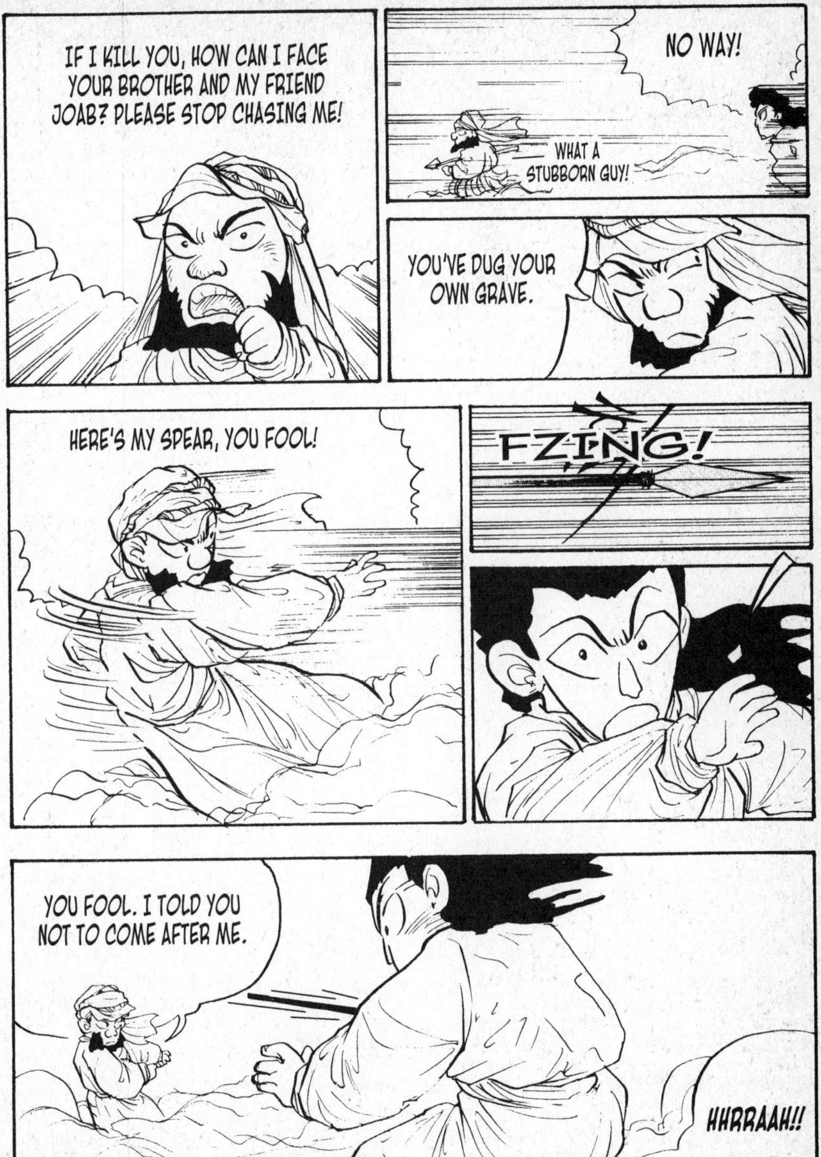
IF I KILL YOU, HOW CAN I FACE YOUR BROTHER AND MY FRIEND JOAB? PLEASE STOP CHASING ME!
NO WAY!
WHAT A STUBBORN GUY!
YOU'VE DUG YOUR OWN GRAVE.
HERE'S MY SPEAR, YOU FOOL!
FZING!
YOU FOOL. I TOLD YOU NOT TO COME AFTER ME.
HHRRAAH!!

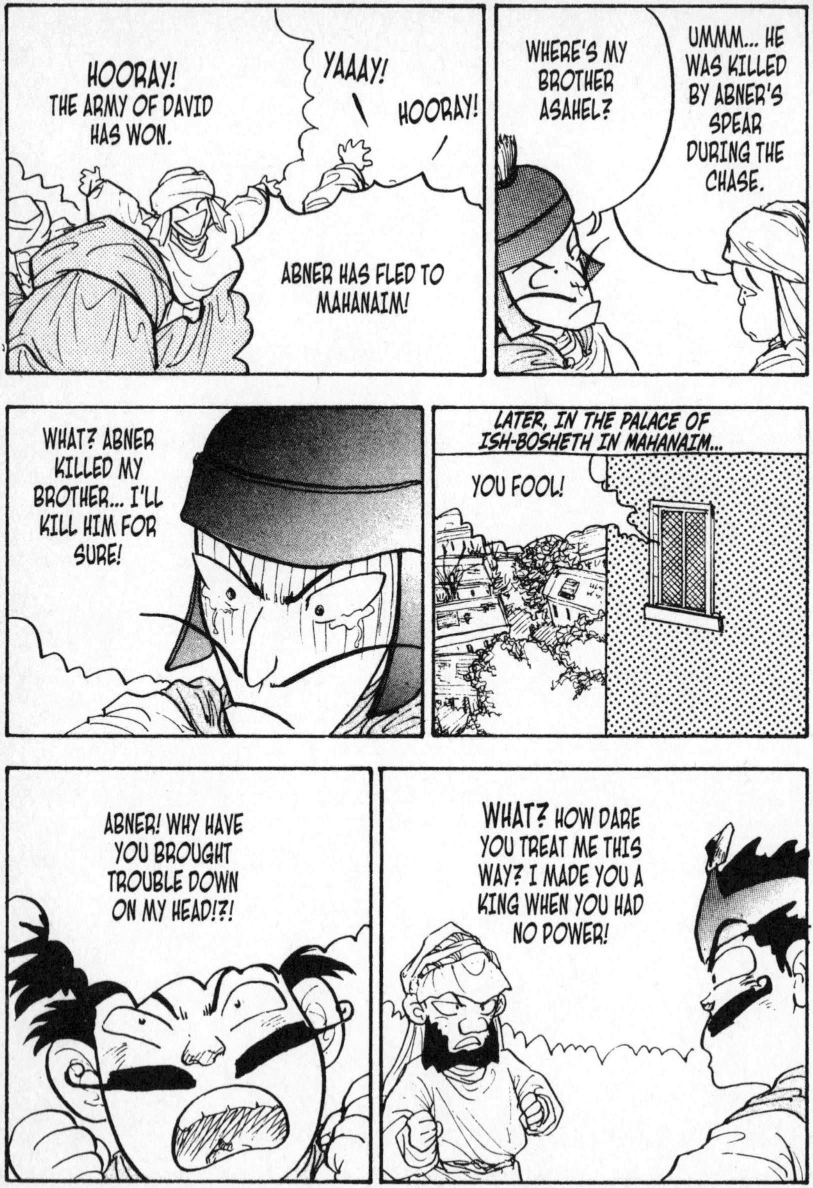
HOORAY! THE ARMY OF DAVID HAS WON.
YAAAY!
HOORAY!
ABNER HAS FLED TO MAHANAIM!
WHERE'S MY BROTHER ASAHEL?
UMMM... HE WAS KILLED BY ABNER'S SPEAR DURING THE CHASE.
WHAT? ABNER KILLED MY BROTHER... I'LL KILL HIM FOR SURE!
LATER, IN THE PALACE OF ISH-BOSHETH IN MAHANAIM...
YOU FOOL!
ABNER! WHY HAVE YOU BROUGHT TROUBLE DOWN ON MY HEAD!?!
WHAT? HOW DARE YOU TREAT ME THIS WAY? I MADE YOU A KING WHEN YOU HAD NO POWER!

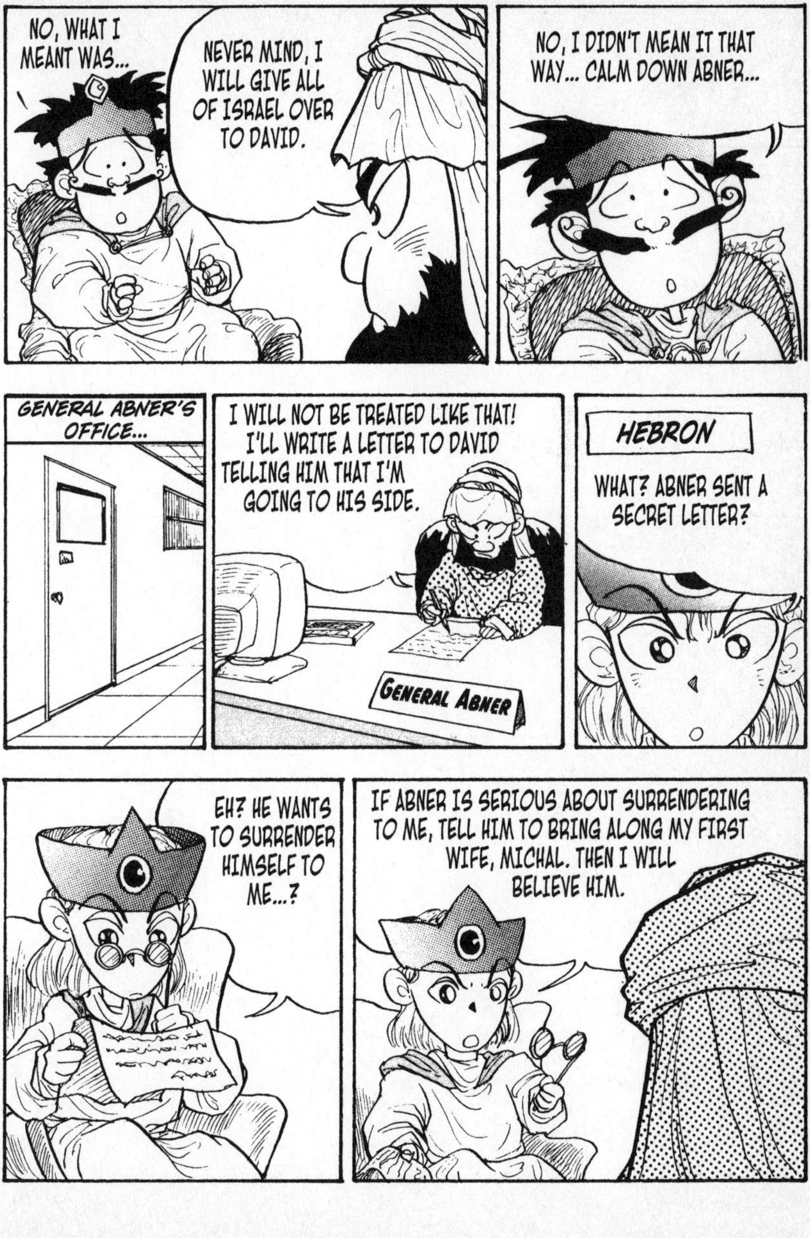
NO, WHAT I MEANT WAS...
NEVER MIND, I WILL GIVE ALL OF ISRAEL OVER TO DAVID.
NO, I DIDN'T MEAN IT THAT WAY... CALM DOWN ABNER...
GENERAL ABNER'S OFFICE...
I WILL NOT BE TREATED LIKE THAT! I'LL WRITE A LETTER TO DAVID TELLING HIM THAT I'M GOING TO HIS SIDE.
GENERAL ABNER
HEBRON
WHAT? ABNER SENT A SECRET LETTER?
EH? HE WANTS TO SURRENDER HIMSELF TO ME...?
IF ABNER IS SERIOUS ABOUT SURRENDERING TO ME, TELL HIM TO BRING ALONG MY FIRST WIFE, MICHAL. THEN I WILL BELIEVE HIM.

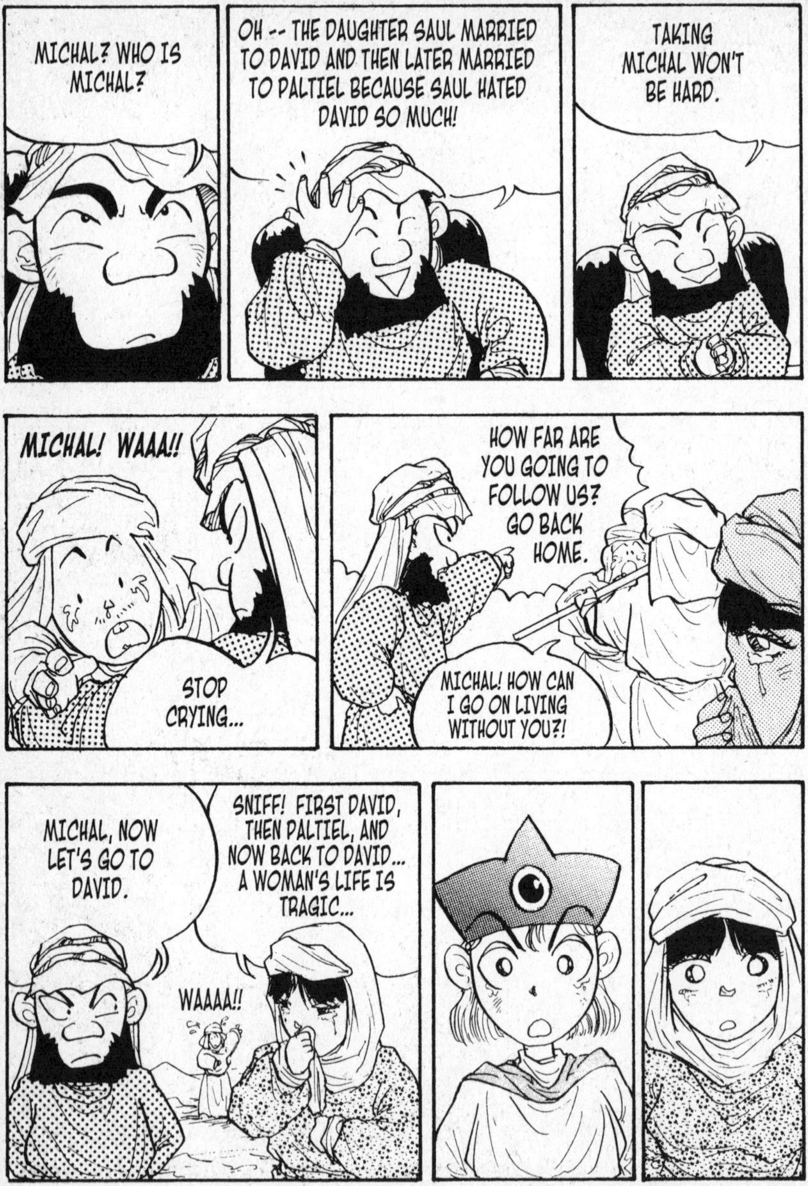
MICHAL? WHO IS MICHAL?
OH -- THE DAUGHTER SAUL MARRIED TO DAVID AND THEN LATER MARRIED TO PALTIEL BECAUSE SAUL HATED DAVID SO MUCH!
TAKING MICHAL WON'T BE HARD.
MICHAL! WAAA!!
STOP CRYING...
HOW FAR ARE YOU GOING TO FOLLOW US? GO BACK HOME.
MICHAL! HOW CAN I GO ON LIVING WITHOUT YOU?!
MICHAL, NOW LET'S GO TO DAVID.
SNIFF! FIRST DAVID, THEN PALTIEL, AND NOW BACK TO DAVID... A WOMAN'S LIFE IS TRAGIC...
WAAAA!!

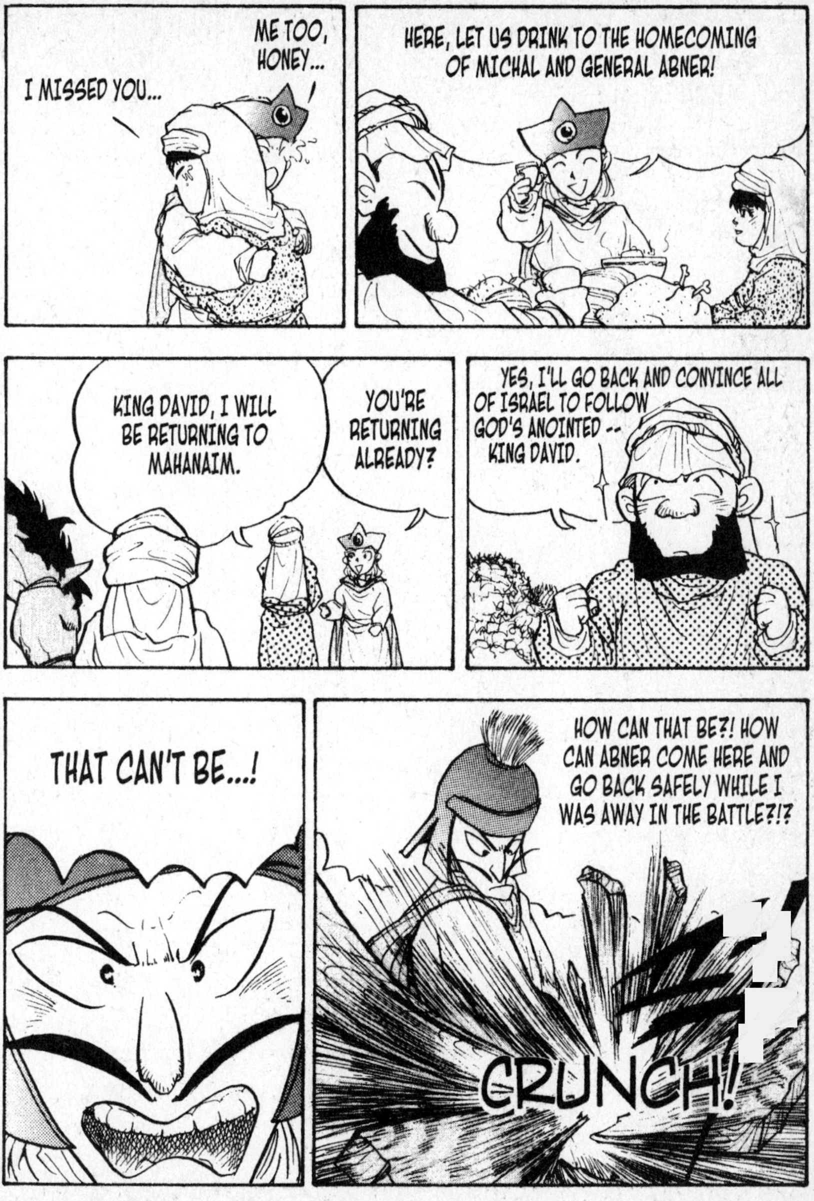
I MISSED YOU...
ME TOO, HONEY...
HERE, LET US DRINK TO THE HOMECOMING OF MICHAL AND GENERAL ABNER!
KING DAVID, I WILL BE RETURNING TO MAHANAIM.
YOU'RE RETURNING ALREADY?
YES, I'LL GO BACK AND CONVINCE ALL OF ISRAEL TO FOLLOW GOD'S ANOINTED -- KING DAVID.
THAT CAN'T BE...!
HOW CAN THAT BE?! HOW CAN ABNER COME HERE AND GO BACK SAFELY WHILE I WAS AWAY IN THE BATTLE?!?
CRUNCH!

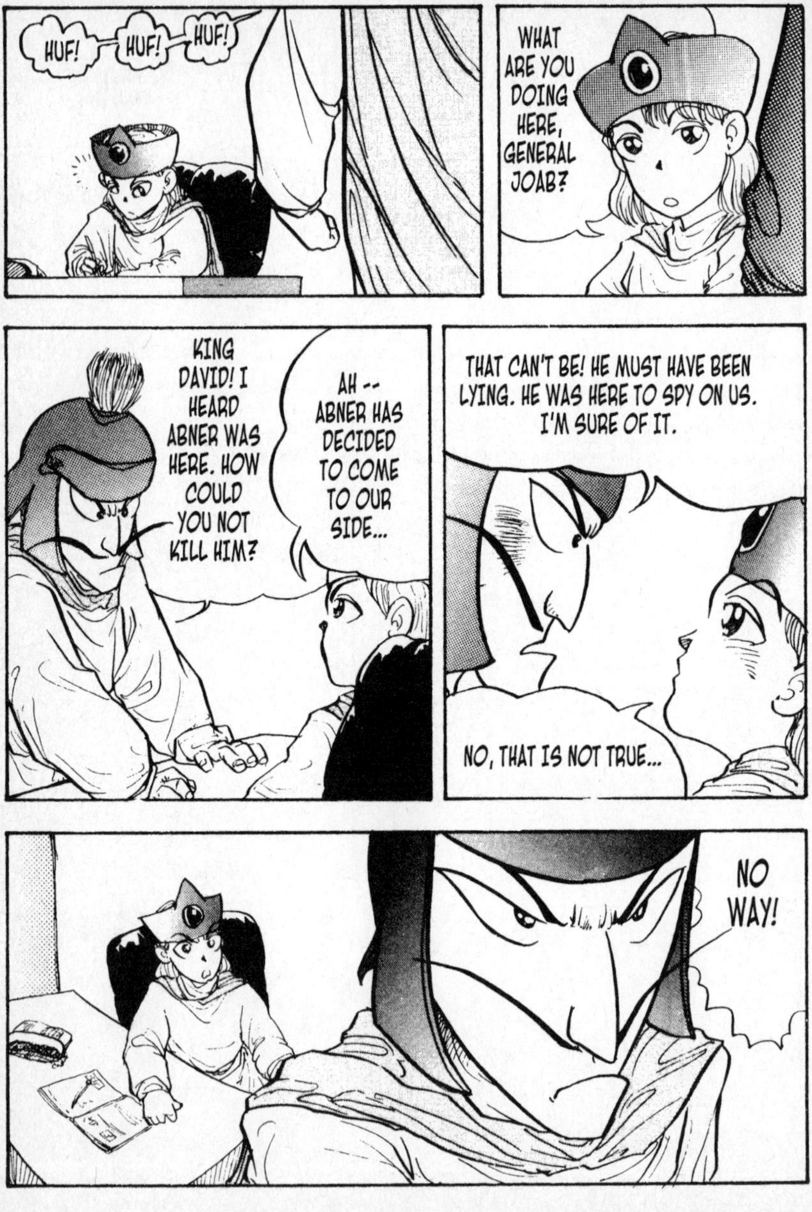
HUF! HUF! HUF!
WHAT ARE YOU DOING HERE, GENERAL JOAB?
KING DAVID! I HEARD ABNER WAS HERE. HOW COULD YOU NOT KILL HIM?
AH -- ABNER HAS DECIDED TO COME TO OUR SIDE...
THAT CAN'T BE! HE MUST HAVE BEEN LYING. HE WAS HERE TO SPY ON US. I'M SURE OF IT.
NO, THAT IS NOT TRUE...
NO WAY!

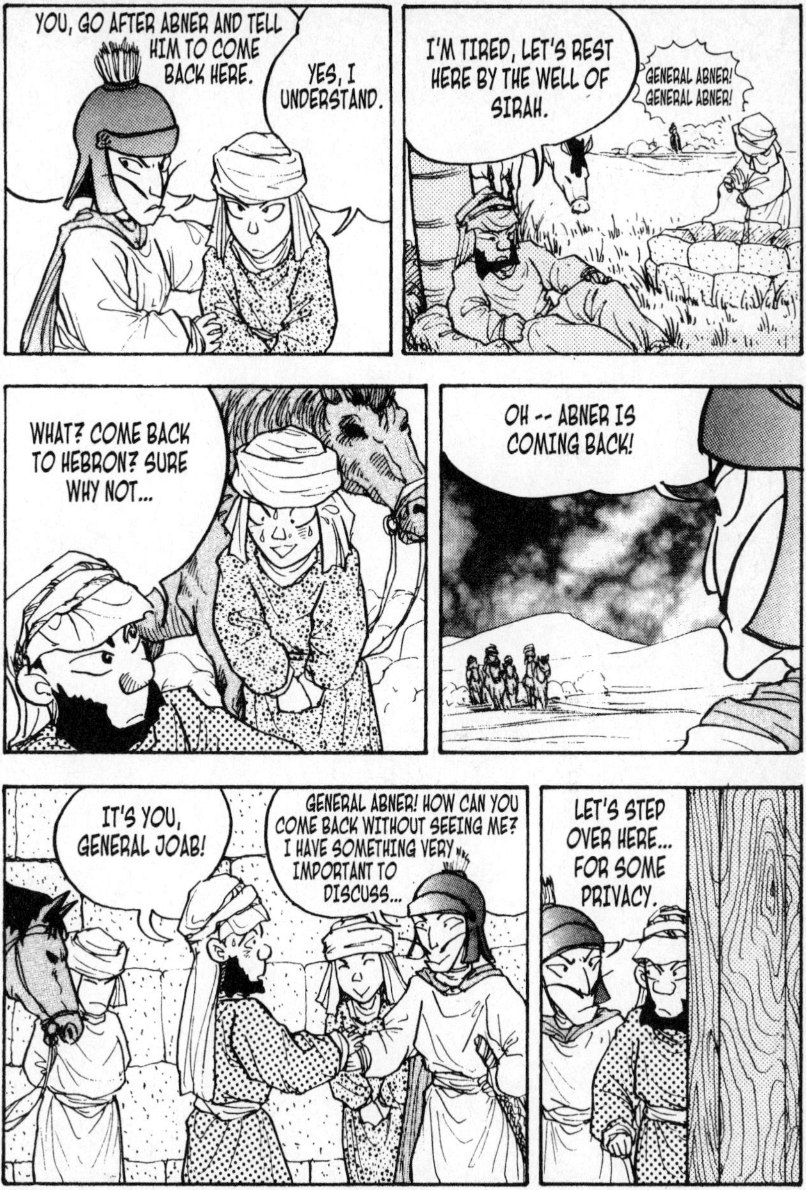
YOU, GO AFTER ABNER AND TELL HIM TO COME BACK HERE.
YES, I UNDERSTAND.
I'M TIRED, LET'S REST HERE BY THE WELL OF SIRAH.
GENERAL ABNER! GENERAL ABNER!
WHAT? COME BACK TO HEBRON? SURE WHY NOT...
OH -- ABNER IS COMING BACK!
IT'S YOU, GENERAL JOAB!
GENERAL ABNER! HOW CAN YOU COME BACK WITHOUT SEEING ME? I HAVE SOMETHING VERY IMPORTANT TO DISCUSS...
LET'S STEP OVER HERE... FOR SOME PRIVACY.

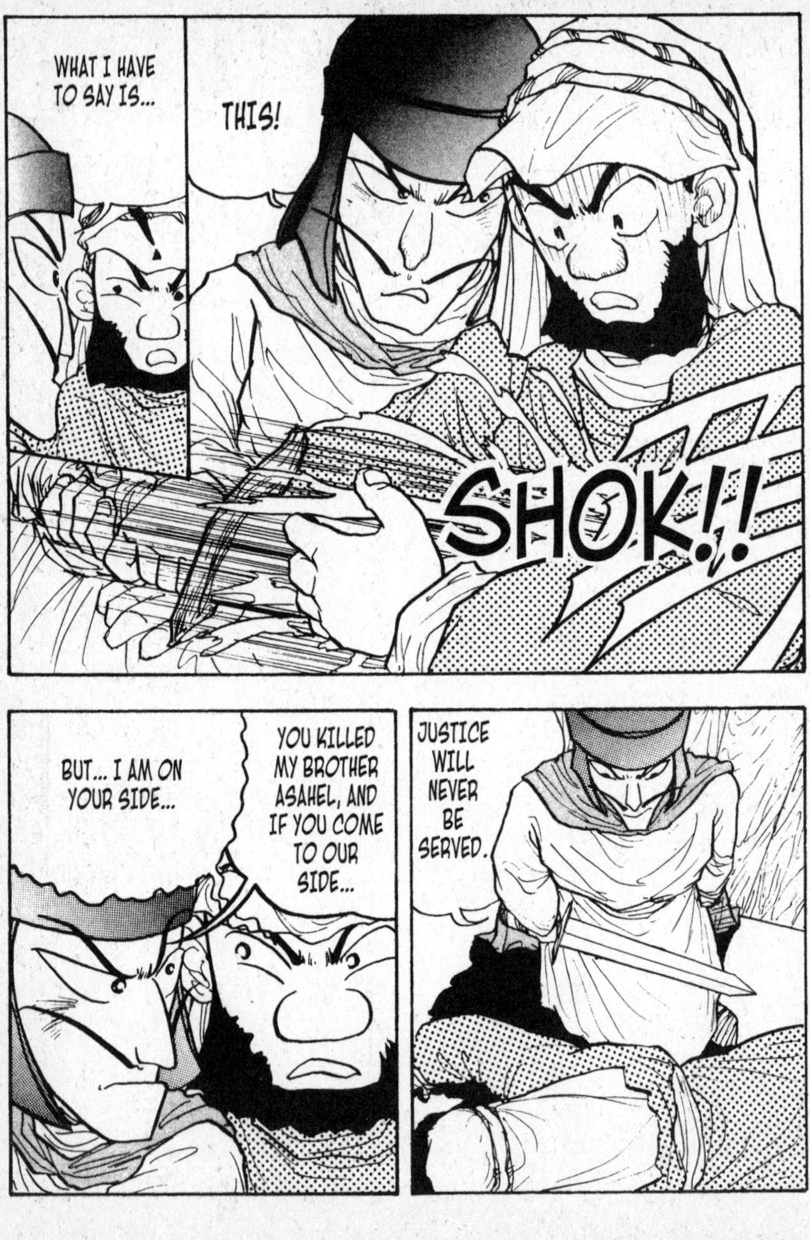
WHAT I HAVE TO SAY IS...
THIS!
SHOK!!
BUT... I AM ON YOUR SIDE...
YOU KILLED MY BROTHER ASAHEL, AND IF YOU COME TO OUR SIDE...
JUSTICE WILL NEVER BE SERVED.

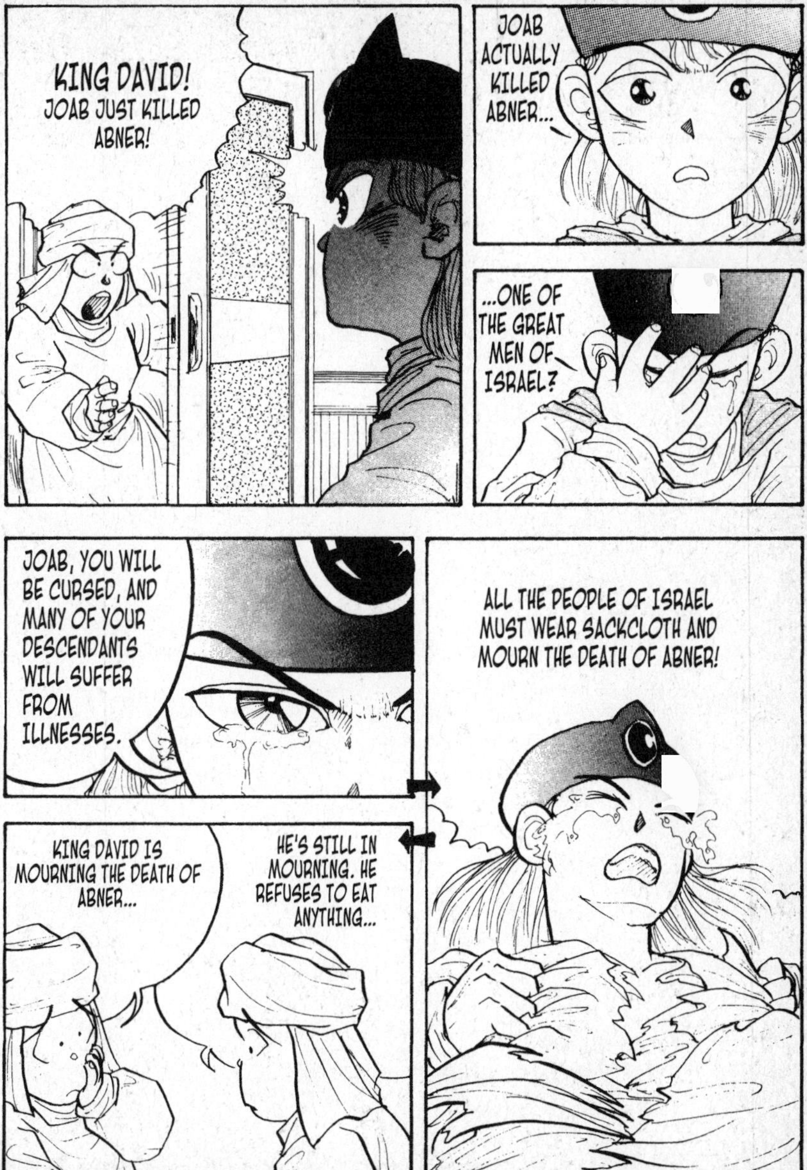
KING DAVID! JOAB JUST KILLED ABNER!
JOAB ACTUALLY KILLED ABNER...
...ONE OF THE GREAT MEN OF ISRAEL?
JOAB, YOU WILL BE CURSED, AND MANY OF YOUR DESCENDANTS WILL SUFFER FROM ILLNESSES.
ALL THE PEOPLE OF ISRAEL MUST WEAR SACKCLOTH AND MOURN THE DEATH OF ABNER!
KING DAVID IS MOURNING THE DEATH OF ABNER...
HE'S STILL IN MOURNING. HE REFUSES TO EAT ANYTHING...

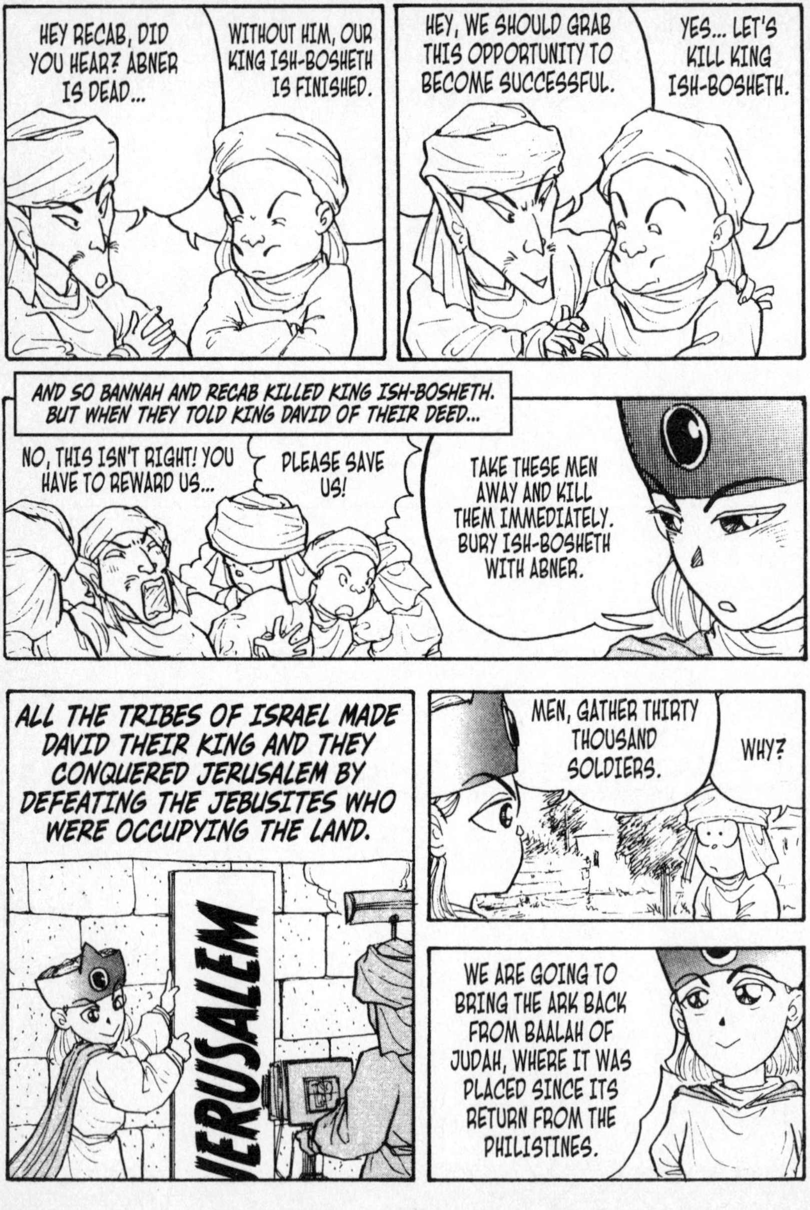
HEY RECAB, DID YOU HEAR? ABNER IS DEAD...
WITHOUT HIM, OUR KING ISH-BOSHETH IS FINISHED.
HEY, WE SHOULD GRAB THIS OPPORTUNITY TO BECOME SUCCESSFUL.
YES... LET'S KILL KING ISH-BOSHETH.
AND SO BANNAH AND RECAB KILLED KING ISH-BOSHETH. BUT WHEN THEY TOLD KING DAVID OF THEIR DEED...
NO, THIS ISN'T RIGHT! YOU HAVE TO REWARD US...
PLEASE SAVE US!
TAKE THESE MEN AWAY AND KILL THEM IMMEDIATELY. BURY ISH-BOSHETH WITH ABNER.
ALL THE TRIBES OF ISRAEL MADE DAVID THEIR KING AND THEY CONQUERED JERUSALEM BY DEFEATING THE JEBUSITES WHO WERE OCCUPYING THE LAND.
JERUSALEM
MEN, GATHER THIRTY THOUSAND SOLDIERS.
WHY?
WE ARE GOING TO BRING THE ARK BACK FROM BAALAH OF JUDAH, WHERE IT WAS PLACED SINCE ITS RETURN FROM THE PHILISTINES.

TOO-TOOOO!!!
JOYFUL DAY
HELLO! REPORTING LIVE FROM BAALAH OF JUDAH! THE ARK IS BEING PREPARED TO LEAVE FOR JERUSALEM IN THE FRONT OF A CROWD OF TENS OF THOUSANDS.
AT THIS MOMENT, THE ARK IS PASSING NACON'S FRONT YARD.
UH-OH -- THE OXEN ARE LOOKING STRANGE...
MROOO! MROOOOO!
WOW! WHAT'S HAPPENING? THE OXEN ARE GOING WILD.

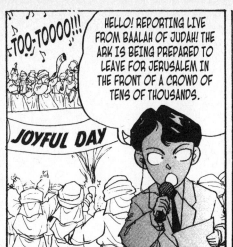

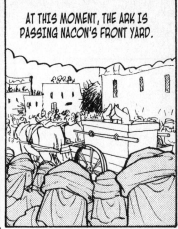

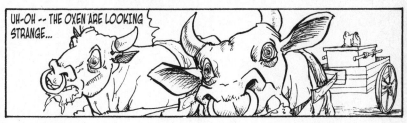

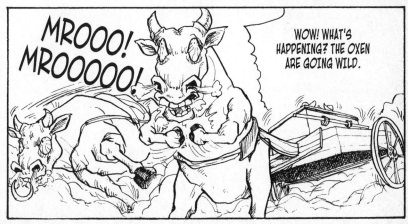

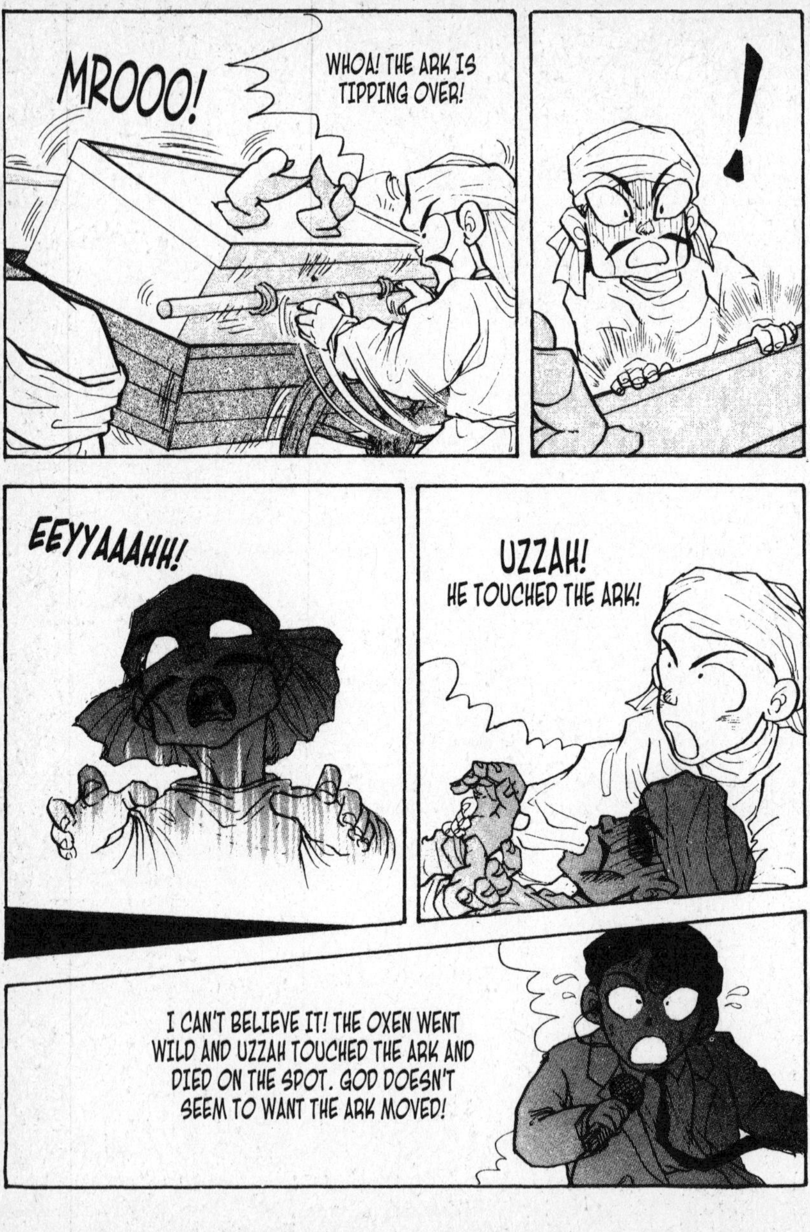
MROOO!
WHOA! THE ARK IS TIPPING OVER!
!
EEYYAAAHH!
UZZAH!
HE TOUCHED THE ARK!
I CAN'T BELIEVE IT! THE OXEN WENT WILD AND UZZAH TOUCHED THE ARK AND DIED ON THE SPOT. GOD DOESN'T SEEM TO WANT THE ARK MOVED!

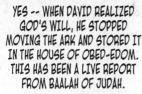

YES -- WHEN DAVID REALIZED GOD'S WILL, HE STOPPED MOVING THE ARK AND STORED IT IN THE HOUSE OF OBED-EDOM. THIS HAS BEEN A LIVE REPORT FROM BAALAH OF JUDAH.

ISRAEL TIMES

OBED-EDOM IS BLESSED

Obed-Edom, who is currently storing the ark, has been overflowing with blessings for the last three months. The sick are being healed and his wealth is increasing every day. Even to this reporter's eyes, Obed-Edom's house is no longer the same as before.

HMM, IT'S BEEN THREE MONTHS. LET'S GO GET THE ARK.

ARE YOU OKAY?

NODDING HEAD

HERE -- MOVE YOUR FEET SLOWLY...

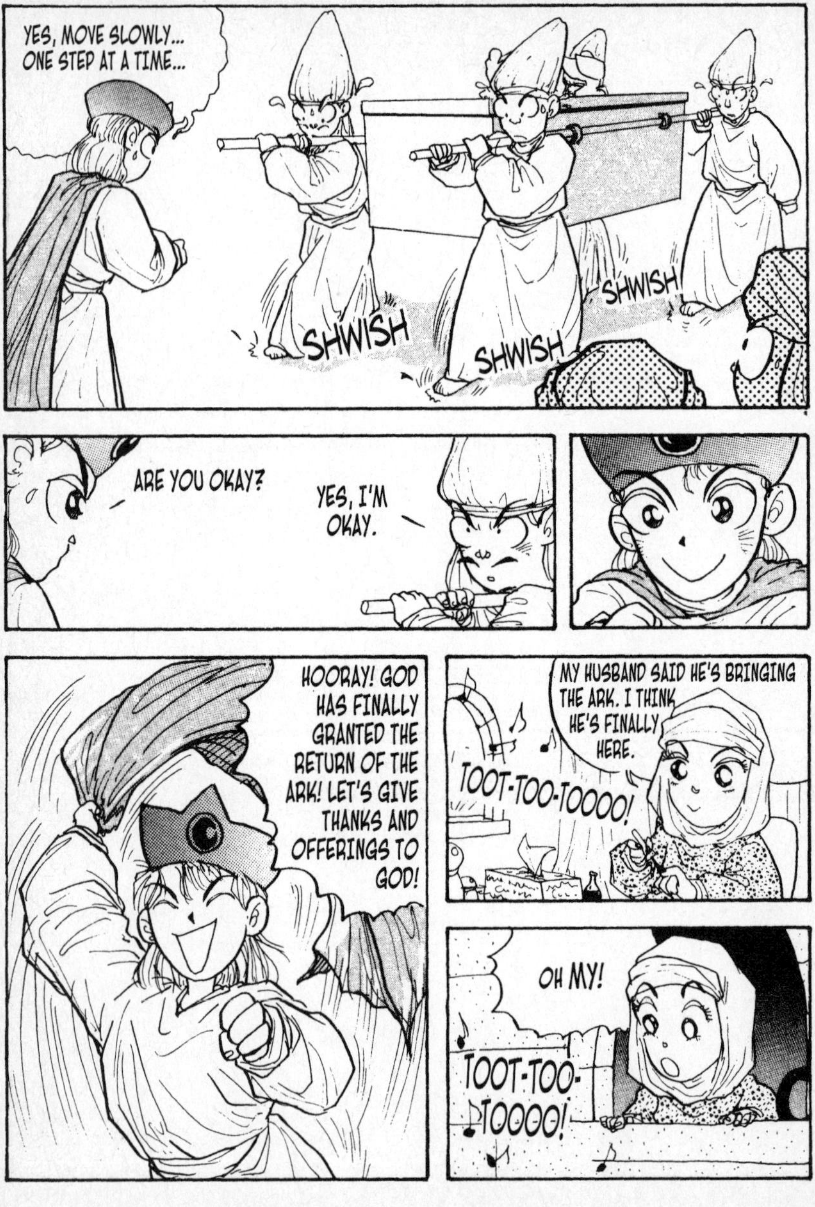
YES, MOVE SLOWLY... ONE STEP AT A TIME...
SHWISH
SHWISH
SHWISH
ARE YOU OKAY?
YES, I'M OKAY.
HOORAY! GOD HAS FINALLY GRANTED THE RETURN OF THE ARK! LET'S GIVE THANKS AND OFFERINGS TO GOD!
MY HUSBAND SAID HE'S BRINGING THE ARK. I THINK HE'S FINALLY HERE.
TOOT-TOO-TOOOO!
OH MY!
TOOT-TOO-TOOOO!

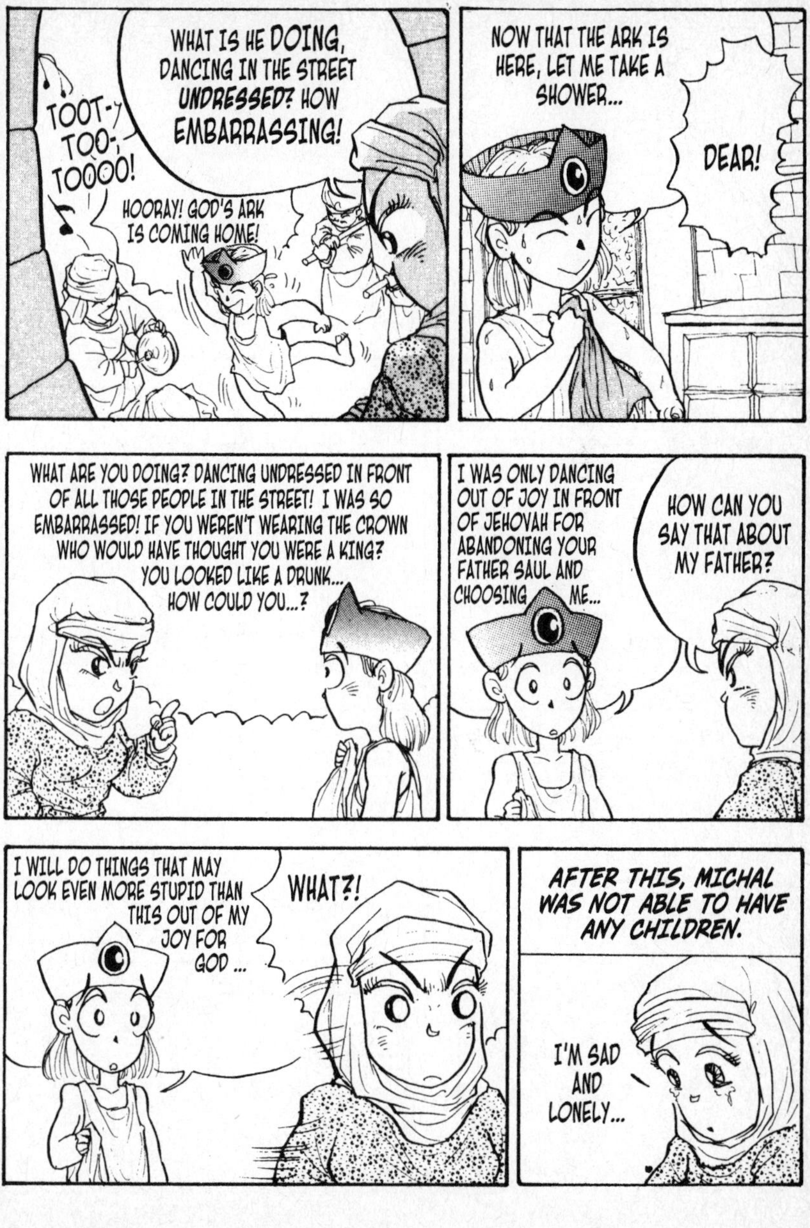

WHAT IS HE DOING, DANCING IN THE STREET UNDRESSED? HOW EMBARRASSING!
TOOT-Y TOO-, TOOOO!
HOORAY! GOD'S ARK IS COMING HOME!
NOW THAT THE ARK IS HERE, LET ME TAKE A SHOWER...
DEAR!
WHAT ARE YOU DOING? DANCING UNDRESSED IN FRONT OF ALL THOSE PEOPLE IN THE STREET! I WAS SO EMBARRASSED! IF YOU WEREN'T WEARING THE CROWN WHO WOULD HAVE THOUGHT YOU WERE A KING? YOU LOOKED LIKE A DRUNK... HOW COULD YOU...?
I WAS ONLY DANCING OUT OF JOY IN FRONT OF JEHOVAH FOR ABANDONING YOUR FATHER SAUL AND CHOOSING ME...
HOW CAN YOU SAY THAT ABOUT MY FATHER?
I WILL DO THINGS THAT MAY LOOK EVEN MORE STUPID THAN THIS OUT OF MY JOY FOR GOD ...
WHAT?!
AFTER THIS, MICHAL WAS NOT ABLE TO HAVE ANY CHILDREN.
I'M SAD AND LONELY...

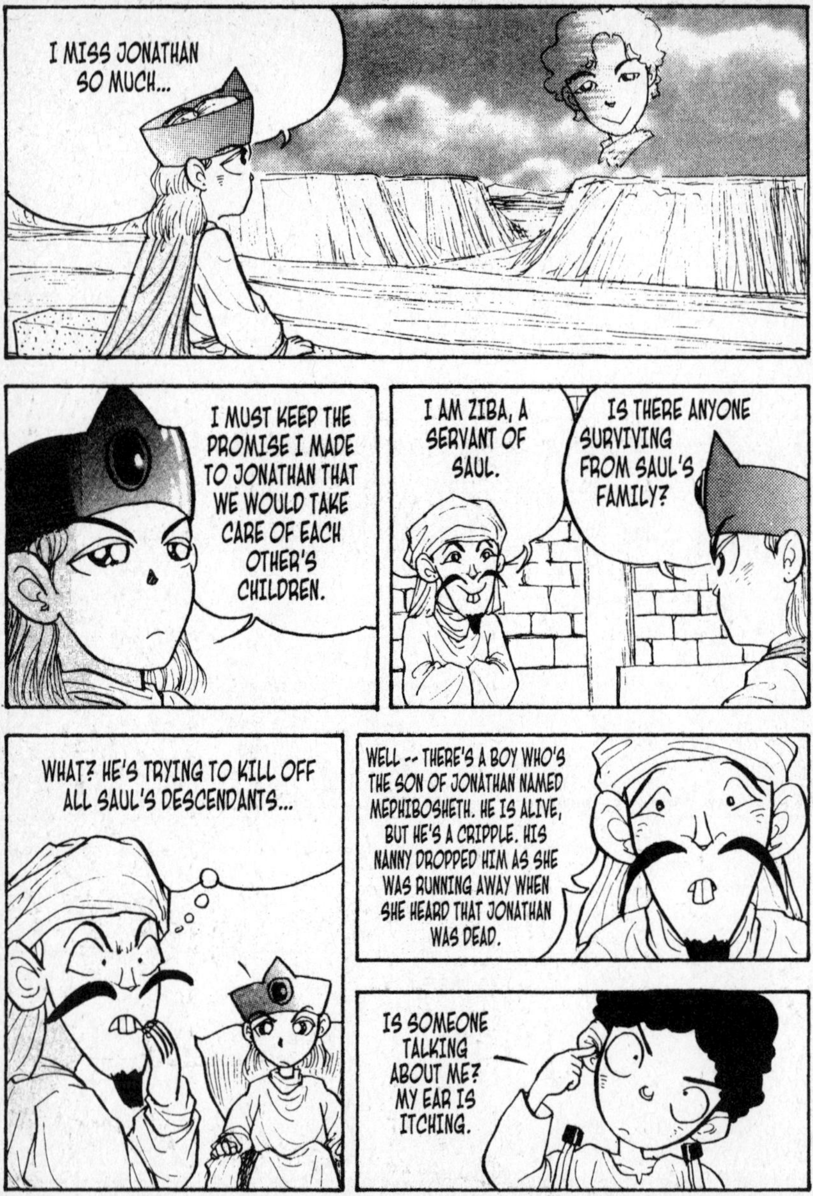
I MISS JONATHAN SO MUCH...
I MUST KEEP THE PROMISE I MADE TO JONATHAN THAT WE WOULD TAKE CARE OF EACH OTHER'S CHILDREN.
I AM ZIBA, A SERVANT OF SAUL.
IS THERE ANYONE SURVIVING FROM SAUL'S FAMILY?
WHAT? HE'S TRYING TO KILL OFF ALL SAUL'S DESCENDANTS...
WELL -- THERE'S A BOY WHO'S THE SON OF JONATHAN NAMED MEPHIBOSHETH. HE IS ALIVE, BUT HE'S A CRIPPLE. HIS NANNY DROPPED HIM AS SHE WAS RUNNING AWAY WHEN SHE HEARD THAT JONATHAN WAS DEAD.
IS SOMEONE TALKING ABOUT ME? MY EAR IS ITCHING.

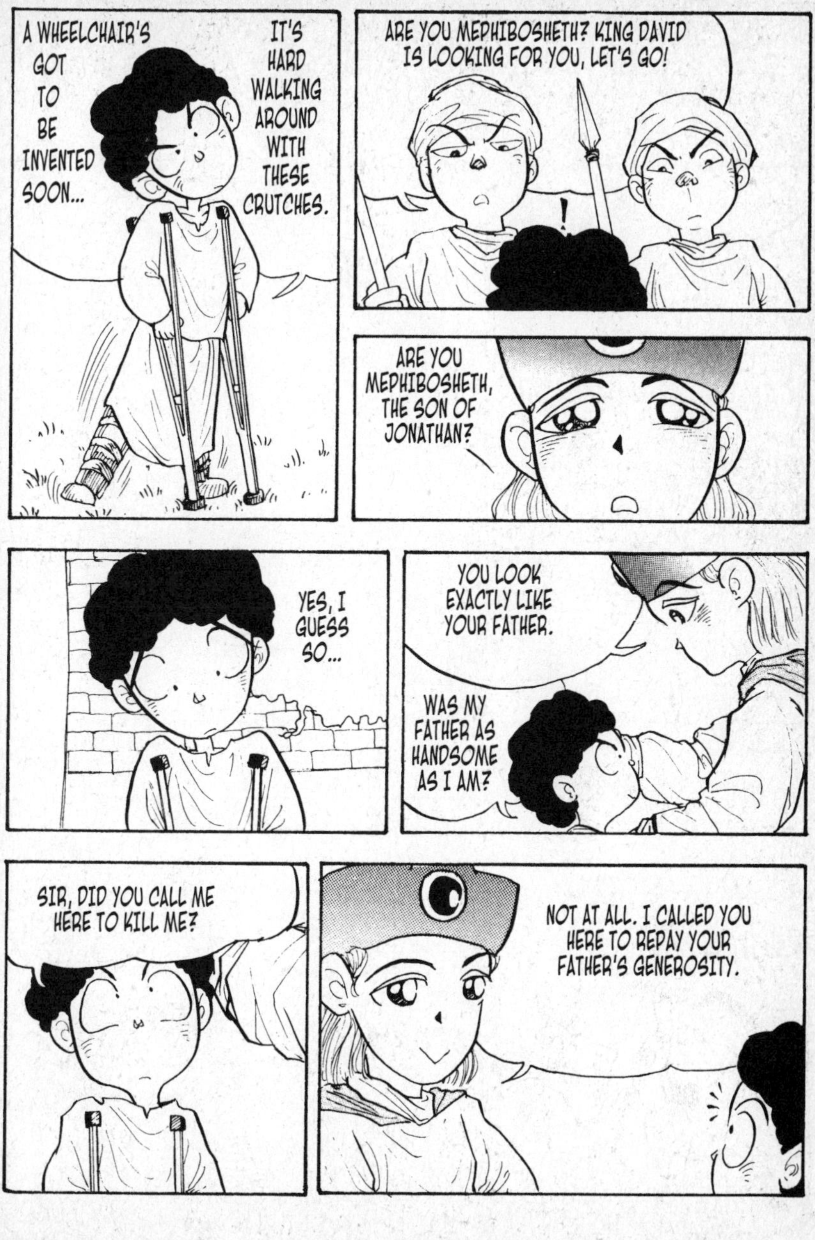
A WHEELCHAIR'S GOT TO BE INVENTED SOON...
IT'S HARD WALKING AROUND WITH THESE CRUTCHES.
ARE YOU MEPHIBOSHETH? KING DAVID IS LOOKING FOR YOU, LET'S GO!
!
ARE YOU MEPHIBOSHETH, THE SON OF JONATHAN?
YES, I GUESS SO...
YOU LOOK EXACTLY LIKE YOUR FATHER.
WAS MY FATHER AS HANDSOME AS I AM?
SIR, DID YOU CALL ME HERE TO KILL ME?
NOT AT ALL. I CALLED YOU HERE TO REPAY YOUR FATHER'S GENEROSITY.

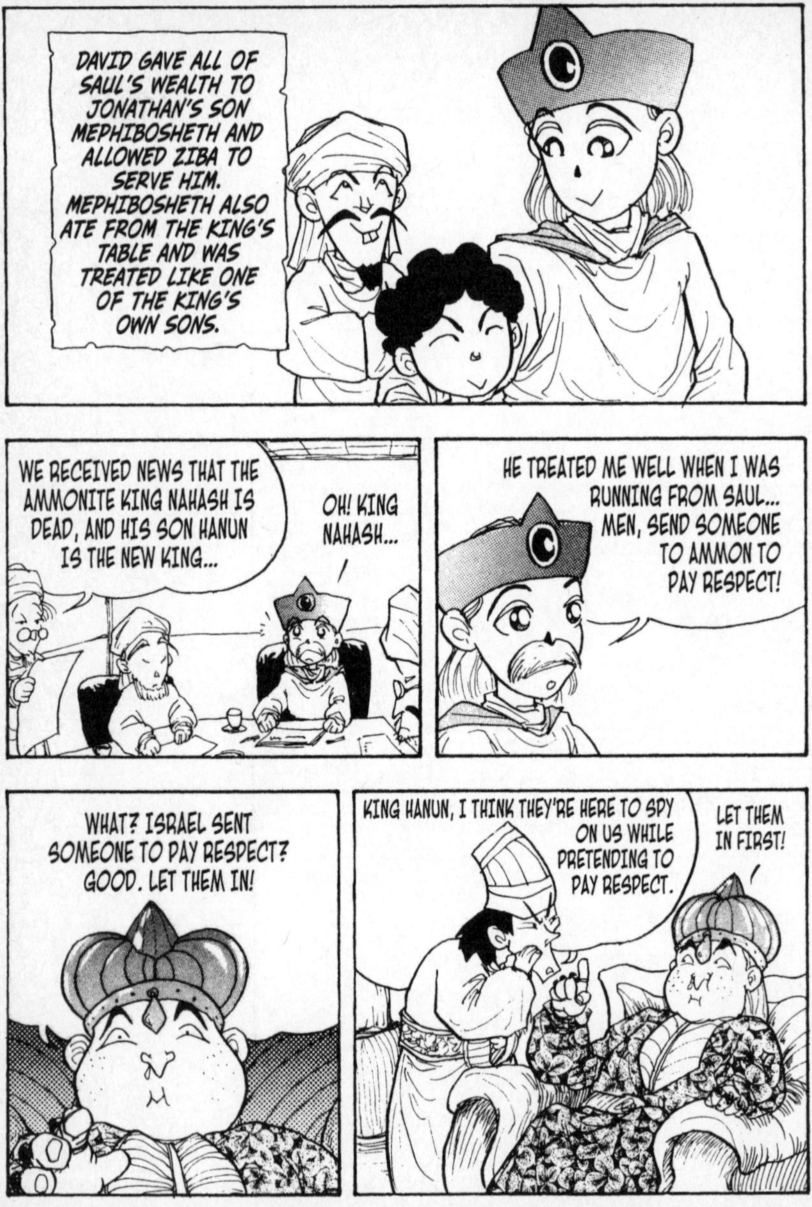
DAVID GAVE ALL OF SAUL'S WEALTH TO JONATHAN'S SON MEPHIBOSHETH AND ALLOWED ZIBA TO SERVE HIM. MEPHIBOSHETH ALSO ATE FROM THE KING'S TABLE AND WAS TREATED LIKE ONE OF THE KING'S OWN SONS.
WE RECEIVED NEWS THAT THE AMMONITE KING NAHASH IS DEAD, AND HIS SON HANUN IS THE NEW KING...
OH! KING NAHASH...
HE TREATED ME WELL WHEN I WAS RUNNING FROM SAUL... MEN, SEND SOMEONE TO AMMON TO PAY RESPECT!
WHAT? ISRAEL SENT SOMEONE TO PAY RESPECT? GOOD. LET THEM IN!
KING HANUN, I THINK THEY'RE HERE TO SPY ON US WHILE PRETENDING TO PAY RESPECT.
LET THEM IN FIRST!

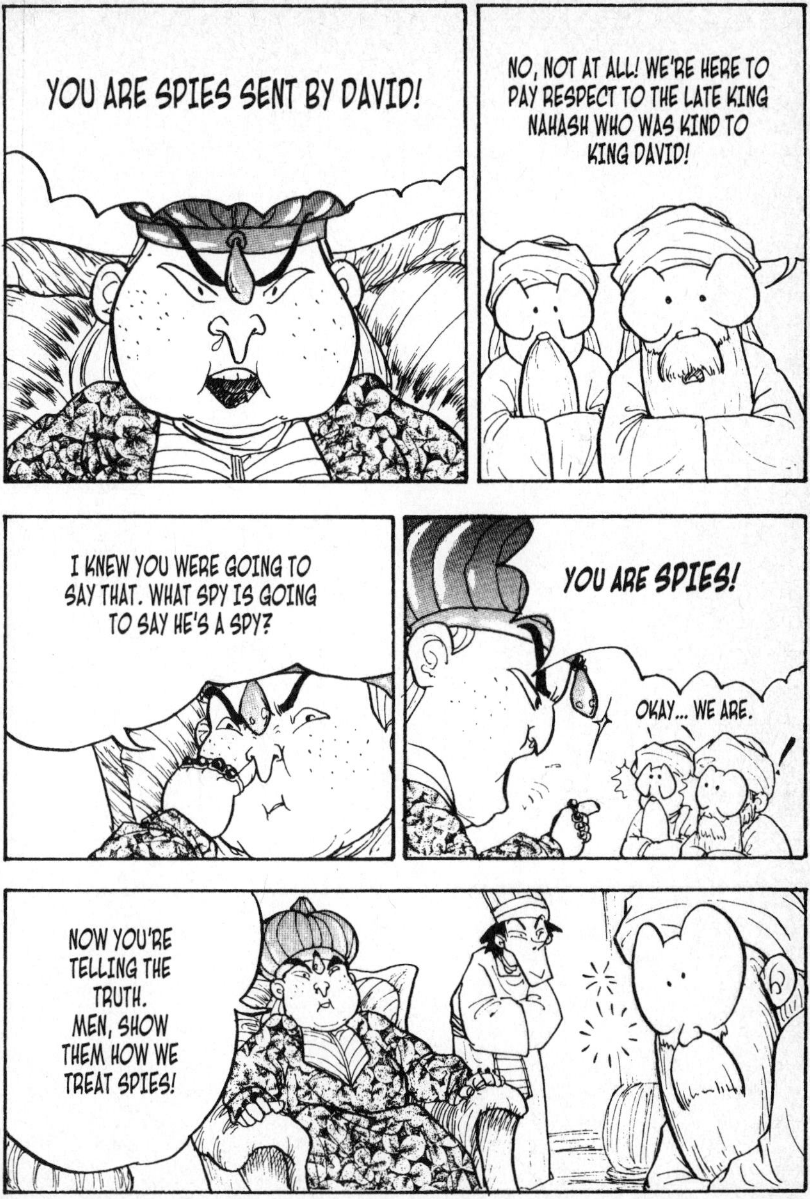
YOU ARE SPIES SENT BY DAVID!
NO, NOT AT ALL! WE'RE HERE TO PAY RESPECT TO THE LATE KING NAHASH WHO WAS KIND TO KING DAVID!
I KNEW YOU WERE GOING TO SAY THAT. WHAT SPY IS GOING TO SAY HE'S A SPY?
YOU ARE SPIES!
OKAY... WE ARE.
NOW YOU'RE TELLING THE TRUTH. MEN, SHOW THEM HOW WE TREAT SPIES!

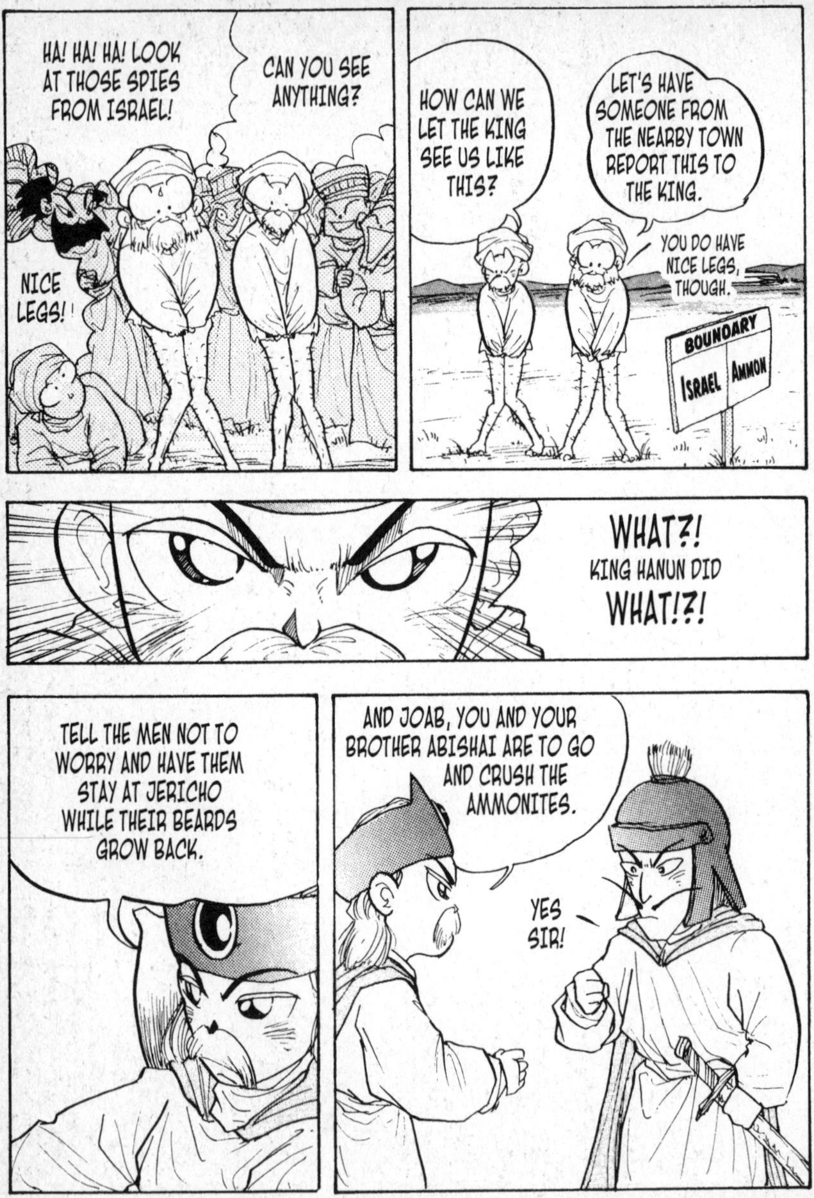
HA! HA! HA! LOOK AT THOSE SPIES FROM ISRAEL!
CAN YOU SEE ANYTHING?
NICE LEGS!
HOW CAN WE LET THE KING SEE US LIKE THIS?
LET'S HAVE SOMEONE FROM THE NEARBY TOWN REPORT THIS TO THE KING.
YOU DO HAVE NICE LEGS, THOUGH.
BOUNDARY
ISRAEL
AMMON
WHAT?! KING HANUN DID WHAT!?!
TELL THE MEN NOT TO WORRY AND HAVE THEM STAY AT JERICHO WHILE THEIR BEARDS GROW BACK.
AND JOAB, YOU AND YOUR BROTHER ABISHAI ARE TO GO AND CRUSH THE AMMONITES.
YES SIR!

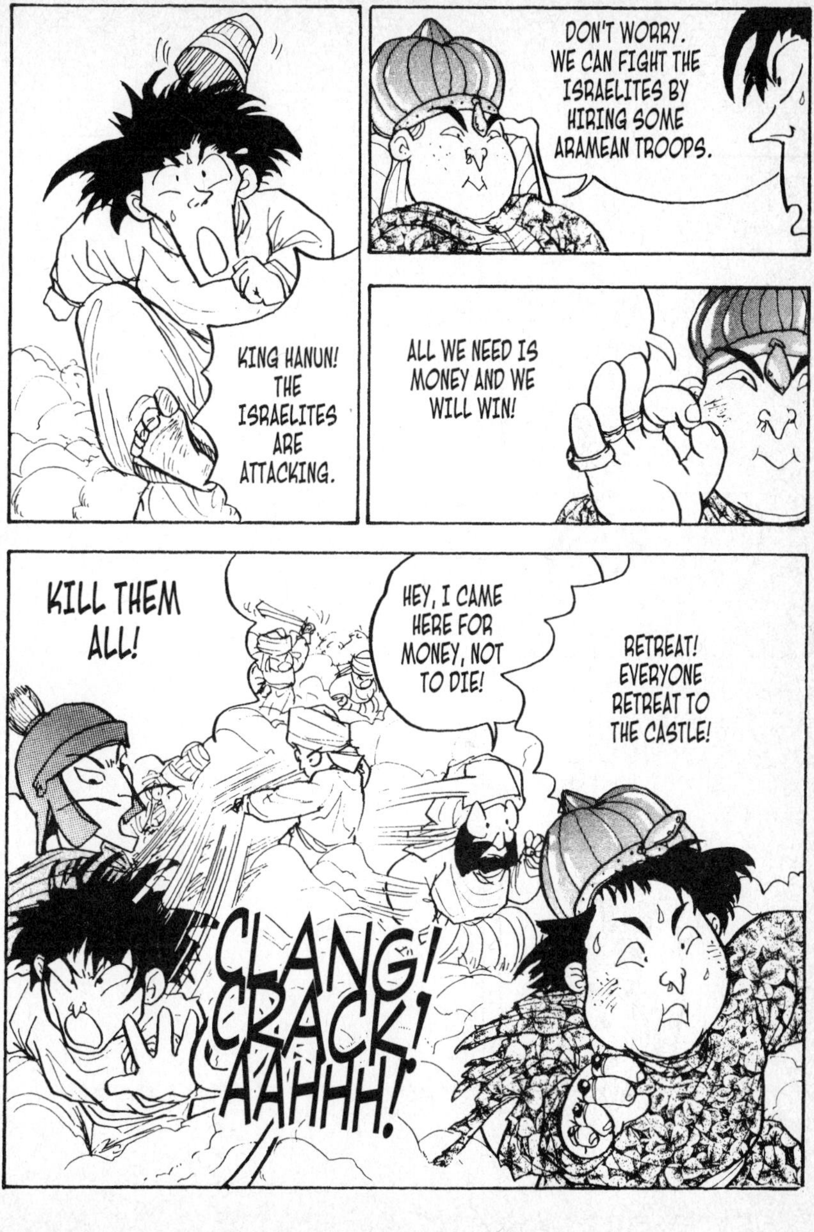
KING HANUN! THE ISRAELITES ARE ATTACKING.
DON'T WORRY. WE CAN FIGHT THE ISRAELITES BY HIRING SOME ARAMEAN TROOPS.
ALL WE NEED IS MONEY AND WE WILL WIN!
KILL THEM ALL!
HEY, I CAME HERE FOR MONEY, NOT TO DIE!
RETREAT! EVERYONE RETREAT TO THE CASTLE!
CLANG! CRACK! AAHHH!

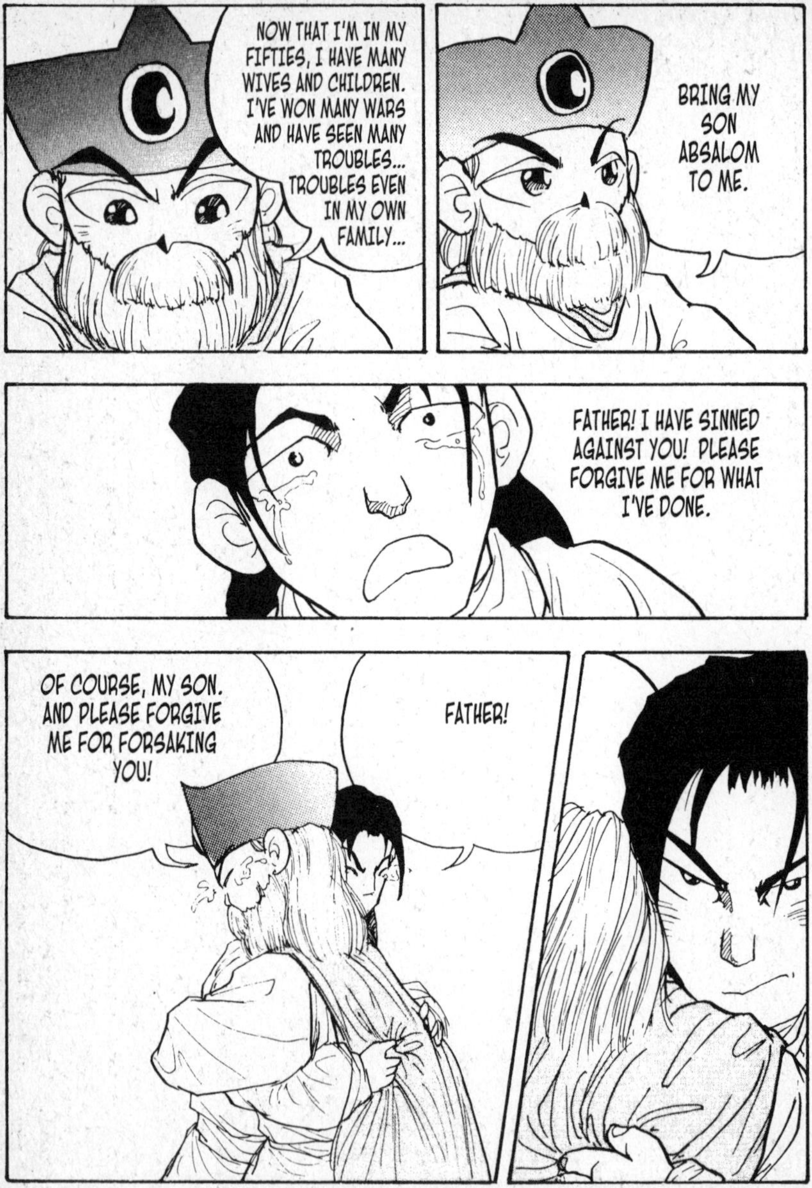
NOW THAT I'M IN MY FIFTIES, I HAVE MANY WIVES AND CHILDREN. I'VE WON MANY WARS AND HAVE SEEN MANY TROUBLES... TROUBLES EVEN IN MY OWN FAMILY...
BRING MY SON ABSALOM TO ME.
FATHER! I HAVE SINNED AGAINST YOU! PLEASE FORGIVE ME FOR WHAT I'VE DONE.
OF COURSE, MY SON. AND PLEASE FORGIVE ME FOR FORSAKING YOU!
FATHER!

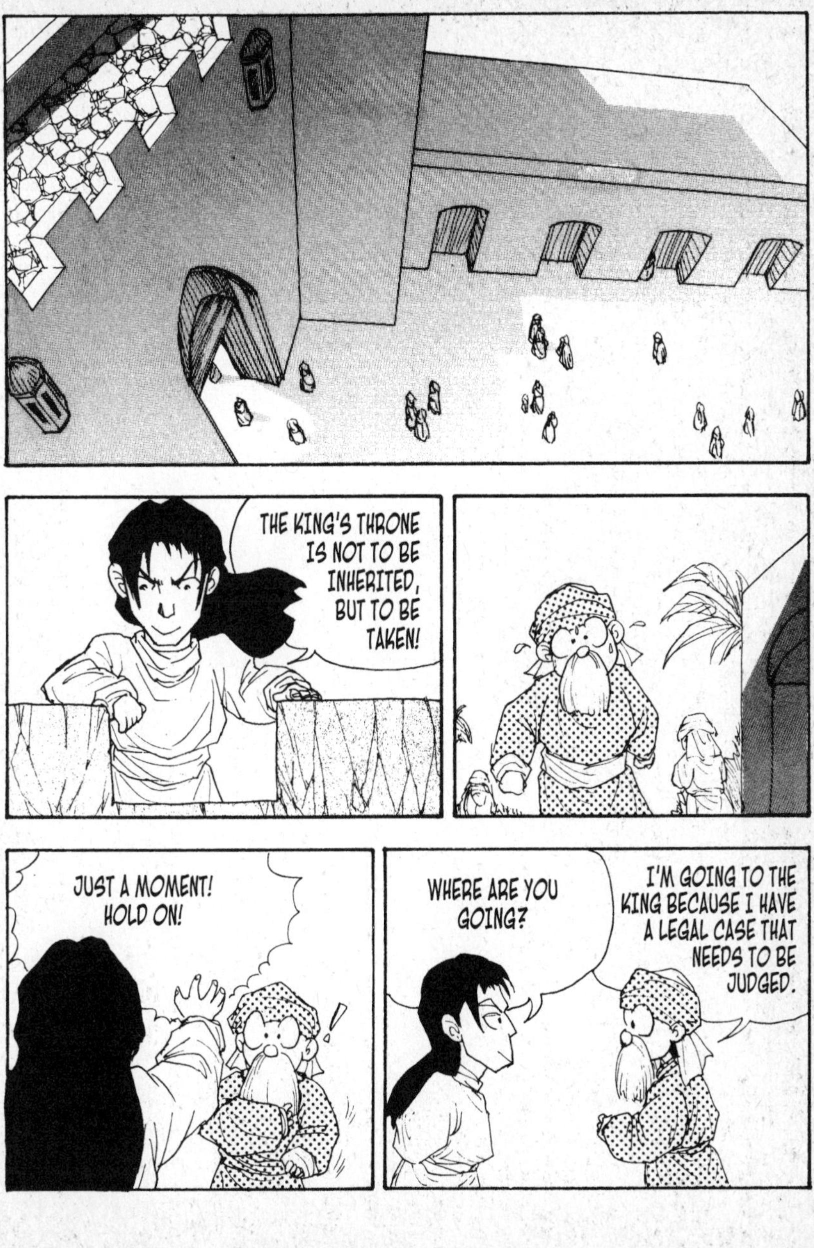
THE KING'S THRONE IS NOT TO BE INHERITED, BUT TO BE TAKEN!
JUST A MOMENT! HOLD ON!
!
WHERE ARE YOU GOING?
I'M GOING TO THE KING BECAUSE I HAVE A LEGAL CASE THAT NEEDS TO BE JUDGED.

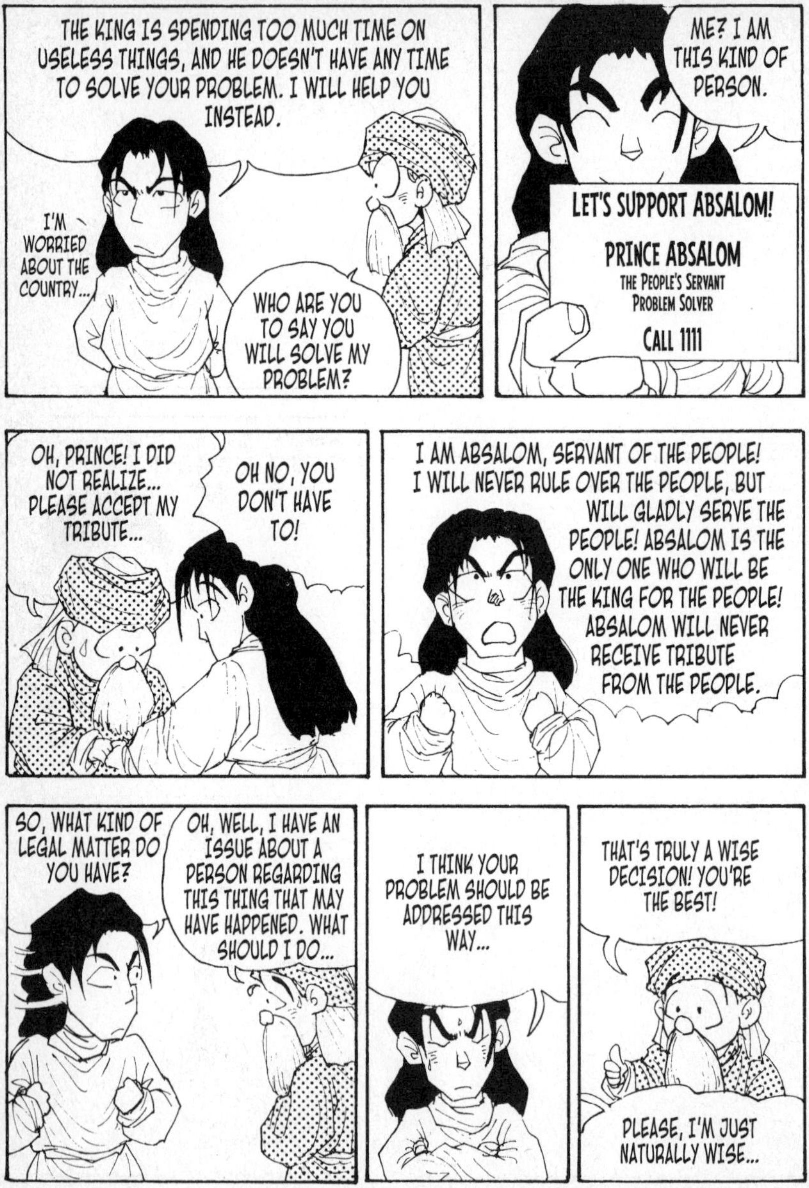
THE KING IS SPENDING TOO MUCH TIME ON USELESS THINGS, AND HE DOESN'T HAVE ANY TIME TO SOLVE YOUR PROBLEM. I WILL HELP YOU INSTEAD.
I'M WORRIED ABOUT THE COUNTRY...
WHO ARE YOU TO SAY YOU WILL SOLVE MY PROBLEM?
ME? I AM THIS KIND OF PERSON.
LET'S SUPPORT ABSALOM!
PRINCE ABSALOM
THE PEOPLE'S SERVANT
PROBLEM SOLVER
CALL 1111
OH, PRINCE! I DID NOT REALIZE... PLEASE ACCEPT MY TRIBUTE...
OH NO, YOU DON'T HAVE TO!
I AM ABSALOM, SERVANT OF THE PEOPLE! I WILL NEVER RULE OVER THE PEOPLE, BUT WILL GLADLY SERVE THE PEOPLE! ABSALOM IS THE ONLY ONE WHO WILL BE THE KING FOR THE PEOPLE! ABSALOM WILL NEVER RECEIVE TRIBUTE FROM THE PEOPLE.
SO, WHAT KIND OF LEGAL MATTER DO YOU HAVE?
OH, WELL, I HAVE AN ISSUE ABOUT A PERSON REGARDING THIS THING THAT MAY HAVE HAPPENED. WHAT SHOULD I DO...
I THINK YOUR PROBLEM SHOULD BE ADDRESSED THIS WAY...
THAT'S TRULY A WISE DECISION! YOU'RE THE BEST!
PLEASE, I'M JUST NATURALLY WISE...

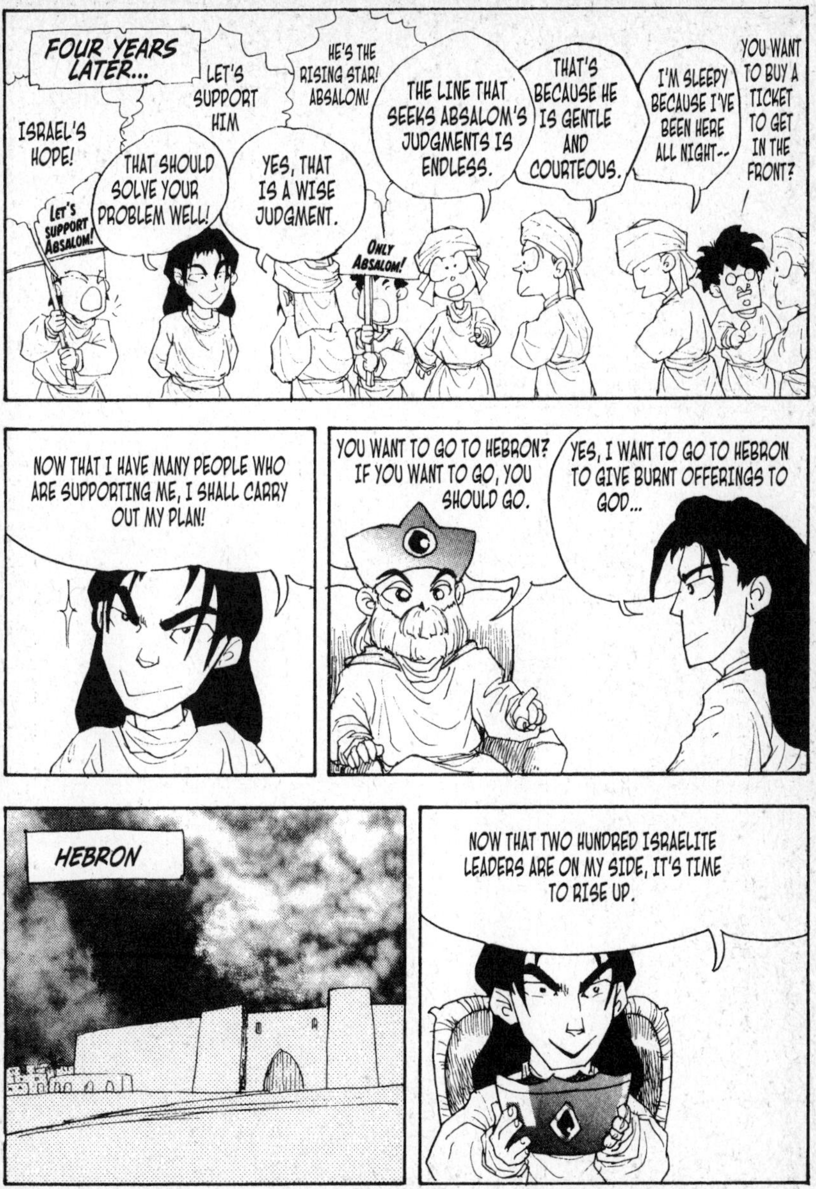
FOUR YEARS LATER...
LET'S SUPPORT HIM
HE'S THE RISING STAR! ABSALOM!
ISRAEL'S HOPE!
THAT SHOULD SOLVE YOUR PROBLEM WELL!
YES, THAT IS A WISE JUDGMENT.
THE LINE THAT SEEKS ABSALOM'S JUDGMENTS IS ENDLESS.
THAT'S BECAUSE HE IS GENTLE AND COURTEOUS.
I'M SLEEPY BECAUSE I'VE BEEN HERE ALL NIGHT--
YOU WANT TO BUY A TICKET TO GET IN THE FRONT?
LET'S SUPPORT ABSALOM!
ONLY ABSALOM!
NOW THAT I HAVE MANY PEOPLE WHO ARE SUPPORTING ME, I SHALL CARRY OUT MY PLAN!
YOU WANT TO GO TO HEBRON? IF YOU WANT TO GO, YOU SHOULD GO.
YES, I WANT TO GO TO HEBRON TO GIVE BURNT OFFERINGS TO GOD...
HEBRON
NOW THAT TWO HUNDRED ISRAELITE LEADERS ARE ON MY SIDE, IT'S TIME TO RISE UP.

NOW LET ALL ISRAEL KNOW THAT ABSALOM HAS BECOME THE KING!

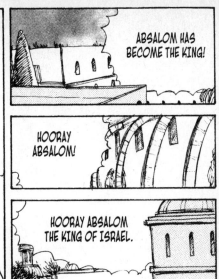

ABSALOM HAS BECOME THE KING!

HOORAY ABSALOM!

HOORAY ABSALOM THE KING OF ISRAEL.

TO AHITHOPHEL,
ALL OF ISRAEL IS ALREADY FOLLOWING ME. YOU SHOULD NOW ABANDON KING DAVID AND BECOME MY CHIEF ADVISOR!

ISRAEL'S NEW KING,
ABSALOM

YES, I WILL GO TO HEBRON AND STAND WITH ABSALOM! THE TIDE OF PUBLIC SUPPORT HAS TURNED TO HIM!

WHAT?! ABSALOM HAS RISEN AGAINST ME?

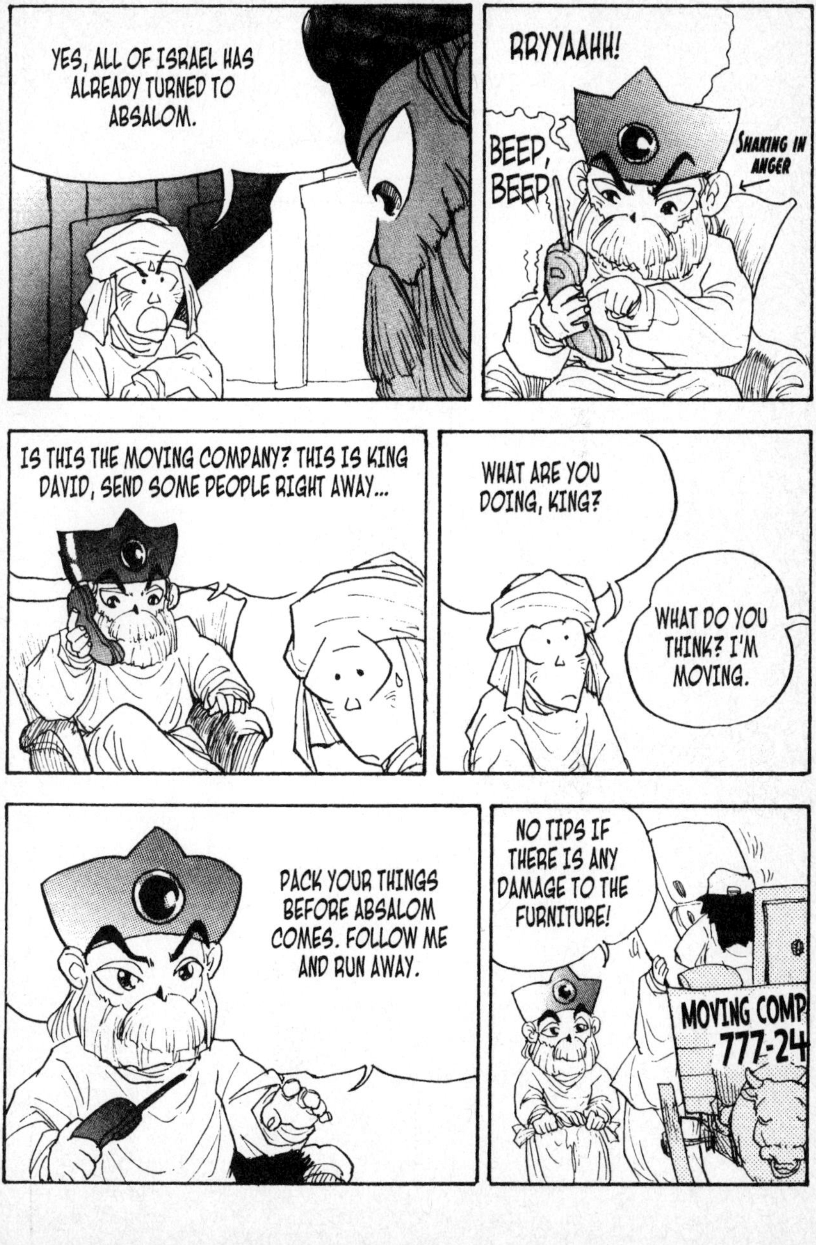
YES, ALL OF ISRAEL HAS ALREADY TURNED TO ABSALOM.
RRYYAAHH!
BEEP, BEEP
SHAKING IN ANGER
IS THIS THE MOVING COMPANY? THIS IS KING DAVID, SEND SOME PEOPLE RIGHT AWAY...
WHAT ARE YOU DOING, KING?
WHAT DO YOU THINK? I'M MOVING.
PACK YOUR THINGS BEFORE ABSALOM COMES. FOLLOW ME AND RUN AWAY.
NO TIPS IF THERE IS ANY DAMAGE TO THE FURNITURE!
MOVING COMP
777-24

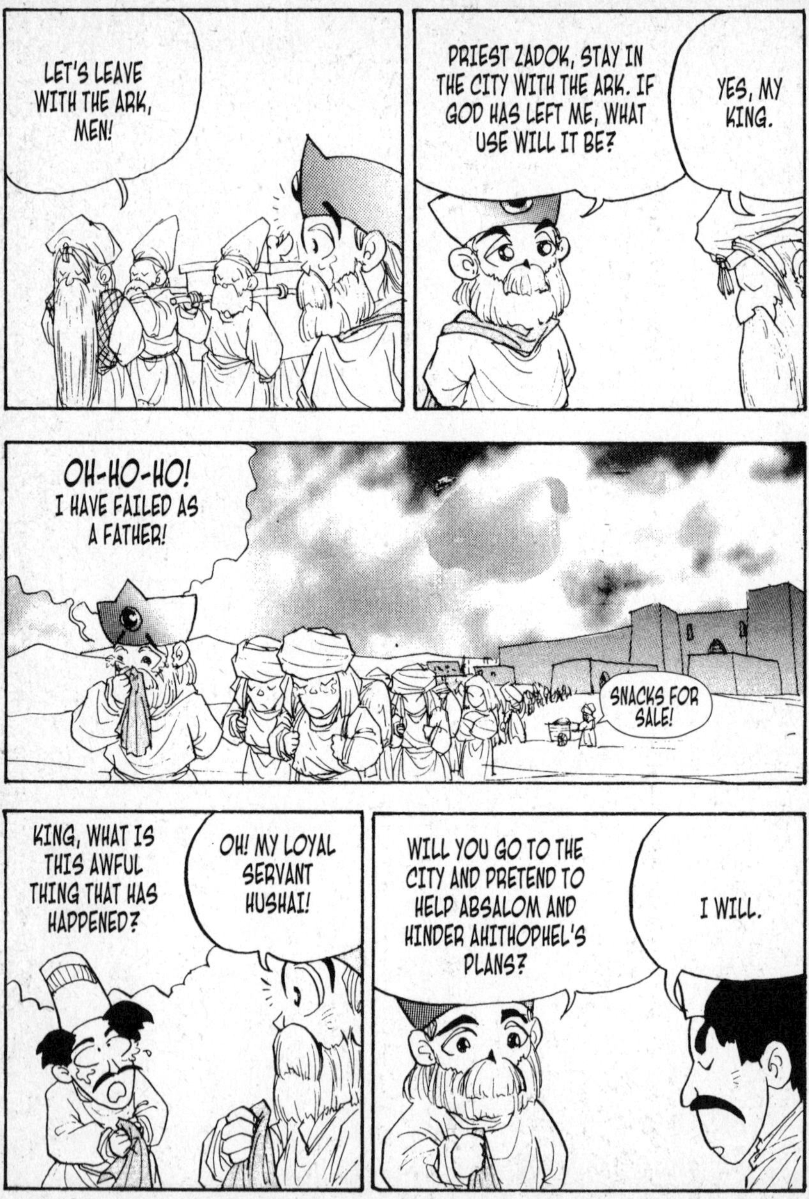
LET'S LEAVE WITH THE ARK, MEN!
PRIEST ZADOK, STAY IN THE CITY WITH THE ARK. IF GOD HAS LEFT ME, WHAT USE WILL IT BE?
YES, MY KING.
OH-HO-HO! I HAVE FAILED AS A FATHER!
SNACKS FOR SALE!
KING, WHAT IS THIS AWFUL THING THAT HAS HAPPENED?
OH! MY LOYAL SERVANT HUSHAI!
WILL YOU GO TO THE CITY AND PRETEND TO HELP ABSALOM AND HINDER AHITHOPHEL'S PLANS?
I WILL.

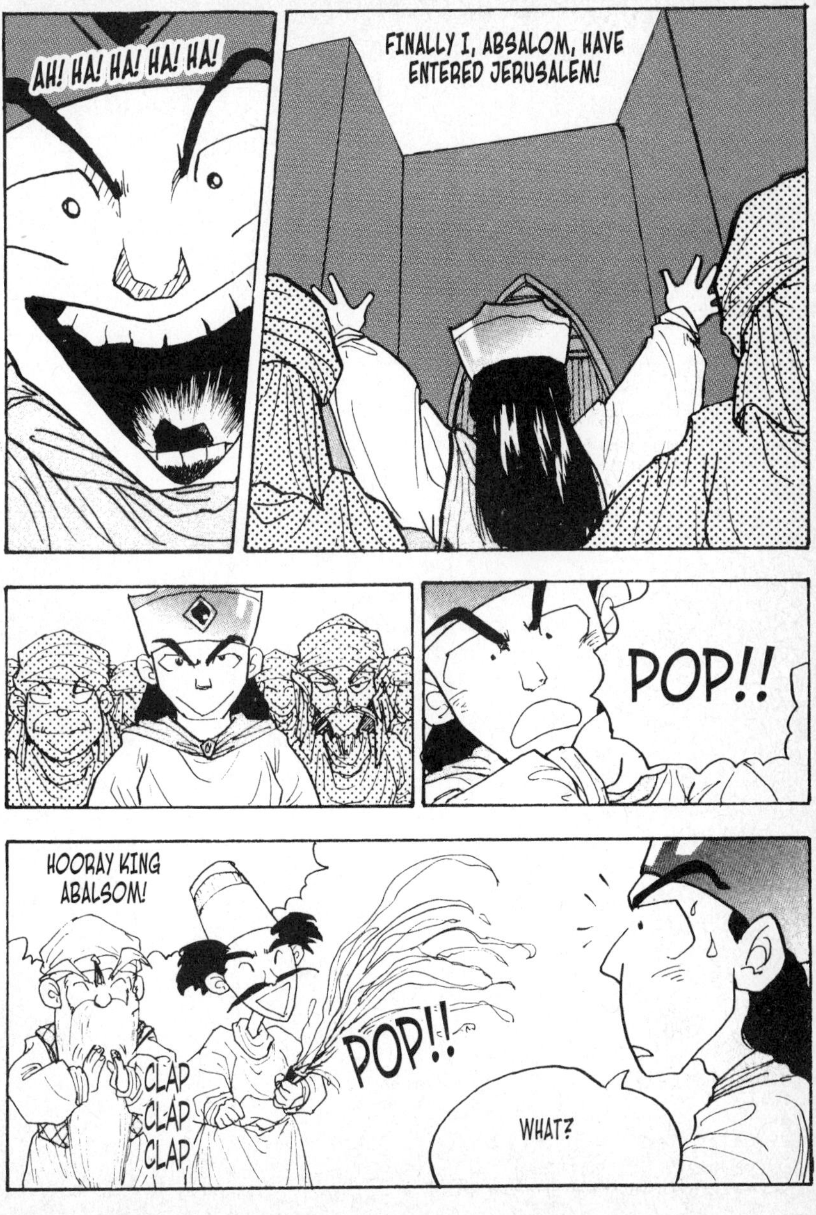
AH! HA! HA! HA! HA!
FINALLY I, ABSALOM, HAVE ENTERED JERUSALEM!
POP!!
HOORAY KING ABALSOM!
CLAP CLAP CLAP
POP!!
WHAT?

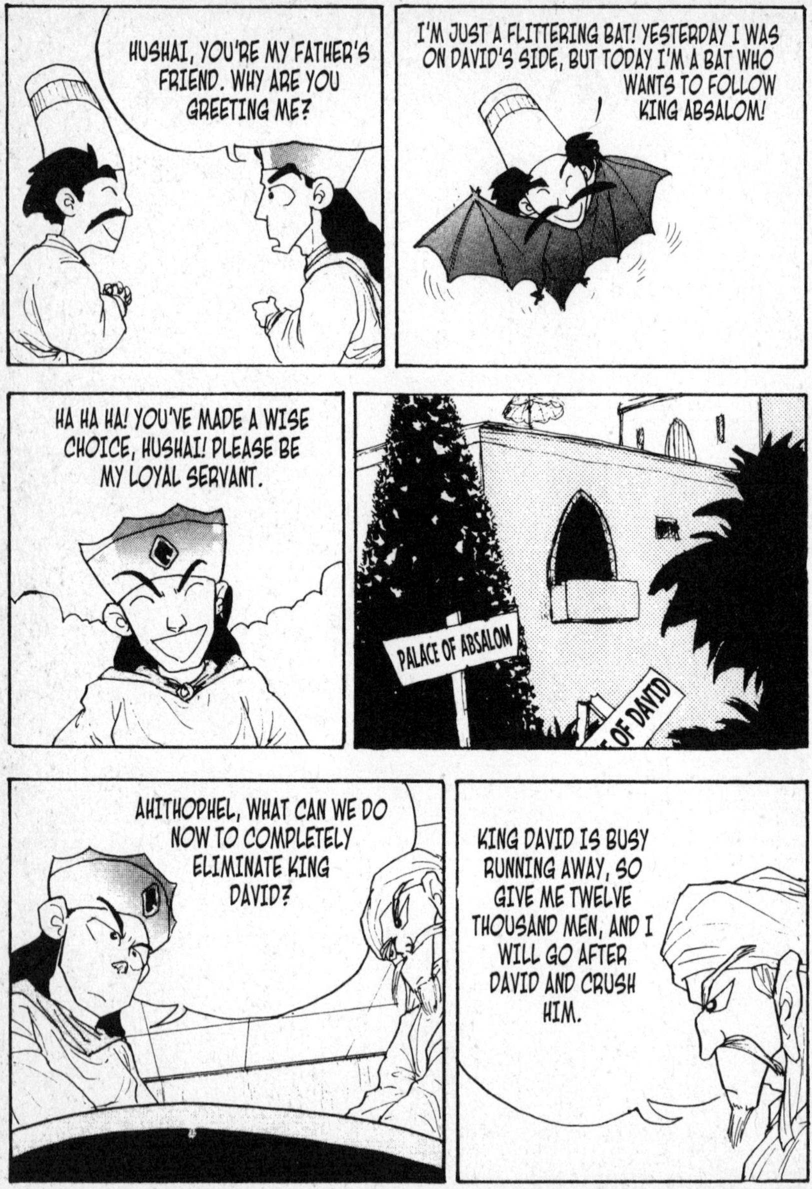
HUSHAI, YOU'RE MY FATHER'S FRIEND. WHY ARE YOU GREETING ME?
I'M JUST A FLITTERING BAT! YESTERDAY I WAS ON DAVID'S SIDE, BUT TODAY I'M A BAT WHO WANTS TO FOLLOW KING ABSALOM!
HA HA HA! YOU'VE MADE A WISE CHOICE, HUSHAI! PLEASE BE MY LOYAL SERVANT.
PALACE OF ABSALOM
OF DAVID
AHITHOPHEL, WHAT CAN WE DO NOW TO COMPLETELY ELIMINATE KING DAVID?
KING DAVID IS BUSY RUNNING AWAY, SO GIVE ME TWELVE THOUSAND MEN, AND I WILL GO AFTER DAVID AND CRUSH HIM.

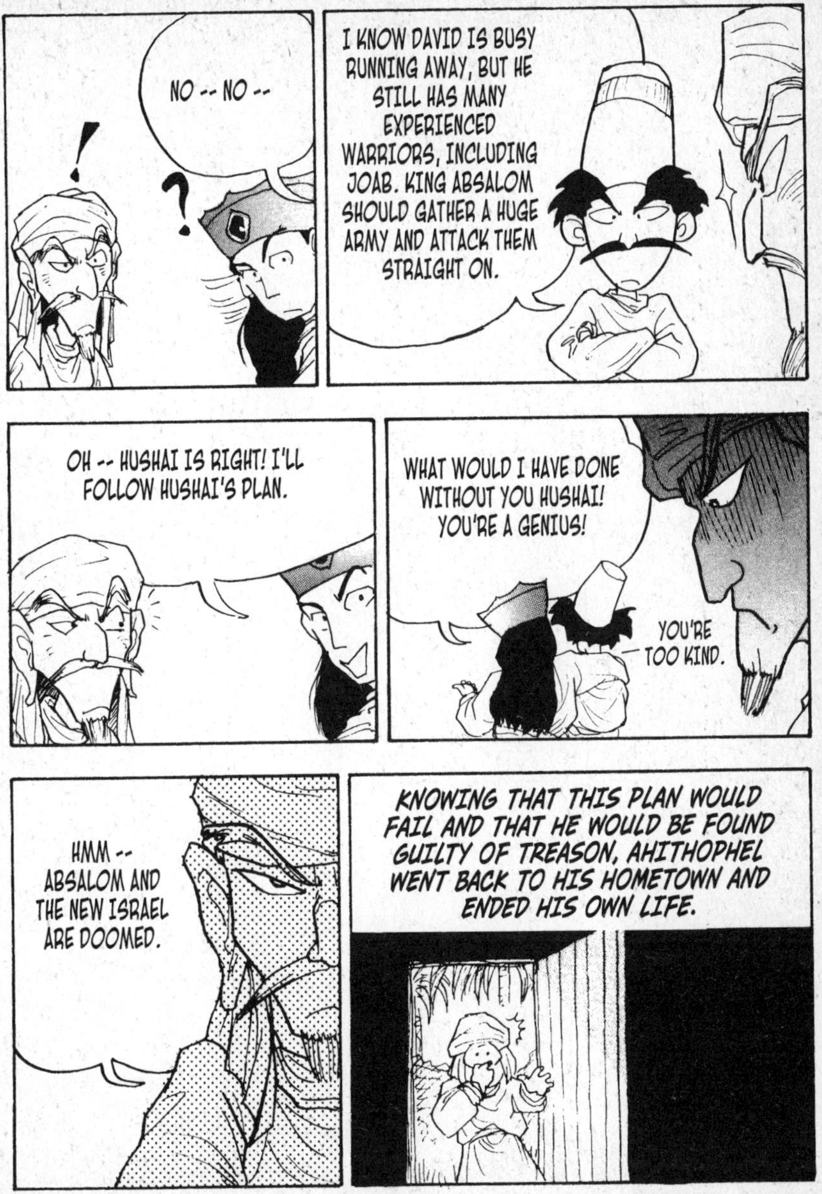
NO -- NO --
I KNOW DAVID IS BUSY RUNNING AWAY, BUT HE STILL HAS MANY EXPERIENCED WARRIORS, INCLUDING JOAB. KING ABSALOM SHOULD GATHER A HUGE ARMY AND ATTACK THEM STRAIGHT ON.
OH -- HUSHAI IS RIGHT! I'LL FOLLOW HUSHAI'S PLAN.
WHAT WOULD I HAVE DONE WITHOUT YOU HUSHAI! YOU'RE A GENIUS!
YOU'RE TOO KIND.
HMM -- ABSALOM AND THE NEW ISRAEL ARE DOOMED.
KNOWING THAT THIS PLAN WOULD FAIL AND THAT HE WOULD BE FOUND GUILTY OF TREASON, AHITHOPHEL WENT BACK TO HIS HOMETOWN AND ENDED HIS OWN LIFE.

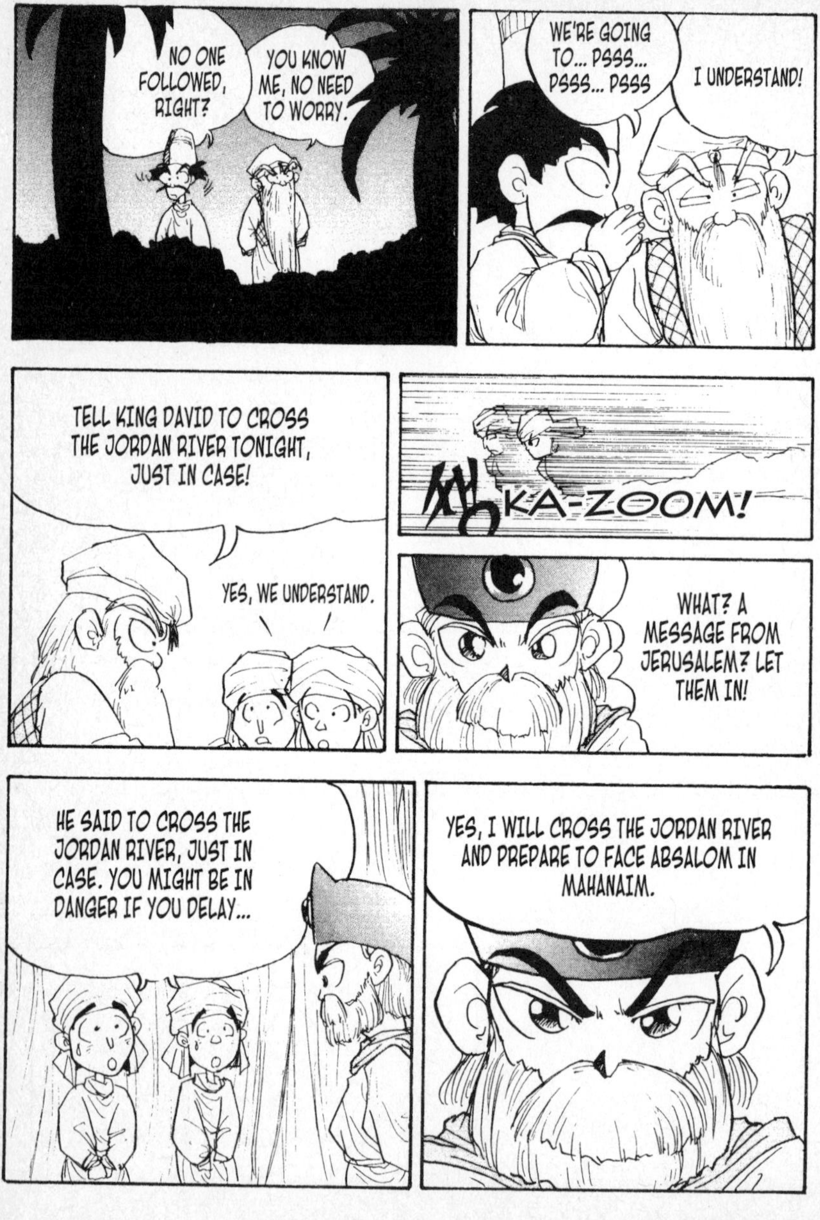
NO ONE FOLLOWED, RIGHT?
YOU KNOW ME, NO NEED TO WORRY.
WE'RE GOING TO... PSSS... PSSS... PSSS
I UNDERSTAND!
TELL KING DAVID TO CROSS THE JORDAN RIVER TONIGHT, JUST IN CASE!
YES, WE UNDERSTAND.
KA-ZOOM!
WHAT? A MESSAGE FROM JERUSALEM? LET THEM IN!
HE SAID TO CROSS THE JORDAN RIVER, JUST IN CASE. YOU MIGHT BE IN DANGER IF YOU DELAY...
YES, I WILL CROSS THE JORDAN RIVER AND PREPARE TO FACE ABSALOM IN MAHANAIM.

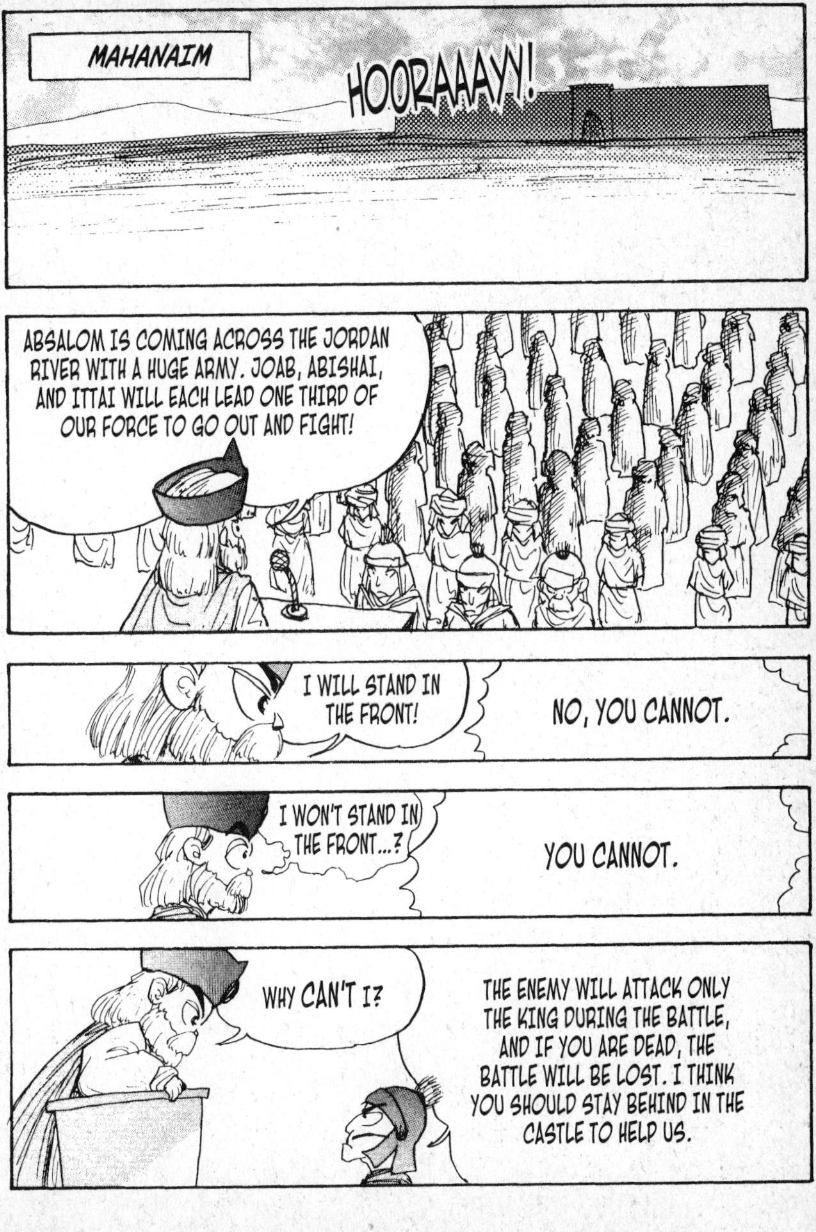
MAHANAIM
HOORAAAYY!
ABSALOM IS COMING ACROSS THE JORDAN RIVER WITH A HUGE ARMY. JOAB, ABISHAI, AND ITTAI WILL EACH LEAD ONE THIRD OF OUR FORCE TO GO OUT AND FIGHT!
I WILL STAND IN THE FRONT!
NO, YOU CANNOT.
I WON'T STAND IN THE FRONT...?
YOU CANNOT.
WHY CAN'T I?
THE ENEMY WILL ATTACK ONLY THE KING DURING THE BATTLE, AND IF YOU ARE DEAD, THE BATTLE WILL BE LOST. I THINK YOU SHOULD STAY BEHIND IN THE CASTLE TO HELP US.

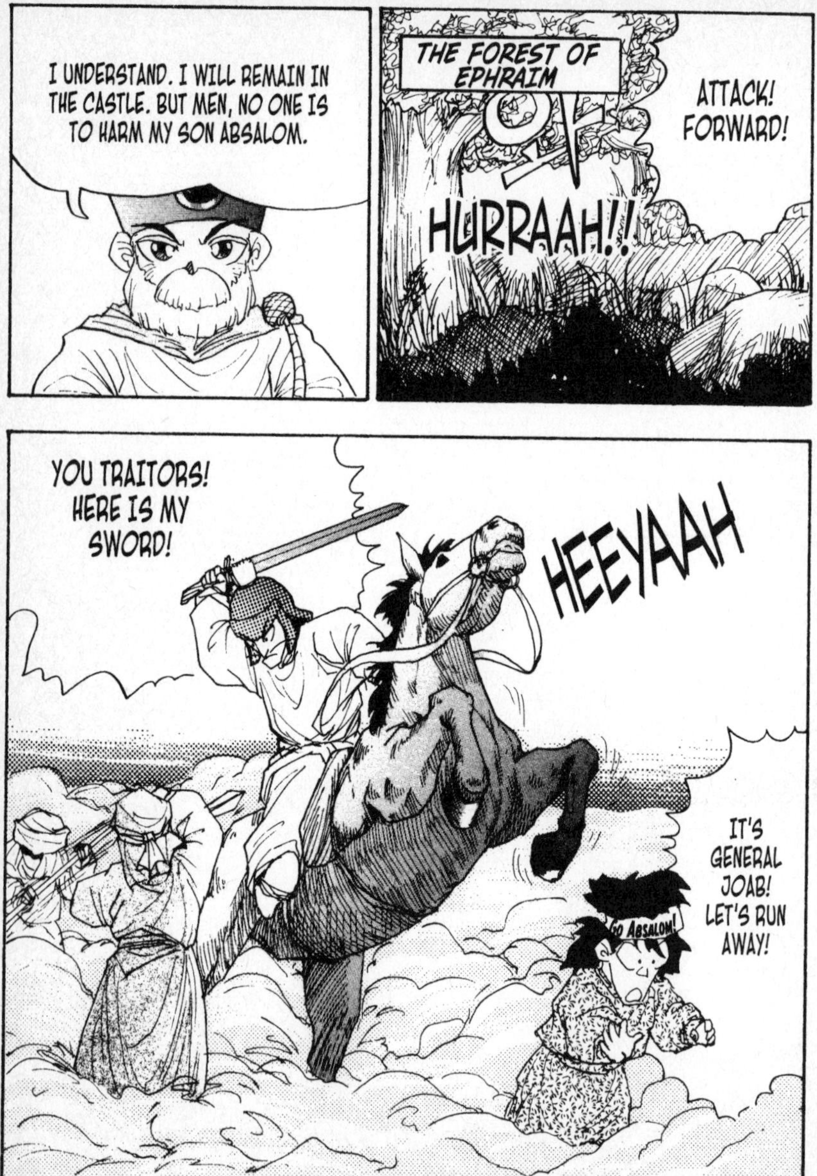
I UNDERSTAND. I WILL REMAIN IN THE CASTLE. BUT MEN, NO ONE IS TO HARM MY SON ABSALOM.
THE FOREST OF EPHRAIM
ATTACK! FORWARD!
HURRAAH!!
YOU TRAITORS! HERE IS MY SWORD!
HEEYAAH
GO ABSALOM!
IT'S GENERAL JOAB! LET'S RUN AWAY!

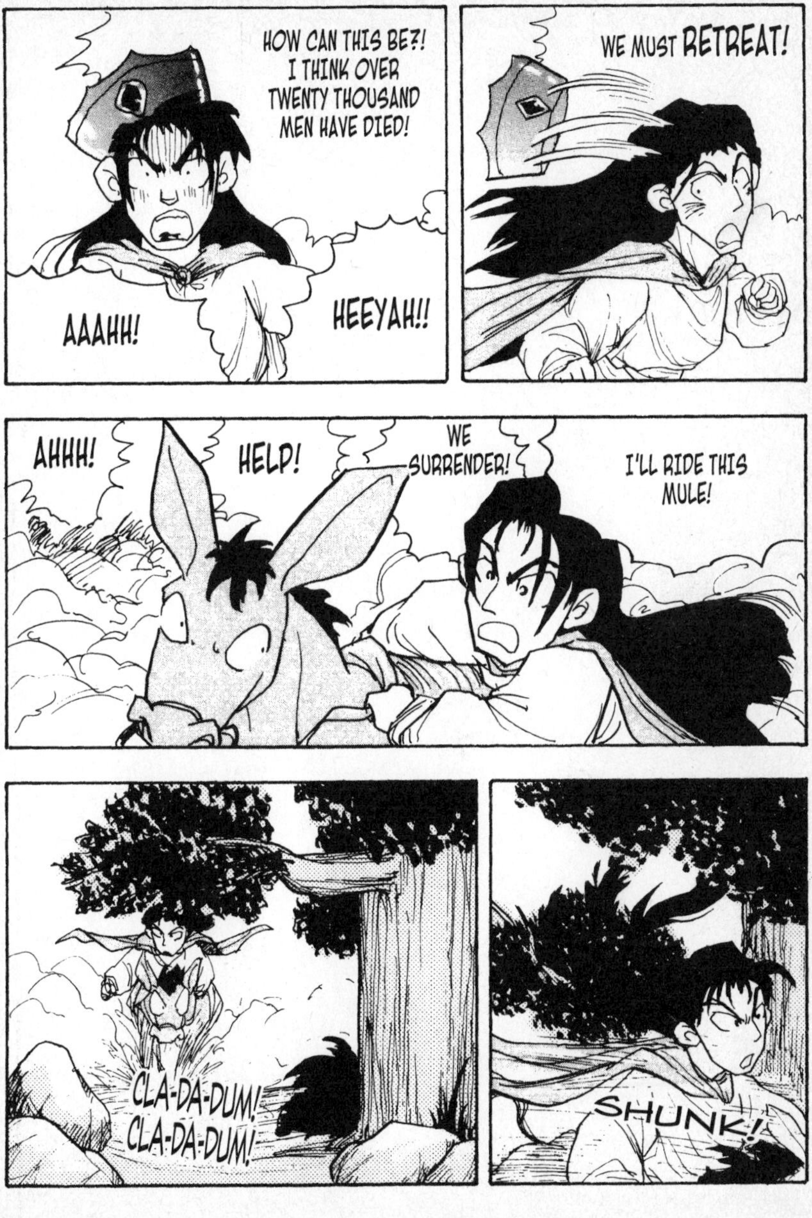
HOW CAN THIS BE?! I THINK OVER TWENTY THOUSAND MEN HAVE DIED!
AAAHH!
HEEYAH!!
WE MUST RETREAT!
AHHH!
HELP!
WE SURRENDER!
I'LL RIDE THIS MULE!
CLA-DA-DUM! CLA-DA-DUM!
SHUNK!

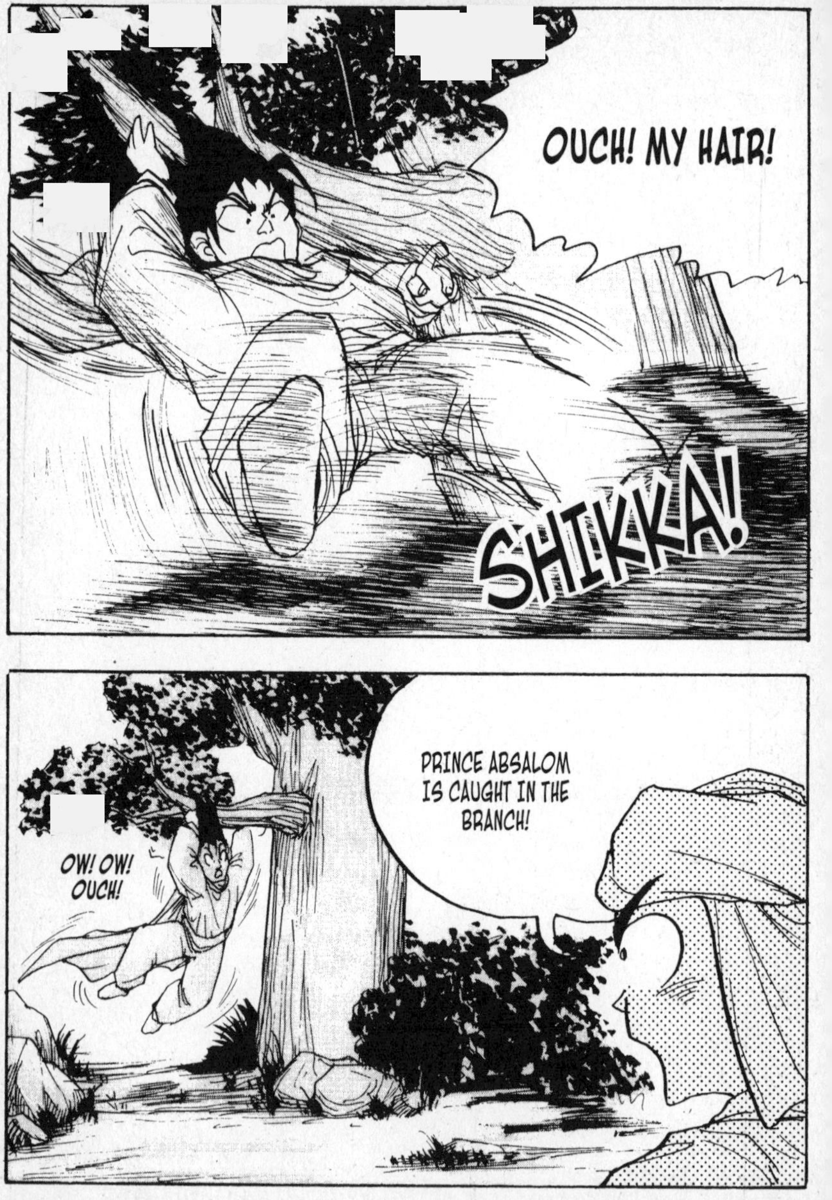
OUCH! MY HAIR!
SHIKKA!
OW! OW! OUCH!
PRINCE ABSALOM IS CAUGHT IN THE BRANCH!

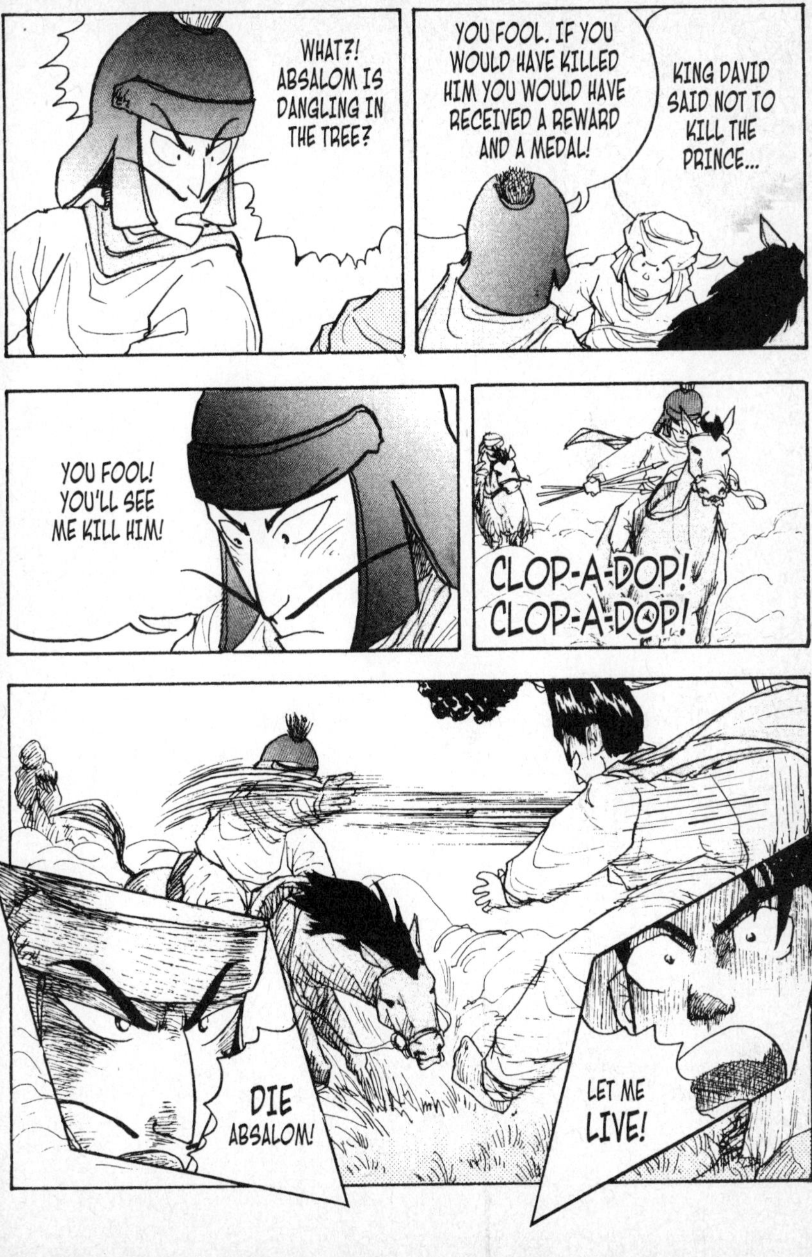
WHAT?! ABSALOM IS DANGLING IN THE TREE?
YOU FOOL. IF YOU WOULD HAVE KILLED HIM YOU WOULD HAVE RECEIVED A REWARD AND A MEDAL!
KING DAVID SAID NOT TO KILL THE PRINCE...
YOU FOOL! YOU'LL SEE ME KILL HIM!
CLOP-A-DOP! CLOP-A-DOP!
DIE ABSALOM!
LET ME LIVE!

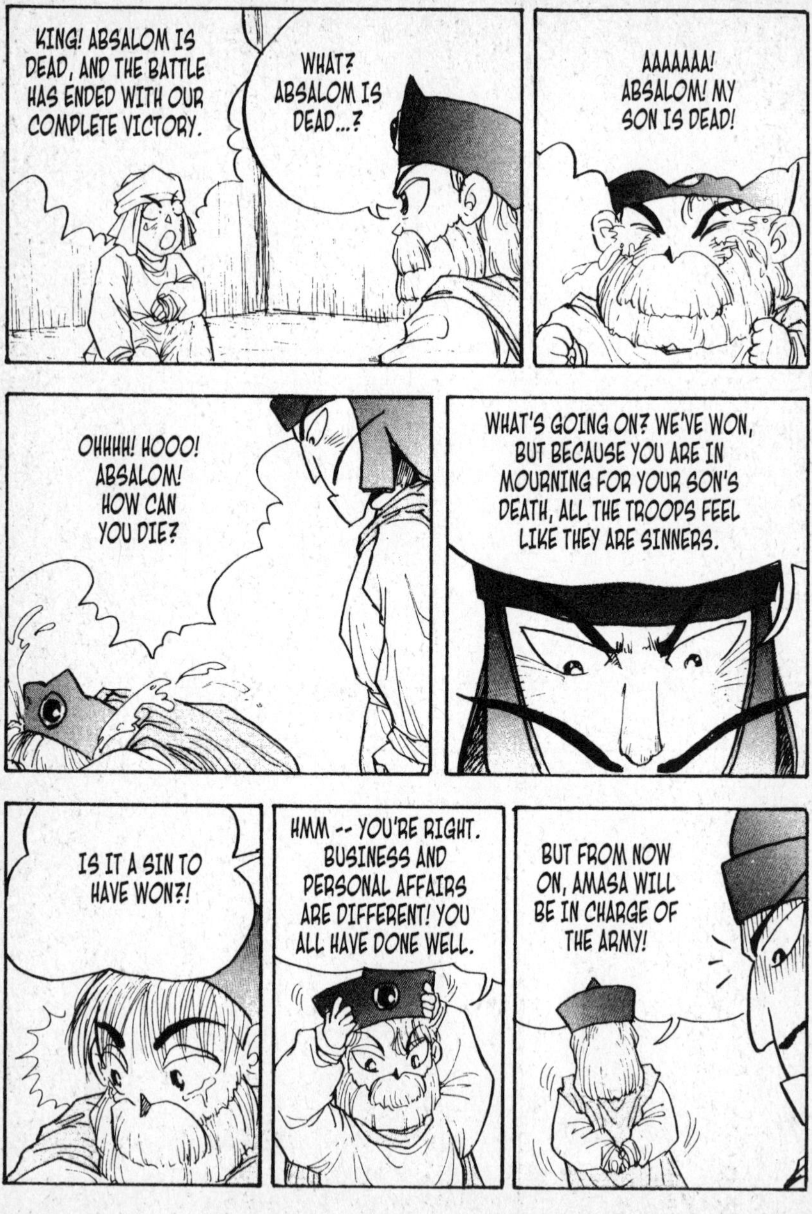
KING! ABSALOM IS DEAD, AND THE BATTLE HAS ENDED WITH OUR COMPLETE VICTORY.
WHAT? ABSALOM IS DEAD...?
AAAAAAA! ABSALOM! MY SON IS DEAD!
OHHHH! HOOO! ABSALOM! HOW CAN YOU DIE?
WHAT'S GOING ON? WE'VE WON, BUT BECAUSE YOU ARE IN MOURNING FOR YOUR SON'S DEATH, ALL THE TROOPS FEEL LIKE THEY ARE SINNERS.
IS IT A SIN TO HAVE WON?!
HMM -- YOU'RE RIGHT. BUSINESS AND PERSONAL AFFAIRS ARE DIFFERENT! YOU ALL HAVE DONE WELL.
BUT FROM NOW ON, AMASA WILL BE IN CHARGE OF THE ARMY!

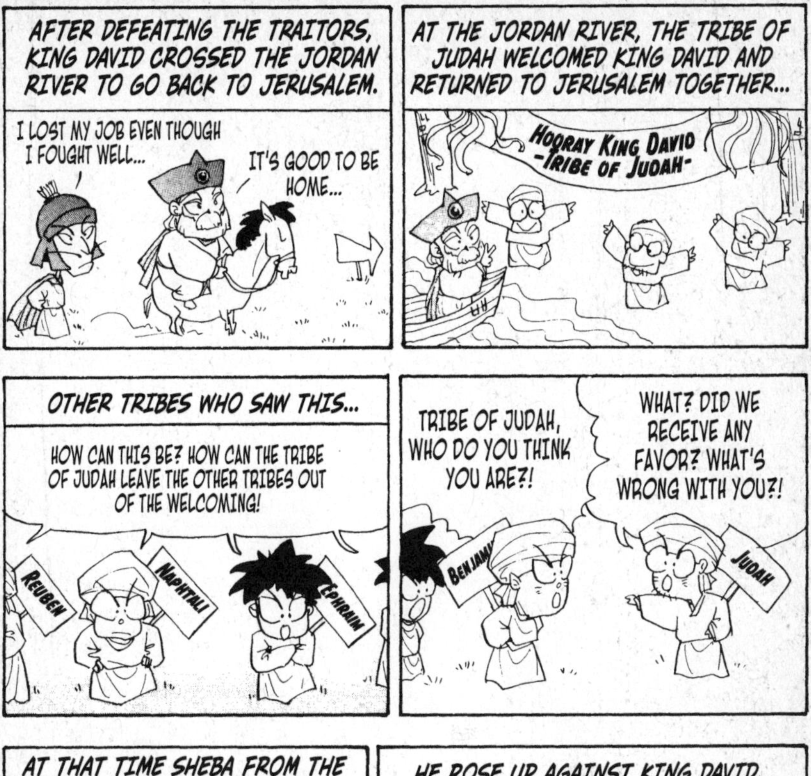
AFTER DEFEATING THE TRAITORS, KING DAVID CROSSED THE JORDAN RIVER TO GO BACK TO JERUSALEM.
I LOST MY JOB EVEN THOUGH I FOUGHT WELL...
IT'S GOOD TO BE HOME...
AT THE JORDAN RIVER, THE TRIBE OF JUDAH WELCOMED KING DAVID AND RETURNED TO JERUSALEM TOGETHER...
HOORAY KING DAVID
-TRIBE OF JUDAH-
OTHER TRIBES WHO SAW THIS...
HOW CAN THIS BE? HOW CAN THE TRIBE OF JUDAH LEAVE THE OTHER TRIBES OUT OF THE WELCOMING!
REUBEN
NAPHTALI
EPHRAIM
TRIBE OF JUDAH, WHO DO YOU THINK YOU ARE?!
WHAT? DID WE RECEIVE ANY FAVOR? WHAT'S WRONG WITH YOU?!
JUDAH
AT THAT TIME SHEBA FROM THE TRIBE OF BENJAMIN REBELLED...
WHY ARE WE TRYING SO HARD TO LOOK GOOD TO KING DAVID?!
HE ROSE UP AGAINST KING DAVID.
FOLLOW ME, ISRAELITES! LET'S GATHER AN ARMY AND FACE KING DAVID!

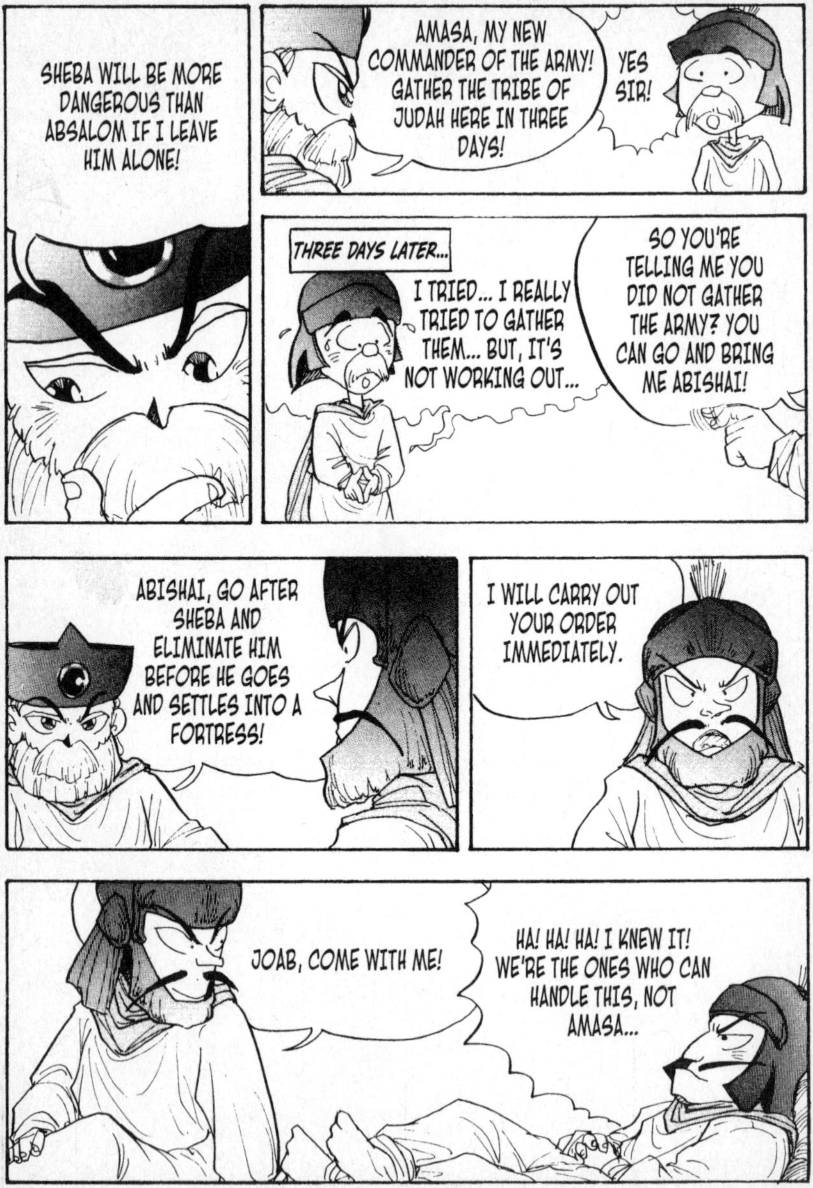
SHEBA WILL BE MORE DANGEROUS THAN ABSALOM IF I LEAVE HIM ALONE!
AMASA, MY NEW COMMANDER OF THE ARMY! GATHER THE TRIBE OF JUDAH HERE IN THREE DAYS!
YES SIR!
THREE DAYS LATER...
I TRIED... I REALLY TRIED TO GATHER THEM... BUT, IT'S NOT WORKING OUT...
SO YOU'RE TELLING ME YOU DID NOT GATHER THE ARMY? YOU CAN GO AND BRING ME ABISHAI!
ABISHAI, GO AFTER SHEBA AND ELIMINATE HIM BEFORE HE GOES AND SETTLES INTO A FORTRESS!
I WILL CARRY OUT YOUR ORDER IMMEDIATELY.
JOAB, COME WITH ME!
HA! HA! HA! I KNEW IT! WE'RE THE ONES WHO CAN HANDLE THIS, NOT AMASA...

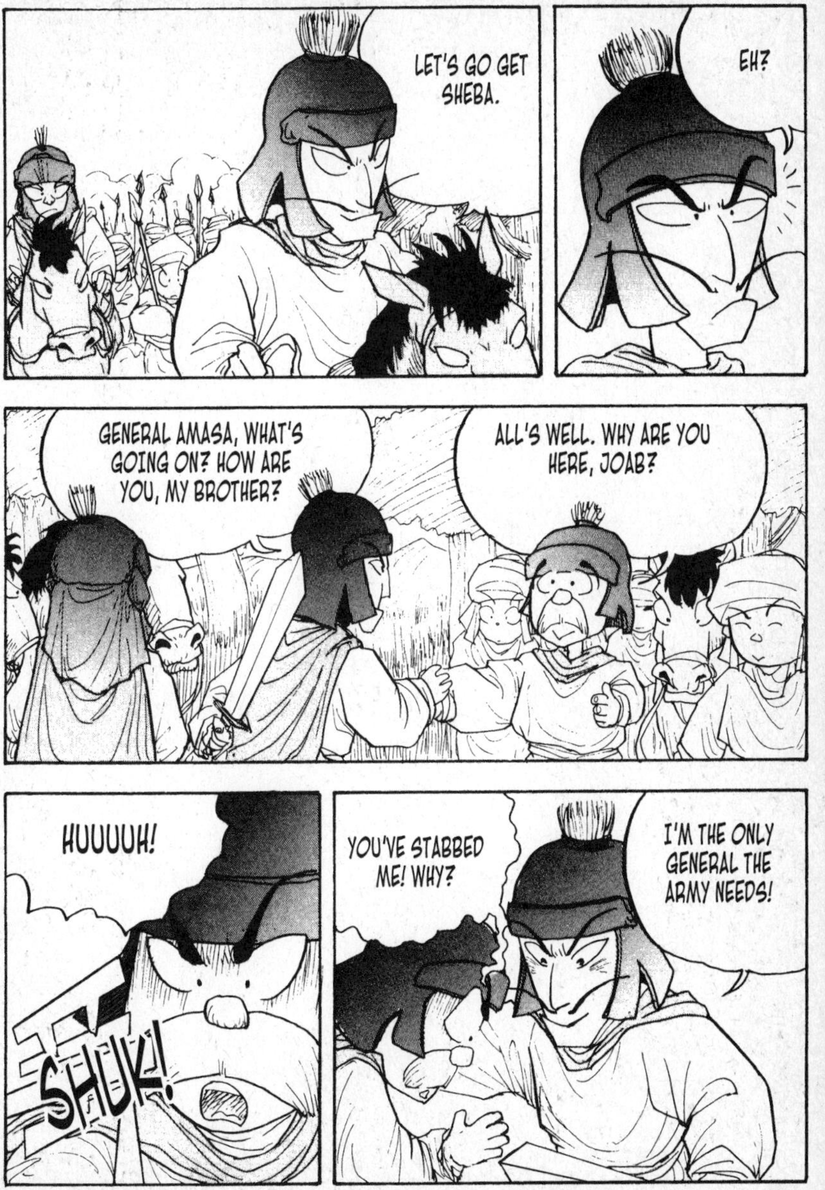
LET'S GO GET SHEBA.
EH?
GENERAL AMASA, WHAT'S GOING ON? HOW ARE YOU, MY BROTHER?
ALL'S WELL. WHY ARE YOU HERE, JOAB?
HUUUUH!
SHUK!
YOU'VE STABBED ME! WHY?
I'M THE ONLY GENERAL THE ARMY NEEDS!

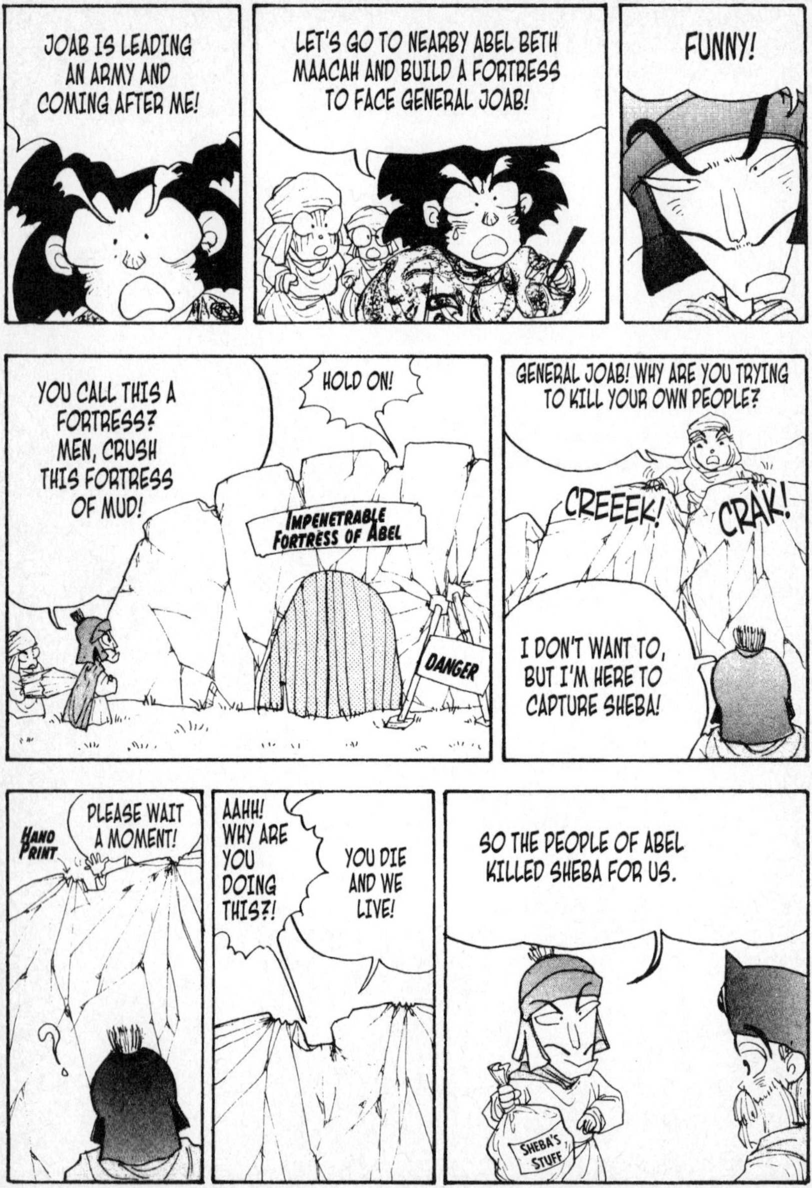

JOAB IS LEADING AN ARMY AND COMING AFTER ME!
LET'S GO TO NEARBY ABEL BETH MAACAH AND BUILD A FORTRESS TO FACE GENERAL JOAB!
FUNNY!
YOU CALL THIS A FORTRESS? MEN, CRUSH THIS FORTRESS OF MUD!
HOLD ON!
IMPENETRABLE FORTRESS OF ABEL
DANGER
GENERAL JOAB! WHY ARE YOU TRYING TO KILL YOUR OWN PEOPLE?
CREEEK!
CRAK!
I DON'T WANT TO, BUT I'M HERE TO CAPTURE SHEBA!
HAND PRINT
PLEASE WAIT A MOMENT!
AAHH! WHY ARE YOU DOING THIS?!
YOU DIE AND WE LIVE!
SO THE PEOPLE OF ABEL KILLED SHEBA FOR US.
SHEBA'S STUFF

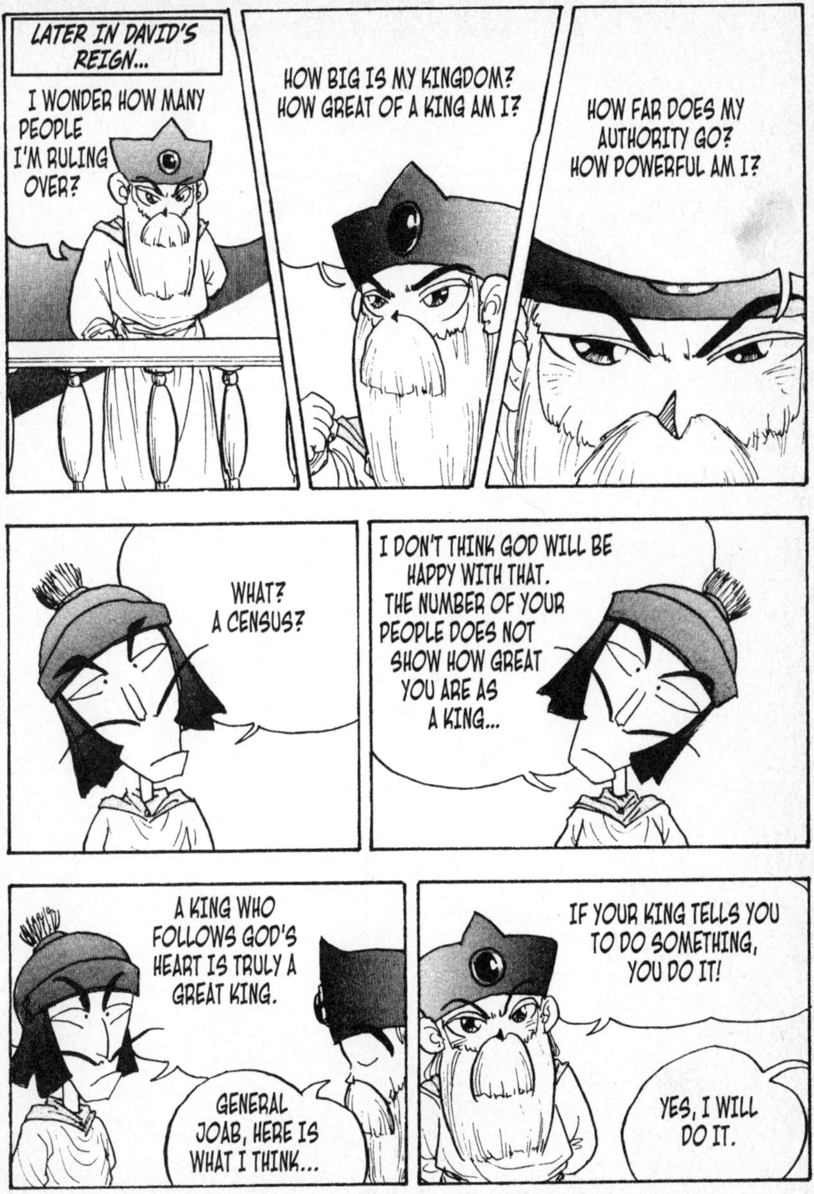

LATER IN DAVID'S REIGN...
I WONDER HOW MANY PEOPLE I'M RULING OVER?
HOW BIG IS MY KINGDOM? HOW GREAT OF A KING AM I?
HOW FAR DOES MY AUTHORITY GO? HOW POWERFUL AM I?
WHAT? A CENSUS?
I DON'T THINK GOD WILL BE HAPPY WITH THAT. THE NUMBER OF YOUR PEOPLE DOES NOT SHOW HOW GREAT YOU ARE AS A KING...
A KING WHO FOLLOWS GOD'S HEART IS TRULY A GREAT KING.
GENERAL JOAB, HERE IS WHAT I THINK...
IF YOUR KING TELLS YOU TO DO SOMETHING, YOU DO IT!
YES, I WILL DO IT.

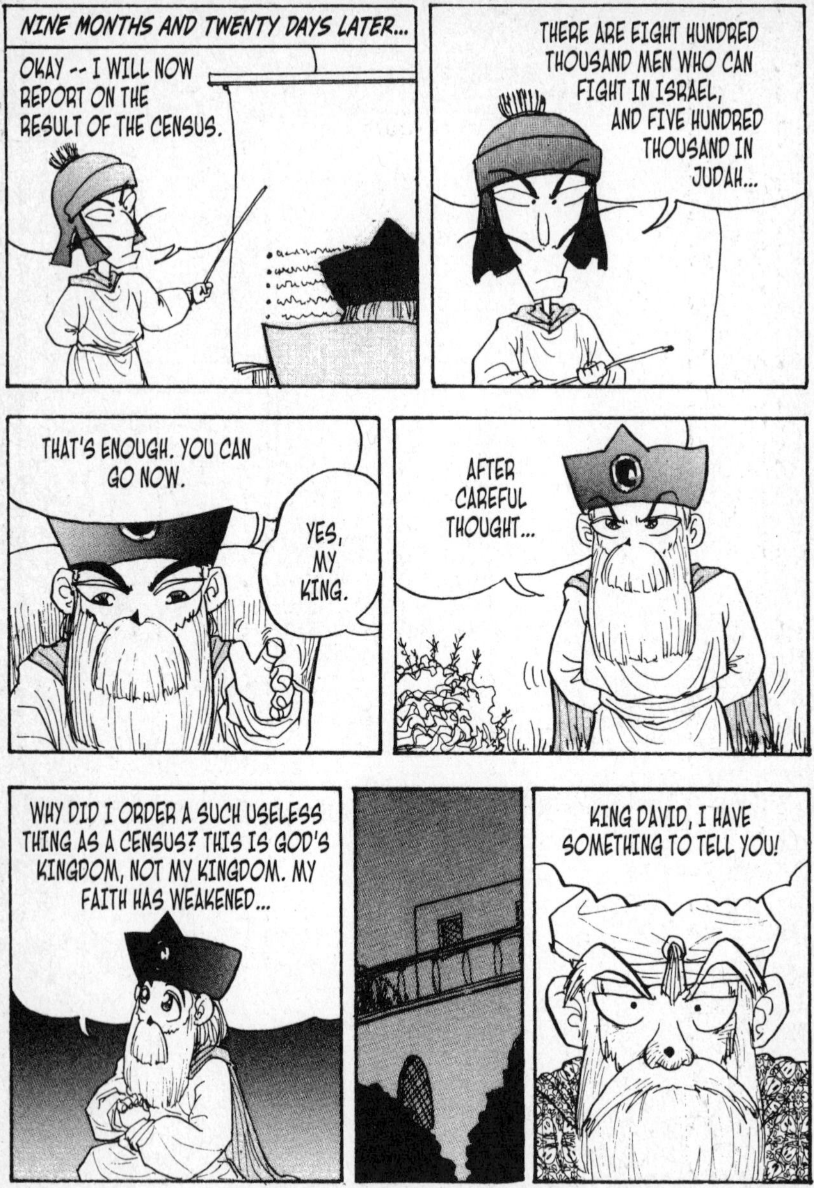
NINE MONTHS AND TWENTY DAYS LATER...
OKAY -- I WILL NOW REPORT ON THE RESULT OF THE CENSUS.
THERE ARE EIGHT HUNDRED THOUSAND MEN WHO CAN FIGHT IN ISRAEL, AND FIVE HUNDRED THOUSAND IN JUDAH...
THAT'S ENOUGH. YOU CAN GO NOW.
YES, MY KING.
AFTER CAREFUL THOUGHT...
WHY DID I ORDER A SUCH USELESS THING AS A CENSUS? THIS IS GOD'S KINGDOM, NOT MY KINGDOM. MY FAITH HAS WEAKENED...
KING DAVID, I HAVE SOMETHING TO TELL YOU!

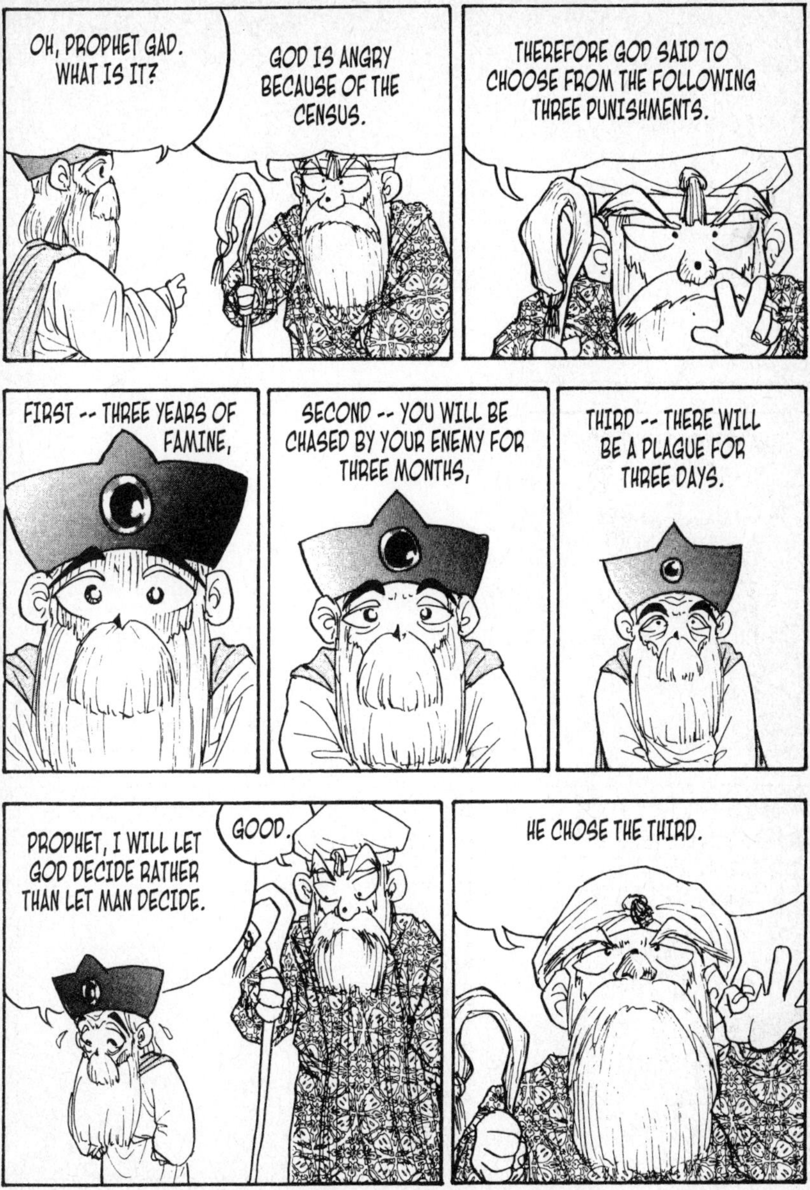
OH, PROPHET GAD. WHAT IS IT?
GOD IS ANGRY BECAUSE OF THE CENSUS.
THEREFORE GOD SAID TO CHOOSE FROM THE FOLLOWING THREE PUNISHMENTS.
FIRST -- THREE YEARS OF FAMINE,
SECOND -- YOU WILL BE CHASED BY YOUR ENEMY FOR THREE MONTHS,
THIRD -- THERE WILL BE A PLAGUE FOR THREE DAYS.
PROPHET, I WILL LET GOD DECIDE RATHER THAN LET MAN DECIDE.
GOOD.
HE CHOSE THE THIRD.

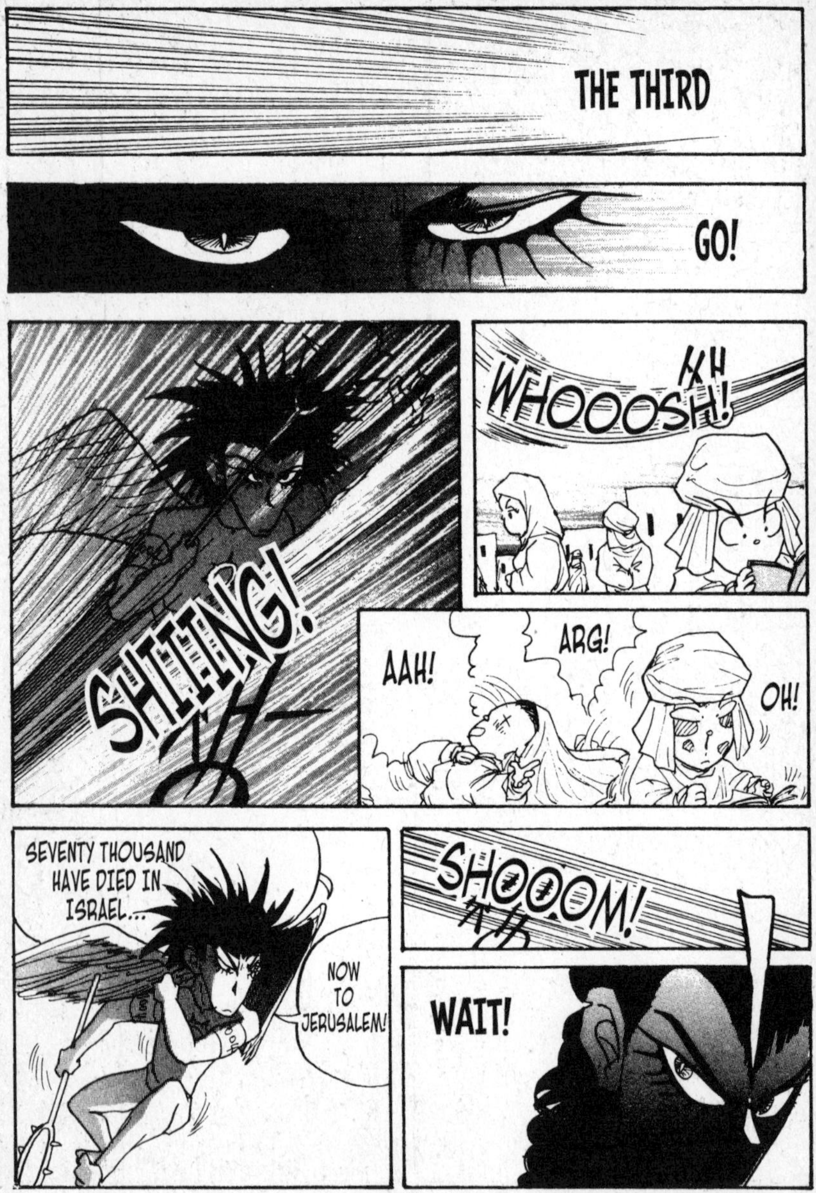
THE THIRD
GO!
SHIIING!
WHOOOSH!
AAH!
ARG!
OH!
SEVENTY THOUSAND HAVE DIED IN ISRAEL...
NOW TO JERUSALEM!
SHOOOM!
WAIT!

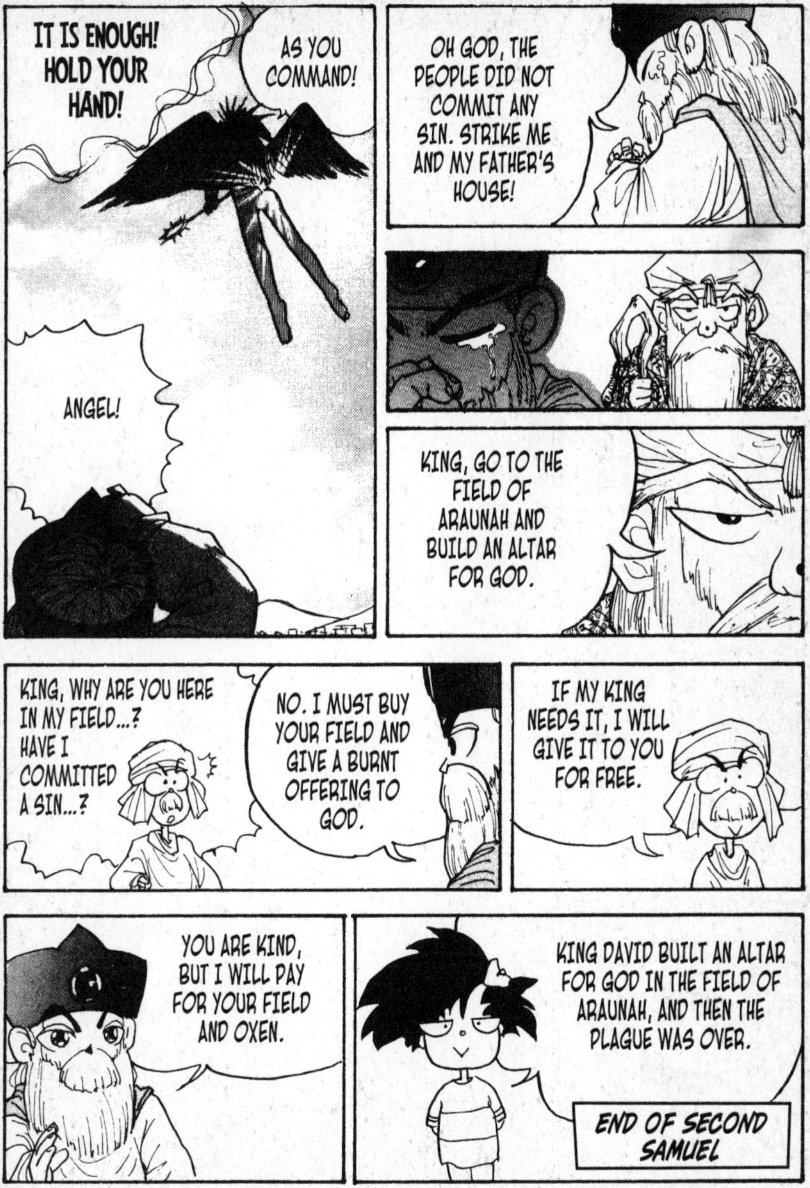
IT IS ENOUGH! HOLD YOUR HAND!
AS YOU COMMAND!
ANGEL!
OH GOD, THE PEOPLE DID NOT COMMIT ANY SIN. STRIKE ME AND MY FATHER'S HOUSE!
KING, GO TO THE FIELD OF ARAUNAH AND BUILD AN ALTAR FOR GOD.
KING, WHY ARE YOU HERE IN MY FIELD...? HAVE I COMMITTED A SIN...?
NO. I MUST BUY YOUR FIELD AND GIVE A BURNT OFFERING TO GOD.
IF MY KING NEEDS IT, I WILL GIVE IT TO YOU FOR FREE.
YOU ARE KIND, BUT I WILL PAY FOR YOUR FIELD AND OXEN.
KING DAVID BUILT AN ALTAR FOR GOD IN THE FIELD OF ARAUNAH, AND THEN THE PLAGUE WAS OVER.
END OF SECOND SAMUEL